REGICIDE

The Completionist Chronicles Book Two

DAKOTA KROUT

ACKNOWLEDGMENTS

There are many people who have made this book possible. As always, the first among them is my *amazing* wife, who always encourages me to do the best at any task I set my mind to. Thanks to her, I now have the remarkable opportunity to work with her every day, and we are able to spend more time with our daughter than we ever thought possible. Speaking of, a small thank you to my daughter, who reminds me why I am working so hard. I hope that I can always be the person you need me to be!

A special thank you to all of my patrons, who not only help me make better stories, but are great friends and people. An extra special thanks to: Steven Willden, Nicholas Schmidt, Samuel Landrie, Justin Williams, Blas Agosto, Andrew Long, Steven Dwyer, Dennis Vanderkerken, Andrew Reagan, Fred Lloyd, William Merrick, and Fawn Crow.

To the amazing readers who have gone out of their way to help manage my social media and/or supply me with sustenance; thanks go out to: Clayton Guerry for the delicious coffee, Dominik Spitzl for the crazy amount of Viennese food, Dennis Vanderkerken and Jessamyn De Vos for not only moderating the discord channel, but for sending me tons of Texan specialties, and last, but not least, to Corey Barron for designing and running the subreddit and discord channel.

Lastly, a heartfelt thanks to you my reader. I could not have done it without you and I hope to keep you entertained for years to come!

PROLOGUE

"Your Majesties." General Armond bowed before the throne, his apprentice doing the same. "The attacks against our defenses have increased in regularity and efficacy. Our guards have been taking serious wounds, but between our healers and a few clerics that have been deemed trustworthy by various Officers, the majority of them are able to return to duty if their wounds are not immediately fatal. Another threat most dire has come to our attention as well. If the number of Racial Traitors we have been finding are any indication, it seems the Wolfmen have been working to turn people against us."

The Monarchs remained unmoving upon their thrones, their impossibly still forms giving credence to the rumors that they were simply statues of the *true* Monarchs. No one still counted among mortals had seen beneath their metal exteriors, but the fact that they *did* move around from time to time proved that at the *very* least they were more than simple effigies.

The King's voice rang out in a rich, deep tone, "What would you have us do, General? With the death of the previous Archmage and the rise of a new one, the fighting force we can muster has expanded to a great degree. Now that our platoons will have reliable magical support, we could either mount an offense or rebuild our defenses. Which way would you have us lean on this issue?"

"With the strange assault of dark creatures that decimated the common Wolfmen for over a week, I believe that the raids and banditry are desperate bids for survival. It would only take a *single* spark to plunge their nation into full war." General Armond hesitated for only a moment. "I wish for a small part of *both* of the options you mentioned. The lands held by humankind have been drastically diminished, and we have been forcibly contained within the walls of this city. Now, though… now we have an advantage that we would be foolish to ignore. I propose that we try to reclaim our outlying population centers."

The Queen's form shifted on her seat, startling those watching. "That course of action is not going to be possible at this time. Though we have Mages joining us and greater access to *enchanted* weapons, the new troops still lack experience. We cannot commit to anything less than a full-blown assault against the Wolfman tribes; even then, not until we have become a cohesive whole."

"I agree, but I think I may have found a solution to this issue. If we were to offer the Travelers a base of operations, an area where they can train in privacy and build their power, we would be able to get the best of both worlds. We would gain not only forward operating base that serves as a training ground as well as a first line of defense, but the guilds would also bring a town under the banner of Ardania." The General's words were passionate and well thought out. All of his strategists had agreed that this was the best, most efficient, and most cost-effective methodology that they could implement.

"You want to give the *guilds* control of a town? The possibility of an abuse of power makes me hesitant to accept this course of action. Unless… perhaps you have a guild that you would recommend right away, a trial run?" The Queen's head tilted a bit as she gazed at her most trusted advisor.

The General looked at his apprentice with a grin, and Tiona–Guild Officer of The Wanderer's Guild–smiled right back at him. "I may already have a group in mind, Your Majesty."

CHAPTER ONE

Joe flinched as a knock boomed against the door to his warehouse. It had been just under a week since his... *altercation* with the Mage's College, and so far, no one had anything negative to say about it. Deep down though, he knew that when someone is raised as a fanatic and another person shatters their worldview... well... history doesn't show that person living a long and happy life. In short, Joe was sure that *someone* was eventually going to come after him. Until he had a person to face off against, he was constantly expecting an assassin to appear. Hence, he was a little jumpy.

"Come in!" Joe called out, putting his ink-stained hands under the table. If someone were entering with less than honorable intentions, he wouldn't hesitate to send thirty points of damage their way in the form of a shadow spike to the leg.

"Can... can you come *out* instead? There's something in the air here." The voice that drifted into the room sounded a bit sickly. Ah yes, his 'Quarantine' ritual would make anyone that got too close to the building super nauseated.

"I have a delivery from the College as well as a personal

message from…" there was a bit of rustling as the man looked at his delivery notes, "Journeyman Fire Mage Cel?"

"I'll be right there!" Joe called, already working on unlocking the door. He typically wasn't an overly paranoid person, it just so happened that he was diving deep into study and experimentation currently. If he were interrupted while trying a new ritual, an assassin wouldn't even need to fight him; the mana feedback could pop him like a balloon as it rebounded into him. "I'm Joe. What do you have for me?"

"Two packages and a letter that I'm supposed to read aloud." The mailman cleared his throat. "This is a quote; it isn't my own words. Understand? Good. Cel says, 'If you want to learn these spells properly, stop faffing around in your creepy room that makes people sick, take a shower, and learn from a Mage at the College. Book learning can only take you so far.' Now, with that done, let me say I agree with the shower comment."

Joe glared at the mailman and subtly sniffed under his arms. It was possible that a shower would not be a terrible idea. Maybe that was why dinner had cost almost half as much more than usual last night. "I didn't ask for your opinion. Just give me the books."

"Here ya go, delivered safe, sound, and on time!" The mailman looked at Joe expectantly, but Joe just glared, maintained eye contact, and slowly shut the door. A message appeared in Joe's vision that made him snort.

Relationship change: -10 with courier #73. You are slightly less likely to gain help or quests from this person.

Bah. With his 'stinky' debuff at… he checked the active effects tab on his character sheet… the fourth rank, even tipping the man a full silver would have only *maintained* a neutral alignment to their relationship. Joe had been hiding out and delving deeper into the secrets of his class ever since the fiasco with the Mages, and it was *possible* that he was a little too intent on his work. With no party to pull him along on quests and an abundance of new material, data, and spell components that everyone had needed a 'license' to purchase before the death of the Archmage... well, it was easy to miss a meal or two. Maybe he was a little less likely to shower or change his underwe-

Joe quickly cut off that line of thinking before scratching at his crusty clothing. It *might* be time to go do other things for a while. On the other hand... he looked at the two thin books that he was holding. There were a few ways to learn a spell. The first–and easiest–was to have someone teach it to you. Normally, this is the route that Joe would have taken, but he had noticed that some people could use the same spell and get different results. This was because the person teaching the spell would teach it in the way that *they* knew it. The teacher would incorporate superstition, unnecessary gestures, and other such fluff. Using a fireball as an example, while some of these components might add a bit of power, maybe heat, or perhaps change the color, it would also lengthen the casting time and increase mana consumption.

The second option was to learn or be granted the spell via a level up or natural ability. Joe had gained most of his magical abilities this way. It was difficult to level up, and it seemed that there was no guarantee that a better way to work the same magic didn't already exist. Also, gaining spells and abilities in this manner might lead you in different directions than you intended to go. A fireball spell wouldn't be super practical to him, for example, because he had high affinity with dark and water magics.

The third option, the least practical for most people, was to find a spell book, specifically a grimoire. This was a detailed accounting of a spell, typically written as accurately as possible by a Mage. It had all the issues of the first option: the superstitions, assumptions, and sometimes tricks thrown in to confuse someone that may have stolen the tome. There was also no person guiding you so your spellform would not be carefully inspected and critiqued. This made an already difficult study nearly impossible, making books the worst options for anyone but enchanters and those who relied on precise lines or drawings.

Joe had an advantage over a normal student of the arcane, and he hoped that his hunch would pay off. He cracked open the first book and read over the first page, smiling as alternating sections glowed either brilliant gold or a murky black light. Joe sighed in pleasure; he loved the occultist profession. Being able to see the truth of written information allowed him to bypass the trial and error associated with determining the fiction and reality of magic. Joe pulled a roll of paper out of the box next to his table, increased the light in the room, and decided that he could put off the shower a *little* longer. Pulling out a quill and ink, he started copying the truthful information from the book onto the scroll.

Hours passed in what felt like an instant, and Joe looked down at the completed scroll. After adding the final details, he attempted to cast the spell it contained. His hands formed the shapes needed, and he *pushed* his mana into the budding spell-form. "Weak acid spray!" With these words, a cone of acid sprayed from his outstretched hands and settled to the floor when it didn't encounter anything else. The ground became a bit pitted after a few seconds, and Joe wrote down a note of how much damage it had done.

Congratulations! You have learned a new spell: Weak acid spray (Novice I). This is a spell taught to the newest Mages, usually used to dissolve garbage, reducing the space taken up by trash heaps. Effect: Deals 5n points of acid damage to anything caught in the area of effect, where 'n' is skill level. Deals triple durability damage to equipment and weapons.

Quest updated: Playing your fake role II. As a Mage, your job is to output as much damage as possible in as short a time as you can. If you want to be a believable Mage, your ambition needs to be even higher than an actual spellslinger! Learn three Mage spells 2/3. Get one Mage-type skill to the beginner ranks 0/1. Kill five enemies within ten seconds by using spells 0/1.

Wonderful, it seemed that writing out the formula would work! It was possible that Joe could learn spells that *no one else* could manage, spells that had been lost to time because there wasn't anyone who could work through powerful grimoires! He could- **Whoosh**. The scroll he had created went up in flames, turning to ash in an instant. He released a high pitched squeal, flailing as he stepped backward and tripped over his chair. Simply lying there for a moment, he looked over the notifications he had been ignoring.

Skill gained: Scribe (Beginner VI). After writing down sentences and formulae instead of single words and doodles, you have proven that your mastery over the written word is at least at the eighth-grade level! +1% writing speed and writing accuracy per skill level.

You have created a spell scroll! A scroll allows anyone with the requisite skill who reads it to learn the spell it contains. Caution! You do not have the skill 'Words of Power (Written)'! Caution! You have not used a type of paper that can contain the magical truths written on it! Oh no! The ink and quill you have used do not have any mana containing or stabilizing properties! The scroll is unstable, chances of spontaneous conflagration, mitigated by materials and skill levels… 99.89%.

Well. That had been informative. At least he knew why four hours of work had just gone up in smoke. Joe went to put away his items, but as he was packing up, he found that his quill had fallen apart and his ink had boiled away. Dang. No more writing until he replaced *those*. Another notification appeared, and he stopped, surprised that it had taken so long. Normally, notifications came in groups.

After review, you have been awarded the skill: Words of Power (Written). You were able to create a scroll, even if it didn't last long. Know that working with me means that you have someone advocating for you! -Tatum. P.S. You should find some information on skill rarity.

Skill gained: Words of Power (Written) (Novice I). Being able to keep bias and personal preference out of spellforms is nearly impossible, but you have managed to distill a spell to its most basic design! By writing out the spellform on a scroll, anyone who reads the scroll will have a chance to learn the spell. Base probability of learning the spell from magical document: 20%. Each rank in this skill increases the chance of learning the spell by 2%, but personal ability will further modify the percentage. Each document will have a minimum characteristic score needed in order to learn the spell. When made properly, scrolls at Novice rank have 90+1n% increased chance to stabilize, -15% per increased difficulty rank. The spell must *be in the basic spellform for the scroll to be valid.*

A one in five chance to instantly learn a spell from a scroll? Joe looked at the pile of ashes on his desk and sighed. It had taken a few hours to complete a single scroll, but it might be worth it to progress this skill. Learning spells was usually the work of multiple days, sometimes weeks or years for higher ranked spells. Even if it only worked every once in a while right now, by the time he had brought it to a high level, he could sell massively powerful scrolls for a fortune. Now, he should… his stomach rumbled, reminding him that he hadn't left his admittedly odious room all day. Did he leave yesterday? No, he was working on perfecting the area of effect for rituals. Really, he still needed to- **Rumble!** His belly was no longer playing around.

Joe sighed and ran his hand over his extra shiny head. It came away disgustingly greasy, and he winced at his own filth. Sorry, stomach. A shower and clean clothes needed to come first.

CHAPTER TWO

Why in the *world* did it cost more to take a bath when filthy? You'd think that with a lowered charisma from being stinky, they would *want* you to be clean! Joe's indignation vanished as he saw two people carrying the tub he had just used. They dumped the water, pouring mud, sweat, various bodily fluids, and blood that had all combined into a viscous slurry down the drain. Oh. That might be why. That had all been on him? The serious debuff was making more sense right now. Joe walked out of the bathhouse in his clean clothes, pleased by how much nicer everyone seemed.

People smiled and nodded as he walked by, and he returned the acknowledgments with a smile of his own. In the last week, news of the fallen Archmage had circulated the city such that when the Mage's College had joined in the fight against the Wolfmen, Joe's reputation with Ardania had slowly increased. It finally settled a thousand points higher than it had been, and he was seeing the benefits of having a reputation of 'reluctantly friendly'. People were nice but didn't go out of their way to do nice things for him, pretty much just common decency. Perfect.

He stopped by a kiosk where they were selling skewers of meat and veggies, buying two and tearing into them.

Basic needs addressed, Joe walked over to the guild hall. Well, the rented army barracks that his guild lived in right now. He had not stopped by in a couple of days, so he was surprised to walk in on a bustling work crew stripping everything out of the building. Noticing the guild leader amongst them, Joe swung over to see what was going on. "Aten! Is the guild hall moving?"

"Yeah, yeah," Aten replied distractedly, not actually looking over at Joe. "*Careful* with that! If that breaks, this whole place goes up in flames! Didn't I tell you not to touch our alchemy equipment yet?"

The unfortunate guild member being yelled at looked down at a bubbling flask that seemed to be getting more unstable. He made a face as the liquid started to churn, and almost dropped the fragile container. Joe had walked over during this exchange and was close enough to take the flask away. He dropped it into his spatial ring, knowing that the distorted time in the ring would allow them to either safely dispose of it or get it back to the alchemist who was working on it. Aten wiped his forehead, removing an increasing nervous sweat. "Ah, Joe. Always a pleasure. Have you finally decided that you want to be guild leader? I would be happy to go on a training spree."

"I could really go for *not* being responsible for a half-million dollar investment like this place," Joe chuckled wryly. "I think I'll leave it in your more than capable hands."

"That's all you think is invested in the guild? Oh, my naive friend," Aten shook his head and grinned as he spoke. "To what do I owe the pleasure? I figured you were out trying to teach the Wolfmen to be friendly or some such."

"Nah, just got caught up in research."

"Learn anything useful? What sort of gains have you seen?"

Joe thought back on his week. "Well, I learned a lot of stuff that will be useful eventually but nothing extra special for the time being. In a week, I've gained zero experience but through my research and trial and error… a total of four intelligence, four wisdom, and two dexterity. Did you know that you gain wisdom faster when you make an unintended effect that is really destructive, then promise to yourself that you won't ever do that again?"

"That's... yeah, I can see that." Aten rolled his eyes. "Anything getting close to the level fifty threshold yet? Also, is that *really* the best method for improving your stats?"

"Mmm. Not really getting close to fifty. My intelligence is at thirty-seven, so I *am* getting *closer*, but I'm not quite there yet." Joe admitted distractedly while looking over his status.

Name: Joe 'The Chosen of Tatum" Class: Arch Cleric (Actual: Ritualist)
Profession: Scholar (Actual: Occultist)
Level: 9 Exp: 37,978 Exp to next level: 7,022
Hit Points: 70/70 (50+(20))*
Mana: 814/814 (12.5 per point of intelligence, +100% from deity, -11% from mana manipulation)
Mana regen: 9.81/sec (.25 per point of wisdom, + 9% from Coalescence)
*Stamina: 60/60 (50+(0)**+(10)***)*
**10 points for each point in Constitution, once it has increased above 10.*
***5 points for each point in Strength, once it has increased above 10.*
****5 points for each point in Constitution, once it has increased above 10.*

Characteristic: Raw score (Modifier)

Strength: 10 (1.1)
Dexterity: 12 (1.12)
Constitution: 12 (1.12)
Intelligence: 37 (1.37)
Wisdom: 36 (1.36)
Charisma: 15 (1.15)
Perception: 25 (1.25)
Luck: 15 (1.15)
Karmic Luck: +5

"Wait a moment, aren't you level nine?" Aten asked with

surprise lacing his voice. "*I'm* level nine and I only need to kill a rabbit or something to get to ten, but my strength, constitution, *and* dexterity are above fifty already."

"Are you being serious right now?" Joe's eyes were round and panicked. "That means… you have at least… four hundred and fifty health and over eight hundred stamina?"

"A bit more than that of each of those plus my bonuses from armor and weapons," Aten confirmed proudly. "You are *way* behind the curve, buddy. These are stats that almost everyone at this level has, while you are still closer to the stats from a level… four? Maybe five? You need to take the time to grind your skills and do training for your stats. Have you asked for stat training from any of the professionals? You can do dexterity training over at the rogue area; they have a really good obstacle course. Talk to the guard if you want strength or constitution training, and… I don't know, the library or Mage's College for mental stats? The others that I know about are for certain classes only, like the rangers, they'll only teach one of their own how to improve perception."

"I didn't even know that was an option. I've just been trying to throw myself into my work, hoping that it would help me get stats…" Joe looked at the ground and grimaced. "I'm betting they have pretty good techniques to help you gain stats, don't they?"

"Yup, any stat below fifty can increase daily if you follow their training plan. The game usually only lets you do the work for an hour or two, depending on what your stats look like. It's seriously grueling stuff but it can even help rank up your skills a lot faster too. My strength training was all about swinging around a copy of a Warhammer that weighed about three times as much as my standard one. The guys there helped me with my constitution at the same time, either tossing ice cold water on me, coals, or doing a bit of light bruising so that I would get used to fighting either Mages or fighters. Simple stuff, really."

Joe felt a little sick. Doing that sort of training with his extra-high perception would be really nasty. He wasn't adverse to a bit of pain, but… even a *little* pain was twenty-five percent more painful to him than a standard human. Maybe that would make the training more effective? "I might go ahead and stick with… the mental versions?"

"Heh. Thought you might," Aten snorted at him. "Anyway, back to your question. The guild is moving. I'm not exactly sure *where* yet; that's for our scouts to determine. Oh. Right. You haven't stopped by in a few days. We got another Noble Guild quest from the palace. If you check your guild tab, you should be able to see the details." Joe was intrigued, so he navigated through his character sheet and opened the quest Aten was talking about.

Guild quest: Base-ic operations. The King has decided that it is time to expand the Kingdom's sphere of influence to its former glory! Do your part by freeing a village or town from whoever is controlling it and bring the village back under the banner of Ardania. After the area is secure, you can set up your headquarters by building, buying, or capturing a structure to use as your main guild house! Rewards: A permanent base of operations for your guild, increased reputation with Ardania. Failure: Increased rent, loss of reputation with Ardania.

"Oh, neat. So we are going to go take over a town?" Joe rubbed his bald head thoughtfully. "And we have not only permission but *orders* to do so?"

"We are, and we do." Aten grinned excitedly. "I'll let you know when we are going to be going; we plan to bring the entire guild. It'll make travel interesting."

"Great! I'm going to have to go find a stat trainer; my methods have hit a wall." Joe sighed and began his journey to the Mage's College. "See you later."

CHAPTER THREE

Joe strolled into the territory controlled by the Mages, the sunlight reflecting from his bald head, attracting the attention of everyone in the area.. Excited conversations followed him as he walked, so he was very glad to get indoors and away from eyes that were filled with either hero worship or bitter anger. Their reaction to his presence mainly depended on how deeply indoctrinated they had been in the manifesto of the ex-Archmage. Some people would never be happy with freedom when they had been trained to enjoy their position in life, especially when that position *used* to be one of power over others.

An unknown Mage was sitting and studying in the reception hall, so Joe went over, introduced himself politely, and asked for directions to an area where he could increase his stats. He was directed to a small room and, unexpectedly, found that Cel was waiting for him. "Hello there, Joe."

"Cel! Good to see you, buddy. How have you been?" Joe replied brightly.

"*Buddy*? I wouldn't go quite that far. While I owe you for freeing me from what would have essentially been slavery, you also used me against my will to power dark rituals as well as experimented on me with healing magic." Cel's face had darkened during his rant.

"Let's focus on the freeing you from slavery aspect!" Joe beamed a brilliant smile at Cel, trying his best to ignore the rest. "What brings you here today?"

"Hmm." Cel squinted his eyes at Joe and reluctantly decided to move on.

Skill increased: Speech (Novice II). Charisma +1! Convincing a person to like you when they are unsure if they should is a great way to climb the social ladder! You sweet talker! Maybe you should be using this skill on fewer men, unless…

Joe ignored the rest of the notification. The notices had been a bit abusive since he had messed up and gotten them set to 'extra snarky' by the AI controlling the game. Cel took a breath and answered Joe's question, "Since I do feel that I owe you a *tiny* bit for your part in freeing us, I asked to be notified if you came in for any kind of training. I assumed you were going to come in for some spell training, but I agree that it is probably for the best that you increase your *intelligence* and *wisdom*." The last few words were heavily inflected, leading Joe to believe that Cel may be trying to hint that he should stop doing stupid things.

"I agree completely!" Joe kept his smile fixed in place, pretending not to understand that Cel was being intentionally rude to him. "I was wondering if perhaps there was anything you have that will also increase perception or dexterity as well…? I need to grow as much as possible."

Cel tapped the table where they had taken seats with one finger while he thought. "We do… but do you understand how stat training works?"

"Not particularly."

"That's fine." Cel stood up and went over to a chalkboard. He wrote a simple division problem on the board. "You *do* understand basic math, I presume?"

"Indeed. Continue," Joe affirmed grandly.

"Mhm. Well, you can only devote either one or two hours a

day to a specific stat–based on which threshold you have passed–to raise it by one point. Otherwise, the system awards you points based on your actions in a seemingly random manner. Studying might give you a point to intelligence, maybe one to perception, or it might not give you anything at all. There is a theory that there are hidden percentage bars that fill with something like experience, and you get awarded points over time."

"*Hidden* percentage bars, you say?" Joe's fake smile turned into a real one. He would be having a conversation with Tatum, his deity, the *Hidden god* about this as soon as he could.

"Yes, please stop interrupting." Cel wrote out 'one divided by one' on the board. "If you spend an hour devoting your time to raising a single stat, it should take one hour to raise it. This only works once per twenty-four hours. If you try to do multiple stats at once…" He wrote out 'two divided by one' on the chalkboard.

"It will increase the amount of time you need to devote by a full hour. Two *uninterrupted* hours. So you can see that it is almost always more efficient to focus entirely on a single stat. If you tried to do all four of the stats you were asking about, it would take you four hours to see any results though all four would increase at the same time," Cel finished his explanation and looked over. "All the time requirements double after the fifty point threshold, and the complexity of the training needs to increase significantly as well."

"I see," Joe thoughtfully went over this lecture for a long moment, "but you do *have* a training aid for multiple stats?"

"We do. Are you sure that you want to use one? You need to devote the required time to them completely until you finish, no breaks allowed or you have to start over." Cel seemed to think poorly of Joe's follow-through for some unknown reason.

"Yes please," Joe solemnly intoned.

"Alright…" Cel sighed and rolled his eyes. "Do I even need to ask? Something that will increase perception, dexterity, intelligence, and wisdom all at once?"

"This is why we are best friends." Joe put his arms out for a hug.

"...Get away from me." Cel sidestepped the attempted ambush as Joe stood and came toward him. "Your funeral. One four-hour-long training session coming up." He walked over to a cabinet in the room, pulling out something that looked like a Rubik's Cube.

Cel looked at the block, rolled his eyes, and handed the cube to Joe. "This is the item you are looking for. Please note that it is covered in dust because no one enjoys four straight hours of intensive studying."

"Neat." Joe turned the cube over and over, trying to understand all of the details it contained. "How do I use it?"

"Have you used a basic puzzle cube? Nine squares on each side?" Cel waited until Joe nodded to continue. "Similar concept but with forty-nine squares on each side. Also, not only do you need to get all of the same colors on each side, but there are equations on each square as well. You need to determine the correct answers and line those up. Then you use the answers to the equations on that face as the input to solve the next side."

"Good *lord*." Joe looked at the item in disgust. "You need a college degree to even start!"

Cel finally cracked a smile. "Pretty accurate statement. That's *why* it's so dusty. People used to use it all the time because there is a rumor that completing the cube gave a special reward. We never found out if it was true."

Joe looked down at the cube again, less apprehensively this time. "That'd be nice. Which side do I start with?"

"That's part of the training. Figure it out." Cel started to walk away. "You can take the cube with you; I'll buy it for you as thanks for helping me remain a free Mage."

"Thanks!"

"Oh, believe me, in this case, the pleasure is *all* mine. Good luck." Cel went off to do other things as Joe started walking back to his warehouse. His rented property was a good halfway point between the College and the city's library, which is where he would go next if this training didn't pan out.

He opened the door, went to his desk, and got comfortable. Putting on the Spectacles of the Scholar to mitigate eye strain from reading the tiny writing, he got to work. Joe started reading each face of the squares, feeling entirely disheartened and full of dread as he found that the questions were far too advanced for him. He thought about working to get all the colors grouped but knew it would be a waste unless he put them in order. He had to flip the square quite frequently during his search, but finally he found a blue square that he was fairly certain he could answer.

"What is the sum of all natural numbers below twenty that are divisible by three or five?" Joe pulled out some chalk and wrote directly on his desk. "Three plus five plus… should be… ninety-eight?" Joe looked over all of the numbers on the cube that were the same color. There was no 'ninety-eight' on any of them. Joe frowned.

"Did I do my math wrong…? No, it's… oh! The question said *below* twenty! I *included* twenty. Let's see, minus twenty, is there a 'seventy-eight'? Yup, there it is." As soon as he said it out loud, the two squares lit up a tiny bit, showing that they were completed and were supposed to be set together. Joe went on to the next problem and kept going until he got a sudden notification.

Characteristic point training completed! +1 to intelligence, wisdom, perception, and dexterity! These stats cannot be increased further by any means other than system rewards, study, or practice for twenty-four hours game time.

Joe looked at the notification, a bit startled. Had it already been four hours? He looked at the clock included on his character sheet. No, it had been… one hour. How…? His class! Yes! He looked at a small portion of the description for his class again, overjoyed that it even applied to this area.

The Ritualist gains skill in their chosen pursuits at four times the speed of an average class due to their vast thirst for power.

His other pursuits had been in attaining skill levels, was this an *active* effect? Did he need to be intentionally trying to increase in these areas in order to increase them? Ugh. There were so many unknown aspects to this system! Joe bonked his head on the table a few times and looked at the puzzle cube again. It was surprisingly fun to try to do the work on the cube, but he was still leery about the more advanced problems. Nothing he could do now, so enough for today! On to other—more important—things.

It was time for Joe to form an adventuring party.

CHAPTER FOUR

"Anyone?" Joe called into the awkwardly quiet room. A few people looked his way, but they quickly turned their heads when he tried to meet their eyes with his admittedly rapidly-approaching-manic stare. "Come on, there's gotta be *some* people in here that don't have a party yet!"

Terra walked over, trying and failing miserably to hide a grin. "There is a reason parties are put together right when people join the guild. You've gained a bit of a reputation as an insane person."

"*What?*" Joe gasped in total shock at her words. "But *why*? All I've done is awesome stuff! The people with me keep getting huge rewards, and we keep-"

"Yeah, but think of all the trouble you've caused, just by being here!" Terra counted off on her fingers. "You were kidnapped by the Mage's College and tortured. Yeah, you toppled the evil Archmage, kudos. A Royal Guardsmen showed up and glared at you, giving you a mysterious 'gift' before leaving. You've died twice in a *safe zone*, not through pvp but because you somehow made NPC's so mad at you that they snapped. Should I go on?"

"I don't understand why that's all a negative," Joe responded calmly, though his knuckles were turning white from his clenched fists. "It's all worked out in the end, right?"

"I'm sure you can see why *normal* people don't want to join up with you though. They just want to have fun and do normal quests or find awesome quests to do where all the credit doesn't go to the bald anti-mage, the 'Chosen of Tatum', whoever that is." Terra arched a hot-pink eyebrow at him.

"You can see all of my titles?" Joe looked at his settings with concern. "I have my privacy settings set up to hide all my information; at best you should only be able to see one title at a time, whichever is equipped."

"Firstly, you have 'Chosen of Tatum' set as your main title. Secondly, I have an ability called 'scan' already into the student ranks. Scan is similar to identify, but works on people." Terra told him how to get the skills when he looked interested, "You need a high enough perception. Then you need to try to look at a person's info. When you are able to see the basics of anyone's information on a consistent basis, it should develop into an ability."

Joe shook his head, "Back on topic! Throughout all of the craziness you are describing, there was only *one* time where I was alone! The other people in my party should be just as famous, minus the Mage's College…"

Terra put her hands up in a classic surrender pose and started to back away. "I'm just telling you what everyone else is thinking. Good luck, crazy man!"

"Ugh." Joe rolled his eyes as he saw that her words were taken as gospel by the others in the room. "Kids these days. You do a few things in a way no one else *thought* to do, and they get all bitter about you solving problems." He walked into the office portion of the building, sidestepping over-eager people who were packing away books and documents. He stopped someone he vaguely recognized and asked where Aten was hiding. A set of instructions and a few turns later, he found the guild leader getting geared up. "Holy moo. What class are you?"

Aten was covered in shining silver plate metal. He pulled a winged helmet down over his head before looking over. "Oh, hey there, Joe! Class? I'm a guild leader. Thought you knew that."

"Wait. I thought that was just a *position*?" Joe looked on in shock as Aten inspected a silver Warhammer that reflected… *no*, it was releasing its own light! His Warhammer was glowing! "Is that hammer enchanted? I haven't seen any enchanted weapons in the game yet."

"Yes, it's enchanted. Yes, guild leader is a class as well as a position." Aten took a deep breath and bounced on his toes, getting used to the huge weight he was now carrying. "Did you need something? I'm off to kill a rabbit and then go for specialization."

"Right, I was wondering if I could put together an official party or be assigned to one. I need to recruit a few people if we go the 'put it together' route." Joe cast one more envious look at the beautiful armor and then tried to let the envy go. He reminded himself that he wouldn't be able to take a single step wearing that shiny, shiny gear.

"Sure. Talk to the admin workers about doing an interview with some guild hopefuls. We've got a bunch of new requests to join, but not nearly enough space for them. I'd offer some suggestions, but I think you are right in thinking that you'd have trouble getting people that are already in our guild." Aten brushed by Joe and waved over his shoulder. "Good luck."

"Thanks…" Joe's voice faltered as Aten vanished through the doorway. "I'm going to take that as permission to bring anyone I want into the guild. He did say admin… where the heck is admin?" Joe had to resort to asking for help a few times, but finally found someone who had files full of people who were hoping to join the guild. All the files were separated out into piles that approximated what position someone would have in a party. Fighter, tank, ranged damage, buffer or healer, and finally, rogue. Joe didn't bother with production classes, people who focused entirely on either collecting or producing goods. Though they had important roles, he was recruiting for his personal team and not the guild.

"Is there a way that we can narrow the selection? Maybe get rid of anyone who plays a standard class? I want people who can wear many hats, fill many roles." Joe tried to direct the man helping him sort through the files.

"We can, I think. Do you mean you want multi-classers or cross-classers?" the friendly, but extraordinarily bland man questioned.

"What's the difference?"

"Multi-classers literally switch between classes. You might have a guy who plays as a warrior in a party but switches to rogue when alone." Even his voice was bland. Joe ground his teeth as the man continued droning, "Cross-classers are different; they might be trying to combine class abilities or unique features into unique classes when they specialize, so they use abilities from multiple classes even though there is a really hefty stamina or mana penalty to do so, something like seven times more expensive. They can also only learn a few skills outside of their area of expertise."

"That one. Cross-classers. I want focused yet driven teammates," Joe quickly responded. The man nodded sleepily and helped sort out the exotic classes. The piles were now much smaller and the people much more… *interesting*. On the forms there was a list of the reasons the person in question had not been accepted right away.

"Really? This guy has everything I'm looking for in a fighter, and he wasn't added to the guild because, and I quote, 'dude's creepy as shnizz'. Who *wrote* this?" Joe only got a shrug in return.

"Fine." Joe took his time going through the pile and picked out a few other likely candidates. "I'm glad these at least have a rough location for finding them."

Reading over the paper, Joe meandered through the streets

until he saw the inn he was looking for. There was a bit of a commotion going on, but he didn't think much of it until he saw that most of the crowd were members of the guard. Joe hurried over, just in case someone had been hurt. He *did* have a deal with the guard to heal them if needed. The strangest sight he had ever seen in a public area greeted him.

"No! Not like *that*!" A smiling man wearing only cloth armor easily dodged a sword that was swinging at him. "Terrible posture! Disgusting form! Tore that shoulder a while ago? You must have hurt yourself overextending like that. Here!" The man's hands wove through the air, striking the guard's joints and sending him clattering to the ground. "That should help, keep practicing boy-o!"

Another sword came at him from the side and he danced around it as if the wind had buffeted him to the side. "Some yellow teeth you have there. Oh, that looks bad. Let me help." He threw something at the guard which stuck into his neck, and the targeted guard dropped to the ground with a gurgle.

A fist struck the smiling man in the stomach, and he was bent over from the force. He bounced back a few feet, put his hands on his gut, and twisted. A moist **crack** could be heard, and he went right back to smiling. "Goodness! That was a lot of force, but the way you twisted… you must have hurt your teres major. That's a muscle in your shoulder… you know what, c'mere." He breezed forward and slammed a palm into the guard's back. "*There* ya go. Seems like a common injury with you sword-flingers."

"Everybody *stop*!" Joe bellowed as loudly as possible when he saw arrows being pulled back. To his shock, they actually did stop. "First of all, is anyone hurt? Next, what in the *abyss* is going on?" He stopped talking, he had meant to say *abyss*. No, not that. He was trying to think *abyss*. *Celestial* and *abyss*. What in the…?

"Hey there, friendly stranger! No one is seriously injured, though there might be minor bruising and tiny lacerations."

The strange smiling man was the first to speak, earning himself glares from the guards as they stepped in to take advantage of his chattiness.

Joe winced as he saw fury and murder in the guards' eyes. "Um. You're probably not who I'm looking for, but you wouldn't happen to be Jaxon, would you?"

"Hey, yeah, that's me!" Jaxon responded brightly. "Can I help you with something? Do you need an *adjustment*?" His fingers started to wiggle as he asked the second question. Not a normal 'jazz hands' wiggle, but independent movement for each finger, like worms attached to his palms.

"Oh, boy." Joe turned to the guards. "Hey all, can you please tell me what's going on? I might be able to fix... whatever this is."

"This is no place for a civilian—ow!" Another guard cuffed the one speaking on the back of the head.

"Quiet, you! That's Joe. The cleric that comes and heals all the guards." There was still a petulant look on the face of the guard who was rubbing his head. "You know, the one who does it for *free*?" Panic showed in the first man's eyes, but they hardened after a moment.

"I know you have a very good reputation with the Captain, but..." the guard hesitated as the others glared at him.

"I'm just trying to clear this up without someone getting hurt," Joe promised with a small smile. He gestured at Jaxon. "I'm actually here to talk to *him*, and I'd prefer not to do it while he is in a cell." The guard still hesitated. "Can I heal anyone who needs it... perhaps while you tell me why he is in trouble? How this started?"

This seemed to tip the guard's mind in Joe's favor, so he nodded and began to talk. "We had a report about a man who was walking around striking people. Never... *attacking* them, per se, but slapping, poking, or grabbing them. When we were told he stabbed someone, we came over to arrest him. Only thing is... we could barely touch this weirdo. Then he started telling us that he was going to 'fix' us and kept attacking us whenever we got close."

Joe turned to Jaxon, who was waiting patiently in the circle of guards while bouncing on his toes. "Why were you attacking people?"

"I *wasn't*!" Jaxon proclaimed instantly. "They needed or asked for treatment and wouldn't get into the proper position to let me help them. So I needed to take matters into my own hands." He wiggled his fingers again. "In fact, I can show you what I'm talking about if you'd like."

Looking around at the wary guards, Joe nodded slowly. "Sure. We'll call this your interview to join my party in The Wanderer's guild."

"Oh, that's what you are here for? Excellent, and a wonderful decision." Jaxon moved forward, *far* too fast in Joe's opinion. His hands launched forward like ballista bolts and landed on Joe's chest and lower back. He pushed and twisted, forcing Joe to move as wet popping sounds filled the air. Jaxon shook Joe's arms, cracked his fingers, finally grabbing his chin and twisting Joe's head back and forth. The guards took a panicked step forward, looking sick to their stomachs. "There you go!" Jaxon finally stated. "You've been slouching, possibly reading or working at a desk far too long. That'll help your posture and energy levels today. We should set up a frequent appointment if you want to stay moving at maximum efficiency."

Joe had to admit, he felt great. There was only one small issue: the abrupt movement had cost him eight points of health. While that didn't sound like much, it was a significant portion of his total health pool. At least now he knew why the guard had been called. Checking his active effects tab to see what had changed, Joe was thoroughly impressed.

Buff added: Well-adjusted. After allowing another man to handle you roughly, you feel great! Not a total surprise, now all of that time you spent in the library avoiding people makes sense. Temporary effect: Charisma, intelligence, wisdom, dexterity, and constitution +2. Time remaining for buff: 35:59.

"Holy…!" Joe exclaimed in happiness and amazement, having learned to ignore the caustic remarks of the system. "I feel wonderful! What did you just do, and why in the world did it give me a temporary increase to *five* different stats?"

"I *adjusted* you," Jaxon explained to him as if he were a simpleton. "I'm a chiropractor and acupuncturist in the real world, and it turns out that the skills transferred here! I just needed to show my real skill, and it bumped me all the way to expert."

"Aren't you level *five*?" Joe looked around at the shocked guards who were all checking their own active effects. Anyone who had been 'attacked' had round eyes and were whispering amongst themselves.

"Yuppers!" Jaxon's smile remained fixed in place without seeming forced, giving him a serial-killer vibe. "In my own humble opinion, I should have at least *Master* rank in those skills. I can't seem to figure out what the system needs from me in order to recognize my ability." He walked over to the guard who had crumpled to the ground, pulling out a thin needle. "There you go, fella! That should keep you off smoking for a few days. Try to make it a permanent habit!"

Joe covered a smile as the abashed guard was pulled to his feet. "I'd really like you to join my team. Are you a ranger? Rogue? Your file says fighter, but…"

"No, fighter is correct; specifically, my class is 'Monk'. I've always wanted to try adjusting animals and other creatures, but the ethics committee kept stopping me! Something about a degree needed to adjust animals. But here, not only can I adjust people and test out theories of acupuncture without needing my patient to be stationary, lying down, on a table, et cetera, but there are apparently *humanoids*! Wolfmen, Elves, Dwarves… I cannot *wait* to see how their bones and circulatory systems are differentiated from ours!" Jaxon was breathing heavily and smiling at the sky. "So excited. Oh, and yes, I'll join your team."

Joe hadn't officially invited him, but it was true that Jaxon fit what he was looking for pretty well. Can't be number one if you aren't odd, right? Joe gave him some information on where to meet up in an hour or so, healed any guards that had lost health, and walked away after making Jaxon promise that he wouldn't try to 'fix' anyone until they were in a party.

CHAPTER FIVE

"So, I have a front-line fighter. Good. Next is... the tank. Really gonna need to make sure to choose the right person here. Some good options, though." Joe shuffled through the files he had on people that designated themselves as damage absorbers. He pulled out his favorite and had to shake his head. "Why in the world are you listed as a tank? Alright, let's see what makes you tick." It took about ten minutes to navigate to the Bard's Theater—which was a glorified training building for musicians—but when he arrived he was glad that he had made the trip.

"For goodness sakes, *stop* that!" Joe had walked into a performance room, where people were being judged on their singing ability. Emphasis was on *judge* if the downcast faces in the room were any indication. There was a small panel of gaudily dressed people sitting in the audience, and one of them was shouting at the man performing, "You have absolutely *no* skill in singing! I hated it so much that I dislike you as a *person* now!"

"I'm not *singing*, ya fat peacock!" the man on the stage shouted back with a thick Scottish accent. "I'm gol' darn *chanting*!"

"Get out of here! You fail! *Shoo!*" the Judge shouted while waving his hands at the glowering applicant.

"Ah, get it up ye. Ahm goo-in, and ahm taking back ma fees, ye dobber!"

The Judge crossed his arms haughtily. "What*ever* gets you out of here the *fastest.*"

Joe intercepted the man he was almost *sure* he was here to meet, getting a glare in return for blocking his path. "Excuse me, are you Bard?"

"Apparently *naw,*" the man shouted at high volume back into the room. He turned to Joe and stuck out a hand. "Ahm Bard, whatcha need?"

"I'm forming a party for The Wanderer's guild. I'm looking for a person to fill the role of tank, and your name was at the top of my list." Joe looked back into the room. "Though if you have other things to do, I won't get in your way. Also, I was wondering how you fit the role of a tank as a Bard."

"Pff. Those cowards an' insufferable pricks? Ahm done wi' them." Bard glanced at Joe's body, trying to see what kind of character he was. "Ahm not *a* Bard, ahm Bard. Mah name. Mah class is apparently rare, and the stinkin' Bardic college canno' or *will* naw find a way to teach me their skills."

"Oh? I was told you had already proven yourself as a Bard to the guild…" Joe trailed off leadingly.

"Ahm a *Skald.* Much betta' than ah stinkin' *Bard.*" Bard spat on the floor, ignoring the fact that they were still indoors. "Ah thought ah was gon' be a Bard when ah first started playin', so ah thought it'd be funny tae have mah name be the same as mah class. Ya know, kinda ah play on words. Being ah Skald is pretty similar, but instead of sitting in the back ahm on the front lines chantin', buffin', and slicin' with mah axes."

"If you don't mind me asking, how does that qualify you to be a tank?" Joe quizzed carefully, knowing that this man wasn't in the best of moods.

"As it turns out, nah too many people care for mah chantin'. Ever since ah started playin', people have been *tossing* things at me! Ah've taken so much damage that mah constitution has skyrocketed without trying! I don' even add points to it, but it's double my nex' highest stat." Bard seemed oddly proud of the fact that people had been attacking him since he joined the game. "Ah found that ah don' mind it so much now, and ah can take some serious punishment."

Joe couldn't hide his grin anymore, and a dark look crossed Bard's face when he saw the smirk. "You're absolutely *perfect.* If you would care to join my team, I'm testing a fighter today as well. We're going to have to wait a few days for a full team, but I'd love to see what you can do."

A considering look appeared on Bard's face, but then he looked back at the building they had just vacated. His face hardened. "Make sure it's worth ma time, and ahm in."

"Are you ready now? Or do you need to go get anything ready?"

"Let's goo."

They walked toward the city gates, meeting up with Jaxon as they were exiting. He had been talking to the gate guards, and they were pointing their pikes at him. Joe defused the situation as quickly as possible, and the three men went out into the unprotected wilds. Joe took the daily quest for hunting Wolfmen and shared it with his small party, just in case they came across the ferocious Beastmen accidentally. The trio walked through rabbit territory easily, Joe's level making the bunnies run away in fear even though he wasn't actually overly powerful. They saw a few small red faces but were able to cross through fox territory without having to fight, and after a short half-hour they finally arrived at their destination.

"Alrighty, guys. For our test run today, we are going to hunt some wolves. Are you fine fighting this level of enemy? They will likely be a bit stronger than you, and they will outnumber us. Feel free to let me know if this will be an issue." Joe directed his questions to the two men, getting very different reactions from them.

"Canines? Their joints are going to be difficult to attack

since they typically stand at half human height," Jaxon muttered at a furious pace. "Their knees are too near to their body to easily strike... but their ankles–which are commonly mistaken for knees–should be fairly easy targets. This enemy should be fine for me."

"Hold on ah moment." Bard held up a hand, and Joe was impressed by how improved his accent was when he was calm. "This is yer party, yeah? What is yer personal ability tha' makes *ye* qualified to lead *us*? How about ye give us ah display ah ye power, show us the kinda man that plans to lead us around?"

Joe paused, considering the man's words. That wasn't an... *unreasonable* request. He nodded at the Skald and stepped forward. "I'm fine with that. What are your perception stats at?"

Jaxon spoke first. "Eighteen."

"...Twelve." Bard muttered under his breath, coughing a bit to try and hide his words.

"So... the two of you might have some trouble spotting the wolves in the area, but we won't know for sure for a little bit. The packs like to hide in the underbrush and ambush unwary travelers, so stay together." Joe led the others into the verdant area, and they tried to scout out where the wolves might be hiding. As expected, Joe was the first to notice them. "There is a pack of five hiding right under that tree. This should work, but if it doesn't... well, just be ready to fight."

He moved both of his hands in the pattern needed to cast shadow spike, going a bit slower than usual as he was casting the spell with each hand. Feeling a bit of strain, Joe realized that he *really* should have tested this somewhere where it wouldn't have such disastrous consequences if he failed. Maintaining his concentration, he released both of the spells at the same time. Success!

**Yipe*!* A pained whimper was heard from the Alpha of the pack as two spikes drove into either side of its flank. The damage wasn't enough to instantly kill it, but Joe channeled the spikes so the beast couldn't escape. Within a few seconds, it had perished and fallen still. The other wolves, seeing their leader killed without a chance to retaliate, scattered into the forest and ran away yelping.

*Exp: 12 (12 * Wolf x1).*

Skill gained: Dual casting (Novice I). Not having a weapon in one hand may make it harder to fend off attacks, but you have found a way to make yourself deadly without needing to hold a stick or pointy chunk of metal! Whether casting the same spell or a different one, as long as you only need a single hand for each spell, you are able to cast two at once! Effect: Cast two spells at the same time. Increase casting time by 51-1n% where 'n' is skill level. 33% chance of failing due to faltering spell stability, +1n% spell stability per skill level.

"Whew! There we go." Joe looked over at the two people with him. They had approving looks on their faces, so he felt that he had just won a small victory. "Alright, so my thought for a normal battle is that I'll target a normal pack member right away so that there are only four coming at us. If I don't target the Alpha, the rest will come after us instead of scattering. Jaxon, you need to disable them as fast as possible; let's see how much damage per second you can manage. Bard, it'll be your job to keep them off of us and do some supplemental damage if possible. I'll send a few spells at them if you need it, but I am actually a cleric so my damage dealing spells are limited. I can bring us back to full health if it's needed at the end."

They walked a bit deeper into the forest and began looking for another pack of wolves. The number of animals in the area seemed to be a bit sparser than usual. Was it because there were fewer people in the party, or was something else going on? Joe kept a careful watch, but there didn't seem to be anything sneaking up behind them. He almost breathed a sigh of relief when he saw some wolves in the distance. For a moment, he had thought that something sinister was going on.

"Are we ready?" Joe didn't wait for an answer, simply dual casting his spikes and skewering a wolf five seconds later. The remaining animals snarled and charged, leaving their fallen brother behind.

Bard stepped forward and began chanting a drinking song, "*There's ah man ah meet, walks up our street, works for the city council...*" As he sang, it seemed that the wolves became inordinately angry. Their attention turned away from Joe, and the furious beasts moved as a group to attack the Skald. He held an axe in each hand, a wide smile on his face, and punctuated his chanting with devastating strikes against the canines.

Watching Jaxon fight was... interesting. He marched toward the wolves and came to an abrupt halt right before entering their attack range. He was tilting his head back and forth, and then seemed to reach out casually and jabbed two fingers into a nerve cluster on the neck of the Alpha. The animal went still, and Jaxon turned away and moved to another. This one he attacked with an open palm, striking four times as the wolf tried to latch onto his arm. Jaxon stopped moving after his combo finished, and the wolf got his jaw around his wrist. Try as it might, it couldn't close its mouth. The wolf's tongue lapped at his skin furiously, but its jaw was dislocated.

"Hmm. Yes, yes. That seems correct, a similar response in other species from what I have seen. Mandible structure is similar across the board. Applying pressure at *this* point should result in asphyxiation while the jaw is out of alignment." One last palm strike and the wolf slid slowly to the ground, kicking its legs a bit before going still. Jaxon had already moved on, helping Bard finish off the two remaining wolves. The entire fight was much *louder* than Joe had expected. In Joe's previous battles, there had been noise from blows landing, grunting, and sometimes crying out, but in this fight there had been a stream of consciousness lecture from Jaxon, while Bard had been chanting drinking songs. Quite a difference. Not bad. Just... different.

*Exp: 60 (12 * Wolf x5).*

"Well, that went *way* better than expected," Joe stated casually. "Even with my last team–a full five appropriately leveled people–we'd still sometimes have trouble fighting wolves."

"I've been coming out here alone," Jaxon replied indifferently. "I do appreciate someone else distracting them so that I can focus more completely on my theories and subjects."

"Ye come an' fight these massive pooches all by yer'self?" Bard looked askance at the Monk.

"Well, have you tried testing the joints of an angry horned rabbit?" Jaxon huffed at Bard. "Their bones are *far* too brittle! They usually die after a single adjustment! I needed patients with a bit more... *resilience.*"

Joe watched as the two men argued back and forth about the appropriate way of killing things. Looking at the wolves' bodies sprawled across the ground, Joe nodded a couple times–deep in thought–before coming to a final decision. They had surpassed his expectations by a huge margin; these two would make an excellent addition to his team.

CHAPTER SIX

Though Joe had told his two potential candidates that he was impressed and would like them on his team, they didn't end their training and go back to town right away. Jaxon mentioned that he was very close to level six, so they spent a few more hours hunting wolves. As they finished off one last wolf, an intense gold light filled the air and exploded outward from the Monk. He stood straighter, and for once, his smile didn't seem manic.

"That is an excellent reward feedback system!" Jaxon sighed happily. "Very pleasing. I bet there are already people addicted to leveling up. Back to town then?" The others nodded and began to trudge back to the city, hoping to get there early enough to avoid lines at dinner. Joe glanced at the accumulated experience he had gained, smiling as he noticed that a few stats had also increased.

*Exp: 329 (12 * Wolf x24 + 41 combat healing bonus).*

You have successfully led a three-man team into battle in a five-man area, and stayed there to fight for several hours without your members gaining serious injuries: Wisdom +1, Luck +1.

You have spotted six potential ambushes in two hours: Perception +1.

Joe was happy with the stat increases, though he was slightly concerned that his luck had increased as a bonus for leading his team… was the system still messing with him? Also, even though it had just increased, it seemed that his enhanced luck was not helping him right now.

A strange chuffing sound came from ahead of them on the path, followed by a much quieter yowling sound a short way behind them. Joe looked at the noise behind the team first and saw a… dog? No, that was too big to be a dog. Remembering Terra's advice, he focused on trying to see the animal's stats.

Perception check success! Black Bear Cub (Juvenile). Cubs are notoriously good climbers of trees and like to play games! One of their favorite things to do is run away from their mother and circle behind an unaware group of animals. It enjoys listening to the roars of rage that its mother releases when she notices that someone is trying to 'steal' her cub!

"Oh, *this* isn't good." Joe's eyes widened, and he turned to tell the others to get off the path. It was too late. As his head spun forward, his eyes locked with the momma bear that was lumbering toward them. A deep, menacing growl shook the air like thunder from a distant storm. He tried to see the bear's level but got a very frustrating notice when the information presented itself.

Perception check (partial) success! Furious Black Bear (Adult). Bears can range in level from 3-15 depending on age and strength. This bear is furious that you are trying to steal her cub and will feel 50% less pain until the end of combat.

"That's no help." Joe looked at the other two, "Should we fight or run?"

"Run!" Bard yelped just as Jaxon excitedly barked, "Fight!"

Jaxon continued talking, "Bears climb almost as fast as they can run, and the average bear can reach speeds of up to thirty miles per hour on a flat surface. That's forty-eight point two eight kilometers per hour for you, Bard."

"Ah knoo' how tae convert yer imperial measurement intah' *real* numbers, tank ye very much!" Bard's accent was extra thick right now thanks to a massive dose of adrenaline.

The bear decided that it had gauged their threat level… and it wasn't impressed. She charged at them while snarling, and as the angry momma got closer, it felt like she doubled in size. Even on all fours, her shoulders were level with Joe's chest, and in his amazement, he almost forgot to start preparing his shadow spikes. *Almost.*

Two spikes burst upward and jabbed into the bear's legs, but it seemed entirely unconcerned with this fact. The beast kept moving, tearing up its muscles and doing more damage to itself as it pushed right through the shadowy material. It closed on them, swinging a hefty paw at the Monk who–instead of being proactive about the fight–was squinting at the creature with his hands folded behind himself. He swayed backward, and the paw missed him by a bear inch. Joe shook his head *hard.* No! No puns during combat!

The other paw swung around as the bear pushed itself onto two legs, towering above the group. Bard jumped forward and swung his dual axes into the limb as it got close, driving the metal only about an inch into flesh before the force of the blow sent him flying backward. Somehow he forced himself to retain his grip on his weapons. He hit the ground with an **oomph** and slowly started to wiggle upward.

"Don'... block!" Bard wheezed as he tried to get back to his feet. The others noted his words but kept their attention on the battle.

The bear grunted, dropping down to all fours in an attempt to crush Jaxon with weight and momentum. The man nimbly tumbled to the side, his palm reaching out and hitting the bear on her leg. "Hmph! That's some tough muscle there… we will work on this spot until we can feel *movement*!" He struck the same spot again, then had to tuck and roll once more as a furious swipe passed over his head.

Meanwhile, Joe was preparing another dual cast of his shadow spikes. He released the built-up mana and channeled the attack, trying to hold the bear in place. The bear was pierced on either side, but as Jaxon landed his next blow, the bear finally managed a clean hit on him. Jaxon went down hard as the small, rounded tips of the claws dug into him and the massive paw crunched bone. His chest seemed to cave in, and he struggled to breathe with collapsed lungs.

"Jaxon!" Joe called, preparing a healing spell. He was somehow shocked that the Monk had been hit, though he shouldn't have been. No one can dodge *everything*! The bear took a single step toward Jaxon, reminding Joe that he had released his spikes in an attempt to heal the man in time. It seemed that the Monk's attack had an effect though, because as the bear put weight on its leg... the limb buckled and the bear dropped. It growled in surprise, then decided to forgo using that leg entirely.

"Grah!" Bard's axes slammed into the unsuspecting bear's side. It shrieked but kept its attention on Jaxon. As the animal got in range of the fallen man, it dug into him like a beehive. The paws easily parted the Monk's flesh, and it buried its teeth into his neck. It shook Jaxon back and forth vigorously, and the light rapidly faded from his eyes.

"No!" Joe cast shadow spike three more times in quick succession before his mana failed him entirely. As the bear focused on Jaxon, Bard kept slamming his axes into the bear's spine. The bear finally shuddered, flailed, and sank to the ground, going as still as the Monk.

*You have killed a level 9 Furious Black Bear (Adult). Since your party is so small and under leveled for this opponent, experience gains are doubled. Feat of strength complete! Strength +2, Constitution +1. Exp: 50 (2 * 25 * Bear x1).*

"Well, tha' was interestin," Bard stated, reaching down to close Jaxon's eyes. "Should we do anything for him?"

"No... he'll be back tomorrow; I hope that he still wants to be on the team–wait!" Joe's eyes widened, and a grin appeared on his face. "I haven't gotten a chance to use this yet, stand back!" Joe opened his character sheet and reviewed what he needed to do to cast his most powerful one-use-a-day spell.

He had Bard help pull the Monk out of the pool of blood

and viscera the bear had created and then stood back a few feet. After waiting for his mana to regenerate, he began the spell. Both hands went up in a yoga pose known as 'sun salutation' then down to his sides. Mana began to charge the air around him, and he took a step forward, sinking into a lunge with his arms still held out. He straightened, pulling his arms back so his elbows were tucked to the side with his palms facing forward. Mana began to fluctuate in front of his hands, the air shimmering from the increasing charge. He pressed his hands forward, and they seemed to meet resistance and slow down the closer they came to Jaxon's body.

Joe exhaled through his nose… took a deep breath… and calmly stated, "*Resurrection*!"

The air in front of him seemed to shatter as Jaxon's body vanished. A small portal opened in the space where his body had been, and after a few seconds of hanging in the air, Jaxon stepped through the rift, and it snapped closed behind him. He looked pretty rough; the spell only returned twenty-five percent of his health, stamina, and mana if he had access to it. He did regain twenty percent of his lost experience as well, which still made the resurrection option very desirable.

"How in the world did you bring me back?" Jaxon shook his head in wonder. "I'm glad; I was supposed to have a real-world twelve-hour penalty for not trying to 'defend myself' from the bear. Then the AI called me an overconfident moron for keeping my hands behind my back as the bear came toward me. Has it been mean to anyone else?"

"Yessir, it's super mean for no reason, and yikes! That's a hefty respawn time." Joe winced at that information. Jaxon wouldn't have been back for twenty-four hours from their perspective. That's a lot of lost time they could have used for leveling and bettering themselves. Further words failed him as a notice appeared.

Skill increase: Resurrection (Novice II). You have done a deed that humans were never meant to do! Bringing back the dead is known as the territory of the divine or the work of the vilest of necromancers looking for soul slaves. Be careful when and where you use this spell, for various religions of the available deities may see this spell as sacrilege or heresy. As a Champion of a deity, other champions may slay you for increased favor and experience from their own deity!

Know this! The spell 'Resurrection' is a daily use spell, and as it is a spell granted by a deity, it has special requirements for increasing in rank. As the power involved is not something that is truly comprehensible by a mortal, you cannot gain knowledge of the spell through study or deepening your understanding of it. Instead—until the beginner ranks—to increase the rank of the spell you simply need to use it the same amount of times as its current rank. As an example, to get to Novice III simply use the spell two more times.

Quest gained: No, I'm right! (Continuous). You have learned that Champions of deities may kill each other for bonus favor and experience. You are not excluded from this! Kill or be killed! Champions slain: 0/??.

Oh look, yet another potential enemy he would need to watch out for. Lovely. Joe sighed and walked over to Jaxon. "Give me a minute, and I'll work on healing you up. That spell drains every drop of mana that I have so… just wait a few. There's no real information provided by the tooltip; it just tells me a full day for cooldown, and the mana just shows 'all of it'. So. Not super helpful."

After Joe was able to regenerate his mana to a useful level, he cast Mend a handful of times and brought Jaxon back to full health. The Monk looked far happier and even had his somewhat disturbing smile back on his face. "Ah! Many thanks, Cleric. That was some mighty fine casting!"

"Not an issue." Joe smiled at him tiredly. "Shall we get back to town? I'm pretty worn."

"That sounds good." Bard stood and stretched. "Ah could use a bi' o' healing mahself if'n ya don' mind. Jax, do hittin' the same spot give ya a boost to damage?"

"Yes, it does!" The Monk seemed a bit surprised that Bard had put that together. "You're smarter than you seem! It is a stacking modifier so if I hit the same spot I put stacks of 'torsion' on my enemies. When I want to, I can activate my main class skill 'adjust', and it uses all the stacks to twist the area that I've been hitting. The more hearty my target, the more times I need to stack the skill in order to do damage. A rabbit? Once. Wolf? About four times. That bear was *quite* meaty!" He laughed at the end of his speech, though the others felt a bit uneasy at his enthusiasm.

"That sounds pretty painful…" Joe trailed off as the Monk gave him a 'look'.

"Just like with *all* medicine, you can either hurt or heal with it. Is death by fireball overly fun? Do your spikes not leave *holes* in your target? I'll tell you frankly, that paw to the chest followed by teeth to my neck did not feel particularly pleasing!"

Bard looked over at Joe and shrugged. "Man's go' a point."

"That he does," Joe agreed readily. "I'm just glad he's on our side!"

"You should be!" Jaxon bobbed his head seriously. "I'm wonderful!"

CHAPTER SEVEN

Joe returned to his warehouse, and he sighed happily as he walked through the door and got to work. Thinking back on the information that had led him to this point, he had to grimace a bit. There was a section in the Mage's College library that had been opened to him, but most of the information had been considered taboo for several hundred years. On one hand, it meant he had the entire section to himself. On the other hand, it also meant there was no one to help him find the information he was looking for so finding *any* information pertinent to his situation had been an incredible grind; he had gone through so many dusty tomes that he had leveled his reading skill all the way to Apprentice rank one.

Through the course of his studying, he had been able to find some information about his brand of magic that he had long suspected: rituals were *designed* to be utility spells. They were grand works of magic that were supposed to have powerful long-term effects on the world. Rituals were not *supposed* to be used for attacking, which is why attack-type rituals were so incredibly short-lived, expensive, and single-use. So Joe had decided to create a powerful utility ritual and see the difference it could make for him.

Joe frowned at the complicated ritual diagram that he had been working on for the last three days. It had taken quite a bit of study, but he had been able to narrow down the requirements needed for this powerful work of magic. What he was trying to make was a ritual that would create a 'Feather Fall' effect directly on his body. He was glad he had gone out and gotten some fresh air, but if he wanted to put some of his most advanced skills to use… this was something that he needed to have. Thinking of jumping through the sky and softly landing enticed him greatly. Joe looked over the ritual diagram once more and grunted; he was either going to need to buy a whole slew of mana potions or get a few people in here to share the mana load with him.

Since mana potions had only recently come on the market, there was an incredible backlog of orders for them. Even attempting to bribe the exhausted alchemists he had been able to find had not worked. They simply stared at his money and ever so slowly shook their heads. On a happy note–for them–they were making a *killing* selling their potions. They were working extreme overtime but being paid a premium for their wares. Ah, supply and demand. So wonderful for productive people.

Sadly, the scarcity of potions meant that he would need to drag at least four other people into his plans to make himself powerful enough. Would they be okay with that? Even more concerning was the fact that there really wasn't anyone he trusted enough to join him in his workshop. If Joe still had hair on his head, he would be pulling it off in clumps right now! This circular logic wasn't getting him anywhere. Maybe… a non-disclosure agreement? He winced as he thought of having to use a mana contract; it reminded him far too much of the previous Archmage and his paranoia. It also might be the only thing that kept his class hidden.

Although… did he even *need* to keep his class hidden at this point? The Mage's College was on good terms with him, and rituals were not forbidden anymore. Joe scratched at his chin, deep in thought. Paranoia versus practicality; he sighed, sad that there was simply no real way to tell what would be best. Keeping it hidden seemed to be doing more harm than good to him at this point by slowing down his progress. Right then and there, Joe decided that it would be better to simply trust people and give them the benefit of the doubt. He only hyperventilated a *little* at that thought.

He needed to give himself more time before making his selections for people to join his... cabal? Too many political connotations. Ritual club? Joe chuckled at that and rolled his eyes. Would coven be the right word? They weren't witches, but coven had more than one meaning, and a 'secret group of associates' fit his needs fairly well. That was for the future, though; until he found a few people who met his requirements, he had plenty of other things to do. The biggest among them was finding a way to boost his survivability as well as completing quests. He decided to make a special trip to the Mage's College. Joe opened the door to his warehouse, intent on accomplishing his goals, but the total darkness on the other side stopped him abruptly. Right. It was just a bit past midnight right now.

Suddenly feeling the sleep deprivation that had been creeping up on him, Joe rubbed at his eyes and yawned. To bed first, *then* the College! He went over to the pile of fabrics he had been using as a bed and paused. He had been using *that* as a bed? No wonder his charisma had been dropping so fast; he was living like an animal! Joe sighed and made the trip to a nearby inn as he didn't feel like walking all the way back to the guild at this time of the night. After renting a room, he fell into the deepest sleep he had managed in quite a while. When the sun eventually poked over the horizon and beams of light stabbed his eyes until he woke up, a notification appeared.

After sleeping in a clean and safe environment on a comfortable surface, you are well-rested! 10% skill and experience gained for four hours. 10% stamina and mana regeneration for six hours.

Joe almost *flew* out of bed, not wanting to waste a moment of the increased skill gain. This was just another reason to buy a bed! He hurried downstairs, took breakfast to go, and rushed toward the College. Unlike Joe, the person sitting behind the desk in the entryway of the College had apparently not slept at all and was far crankier than any customer service individual should have been. Joe had an extra fruit tart from breakfast and successfully bribed the Mage to move at more than a snail's pace when answering questions.

"I'm looking for a couple of things this morning," Joe told the man, who stared at him through half-open and barely focusing eyes as raspberry jam began to stain his teeth. "I was wondering if you had any information on how to gauge the rarity of skills or classes, where I can go to learn how to make paper and ink that can hold mana, and finally, where I can find a book on making Mage armor."

The Mage blinked and reached a hand to his aching head. "Ugh, pick *one*. I haven't slept for almost two days now. I'm not making you a map of the building."

"Um." Joe scrambled to decide which would be the best for his purposes. "The paper and ink?" He would just ask someone else for the other things when he got there, but he wanted to learn while he still received a bonus for it.

"Down this hallway, take the first right turn five times then look for the door that has a sign that says 'contract preparation one-oh-one'." The man looked at him and growled at Joe's skeptical stare. "Yes, *five* right turns. The building uses spatial magic, and it messes with what you think of as normal. Expand your mind, plebeian."

Joe nodded and walked down the hall. "See if I give *you* my food again," he muttered very quietly. After taking the fourth right turn, he looked around to see if he was back in an area he had been before, but somehow, it seemed that he was in an entirely new part of the building. Joe kept following the directions, and sure enough, found the door he was looking for. He knocked, but there was no answer. He shrugged and opened the door anyway, a bit surprised to see that there were a few people in the room working on various things.

"Oh?" A head poked up from behind a shelf, and the person seemed ecstatic to see him. "A new student? Did you mean to come here?"

"I…" Joe decided to give a partial answer, "I'm here to learn how to make ink and paper that can contain mana?"

"Then you *are* in the right place!" The man walked out from behind the shelf, revealing himself to be monstrously tall and thin. Joe had assumed he was standing on a ladder or something when he had been peeking out. "I'm Master Slender; I teach Contract Preparation one-oh-one. We don't have very many students these days; most Mages are far more interested in tossing around fireballs. Have you registered for the course?"

"Not exactly, I'm-" Joe tried to explain what he wanted.

"Not an issue, we can do that right now." The man took three steps and crossed the room in its entirety. He pulled a crystalline rose from his desk and then stepped toward Joe. He held the crystal out, and Joe hesitantly reached out for it. Watching the man move around was seriously disconcerting, like watching a praying mantis stalk dinner. Joe steeled himself and touched the rose, a notification appearing instantly.

Would you like to enroll in the course 'Contract Preparation 101'? The fee for this course is 50 gold (-90% from deal with College, your cost for the course is 5 gold), plus cost of materials. Yes / No

He certainly had the money for that. Joe accepted and the crystal flashed blue. Master Slender nodded and motioned him toward a seat. "This class is not an overly long one, depending on your willingness to learn. To pass, all you need to do is show a proficiency in each of the three skills needed for the creation of magical documents. This is the preparation of ink, paper, and quill. A quill is the medium by which we contain the mana within the ink, the magic-filled ink is how we imbue mana into the paper, and the paper itself must be treated to withstand the stressing forces created by structured mana. Any questions so far?"

The lesson began with learning to mix and create regular ink, followed by cutting and shaping quills, as well as how to find flaws in them. Next was how to determine what kinds of paper could handle mana, and then how you could produce such paper on your own. Typically, purchasing prepared paper would be the best course of action until he began making magical documents above the student ranks in terms of difficulty. Then he would *need* to begin making his own, as the cost of buying prepared versions was prohibitive.

"That's all we have time for today, as I need to get back to work." Master Slender patted Joe on the back. "I'm impressed with your dedication! At this rate, you will be passing the course in a week!" A few people groaned as they heard this lie, and Slender winked at them knowingly.

"Is there any chance that you have a book on this subject I could study," Joe inquired hopefully, "so I can be prepared for our next lesson?"

"You actually *want* to study?" The teacher paused as he thought for a moment. "Hmm. No. I want to show you the next steps in person so that you don't get confused. Our next lesson is going to be about turning the standard equipment and skills into the magical equivalent. Be prepared for an all-day event. Though what we just went through was supposed to take four full days of classes, so I *am* honestly surprised at your aptitude."

"What?" Joe looked at the blinking icon at the corner of his vision that he had been ignoring. "I hadn't even noticed…" He opened the notification and a slew of skill gains and increases condensed into their most recent level.

Being trained by a Master of a craft has greatly increased your speed of comprehension!

Skill gained: Quill preparation and maintenance. (Beginner 0). Sharp quills mean sharp and accurate writing or drawing! Each rank of this skill increases quill durability by 2%.

Skill gained: Ink preparation. (Beginner 0). Creating the correct color and consistency of ink is paramount to creating beautiful works of litera-

ture. Each rank of this skill increases ink purity by 2% and decreases time to create desired ink by 2%.

Skill gained: Paper making and selection. (Beginner 0). Just because the paper is available doesn't mean it is worth using! Each rank of this skill increases paper durability by 2% when it is used or created by you.

Skill increased: Scribe (Beginner VII). Learning how to prepare and maintain the tools of this craft have resulted in a skill increase!

"*Three* skills instantly to the beginner ranks, *and* a skill increase to my scribe skill?" Joe was incredulous at the absurd rate of skill increase.

"There are great benefits to being taught by a *Master*. There is a *reason* we have centers of learning instead of just making our own way through all aspects of life." Slender smiled crookedly before shooing Joe out of the room.

CHAPTER EIGHT

After taking a few minutes to stop himself from getting too frustrated for his lack of critical thinking, Joe remembered that he had come here to learn another Mage spell and make progress on one of his quests. He went back to the entrance of the building and was relieved to find that a new person was sitting at the desk. He walked over and asked where he could go to be taught a new spell. After Joe gave his name to the clerk, he was ushered back to a room similar to… Cel walked in. So the *same* room as when he had been given the puzzle cube.

"Good…" Cel glanced consideringly at an hourglass on the table, "…*morning*, Joe! If *just* barely. I was told you finally came here to be taught a spell? You want to learn it *properly*, hm*mm*?"

Joe rolled his eyes at the casual sneer in Cel's voice. "Hey there, Cel. As always, I am overjoyed to see you once more. Yes, I do want to learn a new spell, but I am unsure what would be best right now. I found out very recently that being taught has some great benefits."

Cel nodded at this statement. "There are great benefits in the form of being able to use the spells and skills sooner, but… well, learning them on your own *is* also admirable. Doing your own research on a subject can only help your progress in the long run. From understanding comes knowledge, and from knowledge comes skill."

Joe's eyes almost bled, he rolled them so hard. "How very *wise* and *Sage* of you. Practicing your lectures for new Mages on me, are you?"

Cel's cheeks went a bit pink. His next words were far more hurried, "Anyway, what sort of spell work are you wanting to learn?"

Pausing for a moment, Joe had to shrug. "As much as I'd love to learn everything right off the bat, I guess some defensive spells would be nice…?"

"Hmm. Well, beyond your Mage Armor, what defensive spells do you know?" Cel pondered thoughtfully.

"Why does everyone keep assuming I know how to use Mage Armor?" Joe looked at the Mage quizzically. "All I am actually doing is dodging or jumping away from attacks coming at me."

"…What?" Cel seemed confused which, in turn, made Joe confused. "My Master told me that you survived an area of effect spell from him even after it blasted you onto a roof from street level. How do you survive *that* without Mage Armor?"

"Oh, that." Joe shuddered as he remembered the street suddenly being filled with volcanic flame and concussive force. "No, I didn't get directly hit with that spell. I jumped out of the way, and a bit of the after effect caught me."

No response came for a long moment. "…*Right.* Sure. Let's pretend you *don't* know how to use Mage Armor. I *will* charge you to learn it if you force me to 'teach' it to you." Cel's eyes were narrowed, probably sore from being rolled so many times in such a short time.

"Good, I guess? I'd like to learn it; the spell sounds useful," Joe stated in a straightforward manner. "If you think I was able to survive a wave of fiery death by having that spell, I would *really* like to know what it does and how to make it work."

"*Fine,*" Cel spat while passing over an orb. "Go ahead and

register your request to be 'taught' the spell, Joe. Go ahead. *Pay* me for knowledge you already have." Joe didn't appreciate the sarcasm but still touched the orb and watched a notification appear.

Register to be taught spell 'Mage Armor' by Journeyman Cel? Tuition price reduced: Instructor is not a Master of the spell, additionally your 90% discount has been applied. Price of spell: 1 gold. Accept instruction? Yes / No

Joe accepted, and the orb flashed blue. Cel groaned and pinched the bridge of his nose. "Fine, you insufferable... why did I *ask* to teach you? Let's talk about Mage Armor. As you undoubtedly *know*, the heavier armor is, the more it impedes your movements. This means that it is harder to cast spells unless you have high strength and dexterity. Obviously, those are typically stats that aren't invested in by Mages to a great degree."

"Makes perfect sense." Joe nodded along.

"I *bet* it does," Cel grumbled, obviously not believing that Joe didn't know the spell. "Mage Armor is a spell that frees the awakened amongst us from the need to wear heavy armor in battle. We create 'armor' from our mana and coat our bodies in this power. The armor acts like a solid and a fluid at the same time, allowing air and slow-moving objects to come through so we can still grasp things, but it stops anything moving above a certain speed."

"So it acts like a non-Newtonian fluid?" Joe muttered to himself as he scratched at his ear.

"What now?"

Joe shook his head. "Just rephrasing it in better terms for myself."

"Mmhm. Almost like you *know*... whatever. Well, the armor is doubly effective against spells, but this, unfortunately, means *all* spells. Healing spells from outside sources will be blocked just as much as damaging spells. Let's focus on the requirements for a moment, though. At the first rank of this spell, you can put any amount of your mana into Mage Armor, and it will block that amount of damage from spells and half that from physical impacts. However much you put in, ten percent of that will be reserved from your mana pool to maintain a connection to the spell as well as maintaining the armor itself." Cel paused to let the information sink in.

"Add two hundred mana, and you lose access to twenty mana until the armor is gone?" Joe questioned, showing he was paying attention. "That investment of two hundred mana will block *one* hundred damage from a sword?"

"Exactly." Cel thought a moment before grouchily muttering, "Not that most beginners with this spell can simply toss two *hundred* mana at it…"

"Don't worry about that. Can we work on actually casting it?" Joe impatiently demanded. He was excited to learn this spell; it would effectively double or triple his health.

"Alright." Cel started talking, "First, you imagine a layer of mana over your body, like a bubble but held tight against your skin. Let your mana flow into that shape, filling all the space between your skin and the bubble. It is harder than it sounds because the mana will want to fly off into the air when you release it."

It took quite a while—and annoyed instruction from Cel—before Joe was able to keep the mana around him and not let it just dissipate into the room. It was a struggle, but as soon as he gained the first rank in the spell it became infinitely easier to create the armor. The lost vapor-like mana was *sucked* back into shape around him, and his new Mage Armor solidified. Luckily, the armor turned transparent, and there was no distortion around him thanks to how close the spell was to his skin. At that point, he practiced dispelling the armor and remaking it under Cel's watchful eye.

Spell gained: Mage Armor (Novice V). Being taught the proper way to do things from the very beginning tends to have better results than bashing your head against a problem until it is solved. Now, you can bash your head against anything and not feel it! Please do try it a few dozen times. Effect: For every point of mana devoted to this spell, negate one point of damage from primary sources of magic and half a point from primary sources of physical damage. Increase conversion by .025n where 'n' equals skill level.

"Huh." Joe read over the notification again, *really* looking at the details. "Huh."

"What?" Cel was pleasantly surprised; his teaching skill had increased, meaning that Joe really *hadn't* known the spell. He was feeling a bit sheepish about his condescending words now.

"The description on this one is pretty different from any of my other skills..." Joe trailed off. "Increases conversion?"

"Oh, that." Cel nodded at Joe's words. "It means that every point you add will block more damage. Easier to see in practice than to explain."

"Great, thanks. How do I rank up in the skill?" Joe wanted to put the armor on, but if there was a trick to it, he didn't want to miss out.

"Two ways, but they are both *kind* of the same. Your armor has to take damage," Cel explained easily. "You can increase your rank faster if you work the armor in specific ways, like thickening it around vital areas. There isn't a *direct* rank gain, but the more of the armor that is devoted to blocking an attack, the faster its levels increase. Passive damage reduction is difficult to directly explain."

"Play with the shape of the armor, take damage," Joe cut out all the fluff, and Cel nodded after a moment.

"That about covers it," Cel admitted, a bit frustrated. He was trying to increase his teaching skill, blast it!

Quest updated: Playing your fake role II. Learn three Mage spells 3/3. Get one Mage-type skill to the Beginner ranks 0/1. Kill five enemies within ten seconds by using spells 0/1.

Joe thanked Cel, chatted a short while, and left the College. As soon as he stepped out, he remembered that he had forgotten to ask about skill rarity! He almost went back in, but decided that he had spent too much time indoors recently and it would be a good idea to go train. Before he went further, he activated his Mage Armor, dumping all eight hundred and eighty-eight points of mana into its activation. That should stop just about four hundred and forty points of physical damage! The only unfortunate part of the skill was the fact that spell efficiency didn't work to decrease the mana requirement. Ah well. Can't have everything.

Joe smiled an evil smile and decided to… go for a walk. Today was a Monday in the real world, so a good amount of people that played the game were offline for now. From Joe's perspective, they wouldn't be logging in until tomorrow; so it was the perfect time to start branching out with his training.

CHAPTER NINE

**Thud*. **Thud*. Joe ignored the impacts that barely shifted him, focusing intently on sharpening another quill in preparation for his next class session. He had already mixed three jars of ink, and- **Thud*. Joe turned his head and glared at the rabbit that was doing its best to kill him. It glared right back at him and jumped once again, slamming its horn into his side.

The rabbits had ignored him for a good long time, frightened away by his level. To get around this, Joe had simply taken a relaxed position by sitting down. Technically, he was considered a 'helpless' target, and the rabbits that saw him couldn't *not* attack him. That said, he didn't want a swarm of rabbits around him full-time, so whenever a new one started attacking him, a shadow spike would devastate whichever rabbit had been attacking him the longest. Joe needed fresh attackers to build his shields, not exhausted fluffballs.

This rabbit though… maybe it was the last one in the area because it had lasted a lot longer than most of them had to this point. It was also a little bigger; did this count as a boss monster for the angry rabbits? It was possible. The rabbit stood out a bit for the simple fact that it had a pointed horn instead of a rounded nub, but there was nothing otherwise that screamed 'boss monster' at him. Joe went back to ignoring the rabbit and started going through his reams of paper. Thanks to his recent instruction, he was able to discern which of the sheets could potentially be upgraded to contain mana and which were going to have to remain as doodle paper. He could- **Thud**. "*Ow*!"

Joe jumped to his feet, frantically looking around to find what could have hurt him. The rabbit jumped at him again, smacking against his Mage armor and falling to the ground. Not seeing anything else in the area, Joe opened his combat log and scrolled down past the scores of 'rabbit does damage to armor' messages, finally finding what he was looking for.

Angry Bunnicorn deals 3 damage (Armor penetration).

"You must be *kidding* me." Joe looked down at the animal that was gearing up to attack him once again and decided to study it instead of killing it outright. He rolled his eyes as he read the information he was able to glean with his perception check.

Perception check success! Angry Bunnicorn (level 3). The Bunnicorn, much like the Unicorn, is largely regarded as a myth. They are pure and gentle creatures, unlike their racial enemy, the 'Chic-chic-boom chicken'. It is widely known that killing a Bunnicorn will stain your soul, permanently increasing the aggressiveness of all rabbits toward you.

"So I can't kill you or rabbits will attack me again whenever I step outside the gates? You are the worst kind of enemy. You make weak creatures attack strong ones." Joe chided the rabbit, which had fluffed up indignantly as soon as Joe started speaking aloud. The rabbit jumped at him again, and Joe watched as the sharp horn reached the edge of his armor and skidded off. "Need either a perfect attack or a certain amount of strength to get through the armor, hmm? Well, I should really thank you. I hadn't even thought about armor penetration... in fact, I am sure there is a way to cut right through Mage armor, isn't there? As thanks, I won't skewer you."

Joe decided to get going; he wasn't going to get much more done right now unless he wanted to kill the Bunnicorn, and he had no desire to fight off rabbits all the time. As he walked away, the Bunnicorn squealed at a pitch that made Joe's ears hurt. He turned around angrily, but just then a notification appeared.

Bunnicorn has called for reinforcements! Prepare for a swarm!

"You have *got* to be kidding me!" Joe groaned, picking up speed as he broke into his strange skip-shuffle walk. It looked exceptionally odd but boosted his walking speed by sixty-two percent since he was technically adding his jump skill modifier to his movement speed. His increased pace wasn't going to allow him to escape though; he could already see a carpet of bouncing rabbits closing in on him. If he didn't clear a path, he was going to be in *serious* trouble. Spellcasting while moving wasn't exactly an easy task, nor a safe one, but he really had no choice. He began casting weak acid spray with each hand, releasing a cone of acid from two locations as the rabbits got close.

There was a collective scream of pain from over a dozen rabbits as they were caught in the acid and it began melting them. The spell did five points of damage over a few seconds, and most rabbits had an average of four health. By the time the first among them reached him, nearly all of the affected rabbits had fallen to the ground and begun dissolving fully. Joe had a clear path now, but… he glanced around and saw dozens more rabbits. His armor started taking hits, but he figured that he had time to finish this group off. He dual cast acid spray once again, intentionally keeping the Bunnicorn out of the area of effect.

Over the next two seconds, almost all of the rabbits that had joined in the fray were turning into puddles. Joe finished off the rest with targeted shadow spikes, happy that he had set his class as 'Mage' today. He might have run out of mana in this battle otherwise! Ten seconds later, only he and the Bunnicorn were still alive. It was trembling in fear and anger but continued to attack him. Joe reached down and grabbed the animal by the scruff of its neck, surprised when it stopped moving just like a cat would when grabbed like this.

Joe shrugged and started walking back to the city. Blinking notifications caught his attention, and he read them as he walked.

Quest updated: Playing your fake role II. Learn three Mage spells 3/3. Get one Mage-type skill to the beginner ranks 0/1. Kill five enemies within ten seconds by using spells 1/1.

Skill increase: Weak Acid Spray (Novice VII). Nothing quite like melting down helpless animals to give you a clear picture of what acid does to flesh!

Skill increase: Dual Casting (Novice II) Spells? Lots *of spells! Spells everywhere! Who needs to be careful not to destroy the landscape? Not you! Cast, cast,* cast*!*

A swarm has been destroyed by you; finish off the instigating agent to complete the event!

"Yeah, I'm not killing this thing," Joe muttered as he picked up the pace. The Bunnicorn struggled a bit, but he ignored it and kept walking. As he approached the city gate, a guard stopped him by stepping into his path.

"You can't bring a live monster inside the city without a permit." The guard was looking at Joe with sad eyes like he should know *better* than to do stupid things.

"Look, this is a Bunnicorn. If you want to kill it, be my guest, but I'm not doing it. I have no plans to get another curse on myself. I was gonna see if I can sell it to a pet shop or something." Joe sighed as the guard looked at him skeptically.

"A Bunnicorn? You're messing with…" The guard seemed to sag as he inspected the rabbit. "I can never let my daughter know about this. I can see her searching for one and getting skewered trying to hug it."

"Makes sense," the other guard chipped in. "If she takes after *you*, that's *exactly* what would happen. Better hope she gets her brain from her momma."

"You know *what-*" the first guard started, reaching for his spear.

"Can I go in? It'll keep attacking me until I can get it in a cage or something." Joe tapped his foot impatiently as the guards began bantering. The rabbit was squirming again, and holding it was getting more difficult. Strength was his weakness, and the rabbit was getting heavy.

"Well... exception?" the first guard asked the other, who nodded. The guard turned back to Joe. "Go on through, but try not to make anything like this a common occurrence."

"Thanks." Joe walked into the city, and the Bunnicorn began to squeal. Joe's face turned red as the animal continued to wail especially loudly around any women they passed. He had to ask directions from disapproving passerby–having never been to a pet store–but he eventually found the small building attached to a warehouse.

The pet shop owner offered to buy the Bunnicorn, but Joe waved away all the offers and tried to simply leave the creature there. The ecstatic shopkeeper was insistent that he take *something*, so Joe pointed at a bestiary and asked if he could have a copy of the book. It was only after seeing the hesitation on the man's face that Joe remembered how expensive paper was and, therefore, how expensive books were. He tried to back out of the deal, but the man had already handed him the book and wouldn't take 'no' for an answer. It seemed that the Bunnicorn was even rarer–and therefore more expensive–than he had expected.

Joe left the store without the Bunnicorn, much to his relief. He almost walked right into a person who was waiting at the door but was luckily able to stop himself in time. "Excuse me. Sorry about that!"

"Are you Joe of The Wanderer's guild?" Her voice was strong but oddly stilted, like she had been rehearsing this phrase.

"...Yes?" Joe was on the defensive now; she must have been following him.

She nodded and took a deep breath and said her next words in such a rush that Joe almost couldn't understand them. "I-need-a-team-and-a-guild-and-I-suck-at-talking-to-people-please-let-me-be-in-yours!"

Staring at the furiously blushing woman, Joe almost couldn't think of a response. "I, uh, what's your class and what position do you want? We need a ranged person for sure, and a rogue if possible…" he trailed off as her face got even redder.

"I range! I can be range!" She slapped her hands on her face. "I suck so much! I'm so sorry, I'll just go."

"Please wait, you came all this way… at least make your case!" Joe called as she started to run.

She slowed, stopped, and then came back to him while staring at the ground. She mumbled a few things and nodded at him, clearly thinking he could hear what she had just said. Seeing his lack of comprehension, she tried again, "I'm Alexis. Um. I use poison and crossbows."

"Great! What's your class and level?" Joe patiently prodded. Even if she wasn't a good fit for the team, there wasn't exactly a long line of people looking to join him. A single willing spirit was worth a dozen forced helpers.

"I'm level ten, and I'm an Aromatic Artificer!" Alexis spoke boldly, swallowing hard when she realized she had practically shouted at him. "I'm so sorry, I have so much trouble with my voice when I get nervous, and then it makes me worse and I-"

"It's fine! It's all good!" Joe stopped her before she could self-destruct. "An Artificer? Do you make weapons or trinkets?"

"No, I m-make weapon augments for ranged weapons. I can upgrade them, and well, yes, I can *make* weapons. No one else can *use* the weapons without the requisite skill though, or they… kinda die? It'll shatter in their hands and backlash on them."

"Have you made your own weapons?" Joe was really having fun right now; he remembered when he had been considered an awkward introvert. He had increased his social ability by quite a bit and now he was just called 'strange'. When she nodded, Joe looked at the clock and noticed that they only had a few hours of light left. "Perfect. Can you meet me tomorrow morning at the east gate? Nine in the morning game time? The other guys on the team will join us, and we can see if we work well together."

"That's-great-thanks-bye!" Alexis turned and scampered away.

"...See you then?" Joe called after her in confusion. What a strange day. He went to his room and worked on his puzzle cube for an hour then worked to study, optimize, and memorize more information from his book on rituals. Deciding to go to bed early for once to appease his burning eyes and throbbing head, he returned to the nearby inn and went to sleep. Joe checked his notifications with a smile right before closing his eyes.

Characteristic point training completed! +1 to intelligence, wisdom, perception, and dexterity! These stats cannot be increased further by any means other than system rewards for twenty-four hours game time.

CHAPTER TEN

Joe's eyes flew open, and he looked at the time in full panic mode. He had overslept! Gah! This is what he gets for going to bed at a normal, healthy time; his body takes *advantage* of his thoughtfulness! Joe looked out of his window and contemplated trying to find a way down. He was on the second floor of the building, so it wasn't a *great* option, but going downstairs and around the block just to get to this street again was going to cost him almost ten minutes.

Wait… why *not* go out the window? He was only ten feet off the ground, and he *was* a Master jumper. If that failed too badly, well then, he was also a healer that could fix broken bones. Joe opened the window, stepped out on the ledge, and closed the window carefully. A well-aimed shadow spike hitting the metal clasp locked the window, and Joe prepared to jump down while considering a life of crime. Taking a deep breath and preparing for pain, Joe *jumped*! His body aligned itself without conscious assistance, and just before landing, he did a flip that ate up most of his momentum. He landed heavily but only lost a single point of health due to true damage from impacting terrain.

"That was *awesome*!" Joe whooped and laughed, then took a single step forward and collapsed. His stamina was entirely depleted, likely from the fancy acrobatics. Wait, *definitely* from the acrobatics!

Skill gained: Aerial Acrobatics (Novice I). This is a subskill of 'Jump' and boosts the effectiveness of any mid-air movements. Masters of this skill have been known to remain in the air long enough to cross canyons, and Sages are rumored to be able to walk on clouds. You though... you can do a flip. Effect: Ease of movement while in the air increases by 2% until the end of the Beginner ranks.

It took almost ten seconds until Joe could stop wheezing and start walking. Still faster than leaving the front of the building! At least, that's what he kept telling himself. Joe hurried to the east gate, waving at the two groups of people that were standing a little bit away from each other. "Jaxon, Bard, this is Alexis. She is going to be trying out for a position on our team as a ranged damage dealer."

Bard grunted, and Jaxon nodded in her direction politely if a bit thoughtlessly. It was obvious that they both had other things that they were thinking about. From the way Jaxon's hands were moving, Joe could see that the Monk wanted to get back to trying to adjust the world; Bard remained as inscrutable as ever. Just as the group started to depart, they were halted by a guild member running up to them with a letter.

"From Aten," the messenger told Joe breathlessly. "He said that we have a good location, but there is something strange going on and we need a strange person to look into it. Then he said to just tell you to look into it and not tell you that he called you... strange..." The messenger coughed and looked away, obviously a bit embarrassed.

"Thanks?" Joe opened the letter as the man wobbled off muttering about his running skill stagnating. The messenger did *not* get a tip. There was a pause as Joe read over the missive, but then he snorted and looked at the notification that appeared.

Your guild leader has shared a secret quest with you! If you complete it, you will gain the rewards while the guild receives the renown. Accept? Yes / No

There was no other information about the quest besides the letter unfolding to show a crude map that he'd have to follow. Joe accepted the quest and a proper notification appeared.

*Quest alert: The Secret of Sir Bearington. A town that fits the needs of your guild has been found, but the locals are somewhat hostile to outsiders. Their mayor, Sir Bearington, has refused to let the town fall back under the banner of Ardania. He says it is because they aren't needed and never have been, but something strange is going on! *Note: This is a secret quest and has many possible routes to completion. Rewards will be given based on the information you find... as well as how you use it.*

"Looks like we have a new plan, everyone. I'm going on a quest, and I need my team with me so I hope you all have free time!" Joe told the others triumphantly, calming down a bit when he remembered that they were all in the trial phase. "I *do* understand if you don't want to go, but it's for the guild and if we complete it... let's just say you might be accepted by the others a little easier."

No one decided to stay behind, which suited Joe's purposes perfectly. It was hard to get to know someone with only a few short, action-packed hours. Now they would have an overnight expedition to really *talk*! ... An hour of walking through the forest later, no one had said anything beyond pointing out monsters followed by a short monologue about bone structure from Jaxon. Joe was feeling a bit put out, but perhaps he hadn't thought about the ramifications of creating a party composed of introverts, experts, and expert introverts. He decided that as the team leader, it was up to him to get to know his minions. Teammates. Same difference.

"So, Alexis!" Joe started brightly, startling the others and making them look for whatever was attacking them. "Can you tell us a little bit about your class and abilities? What does an 'Aromatic Artificer' do?"

"I'm. Um. I use crossbows and... bolts." Alexis looked down at the ground. "The 'aromatic' part of it is... misleading. It's a specialization usually associated with people like candle makers. But… with me… it's…"

The others waited, some more patiently than others. Bard loudly voiced his thoughts, and a touch of mana colored his word, "Ach! Jus' goo head and spit it out, lass! No one here's gon' bite yer head off!"

Contrary to Joe's expectations, Bard's 'kind' words had the intended effect. Had he given her a buff? Alexis rubbed her neck and spoke a little more boldly, "Well, I specialized into this class because of the massive bonuses to area of effect that I get. Instead of vaporizing wax and allowing pretty smells to make their way to people's noses… my artificed weapons release a cloud of poison gas that rapidly expands and expends itself. Exceptionally potent against tightly-packed groups."

"How do we avoid being caught in the poison?" Jaxon voiced his first question of the day that did not relate to anatomy.

Alexis blushed and hesitated a little. "You… don't. I just need to make sure not to use these arrows when you are too close to the enemy. I'll soften them up at a distance and then switch to standard arrows."

"How deadly is the poison?" Joe interrupted thoughtfully. "I have a spell that lets me heal poison over time, but it might be a somewhat underpowered ability if your abilities match your level."

"The size of the arrow is the determining factor; it impacts how much poison I can put into it," Alexis informed them, voice beginning to get soft again. "More poison means more spread, but poison can be time-consuming and difficult to make. This means that my smallest poison arrows have the most deadly and concentrated versions, but those also usually get injected. The most dangerous variant is a student-ranked poison, though my weakest is still beginner ranked."

"So what I really need to worry about clearing is beginner-ranked right now?" Joe thought over her words. "It'll take some practice, but I *should* be able to clear it out if we get hit by it. If not, I can heal you up and try again."

"Yeah, thanks..." Alexis was getting close to hyperventilating, so Joe decided to move the conversation onward.

"What did you all pick as your professions at level five?" Joe looked around, mainly getting shrugs in answer. Joe glared at the group until they started to crack from the building pressure.

Bard finally decided to bite the bullet and speak. "Ah took 'performer'. Boosts mah effect when ah chant, speak, dance, or act."

"Should be no surprise to anyone else, but I took 'Chiropractor'," Jaxon announced. "It helps me-"

Jaxon was driven to the ground as a black streak slammed into him from above. There was a rumbling growl coming from what turned out to be a bear, and it was biting Jaxon as hard as it could. As the others turned to fight it off, Alexis beat them to the punch by screaming and using an ability. "*Pinning shot*!" she yelped in an almost surprised tone, pulling at a strap on her shirt. An oversized crossbow–which looked more similar to a ballista than anything–unhooked from her back, flipped up and snapped into place on her shoulder, instantly launching a bolt as long as her arm.

The recoil of the bolt launching sent her staggering backward, but the bear had it far worse. The projectile caught the beast in the side and sent it flying into a tree trunk several feet from its starting location. The bolt dug into the wood, pinning the bear against the tree a few feet above the ground. A soft explosion followed, the arrow exhaling a puff of smoke that quickly spread away from the impact site. It dissipated after a single second, but unfortunately, the fallen Jaxon was still caught within the area of effect.

As soon as the smoke vanished, Joe was at Jaxon's side with a healing spell to stabilize him. It was obvious to all that Jaxon's health was falling rapidly, mainly from the potent poison he had just inhaled, but also from the sudden damage and perhaps a broken neck. Joe activated Cleanse and worked to combat the poison directly. His Cleanse skill was only ranked at beginner zero, but he had a ten percent bonus effectiveness against poison and toxins that were affecting a person so he slowly started to win. Clearing out the poison took a long minute, but Joe was able to stave off the damage for long enough that the blood-curdling effect petered out. He was a *little* frustrated that he hadn't been able to clear it out directly, but Jaxon had survived and that was what really mattered here.

Skill increase: Cleanse (Beginner I). Working to clear out deadly poison is a great way to gain experience cleansing someone! Remember, poisoning your friends isn't a bad thing… if it is for experience!

Jaxon weakly reached up and grabbed his own head. With a sickening twist and several popping sounds, his bones realigned. His voice rasped like a chain smoker, "Don't suppose you can heal these bones? I set them… so…"

Bard gagged and Alexis seemed to be in shock. Joe–though pale–nodded and cast mend on the Monk. Soon he was back on his feet, doing disturbing stretches. "Hmm. Range of motion has not suffered. Good. I am *quite* thirsty though."

"I have water…" Joe paused as he remembered one of the most underused functions of his cleansing ability. "Let me do this directly, if that's okay. Let your neck take a few minutes off." He channeled Cleanse into the Monk, and soon, Jaxon was commenting on the 'well-hydrated' buff. So much so that Joe soon fed water into himself and the other members of the party to ensure that they were all at peak performance.

"That was the cub of the bear we had to fight yesterday," Jaxon mentioned offhandedly. "At least, it had the same bone structure and markings. Perhaps that is a hidden function of fighting bears? If you kill the mother bear and they have a spawn out in the wild it will hunt you down and attempt an assassination at an unknown time?"

"So you are saying that if we kill *one*, we're going to have to kill their whole family?" Alexis seemed aghast and was twisting a chunk of cloth between her fingers. "I'm not sure I like the combat mechanics in this game."

"Was tha' yer *normal* weapon?" Bard waved at the massive crossbow that was once again hidden on her back.

"Hmm? Bertha? No, that's my… I like to think of it as my ultimate ability?" Alexis seemed to be breathing easier around them. She showed two small crossbows that were in holsters like pistols and pulled them out. "These are my normal armaments, but when I'm startled, or stressed… I tend to go overboard and throw everything I have at my target."

"Overkill is the best kind of kill." Joe chuckled as they *finally* found something to chat about. For the next hour of their walk, they discussed their favorite ways to finish off an opponent. It was a good time.

CHAPTER ELEVEN

Joe had never traveled in this direction before; at the very least, he had never gone this *far* to the east. They had swiftly passed through the plains surrounding the city of Ardania. After discussing the quest for a while, they lapsed back into silence. Finally, after a full day of walking, they broke through the dense forests where the majority of animal enemies lived. Now they were walking down a path through cultivated fields, approaching their destination after about ten hours of constant movement. The journey should have been more difficult, but Joe had set his class to 'Mage' and therefore was able to devote plenty of mana to his tiny yet potent repertoire of offensive spells.

"Have any of you been to another town outside of Ardania?" Joe nervously eyed yet another farmer who seemed inexplicably hostile to them as they walked by.

"This is my first time outside of the *city*," Alexis commented, quickly becoming uncomfortable as the others looked at her oddly. "What?"

"How in the *world* are you level ten?" Jaxon voiced the question the others were thinking.

"I completed quests, *obviously*. Beyond that, I also gain a ton of experience from making weapons and get bonus contribution experience when people use the things that I've made to kill enemies. Sure, no one can use my *special* weapons, but I can make augments and poisons for anyone." Alexis kept her eyes on the road as the others exchanged astonished glances. "Fighting is… *inefficient* for leveling. We've only made one hundred and thirty-six experience this entire trip. That's less than a tenth of what I can make in a normal eight hour work day." From there, the conversation began drifting into irritation or awkward silences after a full day of discussing their differences, and they were all tired and in need of a nap.

"There's the town!" Joe called with relief as the first two-story building they had seen since leaving the city came into view. The group had passed a few small farmhouses, but Joe was getting concerned by the dwindling daylight. If they hadn't found a place to stay the night by the time full dark arrived, he would have had to make a ritual to ward off creatures while they slept. This was not the best option because this far away from the starter area there was a possibility that his ritual would actually draw in a creature at a level that they couldn't hope to combat.

A few minutes of more energetic travel later, they passed through the gate of a wooden palisade that encircled the town. Far different from the people in the fields, here people seemed happy; they were smiling and going about their evening while chatting or calling out to each other. Their smiles and relaxed moods faltered as they saw the strangers that had entered their secluded part of the world. Hushed whispers and furtive glances came their way, and as Joe's party moved through the town, the village folk scattered and emptied the streets ahead of them.

"This don' bode well for making friends in tae area," Bard subvocalized, locking eyes with Joe and pointing at a fleeing group with his chin.

"Was this attitude why the guild wanted us to come here?" Joe pondered aloud. He looked over his letter again and noticed that they only had three days before the entire guild showed up, so if they wanted the rewards they were going to need to work fast. They *did* have the Kingdom's blessing to bring outlying towns under their control, and using force *was* an option unless they had already submitted. Not a *good* option, but it was *an* option. "We have a very limited time frame to do this correctly. Let's get a couple of rooms and get an early start in the morning. I think we all need a break."

They found an 'inn', which was a very nice way to say 'dive bar with rooms'. The bartender was *very* reluctant to hand over keys to the room but did so after they paid his exorbitant fee. When they actually got into the rooms they turned right around and took a vote on if they would rather sleep outside. The beds had so many bugs in them that they were *visibly moving*.

The only reason that they didn't leave and sleep in the open was the simple fact that they had needed to pay up front. At least the bartender repeating 'no refunds' so many times made sense now. The vote was set aside when Bard pointed out that it was better to be somewhere that had at least a *modicum* of protection from the elements and marauding creatures.

In an attempt not to be infested or contract whatever diseases were implanted in the bed, the group stepped out of the room and had Alexis fire an arrow into the mattress. A cloud of poison filled the entire space, lingering quite a bit longer than it would have done outside. Unsurprisingly, there was no window in the wall of the tiny room; that might have added some aspect of comfort. After the dangerous miasma dissipated, they stepped back into the room and looked things over.

The bed was no longer moving, but Joe had no interest in laying in it and bringing back bedbug eggs in his robe when he left this place. Using a broom handle, they carefully flipped the bed up against the wall and cleared the floor, lying directly on the ground in the now-open space. Between the poor comfort and the raucous bar scene, none of them slept soundly at all. Even still, morning came too soon.

"Coffee?" Joe was staring at a new bartender, but when the man responded, Joe was simply dumbfounded.

"No coffee in town." The man shook his head in the negative. "Too expensive to import, and we can't grow it 'round here. I've got cornmeal or wheat meal. Milk to drink. Meat is extra."

Joe's eyes had dark circles under them. He tried to process the words coming out of this man's mouth, but they simply didn't have any meaning to him. "...Coffee?"

"Get out."

The team of adventurers walked out of the hovel they had called home for the night and began looking around for anything that may indicate a glaringly obvious method to complete their quest. Joe looked around at the few businesses in the area and grunted. "Granary, sawmill, carpenter, general goods, and a tailor with the smallest selection of clothes I have ever seen. There is a blacksmith that only makes crude household items and horseshoes! Why in the *world* was this town selected to be our guild's base?"

"Outside my pay grade." Jaxon took a deep breath. "Smells nice, though. Better than the city by far. Should we go find this Bearington fellow?" There were only a few non-residential buildings in the entire town, so it wasn't overly difficult to find the city hall. In fact, it turned out to be the smallest building within the town's borders.

"This is a nice change," Alexis stated as they walked into the building. "Government not using tax money to make itself look fancy? Most unrealistic thing about this entire game, and I've seen a man shatter a rock by staring at it."

Their Spartan surroundings allowed them to see the man that must have been the Mayor. Sir Bearington was sitting at a desk talking to two others who were writing out his decrees. He looked up at them as they entered the building, huffing in annoyance at their interruption. Joe looked over the extraordinarily hairy man, a bit confused. His instincts were screaming something at him, and he could feel his skill 'Hidden Sense' going wild. No wonder the person who had scouted this town had said that something strange was going on. This place was sure to be the epicenter of oddity.

"Good morning. Sir Bearington, I presume?" Joe's words were seemingly ignored, so he decided to get to the point. "I am here as a representative of my guild. Within three days, the majority of my guild will be joining us in the area. We have been charged by the Kingdom to bring this area back under the banner of Ardania, and I would love for us to begin our relationship on a positive note. Is there anything that we can do for the town that would allow us-"

The mayor stood, and at full height he was an unbelievable eight feet tall. His eyes narrowed, and he glared at Joe before speaking with a booming voice. It seemed he had a cold, though, because a few of his words seemed a bit twisted. "You walk in here and tell me you want us to be friends at the same time that you are saying that your guild is coming to take over no matter what we do? To me, it seems that you should be treated as invaders coming to destroy our way of life, our entire bearitage!"

Joe had expected this reaction, to a degree. "We are not coming here to take over, nor do we want to destroy your heritage. We are coming to join the town, offer protection against monsters, and grow our communal strength. There will be no coups, no overthrowing of the local government."

"So what do you call coming and changing things without permission?" Thick and hairy hands pawed at the air in agitation. "I'm not going to give you permission to do a dang thing. No land, no sale of goods, no… *no*, forgive me, that isn't fair. I don't want to be overbearing to this degree. Tell you what, mancub. I'm elected. I'll make this simple for you. If you go and get permission from every building owner in the town to come and live here, you can join us with a high reputation. Otherwise, you're gonna be seen as invading outsiders, and we'll do everything we can to make your life difficult here."

"Why can't we just buy some land and use it for our own

purposes?" Joe challenged in reply. "You can keep your government and pipe dreams of not being a part of the Kingdom."

"All the land 'round here belongs to the town. No one needs to own anything more than their house or shop. No outside trade means no need to hoard goods in hope of selling them. We all participate in feeding and clothing our people. You wanna drink? You contribute more to the town in the form of grain, and we make alcohol. Need clothes? Bring them the equal value in food or other goods. We don't want you here. You'll destroy our economy just by existing."

"What economy?" Joe was beginning to get upset. "This entire town is falling apart! Every building I've seen is built by stacking logs! Every winter you must freeze, and I already know for a fact what *summer* feels like! You are all *surviving*, sure, but none of you are succeeding! Everything that I've seen–from the houses to the clothes on your people's backs–is one bad winter away from being completely erased from the world. Just like your citizens. We can change that! We can bring trade, skilled workers, and specialized tools!"

A deep rumble filled the room, but the mayor stopped the roar that was building in his chest. He took a deep breath and glared at Joe. "*Tradition*, boy. We haven't had to change our ways in over a hundred years, when the kingdom pulled its forces and left us to fend for ourselves. *They* abandoned *us*. They basically fed us to the wolves, and we were forced to grin and bear it! Think on that for a bit as you look down your nose and change *our* lives to better fit *your* comfort level."

Joe didn't know how to respond to that, and even though he was fuming, he recognized that the man had made a good point. He shook his head violently. No! They might be content, but they were simply existing. None of them knew better, so they didn't *know* what they were missing! Knowing the mayor wouldn't want to continue their conversation, Joe simply motioned to his team and left. There was a quest notification waiting for him as he walked outside.

Quest updated: The Secret of Sir Bearington. The mayor of the town has issued a challenge to you to get permission from every person in town who owns a building. As this is a 'secret' quest, this is only one possible way of completing this quest. Reward for completing the quest using this method: Ability to join the town with a high starting reputation. Failure: A massive loss of reputation with the town's residents if your guild relocates here.

Joe discussed this method with the other members of his party, and they all agreed that it had a very low chance of success. For now, though, this was the only clue they had been given. They decided that they would go door to door, and if worst comes to worst, they would likely still gain a plethora of small quests. Perhaps they would be able to find some other information that would open a new door for them.

They were right, and also *very* wrong. The party went to the first shop in town, the blacksmith. After discussing amongst themselves, they decided to have Bard do the talking. He had a high skill level in speech as well as a high charisma from his class. Entering the shop, they were given a searching, suspicious once-over from the proprietor. Bard cleared his throat and began to speak, "Goo' mornin tae ye. We're comin here to try and ge' on yer goo' side. 'Ow ye feel about slappin' on ah smile and tellin' the mayor that yer think we'd be ah good addition tae this here town?"

Staring at the Skald sweating from the heat of the forge, the blacksmith tried to parse his words. "You need *me* to give you a pass to join our town? A whole mess of people that'll come here and bring fancy new smithing techniques and run me out of business? You want me to lose my job with a *smile* on my face?"

"Ah mean, ah think we'd be happy to help ye out if ya needed sommat done," Bard stated lamely.

A smile curled the lips of the blacksmith. "Now we can *talk*! In fact, I do have something you could do for me that would make my estimation of you increase heavily. My family used to run a mine in the area, but it was overrun by Wolfmen a while back. They eventually abandoned it, but now, all sorts of critters call it home. You clear out *every* monster in there for me, and not only will I give you a glowing recommendation, I'll give y'all a discount on ores and a few hundred gold."

Quest alert: Foreboding Ferrum. To get into the blacksmith's good graces, he has asked you to clear his family's iron mines. His words don't match the glint in his eyes, and it is likely that you are being sent to your death. Why are you waiting? Accept already! Reward: Reputation and a discount on ores. 300 gold. Failure: Cannot progress in this branch of the quest 'The Secret of Sir Bearington'. Accept? Yes / No.

The party looked at each other uneasily. Joe decided to take the initiative with his favorite phrase, "We'll do it."

"Excellent." The blacksmith's lips curled upward in pure satisfaction. "You have a map? Let me mark the location of the mine for you..."

CHAPTER TWELVE

They were walking away from the sounds of metal being pounded flat when Jaxon suddenly contorted his face into a strange expression. "Did anyone else think that was a bit strange?"

"The fact that *you* are calling something else strange simply proves that it was creepy beyond words," Alexis stated flatly, her irritation overriding her typical shyness.

Jaxon smiled at her with an overjoyed look replacing his previous one. "Thank you for having such faith in my judgment! It… it means so much!" He actually seemed to wipe away a tear.

"Jaxon…" Joe put his face in his hands. "Just… alright. Alright! We are low on time, so we should go to the mine right away. First, we need to find a place to set our bind point so that we don't get tossed all the way back to Ardania if we die somehow."

"Ah saw ah small temple back ah ways," Bard supplied casually. He thought a moment longer. "Less than tha', smaller, mayhap a shrine?"

"A shrine?" Joe grinned at the idea blooming in his mind. "Can you find the way back?"

"Easy." Bard led them through town and out the gate. They walked for a few minutes, to the point that they were sure Bard had no idea where he was going. Just before Joe decided to say something, Bard pointed at an overgrown and rotten shack that stood about ten feet off the road.

Joe walked over excitedly, and sure enough, there was a small effigy contained in the room. He walked closer, and it started to hum with a weak power.

Would you like to make a donation of mana, stamina, or coin to the final shrine of the Spriggan, minor deity of nature and fertility? Yes / No.

There was an odd feeling of hopefulness attached to the words, and Joe nearly felt bad about selecting 'no'. He stepped closer to the shrine, and a different kind of glow washed over him. Another message appeared, this one tinged with panic.

The shrine of the Spriggan is devoted to this forest and is a lesser nature deity. Your status as a Champion has been recognized! If you move any closer to the shrine… you moved closer! Stop! A call for protection has been issued to the beasts in the area. Leave now, and you will not be hunted! …Please go away.

Joe stepped forward and touched the effigy, even though he felt bad for doing so.

You have found an unguarded shrine! As you are not currently under attack, you have the option to rededicate this shrine to your deity. Would you like to do so now? Yes / No

Joe selected 'yes', and the image of a woman formed from a tree warped. Soon, the stone drooped and collapsed into a mud puddle. From the puddle rose a book, the decay and moss that had covered the previous effigy nowhere to be seen. Joe felt a pull on his mana, and a full half of it was drained from his pool of power.

The mana he lost washed outward, reinforcing and repairing the small shack that had been built around the shrine. The shape of the small building began to change; the triangular roof turned into a stone book placed upside down, and the walls became books placed open and upright. It was a beautiful building, eye-catching and somehow subtle at the same time. Soon it looked like a proper rest stop, or a comfortable place you could come and study on a lazy evening.

You have converted the final shrine of a deity! Unless one of their champions can muster the power to undo your conversion, any blessings this deity has given out will be removed, and any abilities bestowed will be turned into skills. Any progress gained by their worshipers will be retained, but all extra effect from the divine will be lost.

You have earned a reward from the continuous quest: Reclamation of the lost. After making a new shrine for Tatum, you have been blessed! You have gained: +1 perception. +1 free skill point. You have gained the buff 'pierce the veil' for thirty-six hours.

Pierce the veil: Illusions and mind-altering effects are 50% less effective. Likelihood of finding rare items is increased by 5%. Time remaining until buff ends: 35:59.

"What did you just *do* to this place?" Alexis gaped at the changed building, running her hands over the smooth marble the walls appeared to be made of.

"I… polished it up?" Joe offered with a too-innocent smile. He tuned out other distractions and tried to follow his 'hidden sense'. After a few minutes of crawling around on the dirt floor, he brushed aside a clump of dirt and found a small symbol. Pouring mana into it, he gained the option to add this shrine as a fast-travel node. "Yes, yes, and *yes*!"

He hid the symbol by replacing a bit of dirt, and watched as a bright white circle appeared around the shrine. No one else reacted, which made him nod in satisfaction. Exactly the same as last time, the circle was only visible to people that had access to it. Joe smiled as he looked around; now this shrine would act as a fast-travel destination! "Looks like we can set this as our bind point. Just walk up to the shrine, and you should get the option." He bound himself here, and the others followed suit. After making sure they were all prepared, the group started walking, following their map to where the entrance of the mine should be.

Sound from the forest started to wane as they approached their destination. There were fewer birds chirping, fewer small animals rustling in the underbrush, and even the vegetation in the area seemed lackluster. Joe noticed that there was a strange fungus growing on some of the trees, and some of the smaller plants were visibly wilting. Was all of this an effect of whatever was in the mine?

They drew closer to their destination and found an overgrown trail that had likely been the main road to the mines in the past. The area around the mine entrance was filled with young growth, mostly long grass and ferns with a few saplings mixed in. This area must have been clear-cut to allow better access, but over time, nature had begun creeping back in.

"I think that's the entrance." Alexis pointed at a hole in the world. It was a logical conclusion; the trail went straight to the hole, and this was where they had been directed. The mine didn't look like much, but Joe supposed not everything had a grand entryway. In fact, seeing the state of the town, Joe would have been far more nervous if there *was* a grand doorway awaiting them.

They trudged over to the mine, nervous energy filling them as they waited for whatever trap this was to be sprung. Nothing jumped out at them, and none of them fell over from unseen attacks. They walked into the mine, finding that after the entryway, it widened enough for two of them to walk side-by-side. Joe inspected the others for signs of claustrophobia but only saw typical wariness. Even if they would be freaked out in real life, there was something about knowing that you would be revived if something went wrong that was… freeing? Hmm, that didn't quite cover it. Was there a word that meant 'the ability to be totally reckless'?

"Wait one momen'." Bard coughed into his fist to clear his throat and started chanting lightly, "*Bones of iron and skin of stone, like calls to like… now leave us alone!*"

For a single moment, Joe felt like the earth was pressing down on him. He felt like he would be smashed into the rock around him, swallowed deep into the mantle. Then it all fell away. Taking in a shuddering breath, he locked eyes with Bard. "What in the world did you just do?"

Bard shrugged and gestured at Joe. "All of ye now have 'protection from earth'. Half damage from any earth based sources! Didja think ah was only some fancy axe-man? Ahm ah *Skald*, blast it!"

"Bones of *steel* you say?" Jaxon looked at his fingers, trying to determine if the buff would have any impact on his abilities.

"It's ah metaphor, and ah clearly said 'bones of iron'!" Bard slapped wiggling fingers away as Jaxon reached for him. "Get off!"

"Really good idea. Thanks, Bard," Alexis muttered quietly. Joe smirked a bit; it seemed their most introverted member had taken a shine to their performer.

They walked deeper into the mine, but while Joe continued walking boldly, the others were faltering. Joe looked at them quizzically, but they didn't return the look or explain their actions. When Alexis spoke up, he found his answer. "Um, did anyone bring a torch, by chance?"

Right. Joe had Darkvision. He waited for the others to answer, but no one spoke up. "No one has a torch? We came to a *mine,* people!"

"*You* are the party leader, are you not?" Jaxon smugly stated into the darkness. "Planning falls on *you*."

"I can see in the dark!" Joe was getting frustrated; his team only seemed to focus in on their areas of interest. Wait… there was something there. An idea. "Hey… Alexis?"

"Um, yes?" Alexis could hear the dark satisfaction in Joe's voice; it added a creepy undertone to his words.

"Why should we all slink into the darkness and fight unknown amounts of creatures? What would you need in order to fill this place with poison?" Joe's enthusiasm faded a bit as she shook her head.

"Taking out the entire mine? I'd need a barrel the size of a man, two hundred sets of my needed herbs, some way to stop the finished product from dispersing, a delivery system, and also a stopper or seal to stop fresh air from getting down here." Alexis was listing things out on her fingers, checking some unknown list in her head. Apparently, this was something she thought about fairly often.

Jaxon spoke next, "Couldn't we build an extra smoky fire in the entryway and poison the place *that* way?"

Alexis seemed to be in her element. "No, that's a simplistic myth. If this was a single-room cave, that might work. A mine tends to have air shafts drilled throughout, not to mention that smoke moves *up*, not down. If you can find a way to block the entrance, keep air going to the fire, and blow the smoke down the tunnel without adding fresh oxygen... *then* that would work."

"So what yer sayin' is tha' we ah gooin' in, and we should naw keep blabbin and telling tae beasties that we're comin?" Bard shook his head and lifted up a thick bundle of sticks. "Ah stepped outside, collected these, and came back in tae time it took ye to fight it out! Didja even notice ah was gone?"

"I *didn't*, I promise!" Jaxon told him excitedly. "Did you get a sneaking skill?"

"Wha? No, ah just..." Bard rolled his eyes at Jaxon's misplaced enthusiasm.

"Thanks, Bard, that was really thoughtful of you." Alexis's eyes seemed to glow as she took a stick and coated it in something. The next instant, flames began crackling across the wood and light filled the tunnel for a few feet in each direction. "Let's find out what's waiting for us down here!"

CHAPTER THIRTEEN

Bees. That's what was waiting for them. Well, 'bee' was a very polite and gentle representation. Whatever these things were actually named, they were the approximate size of large hornets, but their stinger was attached via a tail like a scorpion. As the humans came to find out, each of the insects only had a single point of health, but… there were *thousands* of them. Not only were they furious at the intruders, but their stingers were full of a potentially deadly poison.

As it currently stood, the only reason Joe was still alive was that his Mage armor was perfect for repelling these bugs. Their main damage capabilities were derived from the toxin they were filled with, so even when he was swarmed by the insects, his shielding only dropped by a single point per second. He had his hands full keeping the others alive though.

"*Ow*, ya blasted bugs!" Bard was swiping at the 'bees' furiously, his axes turned sideways so he could use them like giant fly swatters. Each swing killed dozens of the aerial assailants, but there were thousands willing to take their place. Damage was building as the poison stacked, and Joe was hard pressed to

Cleanse his team fast enough to keep them alive between healing spells.

"Just keep me going, please!" Alexis called as she furiously concocted a compound in a mortar and pestle. Her health was draining slower than the others, though she had far less health overall. Joe chalked it up to a hefty poison resistance; there was no other explanation that he could think of.

Jaxon was having the most violent reaction, though. "*I hate bugs*!" He screamed into the air, swatting everything that came near him. Although his palms were coated in ichor and bits of chitin, he showed no signs of slowing down his attacks.

"Are you allergic in real life?" Joe gasped the words out between spell casts.

"Exoskeletons! *Exoskeletons*, Joe! Do you know what that means?" Jaxon screeched, sparing Joe a dark look. "No *bones*! They are *useless* creatures!"

Joe was so shocked by the actual rage in Jaxon's voice that he almost miscast his next healing spell. "You have a serious fixation on-"

"Eureka!" Alexis called while pouring water into the compound. She mixed it once and touched the torch to it. There was a flash of flame, and then a dense smoke began billowing out of the stone bowl. Any bugs caught in the smoke dropped to the ground without a twitch. Smoke filled the entire room, and Joe was soon able to clear the poison from the others' systems. A few more healing spells cleared the puncture wounds from their bodies, and Joe finally looked up at Alexis with a bit of hero worship.

"Thanks for that, Alexis! This whole thing could have gone really bad; without you we might have needed to retreat. Um. What are you…?" Joe's voice trailed off as he watched Alexis crawling around the room sweeping the fallen bugs into a bag.

"It's a *stackable poison*, Joe." Alexis chuckled under her breath as she collected the bugs. "What do you *think* I'm doing? Heck, the only reason it took so long to make that bug-killer was that I had to make sure that even a concentrated dose wouldn't degrade their poison."

"You did research and made a bug-killing concoction... while being literally stung to death?" Joe had to hand it to her; that was some serious dedication to her craft. Even if it had kind of been a horrible experience for the *other* members of the group...

"*Obviously* not." She rolled her eyes, seemingly forgetting that he could see in the dark. "I didn't die. Hard to be stung 'to death' if I survive it."

"Why is everyone around me always so literal?" Joe sat down and cupped his chin in his hands, knowing they would be in this room for at least another few minutes as people recovered their mental energy and Alexis collected her samples.

"Being very careful and *specific* with your words is an important lesson that everyone should learn. If people didn't run their mouths and instead said *exactly* what they meant, there would be much less confusion in the world," Alexis stated as she worked. Bard and Jaxon nodded along sagely, while Joe took a moment to think on what she was saying. "Misunderstandings and miscommunication are the largest contributors to anger and fear. I work with poison, and being very *specific* saves me from respawn at least three times a week."

"You... make a good point," Joe admitted slowly, thinking about rituals and the detailed requirements they insisted upon. If he applied the same care with his words and actions as he did with his diagrams, he might do better in life. Perhaps he would make fewer enemies.

"What do you all think we will see further in the mine? More of these... Scorbies?" Jaxon wondered aloud, scratching at a dead bug in his hands.

"Scorbies? Scorpion bees?" Joe laughed at the term. "I love it! Is that their actual name?"

"No idea!" Jaxon was now squishing the insect in his hands, trying to find some way to do 'tests' on them. He seemed to grow disgusted and crushed the carapace without another thought. "I don't have a high enough perception to glean information about them, and I don't have a scan or identify skill yet. So, yes, Scorbies!"

Jaxon went silent for a moment. "Huh. I just got a notification and a title. The title is... *Entomologist*? No! I *hate* bugs! This is... oh wait, I get bonus damage against bugs, now. This works nicely for me; thank you, system."

"What was the notification?" Bard verbally prodded the distracted Monk.

"Hmm? Ah, yes." Jaxon pulled up his game log. "All it says is: I like your name better; this race has been renamed. Have a title and some experience."

"That's awesome for you." Alexis stood and brushed herself off. "Everyone ready to go?"

"Sure am!" Joe responded to her. "But, yeah, Jaxon. Back to the question, if there aren't more Scorbies, I'm betting that the only other things in here would be creatures that are either immune to their poison... or have such high defense that the Scorbies can't damage them."

"Wha excitin' options," Bard deadpanned as he picked at his ears.

Joe looked at the quest information, "Oh, look at that! There's a progress bar on this quest now. We have apparently cleared ninety-eight percent of the creatures out of the mines."

"Is that a percentage of total numbers? Because there were literally thousands of the Scorbies. Or is that a way to look at it in terms of power? What if we called all the Scorbies we defeated a single monster? Is this based on challenge rating?" Jaxon seemed to be on a roll, trying out new options in an attempt to gain more titles and experience. Joe tried to do so, but only received a notification in response.

Unable to modify progress bars! Learn one of the following skills in order to make status changes: Probability, Monster Migration Habits, or Beast Ecology.

"It seems that we will not be figuring out what the system uses for progress here." Joe relayed the information he had learned, and the group had no choice but to shrug and decide that they would simply need to explore. They moved into the next tunnel, moving as quickly as possible while attempting to remain fairly quiet. This was not a natural cave system, and without powerful geomancers or mining equipment from the real world... well, hand tools can't exactly create massive labyrinths. Plus, this was a small town mine. If Joe's estimation was correct, they could explore the entire mine in an hour at a normal walking pace if they weren't sneaking around at a quarter speed.

They had just begun relaxing and loosening up when a cracking, grinding vibration began to rumble through the tunnel. Exchanging a glance, they crept forward and snuck a peek around the corner. All of them had a long look at what awaited them, backed away, and then retreated all the way back to where they had killed the Scorbies. All was silent for a moment, but eventually, Jaxon spoke up, "Well. I... I'd like to give it a shot."

"You want to try and kill *that*?" Alexis squeaked in horror. "Wasn't that a golem?"

"Ah think it were ah Rock Monster," Bard muttered to the group. "Had ah flash o' insight, pretty sure t'were 'Skaldic Knowledge' firing off."

"So what you are getting at..." Jaxon tapped his chin in thought, "there is flesh and *bone* under that exterior? It isn't an exoskeleton?"

"Yup." Bard nodded at him, and Jaxon's face brightened. "Has real high defense, but tha' *thing* isn't tae beastie we're fighting. That's its armor."

A flash of inspiration shone from Joe's eyes. "Armor? I have an acid spell that deals triple damage to equipment. If I get enough time to melt the armor, do you think we can take it down?"

There was another moment of silent contemplation, but then Alexis shrugged and nodded. "I'm willing to give it a try. If things go bad, at least we changed our resurrection point."

Each of the others agreed, though Jaxon made a stipulation that he would get the body for a few hours afterward for studying and testing. He apparently wanted to map out its skeletal system and find the best way to take it down in the future. Deciding upon a plan of attack, they shuffled back to the room the Rock Monster was inhabiting. Bracing themselves to run away if it were needed, the others watched as Joe slowly moved his hands in the patterns needed to dual cast weak acid spray.

Joe took a deep breath and *pushed*, channeling the spell. A cloud of acid enveloped the monster, but it didn't seem to notice the moisture. The creature heedlessly chewed on a stone while Joe continued bathing it in acid. After four seconds–if the carapace of the creature was considered equipment–the beast should have taken about seven hundred and seven damage. Checking his mana, Joe was surprised to see that he was still over three-quarters full; the forethought of setting his class to 'Mage' when he left Ardania was paying dividends.

After *six* seconds of being bathed in acid, the monster suddenly released a bellow of rage and surprise. It bucked in place, thrashing like a branded steer. Its movements dislodged large portions of the armor its upper body was encased in, and it began taking actual damage from the acid raining down upon it. The monster turned in place and stood, looking for whatever it was that was causing it to feel pain for the first time in its life. Locking eyes on Joe, the Rock Monster charged at the Ritualist. Having found a target, the cries of pain vanished; instead, the beast became silent and focused. The abrupt lack of sound was even more unnerving than the cries of pain had been.

Jaxon rushed forward, taking the initiative and slamming his fists into the now-unprotected areas of the monster. There was very little effect; while the armor was no longer in place, the creature's skin was rubbery and used to immense amounts of weight and pressure. Bard and Alexis had far greater success, their weapons having been designed to either slash or pierce. Arrows sunk deeply into the fleshy portions of the beast, while a single cut from Bard's axe was enough to expose fatty tissue and muscle. Wherever the monster's body was damaged, gouts of blood sprayed into the air. Apparently, the circulatory system was under serious pressure.

The creature collapsed several feet from Joe, never even getting a chance to attack. When it fell, all of them felt a shockwave as the several-ton beast hit the ground. Joe gulped as he took in the massive figure, his brain doing flips as it tried to classify the thing's actual threat level. When it had stood, it was obvious that they had almost been frightened away by a creature they thought was only a third of this thing's *true* size. The Rock Monster was nine feet tall and four feet wide, roughly humanoid, and coated in thick armor that it likely grew over time. It had taken over a thousand damage from acid before even *noticing* it was under attack.

*Exp: 100 (100 * Juvenile Rock Monster x1).*

In any situation where they weren't able to destroy the armor before engaging in combat, this creature would have utterly demolished their group. This was the Rock Monster equivalent of a *teenager*? Joe tried to clear the nerves from his voice, but his words still squeaked a bit as he spoke, "How many of these things are in here, you think?"

Bard's eyes glazed over a bit, but when he next spoke, his voice was filled with surprise. "Perhaps *one* more? If'n we're *really* unlucky? We wen' up tae ninety-nine point five completion on the quest!"

Each of them checked their quest information and were jubilant to discover that Bard was correct. Jaxon poked Joe a couple times to get his attention, "Might I enlist your aid, oh gracious leader? I have a need of a potent acid to remove a bit of armor."

"Sure thing, Jaxon." Joe followed the Monk to the corpse of the Rock Monster and poured acid in each area Jaxon indicated.

Cutting the creature out of its rocky exterior took longer than the entirety of the time they had spent in the mine to this point. After the first layer of stone had been destroyed, they pulled the actual body out of the shell. It was, for lack of a better term, horrendously disgusting. The body was a blob that had taken a humanoid shape simply to acquire limbs as it grew. When Jaxon cut the fleshy portion open, he became far too excited. Ignoring the smell that was so foul that it was nearly visible, he dove into the carcass. Almost literally.

"Its entire skeleton *shifted* when we pulled it out! It *shifted*!" Jaxon babbled as he tore chunks of meat off of the skeleton. "Do you have any idea what this *means*?"

"Not a clue." Joe looked at the others, but they seemed about as bewildered as he was.

"Look!" Jaxon finished dislodging the remainder of the meaty body. As the last chunk came free, the entire corpse changed. Instead of a humanoid form, the body now had a generally spherical shape. "It's a *shapeshifter*! The Rock Monster could have any *number* of forms! If your skeleton and muscles will adjust, you could look like anything!"

Jaxon was giddy, and the dazed look on the others faces was lost on him. Alexis glanced at Bard then Joe before speaking, "If it can look like anything… we might be searching a *long* time for the last enemy."

"Don' think like that! No need tae get down." Bard beamed a smile at her. "Ahm sure it's wanderin' around here somewhere. We jus' need tae find it."

Jaxon stood up at that moment, seemingly disgusted. Joe, seeing the look on his face, made the mistake of asking the Monk what was wrong. Jaxon turned on him, almost shouting. "What's wrong, Joe? What's *wrong*? Nothing! I seem to have found a useless target though. Not only do these bones shift as needed, but they are solid metal! These creatures will never… **sniff**… need a chiropractor."

"Are you *crying*?" Alexis's voice was lowered from shock.

"'I'm just so... *happy*!" Jaxon cried out, reaching down and patting the exposed bones. "I need to open up a few more of these things, see if their skeletons are all the same."

"This is some kind of steel… I think." Alexis was tapping the skeleton with a small chunk of rock. Each time she did so, a ringing sound like a baseball bat perfectly impacting a baseball sounded out. "Joe, this is a *really* high-grade metal material. I can't even inspect it, and material usage is one of my highest skills."

"This is ah mine, and it *was* eating from the walls." Bard looked at the place the monster had been scraping. "Ah think this is iron."

"I bet it eats ores then adds the metal to its body! This must be an alloy of all the metal it had ever eaten!" Jaxon had a renewed interest in the skeleton, and he spent an unsuccessful minute attempting to tear a bone off for future study. When his stamina finally ran out, he dropped and stared at the bones longingly. "Soon, my beautiful metallic ossification alloy."

"We need to get moving. Jaxon, we'll come back for this but we need to get these mines cleared," Joe ordered abruptly when he saw everyone's stamina recovering. They started moving, though Jaxon was rather reluctant to leave his prize out in the open. Joe made him move by reminding him that there was likely another one in the area.

Not finding any other enemies for forty-five minutes, the group was getting discouraged and sloppy. Bard was the worst of the lot, the time underground putting him on edge. "Ahm sick ah this! So tae guild will start with ah bad rep in tae town, what else is new?"

"Um. Joe, I kinda agree. We've been through this whole place." Alexis looked down as she said this, obviously uncomfortable with telling Joe something negative. "There's nothing else here, and unless you want to try destroying every rock in the mines, I don't know if we will find the last monster."

"Back to the corpse! We can use a very—*very*—small part of it for bribing the blacksmith and use the rest to make weapons and slay anyone who refuses to allow our guild to take over the area! Love us or die!" Jaxon turned on his heel and made a beeline for the room the Rock Monster had died in.

Joe followed them out of the mine, trying his best to be reasonable. "First of all, we can't kill the villagers. That's off the table. Next, I *really* don't want to give up on a quest. What do we have but time? We'll find it eventually."

"Let's do some other quests first, how about?" Jaxon smiled a toothy grin at him in a way that said he would not take 'no' for an answer. "We can always come back after the monster has a chance to move around a bit. We will be able to find it more easily that way, right?"

As much as he wanted to remain in the mine and search, Joe had to agree that finishing quests for other townsfolk might be more beneficial in the short term. "Fine, but we *will* come back, right? Remember, this quest chain is pretty much your guild acceptance test."

"Yes, yes, make more idle threats." Jaxon was standing next to the metal skeleton, and his soft words made Joe shut his mouth with a **click**. The Monk pushed and pulled, making the entire thing wobble a bit. "Good. If we work together, I'm sure we can make it back to town by simply rolling this along."

The four of them worked to get the metal ball rolling. The good news was that they were able to move it; the bad news was that each time they made progress, a bit of viscera would **splat** to the floor. The already-rotting meat fell through the skeleton and left a trail of gore all the way back to where the creature had died.

"This is such an *efficient* way to clean these off!" Jaxon happily burbled. "Look! Nothing is attached to the bones; it must simply be a frame that it builds for itself! Ingenious! If only we had a similar system in place! No wonder it needs an exoskeleton as well. Like a whale on land, over time, it would die from crushing itself."

By the time they reached the entrance to the mine, the bones were clean except for a crusted-on layer of dried blood and dirt. A chiming sounded, and Joe watched with wide eyes as a Core fell onto the ground. Joe swooped down and scooped it up. After finding that it was still only a low-grade Core, he promised to pay the others fair market value if they let him keep it. No one seemed to mind, so he put it in his storage ring with a smile.

They exited the mine and took a break, each of them sweating and gasping. Though Jaxon's new toy rolled fairly easily, the ball of bones weighed several hundred pounds and tended to flatten out on the bottom as it rolled. All of this added up to needing a constant amount of force devoted to pushing. Joe was a bit embarrassed that he was only able to push on it for ten seconds per two minutes before needing to rest and recover his stamina.

His need to rest was what allowed him to see the answer to their quest. As he sat with the others to catch his breath, he looked back to the mine and saw something astounding. As he stared, the entrance vanished behind a wall of stone then reappeared. Like the eyelid of an unbelievably massive creature… blinking.

CHAPTER FOURTEEN

"Joe, are you *sure* you weren't just seeing things?" Alexis had frustration evident in her voice. "I know you really want to finish the quest, but we *were* underground for a long time with poison fumes…"

"I *know* what I saw!" Joe barked in a voice thick with frustration, checking himself too late to stop himself from being rude. Seeing her look away and start trembling a bit made him feel like a terrible person. Ever since they had left the concealing darkness behind, she had reverted to her shy personality, and as much as he wanted to complete everything in the game, that was no reason to be hurtful to people trying to help him. "I'm so sorry, Alexis. I wasn't trying to be mean, I promise. I just really want this all to work out."

Alexis simply nodded, choosing not to respond verbally. Joe massaged his temples, mad at himself for his ill-treatment of her. "Alright, well, we have some preparations to make; I *think* we can kill this thing." Silence was his only answer, and the others seemed to be thinking he was having a mental breakdown. "I'll need a little help though, and my methods might be a bit… unconventional. Is everyone willing to at least try? Give me the benefit of the doubt?"

"How would ye feel about tae three of us finishing up little quests for tae town while ye work on this… giant mine monster?" Bard enunciated his words carefully, his accent barely showing through.

Joe was a bit crestfallen that the others didn't want to work with him directly in his schemes, but he nodded anyway. "That would work, but I *will* need your help for a little while this evening. I need to charge up a spell to kill the… mine… and I can't do it alone."

"I have no mana." Jaxon wiggled his fingers in his normal creepy and disturbing manner. "Only *astounding* physical prowess."

Alexis raised her hand. "I can help. I got mana when I specialized. It's not a lot, but I can do it."

"Ah have mana, too," Bard offered hurriedly while grinning at Alexis. "Ahm in."

"Thanks, guys!" Joe's smile had returned. "It'll be worth it in the end… I hope."

The party slowly started on their route back to town, rolling the ball of metal bones ahead of them. It was a slow, exhausting process, and Bard was none too happy about it. "This… **pant**... had better be worth somethin'!"

"For certain! It already has great *sentimental* value to me," Jaxon purred as he caressed the bones.

"Ah meant *monetary* value, ye creepy bone-lover!" Bard rumbled deep in his chest, making Alexis titter with nervous laughter.

When they were back on the main path to the town, Joe remembered that they were close to the shrine. He perked up; he had forgotten to tell them about the option to fast-travel! Trying to be nonchalant, he cleared his throat. "I think this would be put to better use back in Ardania. Don't you agree?"

Jaxon shrugged. "That doesn't really matter though, does it? We can't get it back easily."

"What if we *could*?" Joe rubbed his hands evil-genius style and fibbed a little. "Would you all like to learn a secret of the cleric class?" At his insistence, they left the path and rolled the ball into the shrine.

Would you like to donate this object to Tatum? Yes / No.

"No!" Joe yelped in shock. His team would have killed him if they lost this… curiosity.

No need to be so rude.

Did the system just get *huffy* with him? Joe opened his fast-travel tab and added his party to the whitelist of people that could use this travel point. There were exclamations and curses as a bright pillar of light became visible to everyone. "Everyone ready?" Joe hit the 'travel' option and waited until everyone accepted the invitation. The travel forced them all to blink; when their eyes came back into focus, they were standing in Ardania.

Bard was the first to react. "So… how does one become ah cleric?"

Joe simply laughed, and they started rolling the ball to the guild's building. They attracted *far* too much attention for Joe's liking, and a crowd of bored or shady people followed them discussing the bones. Soon, questions, guild invites, and offers to buy were being shouted at them as the bones clattered against the cobblestone road. They tried to be polite in their refusal, but this only made the people more rowdy. When the guild building came into sight, Alexis ran ahead to get some help. Seeing a large group of guild members marching toward them a minute later, all but the most insistent of the crowd dispersed.

Joe waved at a few of the guild members that he recognized. "Hey, all! Storing this with the guild until we can get it appraised. Anyone know where we can put it?"

With fifteen people rolling the metal, it moved much faster. An entire–albeit small–room was devoted to it. Now at a loss for what to do, the guild members went back to work. Returning to Ardania with the ball of bones had taken an unexpectedly large amount of time, so instead of asking his team to come over and help tonight as originally planned, Joe instead complimented his party on a hard day's work, told them where to meet the next day, and had them take the night off.

Sighing in relief, Joe spent a small chunk of time walking back to his rented warehouse. He quickly looked over the ritual he planned to empower in the morning and found that the chalk markings were still perfect. Excellent. He could make modifications around the current ritual, adding on a third circle. While it would give the ritual an effect that he needed, it would also make this a student ranked ritual and increase the necessary resources quite a bit. It took almost two hours of chalk work to get the next circle completed without errors, but he was proud of the result.

When he was finished, Joe cleaned up a bit since his team would be here in the morning. He took out the trash, changed the sheets on his bed, hid some knick knacks in an empty crate, all followed by devoting an hour to his puzzle cube.

Characteristic point training completed! +1 to intelligence, wisdom, perception, and dexterity! These stats cannot be increased further by any means other than system rewards, study, or practice for twenty-four hours game time.

Name: Joe 'The Chosen of Tatum' Class: Mage (Actual: Ritualist)
Profession: Scholar (Actual: Occultist)
Level: 9 Exp: 38,665 Exp to next level: 6,335
Hit Points: 80/80 (50+(30))*
Mana: 867/867 (12.5 per point of intelligence, +100% from deity, -11% from mana manipulation)
Mana regen: 10.63/sec (.25 per point of wisdom, + 9% from Coalescence)
*Stamina: 75/75 (50+(10)**+(15)***)*

Characteristic: Raw score (Modifier)

Strength: 12 (1.12)
Dexterity: 14 (1.14)

Constitution: 13 (1.13)
Intelligence: 39 (1.39)
Wisdom: 39 (1.39)
Charisma: 16 (1.16)
Perception: 29 (1.29)
Luck: 16 (1.16)
Karmic Luck: +5

Looking over his character sheet, Joe was pleased by the changes. He was lagging far behind others of the same level, but in… ten days or so, he should be able to get both his intelligence and wisdom above fifty points. From there onward, he would simply need to devote quite a bit of time to raising his other stats. If he wanted to get his strength to fifty, he would need to spend *three months* doing daily strength training. Blegh. He was *really* not looking forward to training his constitution either, especially not with a high perception.

Then he saw something that was… wrong. His experience was *too low* for his actual level. He did the math on the floor with a chunk of chalk. Right now, he had just over thirty-eight thousand experience, which should put him at level… *eight.* Why was he level nine? Joe did all of the math again, but no matter how it came up, he should only be level eight right now. He looked over his equipment, he checked active effects… nothing. He needed answers!

In that case… Joe looked at the time and sighed. It was *almost* too late for him to be comfortable going out, but… Tatum should know what was going on. He stood up, exited the warehouse, locked it behind him, and then strolled to the temple district. Once again, not noticing the eyes upon him as he walked through the massive temple, Joe looked carefully for Tatum's statue. When he found it, he was highly impressed. Whereas before it had been a plaque on the ground that was easily missed, now there was a stone book filled with indecipherable, shifting writing which was level with his knee.

Joe touched the book and once again found himself in a

massive temple on a mountaintop. Tatum glanced over, startled at the sudden intrusion, but then a stunning smile appeared on his face that literally caused flowers to bloom. Joe looked at the flowers and saw that their petals were tiny pages. He plucked one, putting it in his ring to study later as Tatum chuckled.

"I'd expect nothing less. Your inquisitive mind is what makes you an ideal protégé, after all. Feel free to take a few of them; they are basically weeds to me." When he had chuckled, the flowers had grown higher, taking on a bit of a golden glow.

"Does this happen to every deity?" Joe questioned as he looked over the strange flower. His herbalism score jumped five points as he did so; apparently, these were fairly high-leveled plants.

"Ugh, yes. The more power we have, the more often it happens, too. Did you know that Chan… er… *Gaia*, the earth deity, is *not* actually an overgrown tree covered in flowers? She just has so many followers and passive power that plants are constantly growing on and around her." Tatum snorted and looked at the flower Joe was placing in his ring. "Still, it is nice to be visibly gaining power again. Those are good for low-level magical documents, by the way. They expand to hold what you need to write. You can only put up to Student rank information on them, at best; don't try to go too wild. You can also plant the seeds to raise your own paper flowers, but they will only grow in a secret or hidden garden."

"Naturally." Joe chuckled at this reminder of the deity's power. "Listen, I found something strange today… would you look at my stats and tell me why I am a level higher than I should be?"

"Oh… you, uh… saw that, huh?" Tatum chuckled and seemed to sweat. Could deities sweat? "So… pretty please don't say that out loud again or mention it to anyone. I might have been doing something I shouldn't…"

Joe waited as Tatum trailed off. "What did you do?" Tatum replied but it was such a soft mutter that it was unintelligible. Joe waited, and Tatum became exasperated.

He shrunk to the size of a thumb, vanishing and appearing on Joe's ear. "I've been artificially boosting your level. You needed the increased stats and access to more characteristic points in order to survive, and *I* needed you to specialize faster than you would have otherwise. Listen carefully, Joe. If you catch the wrong attention with this fact, you might suffer *severe* penalties. When you get to level ten, the experience difference will need to be repaid and there will no longer be an issue. Going from ten to eleven will simply cost you twenty-one thousand points instead of eleven thousand. Please, no more questions about this. I'd like you to continue existing."

Beginning to sweat, Joe glared at the tiny deity that was now on his shoulder. He couldn't decide if Tatum was supposed to represent an angel or a demon. "Not cool, man. Not. Cool."

"So, *anyway*," Tatum returned to his throne and regular size, "how are things going?"

"…Not great, Tatum," Joe growled darkly, relenting with a sigh after a long moment. "We are trying to get our guild into a town, and they aren't playing nice."

"Hmm. Well, I'd suggest you use your natural *blessings* and find a way to manage." Tatum winked conspiratorially, but Joe didn't understand the reference. "I'm glad that you are getting set up in a town though; your specialization will require it. Did you ever go to that place and do the thing?"

"The thing? What place…?" Joe suddenly remembered the tiny mark that had appeared on his map the last time he had been in this temple. "Oh, right. I have, uh, *found* where I need to go, but I haven't been able to *go* there yet."

"Well, since you found where you need to go, I'll give you a quest for your specialization at level ten!" Tatum clapped, and Joe got a message.

Tatum has given you a quest: Building a specialization. Achieve level ten and go to the area that 'you' found to learn how to specialize! Reward: The next steps for specialization. Failure: You will need to find a new way or a different class to specialize in.

"Thanks, Tatum. This talk has been… um. Fun? Yeah, *fun*," Joe reluctantly allowed.

"I'm so glad!" Tatum clapped his hands once more, and Joe found himself back in Ardania. He began sweating heavily and started towards his warehouse as fast as he could. Chills raced down his spine, and Joe could have *sworn* that people were staring at him angrily, but he hoped it was just his imagination. It was only… his imagination. He was *sure* of it.

CHAPTER FIFTEEN

Knock knock "*Bleaugh*!" Joe woke up to the sound of someone knocking and puking on his door. Really *not* a super fun alarm clock. He probably should have warned his people that there was an… anti-intruder effect in place.

"Coming! I'm so sorry, I can fix this for you!" Joe yelled as he rolled out of his sleeping mat, tripping once as he rubbed at his bleary eyes. He stumbled to the door, throwing it open which caused him to yelp and flinch as the unwelcome bright morning light flooded his eyes. "Why is it always so painful to open that *door*!"

Alexis was on all fours on the ground dry heaving while Bard was wisely staying a few feet away with a look of concern on his face. Joe ran indoors, grabbed his chalice, and returned to the waiting people. "Here, I need a bit of blood from both of you, and I'll get you added to the guest list."

Both of them allowed themselves to be cut, giving blood without a second thought. If they had been able to see some of Joe's potential uses for their donation, they likely would have been far more hesitant. After quickly adding the two of them to the 'Quarantine Area', Joe dashed back and invited them in. He looked at Alexis, who was blushing and furious. "Do you have an extra sensitive stomach?"

"Low... *constitution*," she ground out through gnashing teeth. Joe understood her anger when he saw the looks of panic she kept sending in Bard's direction. Ah, yes. Puking in front of a love interest wasn't a great way to get the kind of attention you *want*.

"Entirely my fault," Joe tried to placate her. She had *very* deadly poisons with her, he was certain. "I have a long-term effect in the building that makes people really sick, and it gets *way* worse if they make it further in."

"Wha' kinda limitations does it have?" Bard eagerly inquired.

Seeing someone else interested in his passion made Joe a bit overexcited. "Well, it... uhm, it is expensive to set up initially, but there is no cost to maintain it for a long period of time. Let's see... oh! They are called rituals, by the way. Anyone *can* use them, but if you can't do research on how to optimize them and reduce their cost, you will likely turn to other endeavors. They-"

"Ah meant more..." Bard interrupted the babbling Ritualist, "Ah wasn't hardly impacted, whereas poor lil' 'Lexis here looked like she got hit by ah bus."

"I don't..." Joe's eyes widened as he realized what Bard was getting at. "Your constitution! Higher constitution mitigates the effect of illness and poisons! So this would be almost useless against thugs trying to break in..."

Alexis's glare had waned a bit; staring at anyone that intensely made her squirm uncomfortably. "Can we please get going?"

Joe looked over at her in a daze. "Hmm? Oh! Yes, we are after this ritual over here. It's called 'Gravedigger's requiem'. Well, the basic version was called that, at least. I guess I don't have a name for this one yet?"

"What does it do? It's very pretty artwork." Alexis reached out to touch the chalk lines, but Joe's strangled cry of inarticulate indignation stopped her.

"Er-hem," Joe cleared his throat and tried to talk in a deeper voice to make up for his squeal. He held out a taglock–a fancy name for something that will connect a spell or charm to a person, in this case, an extra sharp needle–for them to see. "The ritual should dig a hole, straight down. When the digging is stopped by finding flesh, it launches *this* down the hole, hopefully into the body. Then the main part of the ritual takes over, and the targeted thing gets dropped about a kilometer into the ground."

"That's *awesome*." Alexis's eyes shone in wonder even as Bard looked disgusted. The Skald held his tongue though, much to Joe's relief. "What do you need *us* for, then?"

"Well, I need people to help me activate the ritual. Adding the extra effect onto the ritual tripled the amount of mana needed to activate it. It would cost three thousand mana normally, but with me leading the ritual we can reduce it. Nineteen point five percent of fifteen hundred… two-ninety-two point five. Add on coalescence and mana manipulation… so minus twenty-eight percent…" Joe put down his chalk and looked up. "It'll cost eight hundred and sixty-nine mana, then we will need to add in a thousand mana to give it enough power to dig."

"You are out of your *mind*! I have four hundred mana *total*," Alexis cried out at the astronomical sum Joe quoted.

"Two fifty," Bard grunted in agreement when Alexis spoke.

"So six hundred fifty extra to work with." Joe cracked his knuckles. "I can invest the points for the main event on my own… how fast can I regenerate that mana?" He looked over his status sheet. "Ten point six three per second. So we can do this if the entire ritual takes at least thirty seconds. That's… manageable. I think we can do this!"

"What can we expect while this is happening?" Alexis nervously looked over the dried bloodstains on the wood.

"*Machines*!" Bard muttered before beginning to snicker softly.

"You say something, Bard? No? Alright. Um, well, you

will start to feel suction from your mana; just do your best to keep it in your channels, and you'll be fine. It'll take *all* of your mana, so you will feel pretty… drained." Joe couldn't think of a better word to describe the sensation. "If I screw it up it might hurt a little, but it's nothing I can't fix. Any questions?"

"*So* many." Bard crossed his arms. "What are channels, first of all."

"Oh my *gosh*, I was *just* going to ask that!" Alexis beamed at Bard and tapped his arm playfully before looking away with a mortified expression on her face. She was a grown woman for goodness' sake!

"No channels yet? Yikes, maybe we should postpone this… but then you'll have less mana…" Joe's brow furrowed and he ran a hand over his shiny head. "Mana channels appear to be a way to improve access to mana and make it so that your magical skills cost less. Talk to Terra if you want the skill, but I should warn you that the two skills she'll teach you will drop your total mana by thirty percent."

Alexis nodded, apparently over her embarrassment or hiding it well. "I'll ask her about it. What happens if we don't have the channels?"

"The total mana depletion will hit you like a truck," Joe stated frankly. "It'll suck for a little while."

Bard shrugged after a drawn-out moment. "At least ya warned us. Ah don' fancy comin' back here to yer house of horrors again; let's do this."

When Joe glanced at Alexis; she nodded as well. "Great, thank you both. I need you to stand here, and you go… here." Joe positioned the two of them around the ritual, walking over to the other side of the diagram to form an isosceles triangle. "Perfect, now, when the ritual gets started it is very important that you don't *say* anything. This rank of ritual magic requires chanting, and incorrect words at the wrong time could make it… explode. Here we go!"

"When you say *explode*-" Alexis began fearfully, only to be cut off as Joe clapped and started pouring mana into the ritual diagram.

As per usual, the first and innermost circle began accepting the mana. Joe's mana poured out at a manageable pace, and he remained calm as the flow subsided momentarily. The second ritual circle lit up, and the pull on Joe's mana doubled in intensity. Having experienced this before, he simply breathed deeply and chanted calmly. His mana channels had been forcibly altered by his time in the Mage's College, so this level of throughput was easily handled.

The other two were watching him, waiting for something other than a light show to happen. Joe braced himself, wincing and nearly faltering in his chant as the third circle began drawing power. He would have lost control of his mana, but the bonus spell stability from his mana manipulation skill saved him from lighting up like a roman candle. Mana poured from him in a torrent, the connection between himself and the diagram becoming visible to the naked eye. Moments before his mana pool dropped below five percent… the ritual was completed.

Joe stood in his designated spot, heaving in great gulps of air as his mana slowly regenerated. His eyes went round as he saw the next portion begin to activate. "Crap, it's only been fifteen seconds…!"

Bard yelped as the ritual connected to his mana pool. He slid to his knees as a torrent of power was yanked out of him over four seconds, and his nose began bleeding freely. Alexis almost ran over to him, but luckily for *all* of them, the ritual connected to her at that moment. The same process repeated itself, but the bleeding was far worse for her. Her body wasn't up to the task of releasing so much power in such a short time, so she began bleeding from her eyes and ears as well.

"It's only been twenty-four seconds!" Joe braced himself as the power draw flipped back to him. All the ritual needed right now was a collection of mana; it didn't need to flow into specific channels, diagrams, or in any fancy maneuvers. What this meant to Joe was that mana could leave his body as fast as it could be collected. By the time the ritual had all of the mana it needed from them, they had each been forced to pay in health points while their mana regenerated. Alexis seemed half dead while Bard simply seemed profoundly angry. Joe was on the ground wheezing, trying to generate enough mana to heal himself before he bled to death.

Ritual created: Unnamed. Would you like to activate this ritual? Yes / No.

Joe exhaustedly selected 'no'. The option to name the ritual appeared, and he waved that off as well.

"What tae *abyss* was *tha*'?" Bard snarled at Joe. The Ritualist waved him off, still wheezing, so Bard threw his hands in the air and strode over to Alexis. "Tae baw's on tae slates, ahm oot."

"I'm… *gasp*… so sorry! *Gasp*. Please don't go!" Joe managed to speak. "It went *way* faster than I expected, and then it kept leaking mana because we lost spell stability! Then it took *more* mana to restabilize. If I didn't generate a *huge* amount of mana that would have definitely killed us."

"This had better have worked because I'm never doing this sort of thing again," Alexis threatened furiously as she tried to get blood out of her hair before it dried.

Joe sat up, groaning in pain as his mana rapidly regenerated. As his power returned so too did rational thought. "It worked. If it hadn't… actually, I'm not sure. I've never failed a ritual. I think dying is likely?"

"*Never again*!" Alexis stated harshly.

"Please don't say that!" Joe begged her, eyes wide and hands clasped in front of himself. "This was a *mistake*; I completely overestimated myself. I should have had another person at the minimum for this or a contingency such as a mana potion. This was worse than any other time *anyone* has helped me with a ritual."

Alexis hesitated and wavered but didn't rescind her comment. "It had *better* have been worth it." She stalked toward the door, growling lightly.

Bard stared after her, a smile slowly spreading on his face.

"Ah think ah like her. See ye at tae teleportin' spot. Bring snacks. Some booze wouldn't go amiss either." He waved nonchalantly back at Joe as he followed Alexis out of the building.

Joe carefully walked to the center of the ritual diagram after they left. Very cautiously, he picked up the small item that had been the focus of the ritual. The needle–the taglock–was humming and vibrating in his hand hard enough to be painful, so he placed it in his storage ring and followed his teammates out with a smile on his face. "*Totally* worth it. *Almost* positive."

Joe trailed after the rest of his group, thinking hard on the next things he needed to do. As they approached the town square, Joe almost slapped himself. He had forgotten to tell Aten about the new teleportation point! He pulled out a piece of paper and quickly wrote out a note, sealing it with a bit of mana. Joe flagged down a courier and paid three silver to make an urgent delivery to his guild leader. He gave access privileges to Aten as well as permissions for the guild leader to allow others to use the travel locations.

Looking up at his impatiently waiting team, Joe realized that he hadn't explained anything that he had been doing. Bleh. Bad habits really unbefitting a leader. He was getting too used to the lone wolf mentality. "Sorry all, I needed to send a letter to Aten before we could go. Everyone ready?"

"We *were*, but Jaxon just noticed a slouching lute player and ran after him," Alexis responded archly.

Panic followed by resignation flashed across Joe's face. "Have the guards gone after him yet?"

"Naw tha' we can see. Yons a right chancer." Bard chuckled as he watched Jaxon at a distance. He pointed him out to Joe. "Ah don' mind if he busts tha' man up a wee bit though. He's ah mean cuss. Slaps puppies around when he thinks naw one's watchin."

Alexis's head whipped around, and she stared at him in shock. "Are you being serious?"

Bard coughed lightly and flushed a bit. "It's… it's jus' a saying. I'll go get Jaxon back here." Alexis and Joe waited awkwardly until Bard came back, dragging Jaxon along with him. Joe looked out into the crowd and saw what he had been expecting: guards were beginning to swarm the area. He was pretty sure he knew who they were after.

"Time to go!" He grinned nervously and accessed the fast-travel point. When all of his teammates accepted the invitation, they instantly vanished from the city without fanfare. Also without being arrested. Perks.

CHAPTER SIXTEEN

Instead of going back to the small town right away, Joe had asked the others to accompany him to the mine so they could activate the ritual. There had been some minor hesitation from Alexis, but the others quickly decided to go with him. It was a short walk to their destination now that they knew the way, and barely fifteen minutes later, they were standing at the entrance to the mine.

"So… how does this work? It seems quite interesting, but I haven't seen anything like it before." Jaxon followed Joe a bit deeper into the mine.

"Well, the ritual will activate and do what it was designed to do." Joe shrugged helplessly. "It is similar to creating a machine that has a singular purpose, like passing the butter. Very simple stuff, at least until the higher levels of rituals when I can hopefully make versatile rituals that would do intricate tasks. The difference between a single purpose machine and a… car, for example."

"How exciting!" Jaxon watched curiously as Joe got to the approximate center of the mine and set up the ritual focus he had been carrying in his ring. Alexis and Bard rounded the corner, having decided that they wanted to see the activation of the ritual they had nearly died to create.

"Hey, guys!" Joe waved happily. "Ready for this? It should move pretty fast once it's going."

"Go for it!" Bard pronounced in a grand, ringing tone. Joe gave him a thumbs up and activated the ritual. A bit of light was released and a high pitched whine filled the area as the stone beneath the ritual focus was shoved apart.

Multi-stage Ritual: 'Unnamed' activated! Stage one: This ritual will dig until it runs out of mana or finds a target. Any excess mana will be used to grant extra effectiveness to the second stage of this ritual. If no target is found, the ritual will pause until mana is supplied. If 24 hours elapses without an influx of at least 500 points of mana, the ritual will destroy itself. Stage two: This ritual will apply the effects of 'Gravedigger's requiem' to the target, boosted by any remaining mana from stage one.

"Wow, that's getting deep pretty fast." Alexis held a torch above her head and stared down the hole as stone was ground up and compressed against the wall.

Jaxon looked around at the others, then cleared his throat. "That's what she said. *No* one else thought that?"

Alexis ignored him. "Joe, have you thought of using this portion of the ritual for more… mundane things? For instance, this might be really useful for making wells in town or something. Get reputation by improving quality of life or some such."

Joe blinked owlishly. No, he hadn't considered that, but now a whole slew of business options were appearing in his head. Once again, he was startled by the transition Alexis underwent when they were in a dark space. She seemed to lose her bashfulness, becoming calculating and focused. "That's an awesome idea! Actually… there are a bunch of rituals that I've never been able to find a purpose for that might be intended for that sort of thing. I've been looking more at combat utility… but…"

Before he could finish his statement, the whine from rock splitting became the horrendous screech of tortured metal. They all clapped their hands to their ears and looked at Joe. He motioned that they should go to the exit, then looked down the hole to see what was happening. The ritual had dug almost forty feet straight down by this point, which should be an indication of how powerful it was. With his Darkvision ability he would have been able to see the bottom quite easily, but right now there was no need for that skill.

At the bottom of the hole was a brilliantly glowing area full of molten metal. This ritual, which had descended five stories through rock in a matter of moments, was barely moving through the thick metal alloy it had reached. Joe certainly had mixed emotions about this; on one hand, he could likely consider this proof that they had found a Rock Monster. On the other hand… how long would it take to get through that thick plate of metal? How dense and strong was it?

Joe looked at the active ritual and was pleased to see that he could tell how much power was remaining. To get a good reading on it, he watched the ritual and took notes for ten minutes. So far, it had gone through four hundred and sixty-seven of its allocated one thousand mana, but the ritual had slowed its drain considerably. Now it was only losing about four mana every three minutes, which *should* mean a loss of about twenty mana an hour. Unless something changed, Joe had lots of time before the power was used up.

Touching the ritual, Joe channeled mana into it until it had returned to a full thousand points. After doing so, he walked outside and healed his ears. He didn't want tinnitus, and judging by the ringing in his ears, he was close to the danger zone. Looking around at the expectant faces, he plastered as realistic a smile on his face as he could manage. "*Definitely* a Rock Monster."

"Excellent!!" Jaxon pumped his fist into the air. "How soon do we have before your magic kills it?"

When Joe didn't respond, the others began giving him dark looks. Had he lied to them about this spell thing? Alexis had to stop herself from reaching for her oversized crossbow as Joe's face flushed and twitched. Finally, he spoke in a rush. "I have no idea! None at all. All I know is that it's going and should continue digging until tomorrow night."

He tensed up, waiting for them to be angry or leave his group but was surprised once again as they simply nodded, calmed down, and moved on. Alexis started walking away, speaking over her shoulder as she strolled along. "Back to the town, then?"

Seeing Joe's reaction to Alexis's words, Bard thumped him on the back. "What? Just 'cause ye can't kill a big ol' beastie in ah few seconds, ye thought we'd be peeved?"

"I guess I expected that you would all want to see results right away," Joe admitted as they walked or, in his case, skipped. He still needed to add his jump modifier onto his movement if he wanted to be able to keep up with even the slowest of his teammates.

Bard snorted while Jaxon replied, "You've been reading too many newspapers. No matter what the media says, people don't *actually* demand instant gratification. That's already intensely improbable, and we all play this game and know what it takes to do big things. I, for one, am impressed that you may be able to reach the monster at all. *I* had no chance of doing it."

"Besides, if we can't complete the quest…" Alexis trailed off momentarily, taking a deep breath to settle her nerves before continuing, "Oh well, I guess? We *were* up for quitting on it yesterday. *You* weren't, but we certainly were."

Joe felt touched and was even more pleased with his current team. They were proving to be good people. Bard coughed into his hand and broke the peaceful feeling with his next words, "By the way, how soon do we start getting paid?"

Terror filled Joe as he remembered that he was in charge of making sure the team had income, and his resolve firmed into steel. "As soon as we finish the quests in this town!" Going door-to-door after returning to the small town proved fairly fruitless. Though they gained a few minor quests and were usually able to complete them within a few minutes, most of the quests in town were locked behind what Bard called the 'reputation wall'. Until they had a high reputation with the town, they could only get to the quests they *really* needed by smashing the wall with a level of charisma they simply didn't have.

As night began to fall, the dejected group teleported back to Ardania. Joe was exhausted, and from the look of them, the others weren't doing that great either. He made a snap decision, trusting his instincts from long years in the military. "Look, guys, we did a whole heck of a lot today. Heck, between all of us we completed twenty-six quests today!"

"An' gained ah grand total o' three hundred and twenty-four experience apiece," Bard chimed in unhelpfully.

"I delivered almost thirty letters today before I found out that the villagers were illiterate and sending an empty envelope back and forth just to make fun of us," Alexis spat furiously.

"Right." Joe lost his train of thought, needing to restart. "We did great work, though. Getting the entire town on our side in three days was simply an impossible task, alright? Let me pay for a night out. I'll get us all nice rooms at an inn; we can drink and get to know each other. You don't have to come, but just so you know, I will be getting you three into the guild even if this whole town thing doesn't work out."

The others perked up instantly at the end of his impromptu speech. Each of them had been a *tiny* bit concerned that they had been doing so much work with so little to show for it. Having assured access to a Noble Guild–and the rare quests they were sure to get to take part in–made the last two days' worth the effort. Everyone agreed to meet at the inn near the square in about two hours, so Joe went over to give a report to the guild.

As he arrived at the guild hall, he was impressed to see three covered wagons being loaded. They were massive affairs, wagons that stood twelve feet high and were wide enough that they must have trouble turning on the city streets. Aten wasn't around; apparently, he was still in the process of choosing his specialization. He was due back the following morning before the caravan departed, so Joe left a report with a couple other ranked guild members and trudged back to the inn.

Sitting down at an empty table and ordering a drink, Joe found that he had a bit too much free time for his tastes. Deciding not to waste it, he pulled out his puzzle cube and began spinning the multitude of faces. He got a few in alignment and was even able to solve another riddle! At the end of an hour, he smiled as the now-familiar pop-up appeared.

Characteristic point training completed! +1 to intelligence, wisdom, perception, and dexterity! These stats cannot be increased further by any means other than system rewards, study, or practice for twenty-four hours game time.

Perception has reached 30 points! Based on your attempts in the past to view the stats of friends and foes alike, you have gained a new skill: Scan (Novice I).

Skill: 'Scan' has acute affinity with the Ritualist class! 'Scan' has been upgraded to 'Intrusive Scan'.

Intrusive Scan (Novice I): Stare deeply at a target, some would say in an almost loving *manner. Those people would be wrong. As you attempt to analyze an enemy, your eyes allow you to view more than a typical scan. Effect: Over the course of five seconds, additional information about your target will appear. In the first second, you will see their name, class, and title. After two seconds, their highest stat will appear. At second number three, you will be able to see any ongoing effects that might be affecting them. No information will appear on the fourth, but after a full five seconds, any weak points your target has will appear as a red light in your vision. Time needed to scan will decrease only in higher tiers of this skill.*

Use caution. After the first second, there is a 20% chance each second that your target will feel your eyes upon them. If they do, they are nearly guaranteed to feel uncomfortable or outright hostile. They will also know exactly *where they are being watched from.*

Joe felt conflicted. Why was it that his extra-useful skills all felt so… creepy? He could already imagine using this skill in the bar portion of the inn and some lady looking over and seeing a bald man in a robe staring at her unblinkingly. Heck, he could complete the creep effect by breathing heavily from low stamina. He rolled his eyes at his thoughts. On a positive note, this was an incredibly useful skill. It seemed to combine all of the abilities he would expect a politician, scout, and assassin to have into a handy–if somewhat odd–skill.

His reverie was interrupted by his new team entering the building. Joe waved them over and started a tab. Promising all of them a hangover cure, Joe bought all the drinks for the table. Sure, he was a thrifty man, but there were times in life that spending time getting to know someone really well simply cost a bit of coin.

It was a good night, and at one point, a red-faced Bard got onto a small stage in a corner and sang some karaoke. There wasn't any equipment for it, but for once, no one threw anything at him; instead, the patrons cheered for him uproariously. He took an unsteady bow and stumbled back to the table. He sat down next to Alexis and put an arm around her, pulling her against him.

Alexis's eyes went wide, and her face reddened. She looked uncomprehendingly at Bard as he leaned in for a kiss… "Hold it, hold it." Joe put an arm in Bard's way and waited a moment until Bard stopped trying to make out with the skin covering his elbow. "None of *that* while drunk. Cleanse!"

Joe had only dealt with the dehydration factor of drinking when using Cleanse in the past, so it was interesting to him how much the booze acted like a poison. It made sense when he thought about it, but for some reason, he hadn't been expecting it. After a few long seconds, Bard was cleared of any effects the alcohol had on him, so Joe then turned and Cleansed Alexis. After doing so, he got up and went to the bathroom to give them a bit of privacy, as well as to… well, he *had* been drinking.

He came back to the table to see two smiling people leaning toward each other and talking animatedly while kissing intermittently. After a moment of confusion, Joe made them get out of his spot and turned to look at Bard and Alexis. "Who were *they*?"

"No idea, they just stumbled over and sat down," Alexis told him while smiling shyly. Joe could just *barely* see that the two of them were holding hands under the table. Now that they weren't making drunken decisions, Joe was happy for them. Knowing how shy Alexis could be, he didn't mention anything out loud. He did give Bard a thumbs-up when she was looking at a different part of the room, though.

As the night wound to a close, Joe rented a few rooms and went back to the table to distribute keys. He paused and watched in silent wonder as Jaxon performed a trick for everyone, perfectly adjusting a pretzel and turning it into a breadstick. Amid the cheering, Joe shook his head and handed out the keys. Bard glanced over at Alexis and handed his back, giving Joe a broad wink. Joe rolled his eyes. He was happy for them, but he really hoped this budding relationship wouldn't impact their teamwork. Or make one of them choose to save the other instead of him if there were a dangerous situation. Maybe he should put a stop… oh, they left?

Joe shrugged and went to his room, taking a luxurious and *private* bath. It was well past the time that he should be asleep, but he couldn't stop himself from pulling out his notes and books about rituals. He read over them in a new light and saw ways of using them that had eluded him in the past. How had he ever thought *this* one was for combat? It was *obviously* an earth shaping ritual for creating the foundations for buildings. *This* one wasn't a fancy way to attack at range, it was a… Joe sat up in bed and stared at the ritual he had previously deemed useless. This was a *remote activation* sequence!

He shook his head, furious at his previous narrow-mindedness. Joe felt the need to increase his knowledge and ability. He opened his character sheet and moved to the skills section. He was at rank nine of the Student rankings. He had been holding off on adding another point because he was worried that he had been pouring too many skill points into this category without exploring his other options. But now… Joe added a point to the skill and looked at the notification.

Skill increase failed! As this is your class ability, it is impossible at this time to increase it via skill points. You are a Student in the study of rituals, and the difference between a Student and a Journeyman is not a simple skill point. There is a qualitative difference, but one that has a simple explanation. Specialization is the road that leads a Student to Mastery.

Well, that was unexpected.

CHAPTER SEVENTEEN

After sleeping in a clean, safe environment on a comfortable surface, you are well-rested! 10% skill and experience gained for four hours. 10% stamina and mana regeneration for six hours.

Joe awoke with a sour taste in his mouth. Shamelessly using his divine-given spell–Cleanse–he cleaned his mouth and whitened his teeth before sitting up in bed. He was still a bit disappointed, but now he had a clear goal in mind. He had planned to specialize in the future, but it was an amorphous concept that he was ambivalent toward. Now his lack of motivation to reach level ten was *actively* impeding his progress in the game.

To that end… Joe opened his quests and looked over the various tasks he needed to complete. There was one that he had been holding onto for a while that he should have already completed, but he hadn't wanted to use his skill points on. Joe debated with himself but then groaned and added seven points to his spell 'Shadow Spike'.

Quest complete: Playing Your Fake Role II. You have learned the basics of spellslingers and walked their hallowed halls without retribution! Part of the reason Mages aren't lashing out at you may have been from killing their leader in a spectacularly brutal fashion, but still, nice job! Reward: Exp: 1500. Intelligence +2. Skill point +1.

Quest gained: Playing Your Fake Role III. Set a new class as your public class. This quest will update based on your choice.

Joe looked over the gains, feeling cheerful. This had been a good way to wake up; he enjoyed opening his eyes to a huge boost in experience. He thought about setting another class so he could get the quest right away, but the only extra class he had access to right now was Jumplomancer; which had skills in the Master ranks already. He had a feeling that setting that as his next quest would be difficult though… it was *sure* to have great rewards…

Then he remembered that the skill he used to do the majority of damage had just reached beginner zero. He winced as he saw the new damage and mana requirement. Without any other skills impacting it, the spell would cost a full one hundred mana per cast. Not only that, but shadow spike would only be that cheap if he had his class set as a Mage. Otherwise, it would be five hundred mana *per cast*. He felt a bit sick to his stomach.

Quickly calculating his bonuses, he found that the spell would *actually* only cost seventy-two mana per cast if he were set as a Mage. That was a bit more feasible; he would get… oh hot dang, with all the intelligence increases in the last few days, he was up to eleven hundred and sixty-five mana! Back on track, Joe parsed out his options. If he used his Mage armor at full power, he would lose access to one hundred and fifteen mana. That meant that he would be able to cast shadow spike a grand total of… fourteen times. Not bad at all, actually.

Changing to his cleric class would reduce that to a grand total of two attacks, though and… he paused as a truly unpleasant thought crossed his mind. Would using Mage armor as a cleric cost five times more mana? He had to check, right *now*. Since he already had his character sheet open, it was the work of a moment to change his public class. Preparing for the worst, he activated Mage armor. Or, more accurately, he *tried* to. The skill seemed… slippery? Almost as though he were relearning how to use it. He pushed through the difficulty he was having, gaining a headache as his mana rapidly depleted.

He *knew* how to use this ability; why was he having trouble? Joe slowed down, analyzing and manipulating his mana usage more carefully. He compressed the mana that was billowing around him, shaping it and applying his knowledge of the skill. He had to stop and let his mana regenerate, but after ten minutes, he began again. He focused his willpower on making the skill work correctly, and after a few moments, it **snapped** into place. Joe was pleased but confused about the struggle he had just gone through. Then notifications began to appear in a swarm.

Skill gained: Divine Shell (Novice I). This skill is a staple for any cleric that wants to be able to walk outside city walls without an escort! So long as your chosen deity does not abandon you, you can use your mana to shield yourself from harmful spells and physical attacks. Effect: For every point of mana devoted to this spell, negate half a point of damage from primary sources of magic and one point from primary sources of physical damage. Increase conversion by .025n where 'n' equals skill level.

Extreme skill synergy detected! The skills 'Mage Armor' and 'Divine Shell' have similar effects. By paying one hundred gold, you can combine these two skills into one single skill. The level of the new skill will be the average of the original skills, and any remaining skill points (rounded up) will be returned as free skill points! If you do not have the necessary gold on hand, you may combine these skills at a later date or choose to have the money taken from your bank account. As this is the first time you have found two skills with extreme synergy, you have been informed as a courtesy. You will receive no further information on skill synergy from the system.

New system menu available! Congratulations! You have unlocked the ability to use 'Soul Forging'! By meeting certain requirements, you can combine skills or even classes! Be careful, as combining skills with low synergy will lower the new skill's efficacy.

"Now that… is an interesting development." Joe opened the new tab in his menu, looking over the options. He currently had twenty-eight skills, but none of them offered any information on synergy with each other. He dragged two skills over to the 'combine' section, but all that appeared was an associated cost. Fiddling with the skills, he found that he could add as many as he wanted, but for each skill added the price doubled. Three skills? Two hundred gold. Four skills? Four hundred gold. He decided that unless he did proper research, he couldn't risk the few abilities he had.

However, he knew for a fact that he had two skills with extreme synergy… and he was *very* curious. He placed Mage Armor and Divine Shell into the combination area, selected the option to pull the money from the bank, and confirmed that he wanted to combine these skills.

You are about to combine two skills: Mage Armor and Divine Shell. Are you sure? Yes / No.

Joe selected 'yes'.

Are you sure you want to combine these skills? This is your last chance. After this point, you will need to relearn the skills from Novice level one! Yes / No.

Joe rolled his eyes and selected 'yes' once more. So what if he would need to relearn the skills, he knew how it was done now. As soon as he pressed the button, both of the skill names turned grey, and an icon of a cauldron appeared. Both skills dropped into the cauldron, and a notice appeared.

Time until skills have combined: 12 hours.

Title Gained: Never satisfied. By gaining access to the Soul Forge before specializing–as well as creating a new skill–you have proven your burning desire to improve! What style, what passion! What a disaster in the making! Still, there are benefits to forging ahead of the competition. Effect: Gain a permanent +5 to Wisdom. After creating ten skills or three classes, this title will turn into a skill which allows you to gauge skill synergy.

Caution! Nine of a possible ten titles have been gained!

Of course there was a timer until he could use his skills again. At least *this* process didn't hurt, and… that title was *amazing*! Joe stood and prepared to start his day. He switched back to his Mage class, pouring mana into his Mage Armor… and got no effect. So he couldn't use the skill while it was being combined? He opened his status once again. No, it seemed that the skill was unusable because he didn't have it anymore. Alright, he would just do the same thing he did before and… how had he activated Mage armor last time? Pumping mana into the air around him, right?

Joe tried to remember exactly how to do it, but he just… couldn't get the hang of it! He'd need to go back to the Mage's College and buy the training again, he just knew it. With a frustrated growl he stood up to storm away, but he calmed himself with the knowledge that in twelve hours he wouldn't need the skill anymore anyway. He opened his door and went in search of his team, finding them nursing cups of coffee in the dining area.

Jaxon had a dissatisfied expression on his face for the first time since they had met–excluding when he had gotten his neck broken by a bear–leading Joe to believe that he was feeling absolutely terrible. He went over and Cleansed the Monk's hangover, and soon, a terrifying smile had returned to the man's face.

"Are we all ready? The entire guild is moving to the town today; we should go be part of the fun," Joe announced as they all finished eating breakfast. They stepped out of the inn, and it was only a short distance to the town square, so they made idle conversation for a half hour before the first carriage of the convoy trundled toward them.

It took ten minutes of slowly moving through the narrow streets, but eventually, all three wagons were in the square, as well as most members of the guild. Aten noticed Joe and smiled, walking over to him with a wave. "Good to see you! Notice anything different?"

"About you, or the area in general?" Joe looked at him and didn't see anything new, but before he opened his mouth he remembered his new skill. Activating Intrusive Scan, he stared intently at Aten. One second passed.

Name: Aten. Class: Guild Commander. Title: Noble Guild Master.

"Oh, a new class! Congrats!" Joe clapped Aten on the shoulder, wincing as his armor sparked and shocked him. "Ow! Jeez, warn a guy. How's the class? Like it?"

Aten grinned and tapped his breastplate. "Sorry buddy, she has an enchantment to zap any attackers, so the sudden slap musta startled her. The class is amazing; it provides bonuses like you wouldn't believe, and it's augmented even further by being the leader of a Noble Guild."

"Anything *extra* special?" Joe waggled an eyebrow at him, making Aten laugh.

"Well, ranking up let me double the amount of people that can be in the guild and gave me a once-weekly skill that lets me borrow the stats of all guild members in a certain range for a full minute. I tried it out when I first got it, and *all* of my stats jumped to over two hundred!" Aten's eyes glinted as he spoke, obviously relishing the memory. "A bit of a downside to that, though… they lose their stats while I am using them. So I become super powerful, and they become weaker. This doesn't debilitate them; it only drains them down to their nearest threshold."

Joe gulped at that thought. His nearest threshold was *ten* for all of his stats. What would happen if he lost all of his intelligence and wisdom while a fight was going on? The conversation only reaffirmed his choice to get those stats above fifty. Right away. "That's a really… *cool* skill; any idea when you'd need to use it?"

"It's a last resort spell, so beyond using it to rank it up, I would use it if I were in single combat, finishing off a boss monster or if I were in a situation which would otherwise be fatal." Aten smiled at the sickly look on Joe's face. "I'm not going to use it carelessly, Joe. I can only use it once a week, so my need will have to be pretty severe."

"Is it bad to say that I hope you never use it?" Joe grumbled, making Aten roll his eyes. "Anyway, I have three people that have been in my party and doing quests with me. I'd like to have them added to the guild."

Aten's face turned serious. "Are you certain about your

choices? As an officer, you *do* have the right to make a party, but all that really means is that you get to add a total of four people to the guild. Anyone after that can only be a recommendation, so be *sure* that the people you add are going to *stay* in your party."

Joe hesitated only for a moment before nodding. "Yeah, they are good people. Fun, too."

"Alright." Aten's eyes glazed over a bit, showing that he was looking at his status screen. "There you go. I gave you privileges to add four people to the guild with no questions asked. Hope you made the right choice!"

"Me too," Joe quietly stated as he looked at the team he had assembled, sending them guild invites which were just as quickly accepted. "Should we get going?"

"Yeah." A messenger ran up to Aten and handed him a note. Aten tipped the man a silver and read the information, laughing darkly halfway through. "Ha! There's a huge blockade waiting for us! Looks like a few of the PvP guilds are joining together to ambush us and our caravan when we leave the city."

Another guild member nearby seemed troubled by Aten's happiness. "And *why* is that a good thing? If there are enough of them we could get overrun! We have *all* of the guild's stuff with us!"

Aten looked at the speaking man as if he had never seen him before, a distinct possibility with their recent surge in recruitment. "*Obviously* because we don't have any need to worry about it."

As Aten finished speaking, the guild officers that had access to the new travel point–which Joe had shared with Aten–finished corralling everyone they were responsible for into the area. A notification appeared in front of each person in the guild, asking if they would like to fast travel to a new area. This notification was met with excitement as well as outrage when people realized there were better modes of travel. Aten waited a few moments for everyone to accept the transport, pressing the button to teleport when he figured enough time had passed.

In an instant, the city square that had been filled with people was nearly empty. All that remained were confused players that had been passing through the area. Outside of the city, scores of people wearing identity-concealing garb waited… and waited. It would be hours before a report got to all of them that their intended targets had simply… vanished.

CHAPTER EIGHTEEN

Joe looked around at all the people emptying their stomachs on the ground. The area was beginning to smell sour and acidic, causing the people that weren't *already* sick to quickly get there. Joe's flabbergasted face was the only reason Aten wasn't shouting at him right now and demanding to know why he hadn't warned them. Aten held his temper in check and looked at all the people on the ground covered in filth. "What *happened* to all of them?"

Throwing his hands up in a helpless gesture, Joe showed that he had no idea, even though he was feeling a bit sore as well. Looking at the people and trying to establish a pattern for their sickness, he saw that those that were nearest the wagons were the most impacted. He hastily opened his status sheet and looked over his stats, wincing as he realized the issue.

Name: Joe 'The Chosen of Tatum" Class: Mage (Actual: Ritualist)
Profession: Scholar (Actual: Occultist)
Level: 9 Exp: 40489 Exp to next level: 4,511
Hit Points: 80/80 (50+(30))*

Mana: 200/1165 (12.5 per point of intelligence, +100% from deity, -11% from mana manipulation)
Mana regen: 12.26/sec (.25 per point of wisdom, + 9% from Coalescence)
*Stamina: 75/75 (50+(10)**+(15)***)*

Characteristic: Raw score (Modifier)

Strength: 12 (1.12)
Dexterity: 15 (1.15)
Constitution: 13 (1.13)
Intelligence: 42 (1.42)
Wisdom: 45 (1.45)
Charisma: 16 (1.16)
Perception: 30 (1.30)
Luck: 16 (1.16)
Karmic Luck: +5

"Wow." Joe shook his head. "Aten, that little trip cost me about nine hundred mana. I have no idea why I'm not in *incredible* pain right now."

Aten frowned and grimaced at his own status. "Almost a thousand stamina from me. You think that the normal draw for fast travel was amped up due to the wagons and horses?"

"I had no idea the energy needed to travel would jump like that," Joe promised apologetically. "On the plus side, now we know better than to try doing that before going into battle."

"I *had* been hoping this would be an awesome delivery system for when wars happened," Aten admitted as he watched his guild members slowly picking themselves off the ground. "We just got a few crafting guys that are trying to find ways to make battle golems or something like that, but if the cost is this high with just *wagons*… we may need to rethink that."

Aten walked off, giving orders and getting everyone into formation. Within a few moments, the guild was rolling toward the town. Joe looked over the area–which was covered in vomit and horse turds–and shuddered at the thought of coming here via teleportation and landing in this filth. He looked over at the shrine and a devious thought made him chuckle maniacally. Walking up to the shrine, his grin turned to all-out evil laughing as a notification appeared.

Would you like to donate the alchemy material 'Acid' and 'Various Digested Food'? Yes / No.

"Oh, yes. Yes, I would." Joe accepted, and the area was once again clean in a perfect circle around the shrine. He quickly jogged away to rejoin the caravan, speeding up as another message appeared.

Message from Tatum: Joe! What in the abyss *did you just send to my temple! You little-*

At that moment Joe got too far from the shrine, and the remainder of the message didn't appear since Tatum would have needed to use some of his personal power to continue the conversation. Joe jogged to the trailing end of the convoy laughing the entire time which increased his stamina consumption by a third. Even though everyone was more than ready to set up and start the next chapter of their guild's life, it took forty minutes to walk the remaining distance to the town due to the slow pace of the wagons. As they approached the small settlement, the wooden gates swung closed with a rattling **boom**. Although the others became a bit leery about continuing, Aten had the group roll forward, only stopping about ten feet from the wall as townsfolk appeared over the wooden palisade with arrows on their strings.

Sir Bearington lumbered into view, glowering down at the assembled warriors. "Have you lost your bearings? I cannot otherwise imagine a positive situation where a large assemblage of people would show up at *my town* geared for war."

Aten stood forward with a dazzling smile, using his charisma to its fullest. "Sir Bearington, I presume? I am Aten, Guild Commander of the Noble Guild 'The Wanderer's'. You cannot *truly* tell me that you weren't expecting us. We have had at least five groups come through here recently, and all of them have told you of our plans to return this area to the control of Ardania."

"That you have, that you have," Sir Bearington growled while nodding at the words. "And *you* know I have always replied with the requirements they would need to fulfill in order to have your guild be treated with forbearance. This form of welcome is the result of arriving *without* the consent of the people. If you want to fight for the area in which we have lived for generations, we shall oblige."

Aten went silent, chewing on his thoughts as he tried to keep his temper. Joe decided to step in, earning himself a sharp glance from Sir Bearington as well as his guild members. The guild members retreated a bit, knowing his reputation for dangerous tactics. "Sir, I will admit that *you* are trying to be a reasonable person. *You* gave us a task that we *should* have eventually been able to complete."

Sir Bearington nodded gravely at his words, but a suspicious look was growing on his face because the speaking Traveler was obviously not finished. Joe continued, voice rich with righteous anger, "Conversely… your *people* have not been so forthright with us, sending us on pointless quests to humiliate us, having us do tasks specifically to cause us harm, or even setting seemingly *impossible* tasks that will actively impede us, all the while promising to reward us with gold, praise, and recommendations of the highest order at the end."

Sir Bearington looked down at Joe with a great deal of concern on his face. To the surprise of all the guild members, his next words were not at all what they had been expecting. "Lad… I need to know *right now* who in this town offered to bear the burden of rewarding you with gold."

"Is that all you are taking away from this conversation? That someone actually offered to *pay* us? There are far more serious issues at hand right now!" Joe sputtered his reply, face going red with indignation.

"*Not now*, boy!" Sir Bearington's voice boomed over the assembled people. "There is *no one* in town that has the koalafications to reward you with gold! There is a *single* gold piece in the entire town, baring what your people have paid for supplies. I *need to know* who did this!"

Joe was stunned at this outburst as were all the onlookers. "The… smith. He gave us a quest to clear out his old family mines."

Most of the people on the wall heaved a great sigh of relief, a few of them even showing a relieved smile or letting out a laugh. Sir Bearington, however, cared not one whit for this revelation. He turned to the guards and made a motion. "Go, bring me the smith, and inform him that he is about to be on trial for beartrayal of the people."

A few tense minutes passed before the smith's head appeared above the palisade. It bobbed up and down as he walked toward the gate, and he was glowering at the mayor the entire time. "What nonsense is this, that you would call me a betrayer?"

"Technically, he called you a bear-trayer," Joe called up with a chuckle. A few people looked at him in confusion, and Jaxon even came over and adjusted his ears. "Ah! What was that for?"

"Either you are making light of the situation, or you haven't been able to hear him correctly." Jaxon patted him on the shoulder and stepped back. "I adjusted your ears just now so you won't be able to say you didn't hear him properly. Now I will know for sure what you are trying to do. I'm testing social interactions in-game, carry on."

"All gathered shall bear witness to these proceedings. Smith, is it true that you have offered a quest to some people that would pay out in *gold*?" the mayor questioned in a rich baritone filled with concern.

The smith shifted uncomfortably. "Well, yeah, but you know that completing the quest isn't possible. It's just a little joke to make them clear out the bugs and such that get in there over time. Usually, we can get a good couple months of mining done after someone goes through there."

"So… you are admitting to offering an *impossible* quest?" Sir

Bearington rumbled. "You do know that we are not able to give forbearance with these kinds of charges. Smith… you are looking at jail time. Give me a reason not to make it happen."

"Oh, come on!" the smith cried out, throwing his hands in the air. "It isn't *impossible.* They *could* complete it… if they spent a few years going at it, digging to the last beast, and finding some way to kill it through its regeneration! I was just trying to get them to go clear out what they could before they were warned away by other people who had tried and failed the quest." He tried to laugh at the end of his short speech, but his joviality quickly died as no one else had joined in.

"So then you admit that it is *not* impossible. That someone *could* complete the quest you set out for them. This is becoming teddyous." The mayor stretched to his full height. "We live as a collective! Our people have made a pact to share in the successes and downfalls of our lives! You *know* what the system would do to us, the punishment it imparts for those who cannot fulfill the promises of their offered quests! You have endangered this entire town. You will go down there, *now,* and give them all the other rewards that they were promised. Count your lucky stars that they *didn't* complete the quest!"

Sir Bearington looked down at Joe. "Thank you for calling attention to this issue. Please, I beg you, accept the reward for partial completion and allow the quest to vanish. We will open our doors to your guild out of thanks for you bearing with us during this trying time."

He wanted to answer, to accept, but Joe couldn't stop himself from asking one more question. "Are… are you making bear puns?"

Perception +1!

That confirmed it. Why was no one else commenting? Joe shook his head and stared up at the overly hairy person speaking to him, and this time, he began using Intrusive Scan. He only was able to maintain the skill for three seconds before stopping out of shock.

Name: Sir Bearington. Class: Politician. Title: Champion of the Spriggan.

Highest stat: Charisma.

Ongoing effects: Conversion to Humanity. Enhanced Acting. Enhanced Disguise. Forced pun-maker.

"You are... not a human? Are you actually a *bear*?" Joe's shocked voice rang through the suddenly silent area.

Quest complete: The Secret of Sir Bearington. You have discovered the startling truth about Sir Bearington! How you use this information is up to you. Reward: Knowledge is its own reward. What do you mean give him something tangible? ...fine. +10 ranks in the skill Hidden Sense for completing the quest in an unintended manner. Your guild has gained an area it can build or buy a guild hall in!

Skill increased: Hidden Sense (Beginner II). You have learned to trust your instincts no matter what anyone else is saying, no matter how insane it makes you appear! Finding hidden knowledge, items, or locations is now far easier.

"What? Look, your issue is with *me,* kid. Don't go saying nasty or weird things about the mayor. He's a better man than you'll ever be!" the smith shouted at Joe as the gates opened to let him out. "Let's just get this over with already."

As the smith walked toward him while rolling his eyes and pouting, the earth trembled violently, causing everyone to stumble and a few to cry out with shock. Several of the worse-off buildings in the town collapsed, and the palisade sagged in a few places as the earth seemed to drop a bit. Joe got back into a standing position a few seconds after the others around him thanks to his low dexterity. Looking around at the damage, then the pale faces of the villagers, Joe asked the obvious question, "What just happened?"

*You have killed a level 32 Rock Monster (Ancient). Heroic feat completed! All stats except Karmic Luck +2! Exp: 3,000 (.3 (immobile/helpless enemy) * 10,000 * Rock Monster x1).*

For defeating an opponent more than 20 levels above you, each member of your party gains the title: Legend.

Title gained: Legend. You have killed a being more than twenty levels above your own! Your name will be whispered through history; will the whispers be full of admiration or loathing? Effect: Doubles reputation gains and halves reputation losses. +25% damage against opponents who have a higher level than you. -25% Damage against opponents who have a lower level than you.

Caution! All ten slots for Titles have been filled. Upon gaining a new Title from this point forward, you will need to permanently delete a currently held Title.

"I know what has happened. This blasted smith's *joke* just doomed us all," Sir Bearington stated heavily. "I hope that our punishment isn't *too* grizzly. Pre… *sob*... prepare yourselves."

Quest complete: Foreboding Ferrum. You have earned a reward: Reputation, 300 gold, and a discount on ores. Return to the smith to collect!

The smith's jaw was working, and his complexion was ashen. His shaking eyes locked onto Joe's, and he managed to ask a question while he slid to the ground with his hands coming up to grip his hair... "Y-y-you *cleared* the mines?"

"That is what we had been asked to do, so that is what we did," Joe stoically responded, unsure of what was happening. He was *pretty* sure they weren't getting paid though.

"No! It… it was supposed to be *funny*! I… I… I can't *pay* you-" A tear trickled down the smith's face as he was suddenly *sucked* back into the town through the gate which slammed shut behind his limp form. A hurricane-force storm appeared above the city with a **clap** of displaced air. Howling winds threw debris into the air as lightning struck over and over within the city. The wooden wall transformed as the strangely colored lightning wreathed it, the wood writhing ten feet higher and morphing into dark stone that dripped with moisture as rain fell over the town in a flash-flood.

There were sure to be changes behind the wall as well, but no one could see what was happening. The freakish storm vanished as fast as it had appeared, and the shocked onlookers read the notification that appeared in front of them.

You have found an instant dungeon! As recompense for the failure of its inhabitants, the guild 'The Wanderer's' has been granted exclusive access to this dungeon for as long as it exists! Double experience will be awarded in the dungeon to anyone currently in the party of 'Joe Legend', and one additional individual can join the party and take advantage of the experience increase! This dungeon may be entered for 24 hours, after which point the area can be claimed for incorporation into a guild. So long as a party is in the dungeon, it will not vanish. Happy hunting!

CHAPTER NINETEEN

"What just *happened*?" Aten's breathless shock summed up the feeling in the air admirably. Joe frantically opened his combat log and scrolled through the most recent notifications. He saw the messages waiting for him and grimaced, sending a screenshot of them to Aten.

Ritual 'Unnamed' has encountered a creature! Taglock deployed ... success! Taglock has encountered Rock Monster (Ancient). Gravedigger's Requiem effect activated!

Critical success! As the Rock Monster's bones and carapace are entirely made of earthen materials, all other portions will vibrate past them!

Calculating... due to having no skeletal structure or carapace to protect from the crushing weight of the earth above, Rock Monster (Ancient) will take 1000 points of crushing damage per second!

Rock Monster (Ancient) takes 1000 crushing damage, Rock Monster (Ancient) regenerates 200 health, Rock Monster (Ancient) takes 1000 crushing damage...

Joe had seen enough. Giving off a nervous chuckle, he explained what had happened to the people around him. The Guild Commander stared at him, eyelid twitching a bit as his hands clenched into fists and relaxed over and over. Aten took a deep breath and bellowed a deep laugh. "Ha! Instant dungeon, just add water and a dash of betrayal! So what you are telling me is that we now have access to an instant dungeon, a mine with a huge amount of the densest and most difficult-to-damage metal we have ever seen, and somewhere in that same mine will be a Core from a level thirty-two *Ancient* creature? Couple that with the fact that we can directly *claim* this area tomorrow? Don't be nervous, Joe, you're getting a raise!"

"But… all those villagers…" Cheering erupted around them as the guild members heard Aten's words, so Joe went unheard by the people.

Aten smiled around at the excited members of his guild and gave an order to set up a campsite. He pulled Joe aside and asked if it were possible for him to place some protections around the area, or else it was fairly likely that they would sustain some losses overnight. Joe agreed to do the work so long as the materials were provided by the Guild, and soon, he had a pile of goods to work with as well as a high-quality health potion. Aten wanted to see if the grade of the optional potion would impact the potency of the ritual. The use of such an expensive potion drew no complaints from Joe, as he too was fairly curious to know what would happen.

While the temporary barriers and tents went up, Joe focused on drawing out his ritual. He had been given a fairly large chalkboard to work on, and he was using his own chalk to fill in the aspects of the ritual that he needed. Checking his notes again and again, he made sure that there were no errors in the design. Joe chuckled as he made a small change which allowed him to specify the area that the ritual affected. The last time he had made this ritual for the guild, he had simply made a massive ritual circle around the entire building. Now, he added the magical equivalent of specifying the radius, and he had a ritual that would work the same if not better.

He walked to the center of the camp, placed the chalkboard on the ground, and added the needed components. Making sure they were in the correct formation, Joe then began pouring mana into the ritual. This was a Novice ritual, so powering it by himself was not an issue. In fact, his mana didn't even dip below half by the time it was complete. Joe pocketed the Core he was supposed to use up in this ritual, figuring that the people that had handed it over to him most likely hadn't expected it back… and either way, they would be repaid by the guild.

Activate ritual: Predator's territory? This ritual will cause creatures of level 19 or below to avoid the area, but any creature level 20 or above will be drawn to you. For using a high-grade healing potion, anyone who sleeps in the area will recover wounds 50% faster, and sleeping in the area for 3 consecutive hours will grant the 'Well-rested' effect. Ritual will last for 8 hours upon activation. Yes / No.

Joe selected 'no', as it wasn't anywhere near nighttime right now. He set the ritual so that any guild officer could activate it, then looked up from his work to see a man waiting patiently to speak to him. The unknown person cut a rather dashing figure, well dressed and wearing a wide-brimmed hat with a large feather coming out of it. "Hello there, can I help you?"

"Pardon my forwardness, but it is *I* who is hoping to help *you*." The man unleashed a dazzling smile, making Joe wonder how high his charisma stat was. He swept his hat from his head and took a deep bow. "My name is Papadopoulos Whisperfoot, rogue extraordinaire! I have heard tell of your group searching for an additional member and was hoping that I could throw my hat into the ring, as they say."

"You do not have your own team? If I might ask, how are you in the guild without a party, pop… papa… Mr. Whisperfoot?" Joe stumbled over the name a bit, but he thought that he recovered admirably. He had to blink a few times even during that short discussion; the bright colors that the rogue was wearing were starting to hurt his eyes.

"Ah, yes, I can see the confusion. I was added to the guild simply because I know Aten in real life. I have tried out a few teams, but none of them were… hmm… how to say it… *right* for me? Also, please call me Poppy, nearly everyone does when I give them the chance." Poppy grinned as he stood tall. Obviously, he had chosen his name to mess with people, making Joe feel a bit nostalgic about his old teammate, Guess.

"Alright, Poppy. We *do* need another member, but I can't promise that it'll work out. If you fit in well, that'd be great. Now, we try to work as democratically as possible, so I need to ask the others before *really* giving you the green light, but I don't think there will be an issue if we call this a trial run. Can you tell me your class and level? A bit about yourself if possible?" Joe sent a party invite to Poppy as he spoke.

"Excellent!" Poppy thought on his words for a moment. "I am a level seven Duelist. My class grants me excellent bonuses against enemies if I am fighting them one-on-one. Hmm. My main weapon is a rapier, which grants armor penetration like you would simply not *believe*. Careful attacks allow me to fight well-armored foes as easily as if they were fighting me nude, simply making them slower targets for me."

"Do you often find the time for careful attacks when a battle is ongoing?" Joe wasn't trying to be insulting; this was something he would need to figure out eventually. Technically, he could learn any skill from any class. In time, he expected that he would learn swordplay. Sure, it might be a hundred years or so, but…

"There is always time to carefully choose a target," Poppy gushed ecstatically. "In fact, it is far more efficient and economical for *anyone* to fight in a manner that uses skill instead of power... wait… I think Berserkers and the like are able to do extra damage from wild blows?"

"Makes sense to me." Joe shrugged and started walking. "We are planning to go into the dungeon in a little while; do you need anything before we go? Sleep, food, or healing?"

Poppy went thoughtfully quiet for a moment but ultimately shook his head. "Unless we wanted to get a few hours of sleep before we went, I can't think of anything. We don't know how long we will be in the dungeon, but if we wait too long it will be nighttime and the creatures may become harder to fight."

Just then, they came upon the remainder of the group, and

Joe made a few quick introductions. Bard was the only one who had anything to say about taking in a new member. "Ye joinin' tae group just ta walk with legends? Ye here ta take advantage o' tae double exp? Or are ye actually gonna stay in tae group?"

Jaxon smiled at Poppy, the ghoulish expression on his face almost causing him to leave the group right then. "Anything you choose is fine, though I would like to know as well. If you won't be around very long, I don't need to be on my best behavior around you!"

"I'm staying!" Poppy quickly squeaked, hand on the hilt of his rapier as he stared at the wiggling fingers inching toward him. "If I'm allowed to, of course. Jaxon was it? Would you mind telling me what your charisma stat is at?"

Frowning, Jaxon cocked his head to the side with the swiftness of a bird looking at a worm. "Does it matter? I see that it does matter to you. Let me see, I've gained two points since joining this group, so it is now at... four."

"*Four*? You only have *four* points in charisma?" Joe sputtered, incredulous even as Jaxon's past actions became much more understandable.

"Well, yes." Jaxon was now looking directly into Joe's eyes, not blinking at all. "When in character creation, I had the option to reduce unneeded stats to boost others that were more necessary. Didn't you do the same?"

"It's all becoming clear now," Alexis muttered into Bard's ear, quickly looking away before Jaxon could meet her eyes.

"Jaxon, when your charisma is below ten... you have serious penalties to any kind of normal interaction. The worst part is that you can't tell what it is that you are doing wrong, so you just get in trouble for what you think is no reason at all," Joe explained succinctly to the Monk.

"Ah, that would explain why the guards kept showing up when I adjusted people, even though they kept asking me to help them feel better?" Jaxon seemed to be deep in thought–nodding at some internal process–and missed the wince that passed over the others faces.

"Adjusted?" Poppy spoke out loud, causing the others to look at him with wide eyes while shaking their heads rapidly.

"Sure, I'd be happy to!" In a flash, Jaxon was beside the Duelist, hands flashing outward. His fingers and palms struck at full force, instantly leaving bruises. Poppy took a sharp breath, but in that same moment, Joe healed him. The pain vanished, leaving behind an excellent buff. Poppy had a look of wonder on his face that turned to fear as a set of long needles appeared in Jaxon's hand.

"How's that? Do you have any habits you'd like to break?" Jaxon blinked and then smiled. "Oh, look at that! I gained yet *another* level in a charisma-based skill! Thank you all for your concern, this talk has already been beneficial."

Poppy coughed, stepping back as Jaxon lifted his needles and stared at him. You could see the question in the Monk's eyes–he was wondering if this 'Poppy' fellow was a smoker. "What… um… what was the skill you just increased?"

"*Intimidation.*" The word seemed to shake the air like a lion's roar as Jaxon spoke it. "Oh, look at that! There is an active component as well! Who would have guessed?"

"If we ever find some charisma-enhancing gear, I vote that we force Jaxon to wear it. All opposed?" Joe looked around, but there were no nay-sayers. Jaxon was preoccupied reading over his skill again, else he may have had something to say.

"Speaking of gear, fearless leader, are you wearing anything beyond the starting clothes under your lovely robe?" Poppy already knew the only answer he would accept; he had been able to inspect and assign a value to all of Joe's gear by this point.

"No, my strength is too low for me to…" Joe slapped himself on the forehead hard enough to do damage. "I *used* to be too weak to put anything else on. I bet I could even get a new weapon!" He looked at his cleric scepter, thinking, not for the first time, that it looked quite a bit like plywood.

"There are a bunch of merchants in the guild; I can show you where to go if you'd like," Alexis offered quietly. "We should really be prepared when we go in the dungeon. I get a bad feeling from this place."

"Maybe it was the lightning." Jaxon looked at the walls and nodded. "That was what did it for me."

They made their way over to the merchants, and even though the man gave Joe a good price, getting equipment for his level that he could also *wear* cost him a solid chunk of gold. Joe didn't buy anything *too* extravagant since he was going to specialize soon, but he did take Alexis's advice to go into the dungeon well-prepared. He walked away from the mobile store wearing a new set of clothing that increased magic resistance and mana regeneration by a point, a pair of shoes that increased movement speed by ten percent, and best of all, a new scepter!

Cleric scepter (Blessed Oak). Adds 10-15 blunt damage on strike. -15% cast time when casting Cleric spells. 20% chance to use ability [Turn undead] on strike. To cast cleric spells while holding, simply focus your will, intent, and mana into the scepter; it will do the rest. +1 piercing damage. (Augmented with Titanium Taglock)

Joe tried to cast a shadow spike with the hand that was holding the scepter but found that he was unable to do so. It was understandable that he couldn't use the weapon for a different style of spells, but it still sucked. This was a tool devoted to usage by *Clerics*, and… he skid to a stop and turned around. Against the protests of those waiting, he jumped to the front of the short line that had started to form and blurted out a question. "Are there single-hand tools that Mages use for casting, and do you have any?"

The merchant could have been angry that Joe had stopped the flow of customers, but he had just made a hefty profit off of him. Joe had no bartering skills, and since the merchant was a player, his charisma and speech skill did nothing to save Joe money. With a wide smile, the merchant gave his answer, "I sure do! Let me see what I can find here… level nine? Mhmm… here we go! What we have *here* is called a 'casting orb'. All you need to do is cast your spells into this orb, and it will save an imprint of them. Then you pass mana into the orb, and you will be able to cast the spell over and over."

"Single-use? Is it just a bank of spells to use?" Joe was uncertain about the usefulness, and the merchant seemed to smell his hesitation.

"Oh, no, no! Here, you can test it. Cast the spell into the orb, then hold it and try to cast your spell without the hand motions." The merchant pressed the orb into Joe's hands, causing Joe to nearly drop the sweat-coated glass ball.

"Was this in your pocket...?" Joe gagged softly as the merchant merely shrugged. Joe looked at the baseball-sized orb and turned his mind away from gross images, casting shadow spike into the Mage's tool. The sphere went completely dark for a moment, slowly lightening over a long second. The previously slightly-pink but clear orb now had a dark pattern in it, clearly the diagram of the spell, though it was too tiny to make out details. Joe looked around for a suitable target and spotted a large boulder in range.

The area around them went silent as the boulder exploded into gravel. For the remainder of a single second, a barbed spike stood in the shower of gravel. The spike had grown since the last time he had used it and now stood waist-high on Joe. He cast the spell a second time and was pleased to note that the orb functioned much as his scepter did, simply speeding up his casting time. He looked back to smirk at the pale face of the merchant. "I'll take it."

Casting Orb (Rose Quartz) (Uncommon). Adds 5-10 blunt damage on strike. -8% cast time when casting Mage spells. To use, simply cast the spell once into the orb to attune it, then cast the spell as normal through the orb. Note: This is a single-hand item. Spells that require two hands to cast require a different orb.

As Joe's group walked to the entrance of the dungeon, Alexis looked at him and coughed. "You know that he was totally ripping you off, right?"

"Yeah, but I still got the stuff below fair market value," Joe responded with a calm shrug. "I know how expensive it is to play this game, so I'm not going to begrudge someone a bit extra if it doesn't hurt me *too* much. I'm still going to tell Aten to keep an eye on him, though. Just because I'm not hurting for cash doesn't mean some other naive person won't be."

"You know, we still haven't gotten any pay, right?" Alexis smiled dangerously at the Ritualist, who kept his sweating face pointing forward as they approached their goal.

A representative of the guild was waiting for them at the entrance to the dungeon. He looked up from a packet of information, grimacing when he saw the variation in their levels. "Hey, guys. *Couple* of things here. This dungeon is instant and instanced. That means several things, but here is the main one: the creatures in there are going to be really strong and set to be a challenge for the highest level party member. That is the 'instant' portion. The *instanced* portion is a bit… stranger. All the monsters in there are going to be intelligent, but as more parties enter, they will become less intelligent and more ferocious. Their mind and intellect get split to deal with the various parties."

"Is there a limit to the amount of parties that can go in?" Joe questioned the man.

"No, but you cannot leave until you complete the dungeon or die," Joe was promptly informed. "So we don't yet have any good information on what's in there."

"Don' worry about it!" Bard clapped Joe on the shoulder when he noticed the hesitation on Joe's face, causing the party leader to stumble. "We can handle it jus' fine!"

These words would be thrown in his face soon enough. None of them were mentally prepared to handle the horrors they would face in this cursed village.

CHAPTER TWENTY

"So… are they undead, or what?" Poppy whispered *far* too loudly for comfort. They were looking at the monsters that were wandering around shrieking into the air intermittently. Every once in a while, they would act differently, thrashing around as if they were fighting an unseen enemy. Often, the thrashing would stop, and they would seem to become a bit more intelligent. Rarely, they would crouch down and feed on an intangible and invisible feast. Joe winced at the thought of one of his guild members being chewed on.

"Not a clue," Jaxon said in a normal tone of voice. "Though from the description the gut out there gave us, they are currently most likely fighting in alternate 'dimensions'. When they lose in one scenario, they get more intelligence devoted to the remainder of their many forms. Their minds become less spread out. If they win… looks like they're hungry. We should be extra careful of the ones showing heightened awareness, they might be crafty."

"Did you call the helpful guy outside of the entrance a 'gut'?" Alexis hissed. "Did you forget how to say 'guy'?"

"Did he forget how to control his calorie intake? How did

he even do that to himself in the short time this game has been running?" Jaxon rebutted heartlessly. The others rolled their eyes and chalked up another reason to get him some points in charisma.

"That's a terrible thing to say," Joe admonished his teammate. "He could have designed his character that way, or maybe he just struggles with his weight."

"If he struggled with *weights*, he wouldn't struggle with weight," Jaxon responded with great satisfaction. Joe had to resist the urge to slap him. Due to Jaxon's deplorable charisma, there was no way of telling what he thought people were saying during this conversation, so getting mad would just be helping the developers get their laughs.

Their conversation had the unfortunate effect of drawing the attention of the nearest foe, which rushed at them with a howl filled with insanity. It looked like a normal person that had been encapsulated by a rapidly growing tree. The creature came at them swiftly, its attacks wild and brutal. Each swing of its arm was enhanced by the thick wood that twined around to form a club-like weapon, and roots protruded past its feet allowing it to spring forward at high speeds.

"This looks like mah kind o' enemy!" Bard laughed as he stepped forward, axes held out to each side. He swung hard, landing a blow that was blocked by a wood-covered arm. The metal gouged deep into the fibrous armor and tore out a chunk of wood, but Joe realized that they were in trouble when the creature casually counterattacked with a backhand that knocked Bard a full two meters backward. Bard landed hard, coughing up a mouthful of blood from the force of his landing. A healing spell landed on him, and his breathing came a bit easier. The Skald rushed to rejoin the battle.

Alexis fired a crossbow bolt that tore into the exposed flesh of the humanoid, knowing almost instantly that her poison was having no effect. "Immune to poison or at least this kind! This thing must be undead; be careful!"

"Undead? Excellent! My favorite!" Poppy sprang forward,

his rapier hissing through the air like a striking serpent. He skillfully sank his blade into exposed flesh, tearing open a hole that slowly dripped black blood. Jaxon appeared beside the creature, landing a devastating kick to its knee. With a sickening crunch, the joint twisted sideways, but the wood covering simply constricted and realigned the leg before the monster could fall.

Jaxon leaned away from a blow that should have taken his head, and Poppy rammed his rapier into another unarmored location. Bard was back on his feet, charging into the fray within moments of being healed. Joe was preparing to use a shadow spike when their opponent suddenly stomped, one foot after the other. The roots that had given it so much mobility now sank into the ground, and its wounds began closing at a visible rate.

"Get away from it!" Joe called, staring at the creature and activating Intrusive Scan. He watched the creature for five full seconds while it snarled at them, unable to move for the time being.

Name: Lumber Jack. Class: Livingwood Ghoul. Level: 10.

Highest stat: Constitution.

Ongoing effects: Living Armor, Undead, Cursed, Sacrificial Defense, Absorb Nutrients.

After five seconds, the Ghoul's weak points lit up in Joe's vision, and he hurried to point them out before combat reignited. "Anyone know what Sacrificial Defense means? Also, Alexis, its armor is alive even if the creature isn't!"

"I have something similar to Agent Orange; it works on plants and meat! No need to worry about poison immunity if its flesh falls off!" Alexis began to dig through her pack. "Make sure not to breathe this in after I use it if you like having lungs!"

A tiny halo of copper light appeared around Bard's head for a moment. "Ah! Skaldic Knowledge kicked in! Sacrificial Defense means that armor will be continuously repaired using the health of the person wearing it. Killing the armor should kill the creature as well!"

"Alright, but when it is standing still like that it is healing by pulling nutrients from the ground," Joe told them, watching as the wounds on the Ghoul closed. It was staring at him with frightening intensity; his intrusive scan must have built up a lot of aggro.

"I'm gonna launch the herbicide," Alexis told the group as she put a new bolt in her hand crossbow. "As soon as it clears up, go for the kill."

The melee fighters got into position, getting ready to charge the undead that was eying them like dinner. **Thwack** At this range, there was almost no time between when Alexis fired and when the bolt landed. As the cloud of toxins settled on the wood, the Ghoul released a shriek of fury. The wood and exposed flesh began to bubble, and the wood armor thrashed in place while uprooting itself. The Ghoul's already thin body became skeletal as the wood absorbed muscle and fat to restore itself.

As the air cleared, the fighters launched themselves forward. Bard began using his axes to take chunks of wood from the armor, forcing it to kill its host in an attempt to recover. Poppy aimed for the critical points that Joe had mentioned and Jaxon continued to try and tear off limbs by forcing joints to rotate over and over.

*Exp: 300 (2 * 150 * Jack x1).*

The attacks stopped as the notification appeared, everyone breathing heavily as the adrenaline began to wear off. Bard smiled happily as he exclaimed, "I go' five *hundred* exp off that shan beastie!"

The others seemed happy with the gains from fighting the Ghoul, but something was bothering Joe. He snapped his fingers as it came to him. "Aha! Guys, we only beat half the enemy! That armor is alive, remember? We were fighting 'Lumber Jack', but we only got experience for 'Jack'. Let's kill the armor!"

Joe started the attack, spraying a gout of acid onto the wood. He was pleased to see that it took extra damage, as it was apparently considered equipment even if it was alive. He would remember that in future battles. Bard came in next, using his axes to chop the wood into manageable chunks. The others stayed back, their attacks not very useful against this kind of enemy. On the plus side, without a host, the armor was immobile. In moments, a new notification appeared.

*Exp: 150 (2 * 75* Lumber x1).*

"I am loving this double experience," Poppy sighed happily. "Two hundred experience for an immobile enemy? Awesome."

"Ah got three," Bard told him smugly.

"I'm glad for you, but doesn't that just mean you are at a lower level?" Poppy's seemingly pleasant words caused Bard to grimace, a bit of color that he tried to hide coming into his cheeks.

Jaxon seemed troubled. He looked around the transformed town, sighing as he saw mainly enemies similar to the one they had just fought. "I am uncertain how useful my skills will be here. Unless we encounter enemies without limb-assisting mechanisms, most of my skills will be countered quite easily."

"I'm sure there will be something out there for you, Jaxon. If nothing else, you apparently have a really high skill in dodging. You could serve as an alternate tank if you needed to." Joe patted the despondent Monk on the back, hoping to cheer him up.

"Joe, there is something you need to see." Alexis had moved forward to do a bit of scouting, and the way she hurried back was concerning.

"What's wrong?" Joe responded instantly, putting on his 'serious' face.

"I think we are in trouble." She motioned for everyone to stay as quiet as possible, and they followed her. They peeked around the corner, horrified as they saw the mass of ghoulish enemies clustered in the area. While none of them were exactly the same, it was obvious that they would be at *least* as strong as the first ghoul they had fought.

They moved back to the entrance, regrouping around the bubbling remains of the ghoul. Poppy was beginning to panic, and his words were filled with a mix of fear and frustration, "How are we supposed to fight *that?* This is stupid! Much as I love fighting the undead, there must have been two dozen of them clustered in the town square!"

"Calm down," Jaxon demanded, surprising the others. "If you attract them over here like that, I am going to make *you* hold them off."

"Take it *easy*, Jaxon." Joe was getting concerned; had he made a mistake adding Jaxon to the party? It seemed that whenever he wasn't talking about things that he was passionate about, he was... kinda *mean*. Though... something was... off. Jaxon was looking at him with a strange, uncomprehending expression. "Jaxon... what did you just hear Poppy say?"

"What are you talking about?" Jaxon pointed at the Duelist, who seemed quite offended. "You were right here! He said, 'How can we not fight that? Don't be stupid; there are only two dozen of them, and we can lure them from here.' I thought that was a terrible idea, and if he wants to draw them in like that he is going to need to hold them off if things go wrong. It's only fair."

"Oh, this is so cool," Alexis whispered, eyes alight with interest. "I read in the forums that people with negative stats in certain areas have different gameplay, but I've never seen any posts from people with low charisma! Oh, that's insidious. I love it."

"What do you mean?" Poppy didn't take his eyes off of Jaxon, who seemed to be studying his fingers again.

"Well, people with below ten strength or constitution have a really hard time getting around or doing *anything* physical," Alexis started, only to be cut off by Joe.

"I can attest to that." Joe held up a hand. "I only recently got above ten in those two stats."

"Right, and people with bad dexterity fall a lot or hurt themselves trying to work with intricate stuff," Alexis continued while Joe nodded along almost nostalgically. "Warriors that didn't think intelligence or wisdom mattered have reported that when people talk, they only hear the simplest words; everything else comes out as 'blah, blah, la-la'. Baby talk. Apparently, it is really upsetting. Bad wisdom? They attack things that they *really* shouldn't, like rocks, thinking they are the enemy they were seeking."

"So what you are saying…" Joe realized where this was going. "Low charisma means that they just think everyone *else* is being a jerk!"

"Exactly!" Alexis smiled, though it faltered a bit when she saw that she was the center of attention. "Ah… so, Jaxon really thinks he is doing nice things for people, and he might not even be saying mean things, but the game is transforming what he says to meet his low charisma."

"Insidious. Ye weren't jokin'." Bard looked at the smiling Monk. "I'll see if ah can't find ah spell ta buff charisma when we get outta here."

"*If* we get out of here," Poppy muttered, looking away.

"That's something we should talk about." Joe heaved a sigh as a plan formed in his mind. "Not that I don't have faith in our team, but… I don't think we can beat this dungeon."

"What are you saying?" Jaxon seemed shocked at their leader's lack of faith.

"I think that we should play it safe and pick off individual enemies for as long as we can. But if we can't leave except by winning or dying… we should make sure that we get enough experience not to drop a level before we take any chances. Let's look for any items or money, but if we have a total party wipe don't be upset."

"Joe, if we plan to fail, we will," Alexis spoke up uncharacteristically vehemently. "We will play it safe, but we *will* beat this dungeon. Even if it takes a week or a month of grinding and going slow, we will *all* walk out of here together. Alive."

As she finished her speech, the group was coated by a spray of liquid. Jaxon fell to the ground, his head landing a moment later. Behind his falling corpse was another ghoul, but the wood covering this one's arms was curved and sharp as if it held a scythe in each hand.

"I take it we forgot to set a guard?" Joe quipped as they rushed to get into a battle formation. Contrary to his flippant attitude, Joe was furious with himself for failing to take care of his people. He readied a spray of acid, planning on skewering this foe with a shadow spike as soon as it was distracted by the destruction of its armor. Poppy parried a swing from the ghoul, using the opening to create a large hole through its neck.

"That didn't count as a critical!" Poppy warned them. "I forgot for a moment, head or heart with the undead." The creature spun rapidly, its other arm coming down on Bard, who failed to properly block in time. A fresh shower of blood wet the ground as a huge wound opened up on Bard's arm.

"Argh! Yer maw's got baws 'n yer da' loves it!" The Bard shouted at the ghoul in rage and pain. The ghoul took on a red tinge as Bard unexpectedly enraged it. Joe finished with his cast, and the ghoul was coated in weak acid, its armor instantly trying to fix the damage by tearing into its host. Joe quickly aimed his scepter at Bard, sending a focused heal into his arm as the ghoul began to swing at the Skald wildly.

Bard's motions became much more fluid as his arm stitched itself together. "Gimme ah minute wi' this beastie! Mah dodge skill has been stagnatin'. Jump–**swish**–in if'n–**swish**–ah look like ahm gon' die!"

The group tried to heed his wishes but kept attacking in order to whittle down the ghoul's health. A scythe came too close to killing the Skald once, slicing open his cheek deeply enough that his teeth could be seen through the hole. Though they threw a few attacks in every once in a while, they made sure to let the focus stay on Bard until Joe saw the ghoul begin to lift its foot. Instantly reacting, he began to cast shadow spike.

Slam. The first foot came down, driving the roots into the ground. Joe had timed his spell perfectly because as the other foot raised and lowered, a spike was formed right under the stamping heel. A sound like a tree splintering cracked through the area as the ghoul drove its foot down as hard as it could, allowing the spell to drive upward all the way to its knee. The spike vanished a bare second later, and the ghoul would have fallen if its other leg weren't already stabilizing it.

"Brilliant cast!" Alexis laughed in exaltation, firing another bolt into the ghoul's wood-covered face.

Bard took the initiative and hacked into the rooted leg like it was a sapling. After a few moments of this, the ghoul dropped to the ground. Bard and Poppy finished it off by chopping off the ghoul's head in honor of their fallen comrade. This had the added benefit of killing the armor at the same time, so they decided to remember this trick for the future.

*Exp: 450 (2 * 225 * Plank McGee x1).*

Joe looked sadly at the grey matter leaking from the ghoul's split skull. "If only I had a way to preserve that! I have so many uses for an undead brain…"

Alexis looked at him oddly but didn't say anything. Bard gestured at Jaxon's body. "Well?"

Joe nodded in reply, sitting down for a minute to regain his mana. "This is going to be the only time I can do this today, so we really need to be *extra* paranoid from now on. Guards, cautious steps, the works."

"Do *what* today?" Poppy questioned as Bard nodded in understanding. Alexis made a 'no idea' gesture as Joe stood up.

"Alrighty, here we go." He began going through the myriad of movements needed, finishing up by pulling his arms back so his elbows were tucked to the side with his palms facing forward. Once again, mana began to fluctuate in front of his hands, becoming visible and seeming to hold great depth. Joe pressed his hands forward slowly as he took a deep breath, "*Resurrection*!"

As had happened the last time he used this spell, a rent in the air appeared, a portal to *elsewhere* forming. A second passed, then two, but soon Jaxon stepped through the breach. His corpse vanished from the ground before his foot had touched the first speck of dirt. "Didn't think anyone made it! I do have to say, the time dilation makes the wait *much* more manageable."

"Gotta stop dyin', Jaxon." Bard rolled his eyes. "If ye already complain about tae time it takes ta magic ye back..."

"Yes, yes, don't make dying a habit." Jaxon waved Bard's words away. "I would really prefer *not* to, but if I do go down, I much prefer a speedy return."

"*You can resurrect people*?" Poppy gasped with glee. "I don't even... do you know what this..."

"That's a neat trick." Alexis gave a half smile, her cool attitude sobering Poppy.

"I like it." Joe shrugged nonchalantly. "C'mon, guys. Let's try to find a safe area; we need a plan of action."

CHAPTER TWENTY-ONE

By going left instead of taking a right into the town square, they were able to avoid the densely packed enemies. Joe had a sinking suspicion that they would still need to go into that area if they lasted long enough. Most of the buildings that had been in the town were still standing, though they had been twisted, malformed, and–strangely enough–reinforced. Even with the strange new look, the building they set up in felt far less rickety and likely to collapse than they had expected.

They crept around, and after ensuring that there was no one hiding in a corner waiting to jump out at them, they closed and barricaded the door. Bard sat down, heaving a huge sigh. "Two foes in an' we're near ready ta drop."

"I'm still shocked how something as large and nasty as that thing could move so silently," Jaxon complained heatedly. "I normally have *excellent* situational awareness."

"We got too caught up in discussing game mechanics." Joe waved Jaxon over to sit with them. "We got too loud, too focused on other things. We won't let it happen again, but right now, we need to make a plan. I'm not sure what the requirements for beating this dungeon are, but if it's anything like other games we need to find and beat the dungeon boss."

"Most likely still true here." Alexis sank down to the ground next to Bard. "In my opinion, there are two choices for who the boss would be: either the highest leveled person in town–Sir Bearington–or the person who set this whole thing into motion, the smith."

"The mayor is a bear," Joe flatly stated. The others ignored his inane comments and continued talking.

"Could we set up traps?" Poppy didn't direct the question at anyone, simply voicing his thoughts.

"Aye, we could, but with what?" Bard scratched at his beard, deep in thought. "Ah doubt tha' 'Lexis has tha' volume o' poison. Joe might be able ta do sommat, but ah don' wanna spend ah week here."

"Hey!" Joe started indignantly, pausing and thinking about what Bard was saying. As he parsed the accent, Joe realized he had actually been complimented. He finished with a grudging, "Carry on."

"In my opinion, the issue isn't with fighting the Ghouls, it is with fighting all of them at once," Jaxon stretched forward, cracking his knuckles. "We either need to split them up or get them into an enclosed area where their numbers are meaningless. Heck, bring them into here."

"If we can get them into an enclosed area, my poison would be more effective." Alexis nodded along with Jaxon's words. "The issue in that instance would be that there is no other exit from these buildings that I have seen."

"Unless we had another way out, that would be ah death sentence." Bard looked at his axes then the back wall.

"Cutting through the walls would take a long time, alert the ghouls, and reduce the effectiveness of Alexis's poison," Poppy was quick to say when he saw the decision forming in Bard's eyes. Bard simply sighed and leaned into Alexis for comfort.

"This building has two floors; we could hop out a window if we needed to," Jaxon offered cheerfully.

"That opens us up to true damage from falling. Terrain damage." Alexis shook her head, sighing as she realized that surviving this dungeon was becoming more and more unlikely.

"I might be able to help with that…" Joe slowly stated, looking a bit uncomfortable. "Do any of you have the skill 'jump'?"

"This should be good. Look how he's blushing." Alexis smirked at the uncomfortable look on Joe's face. "I don't have it; is that an issue?"

"No, actually. That's a good thing." Joe made everyone stand up, his face bright red. "I'm going to try to teach you all how to get the jump skill, alright?"

"Do we just jump?" Jaxon crouched, but Joe quickly stopped him.

"No, no, listen to my instruction before doing anything, ok?" Joe looked at the others, who had various versions of a smirk on their faces. "Alright… point your hands down and put them slightly below your hips, bend your knees… and straighten them as quickly as possible. Repeat as necessary."

"Are ye messing wi' us?" Bard grumbled with a snort.

Jaxon followed Joe's instructions right away, jumping lightly into the air and landing easily. "Huh." Joe blinked as a notification filled his vision.

Skill gained: Teaching (Novice V). While others are content to simply learn a skill, you never stop until you are good enough at it to teach that skill to another person. Anything worth doing is worth passing on to someone else, am I right? What amazing altruism! Oh, wait. You are going to start charging for this, aren't you? Effect: Boost the speed at which a person you are teaching can learn a skill by 10%. Based on your own rank in the skill, your student may acquire the skill at a higher ranking than normal.

"I just gained the skill 'jump' at *Beginner* zero," Jaxon spoke thoughtfully, tapping his fingertips together. "How intriguing. The notification tells me that there are benefits from learning from 'a Master'? Do you have the jump skill at the *Master* rank, Joe?"

"Yeah." Joe smiled as the others began jumping, expressions

ranging from delight to wry annoyance. "Keep going guys, bend your knees and straighten them out quickly." Jaxon began jumping in place along with the others, and Joe repeated his words every once in a while. Each time he did so, the people rolled their eyes at him, but he knew that 'instructing' them would boost their learning speed and boost his teaching skill. By the time they stopped, Joe had increased his teaching skill by a surprising amount.

Skill increased: Teaching (Beginner II). Effect: Boost the speed at which a person you are teaching can learn a skill by 20%. Based on your own rank in the skill, your student may acquire the skill at a higher ranking than normal. Extra effect: Passionate instruction. As you have not been teaching others for profit but simply to help them, when you initially teach a person a skill, the boost to their starting rank will be significantly higher if you do not charge for your services.

"And just like that, my dreams of making a profit vanish once again," Joe grumbled good-naturedly. He didn't really need extra money, but it would be nice to have the option for once. "How is everyone feeling?"

"I got to Beginner nine. *Nine.*" Poppy shook his head, a goofy look of glee on his face. "I got an extra effect that reduces fall damage by twenty percent because my 'instructor' has something similar."

"Same here," Alexis stated, followed quickly by the others. "How in the *world* did you get your jump skill to the Master ranks? I've never even *seen* you jump."

"I'd *really* rather not say." Joe quickly killed *that* awkward conversation. "But I jump all the time. You've seen how I walk? How it seems that I go further than I should with each step?"

"You mean *skipping* counts as jumping?" Jaxon had a look of glee on his face. "I can't wait to work on increasing the rank of this skill!" The others had a sudden vision of the Monk skipping down the road with a skeletal smile on his face, fingers wiggling as if he were gripping a handful of snakes. *Also* appearing in all of their premonitions were angry guards with drawn swords chasing the man.

"You know, I think that will be fun," Poppy snickered evilly. "I love that I joined this group."

"We should get started setting up some traps and figure out how not to get caught in them." Joe coughed into his hand, hoping that he hadn't just made life harder for Jaxon. "Who here can run the fastest? You are going to have to be bait for the Ghouls. Not Alexis, though; she and I need to work on traps."

"I'll do it!" Jaxon happily stated, turning toward the door. "Just tell me when!"

"Wait a bit," Joe instructed as he turned to Alexis. "What do you need from us in order to make this work?"

"I need a vat of some kind," Alexis told them. "I'm going to dump the majority of my ingredients into it, then when Jaxon comes back through here he can toss in the final aerosolizing agent into it. The entirety of the first floor will quickly be filled with a choking poison, but it is heavier than air so most of it shouldn't filter into the air upstairs. We need to be really careful though; once the air is filled with this stuff, it will explode if it comes in contact with an open flame."

"Can we use that as a part of the trap?" Joe inquired right before Poppy could ask the same question. Poppy caught his breath, snorting because he had been beaten to the punch.

"I mean. If you want to go kamikaze?" Alexis rolled her eyes. "If you are close enough to light it on fire, you will be caught in the blast. It'll be *indoors* remember? That amount of force would blow the roof off, and we will be between the blast and the roof, so…"

"Ah found ah bathtub o'er here!" Bard called from another room. "Will that work as ah vat? It's moveable, an' has no drain!"

"That's perfect sweet- **ahem**, that's perfect!" Alexis's face turned crimson. She looked around at the others. "Um. We're dating now."

"Got that." Poppy chuckled at her murderous glare. "No need to be embarrassed, I wish I were as lucky."

Before Alexis could say anything, Jaxon nodded and agreed

with the Duelist. "Yes, we would all be lucky to have a partner as competent and caring as Bard. He was an excellent choice of mate, Alexis."

A half-snort, half-laugh came from both Joe and Poppy at his words. Alexis simply covered her face with her hands and tried not to throw something at the Monk. "I hate you all," she groaned weakly.

"Alright, coulda used ah hand wit' this, that's fine, I'll just do it alone," Bard grumbled as he dragged a copper bathtub into the room. "Where do ya want me to put 'er?"

Joe couldn't help himself. "Put it over there, shnookums." The crossbow bolt in his foot made him screech, but he considered himself lucky that she used a non-poisoned projectile. He healed his foot over a few seconds, ignoring the glare on Alexis's face and the shock on Bard's. "Worth it," he stage-whispered, locking eyes with Poppy and winking.

"We are going to want it near the stairs." Alexis directed the placement of the tub, then Joe channeled his healing water into the tub to fill it up. After a few moments, the magical component of the water faded and left behind regular but very pure water. Alexis tested the water with a strip of something that she pulled from her pack. "This is a perfect base for potions and especially for poison. This is strange; I've never run into water with such a high affinity for darkness before."

"Is that good for what you do? Making potions and such?" Joe examined the water with interest; he hadn't known it would keep any properties.

"Good enough that I'd really like to use this water in the future whenever I'm making poison," Alexis informed him with a pleading glance.

"Hmm. Maybe don't *shoot* me then?" Joe countered the puppy-dog eyes easily. "How long will this take?"

"This is a simple poison with limited usage. A plant killer, mainly, so it'll only take about ten minutes to steep and integrate the reagents. We are counting on it being highly concentrated so that the wooden armor eats the Ghouls as they wither;

I think the Ghouls are largely immune to my poison, being undead, so I am maximizing this against their armor. All Jaxon will need to do is dump in the powdered beast Core when he comes through." Alexis fished out a small bag from her satchel. "Then poof. Within ten seconds, the contents of the entire tub will have turned into a fog. It'll fill this space *really* thickly, so you are going to need to move *scary* fast, Jaxon."

"Run up the stairs as fast as I did when I was a child and had to turn off the basement lights. Got it." Jaxon was limbering up, the cracking of his joints making Alexis wince.

Joe shifted the conversation to the next talking point. "Poppy, any information on an emergency exit point?"

"I snuck out back, and we have two options. We can either jump to ground floor or if we are feeling really lucky we can try and get over onto the roof of the next building over. Not sure if it's clear, so I say we go to the ground and around that building." Poppy waved his hands as he spoke, obviously thinking that the wild motions were helping them understand what he was saying.

"Works for me. Anything to add, Bard?" Joe looked over at the last member of the party.

"Ahm gonna add a buff ta ol' creepyfingers here; it'll boost his aggro rate. That way he should be able to get *all* the Ghouls instead o' just ah part of 'em." Bard chanted a short incantation, and a red film descended over Jaxon.

"Thanks!" Jaxon got into position by the door. "Are we all ready?"

Alexis stirred the tub of purple liquid with the broken-off leg of a chair. "Ready over here. Just make sure to push *this* bowl into the tub when you come back and run *hard* up the stairs."

"Got it." Jaxon took a deep breath and threw open the door. "Here I go!" He skipped out into the hazy late-afternoon light.

The remaining members of the party watched the spot he had just vacated, hoping that they hadn't just invited their doom to visit. Also, watching Jaxon skip away had been just as disturbing and hilarious as they had imagined it would be. The general consensus was that there was nothing else to do at this point, so after a minute, they simply filed up the stairs and waited. From the noises outside that were quickly approaching, the wait would not be a long one. "Tasty, tasty Monk! Come get me while I'm warm, yum-yum-yum! Hey! Anything I may have missed! Over *here*!"

"We're dead," Alexis whispered, paling at the sight of the platoon of Ghouls chasing after Jaxon.

"Let's get ready for plan B." Joe opened the back window just in case they didn't understand.

"A *little* faith in the plans you concoct would ease my tension significantly," Poppy joked halfheartedly. "I don't suppose you have any advice for when we jump out of the window?"

Joe looked directly into Poppy's eyes and nodded. "Do a flip."

"Wow."

"It'll give you a skill; I'm not being a terrible person!" Joe huffed at the shocked looks that were thrown his way.

The door on the first floor was slammed open, and thundering footsteps announced Jaxon's return. "I think I got their attention!"

"Get up 'ere, ye weapons-grade idjit!" Bard shouted down the stairs when Jaxon didn't immediately run back to relative safety.

"One moment, please!" Jaxon called back. "Where did you put the powder?"

"It's on the nightstand next to the tub!" Alexis called down impatiently.

Smashing sounds filled the air as the Ghouls began entering the building. Jaxon called up to them in a sing-song voice, "I don't *see* it!"

"Oh. My. Gosh." Alexis slapped the wall. "To the *left* of the tub, on your way up the stairs! It's in a bowl! It's purple! Filled with shiny powder!"

Crash **Tinkle** "I found it! Adding it now!" Jaxon practically flew up the stairs, Ghouls on his heels.

"Does that taunt impact teammates, or do I just naturally want to hurt him?" Alexis wondered as she glanced out the window and saw the last few Ghouls forcing their way into the building. Bard just shrugged as Jaxon–looking much the worse for wear–burst into the room.

"I think **gasp** we're trapped. **Wheeze**. There are dozens of them!" Jaxon almost fell to the ground, stamina completely drained. Joe threw a healing spell at him to take care of the few injuries he had gained; both Bard and Poppy were already completely engaged with the enemy, doing their best to hold them off at the doorway.

"It's okay, Jaxon. Those dozens of poor suckers don't know they just walked into a trap. There's *five* of us here waiting for them." Joe pulled Jaxon to his feet.

"Right, the poison. Yes." Jaxon struggled into a fighting stance, getting closer to the door.

"No, the trap is that there is five of… yeah, the poison." Joe had been wanting to use that joke all day, and now it was spoiled.

"I'm getting damage notifications, but the poison isn't doing as much damage as it should be. It isn't going to be killing them anytime soon." Alexis looked away from her combat log with wide eyes. "They must have torn part of the wall off down there."

"They did," Jaxon informed them, looking around at the group. Bard took a heavy blow just then, stumbling back and opening a hole in the human barrier they had established. A root slammed into the floor below them, penetrating through and opening a small hole. Jaxon nodded sharply as if understanding something. More roots tore into the floor, then the doorframe. "You all need to go out of the window–right now."

"Jax–what are you *doing*?" Joe cried as Jaxon pulled an unused torch from his bag and lit it. "That'll kill us all!"

"No… just me. Go, now, all of you. I think we all knew that

this was a possibility. No, that it was *likely*." Jaxon seemed determined, the firelight reflecting in his eyes along with his perpetual smile giving him a terrifying visage. "I'm exhausted, my stamina is bottomed out, and someone needs to give you all time to escape. In five seconds, I am dropping this torch down that hole, and I hope you all beat this dungeon. Four."

Bard pushed Alexis toward the window, and with a glance backward, she leapt. Bard followed closely, but Joe tried to stay with the crazy Monk who continued his countdown, seemingly oblivious to their peril. "Three." Poppy shook his head and pointed, stabbing once more before turning and going out the window. "Two." Joe sighed when he saw that Jaxon wasn't even looking at them anymore. Joe turned and *jumped* just as Jaxon was overwhelmed.

"*One.*"

CHAPTER TWENTY-TWO

The world seemed to lose all color but white and orange as the building erupted in flames behind them. With the wall being torn open, there had not been enough flammable material in the air to make the entire building explode, but it was unlikely that anything inside the building was going to survive the sudden inferno if they weren't right next to an exit.

Joe did a flip right before landing, arresting some of his momentum and allowing him to reach the ground without injury. Before he touched down, he got a notification that Jaxon had died. Joe cursed loudly, looking back to see fire flowing upward from the windows like a reverse waterfall. "We need to get ready to cut down any survivors. We haven't gotten any experience yet, so combat must be ongoing."

The response was muted acceptance, and they hurried around to the front of the building. One Ghoul was standing stock-still, roots buried as it tried to heal through regaining nutrients. Another one–badly charred–was planting itself as a third wobbled out of the building, barely holding itself together. It fell forward, and Joe met the downward descent of its head with a shadow spike, instantly finishing it off by letting it skewer itself. The least damaged one growled menacingly at them, its vocal chords badly mangled by poison, fire, and smoke.

Poppy and Bard circled past that one, their weapons digging into the other as it tried to hurry its regeneration. Arrows buried themselves into the Ghoul's flesh, and though the poison wasn't very effective, it still sped the Ghoul towards death. The creature died, still standing upright as the armor it was wearing ate the body for nutrients. They didn't bother to chop up the living armor just yet, focusing instead on the remaining monster. It watched them without moving, trying to heal as much of the damage it had taken as possible before joining combat.

Joe took the lead, channeling weak acid spray on the Ghoul. Over five seconds, he used one hundred and forty mana to do one hundred seventy-five damage to the Ghoul and five times that to the armor. The wood was melted almost completely off, and it was child's play for Bard to take the Ghoul's head with a single clean swipe.

They returned to the other standing armor and simply tossed it back into the inferno then waited a few moments to be sure that they had gotten every enemy. The notification appearing in their vision confirmed for them that combat had ended.

*Exp: 3,780 (2 * (225 * .3 (Indirect combat)) * Sapling Ghouls x28).*

*Exp: 1,350 (2 * 225) * Sapling Ghouls x3).*

Level increase postponed due to being in a dungeon.

Skill increased: Weak Acid Spray (Novice IX). No longer content with small animals, you now test on larger and larger creatures! The sign of a truly dangerous individual's disturbed mind.

Skill increased: Aerial Acrobatics (Novice IV). Oh look, he did another flip. At least you didn't hurt yourself this time, showing that you are making actual progress.

"Level up *postponed*?" Alexis complained bitterly. "That's stupid! I have enough now for level eleven!"

"This is actually a safety feature if I am not mistaken," Poppy interjected before the conversation could spiral downward. "If we die, we lose experience as though we were still at our original level. If we *live*, we are given as much Exp as if we were still at the lower level as well. This is a win-win-win situation for us because it will also keep the monsters from getting stronger. Also, I totally did a flip and got a new skill."

"Yer ramblin, Poppy. Take ah deep breath." Bard swatted the Duelist on the back, making him sputter.

"I'm good, I'm good." Poppy calmed down, whether it was under his own power or an effect of Bard's charisma was unknown. "We should get moving, get away from here. The smoke and light will draw in anything that is still out there wandering around."

"Agreed." Joe looked at the walls surrounding the dungeon, specifically the fact that the sun was dipping below them. "We should *really* hurry. I don't want to be in here after full dark."

The party moved away from the area, back toward the town square. They looked around, but the square was now empty except for the trees that lined the paths to the new city hall. Of all the areas in town, this one had been changed the most. Where before the city hall was a simple building shoved in among many others, now it was a grand affair that sat alone in the middle of an otherwise empty lot. Only the vegetation and rustling trees kept the lonely manor company.

"I see nothing that'll attack us," Joe quietly told the others. Whispering was a bad idea when attempting to be sneaky, as the hissing vowels would draw attention far easier than simply speaking in a modulated tone. "Anyone see something I'm missing?"

Of course none of the others saw something he had missed; at thirty-three, his perception was higher than anyone else's in the group. They began moving cautiously toward the doors, keeping their eyes open for enemies or traps. Not only did they scan the ground, they watched the trees above them. Unfortunately for all of them, they were simply looking for the wrong size of enemy.

"Ow!" Alexis called, slapping at her neck. The others

instantly had their attention on her, trying to figure out what had happened, why she was so loud. Her hand came away, leaving behind a path of blood, both red and blue. Metallic thread-like streaks were also visible, but they didn't understand what they were. "It's a… spider? Oh… oh no."

Alexis was beginning to stiffen, her head already hard to turn. Her words were forced, panicked, and starting to slur, "It went right through mah 'oison resiss! 'Ook ow!"

Hearing her warning, the others moved quickly. If the spider had gone through *her* poison resistance that easily, it must be a deadly concoction indeed. Joe's vision shifted slightly as the sun fully dropped beyond the horizon, and shadows cloaked the dungeon. Either Darkvision allowed him to make out the details of the spiders better, or they had stopped concealing themselves with the onset of night.

The spiders were large for their species, about the size of Joe's middle finger. This was not the disturbing aspect of them, oh no. Beyond their size was their form; the arachnids had the torso and head of human women but no human limbs. Instead, they had the legs of spiders, if spider legs were made out of syringes. Yes, the legs on the spiders were made out of *hypodermic needles*. That was enough for Joe. Nope, nope, nope. He raised both hands, dropping his scepter and dual casting weak acid spray. A fountain of acid shot upward, killing spiders and mutilating the foliage. Some splashed down on him, but the damage was small enough that he ignored it.

Still channeling the spell, he turned in place and continued washing the area with the destructive fluid. Just as he stopped, panting, he heard a muffled scream of terror from Alexis. She had fallen over, and a dozen spiders were on her back staring at the others in the party. Before anyone else could make a move, the tiny creatures suddenly pulled *hard* on the threads connecting them to the branches above and shot into the air, pulling Alexis with them. There was a moan of terror… and a moment later she was dropped, having been slingshot and released above the tree's foliage. She landed heavily, head first, dying instantly upon impact.

The remaining members of the party simply stood there in shock. In the space of a few seconds, everything had moved from not dangerous at all… to a teammate being dropped out of a tree by freaking *needle spiders*. Bard looked at Alexis's body in horror then glanced back at Joe a simple question on his lips, "Fire?"

Joe shook his head. "I'll walk ahead blasting the trees with acid. We need to clear a path right away; they got bolder with darkness. Keep an eye out; if they come at us across the ground we might be screwed if we don't see them." He put his plan into action, stepping forward briskly while keeping a stream of acid angled above himself and toward the building. There were tiny high-pitched screams every once in a while, letting Joe know that he was doing the right thing.

"Nothing on the ground; looks like they really don't want to walk," Poppy announced quietly, shuddering at his next words. "I think their legs are more for *landing* on things than for walking."

"Ah've got tae creepy-crawlies like ye wouldn't imagine." Bard scratched at his arms angrily. "Nasty little things. Poor 'Lexis. That musta been ah terrifyin' way ta go."

"I'm sure it won't be an issue," Joe grunted, remembering that the game had a way of making you… *ignore* past horrors. Maybe not *ignore*, perhaps *heal* from the trauma? Joe almost missed a step as that second thought crossed his mind. That thought *hadn't come from him…*

Skill gained: Mental Manipulation Resistance (Novice I). This skill is a staple for the paranoid and frightened. While it might be useful in certain situations, all that you are doing is hurting yourself. Effect: Grants 10+1n% direct resistance to mental manipulation where 'n' is skill level. This will help you block out effects of skills such as fear, control, and magical seduction. At rank ten: 2n% less experience lost upon death. Caution: Frequent use of this skill may lead to a damaged mind. It isn't normal *to walk away from a fight where you were killed. By removing some of the mind-altering effects of dying and coming back, you lose experience. With this skill… you lose some of the protections granted to the minds of Travelers. At the beginner ranks, you may start to go insane upon dying.*

You have gained a class: Psychomancer (Restricted). A being that inspires fear into the hearts of foe and friend alike, the Psychomancer works to directly control others. Unlike a Bard who evokes reaction through emotion or a necromancer who controls empty bodies of the dead… a Psychomancer controls the living, easily being able to turn groups into puppets at higher levels.

Psychomancer has been absorbed by class: Ritualist. All bonuses from having this class are negated. Caution! This class has the rarity (Restricted). If an official of the Kingdom of Ardania sees this class active without permission from the King or Queen, you will be jailed immediately. To make an appointment with one of the Monarchs, find a trusted governmental official and inform them of this development.

Quest Gained: Please Don't Kill Me. By gaining a Kingdom-Restricted class, you have set yourself up to become an enemy of the Kingdom and, therefore, humanity as a whole. Proceed to a government official and turn yourself in. Reward: A fair trial by the Monarchs. Failure: If caught, you face jail time or Sealing.

Quest Gained: I Do What I Want! By gaining a Kingdom-Restricted class, you have set yourself up to be an enemy of the Kingdom and, therefore, humanity as a whole. Find a class trainer. They are well-hidden for obvious reasons. Reward: Advancement of your new class. Failure: Loss of access to hidden Psychomancer trainers. This quest is automatically failed by completing quest 'Please Don't Kill Me'.

"One thing after another," Joe grunted, pausing his forward movement to let his mana recover. Gauging the distance to the building ahead of them, Joe took a deep breath and continued forward, acid once again gushing from his hands. Once they stepped out from under the trees, Joe sighed with relief and dropped his hands. They had been getting heavy.

Skill change: Weak Acid Spray has become 'Acid Spray' (Beginner 0). After using this spell on living beings constantly, it has shifted slightly to be more dangerous to living material! +5 acid damage per second to living things.

*Exp: 1,620 (2 * 30 * Phobic Spiders x27).*

"As horrible as this has all been, I'm getting excellent returns," Poppy announced, looking over the notifications that were appearing. "The horror of coming face-to-face with so many phobias all at once is mentally draining, though." He turned the door handle, threw open the door, and his top half vanished into a fine red mist as a paw the size of a manhole cover blew through him.

Poppy's legs toppled over, crunching against the ground as a bear the size of a truck stepped out of the open door and used the limbs as a welcome mat. Joe stared at the bear as it came into view, unconsciously activating his intrusive scan.

Name: Sir Bearington. Class: Raid Boss. Title: Cursed Champion of a Fallen Deity (Spriggan).

Highest stat: Strength.

Ongoing effects: Enraged. Bear. Grizzly Damage. Triple Speed. Forced Sentience. Enlarged Bear. Jailor. Boss Monster. Item Destruction. Run.

"See you tomorrow, Bard." Joe winced as a bloody paw whipped toward him. He took the hit full-on, entirely unable to dodge or block the strike he could barely see coming toward him.

Critical hit! You have taken 835 blunt damage! Undying Robes effect activated. Health set to 1!

Joe slid to the ground bonelessly, nearly literally. He had so many notifications for broken bones… Joe cast lay on hands on himself, instantly raising his health to forty-one of his possible one hundred. Using the insight he had gained from learning how to mend bones with his main healing spell, this spell instantly ranked up.

Skill increase: Lay on Hands (Beginner VI). Having proven that you are more knowledgeable about the intricacies of healing, your previous skill level has been changed to reflect your actual skill level.

Wow, he must be in a *really* bad situation if the prompts weren't even being mean to him. Joe pulled himself into a sitting position just in time to see Bard get flattened. The Skald survived the first hit, but the follow-up blow sent him into a tree.

Into a tree. Not into the branches but actually creating a hole in the trunk from the force like a bad cartoon. The bear started to turn around, chuffing in dissatisfaction at a boring fight and caught sight of Joe sitting up.

It lumbered toward him, rage flaring in its eyes. Just before crushing him, intelligence shown through, replacing the fury that had filled the massive beast. With a strange, crafty facial expression, one paw came down on Joe's robe while the other scooped him out of the garment. The twisting torsion ripped Joe's arm off, but the bear grabbed that as well. Then the bear's jaws opened and closed around Joe's face.

You have died! Calculating... you lose 1800 experience! Your item 'Undying Robe' has been destroyed! You will respawn in 6 real-world hours. Enjoy the relaxation; we are sure that you have earned it!

CHAPTER TWENTY-THREE

Sitting in the respawn room, Joe couldn't do anything that could impact the game. No chatting with people in the guild, no researching the strange quest lines that he kept coming upon. Did other people have such strange things happening to them? They *must*, Joe decided firmly. He was not the smartest, strongest, or best player out there, and yet he was stumbling upon strange and overly high-powered quests. He decided to go online and look for any information that might have made it through the restrictions the creators of the game put in place.

To his shock—and a tinge of pure jealousy—Joe found that there was now an official game news channel that had all sorts of general information. The official reason was that the Mage's College had been powering a spell that prevented 'scrying into their world'. Now that the College had instituted a leadership change, they were 'fine with outsiders being prepared for the challenges they might face'. Joe rolled his eyes hard enough that he almost fell over at that one.

Trying to play catch-up was a bit fruitless, but his anger mellowed as he learned that all that was offered online was *really* general information: guild names, simple maps, and a few plans for the game. It seemed that people were hiding their class paths still. He also found a site filled with lore and learned a bit more about Ardania itself, which was nice. For instance, he found the reason that he had only ever exited via a single gate of the city: as it turned out, Ardania was *massive*—easily the size of New York City—with entire quest lines through the urban sprawl which allowed you to never step out of the walls and still gain levels while experiencing combat. The next gate out of the city was literally miles away.

Another interesting topic in the news was that the company running Eternium had ramped up production of pods and VR setups, and even with all of the new gear, they were backlogged for at least two years. Apparently, there were huge shipments of the data Cores being distributed to government buildings, though. Miraculously, none of the high-priced items had been stolen even though there had been attempts to do so. An expected quarter million players would be joining the game every *two weeks* from now on, and Joe felt extra thankful he had joined the game when he did.

Joe closed his browser and decided to do other things. After the obligatory call to his mother, he felt better about diving into some practice. A bit frustrated that he had closed everything down before making his call, he got back on the internet and found some instructional videos and practical exercises for learning to draw. This was a skill that he didn't really think about much, but it was very important to his class. He had a feeling that simple chalk wouldn't work for him much longer, and being able to add more detail into a smaller space was going to be important.

When he finally was sick of working, he took a short nap. His alarm was set for five minutes before he was going to be allowed back into the game, so Joe forced himself to relax and get some shuteye. He was awake and ready when the portal reappeared, immediately stepping through it into the small shrine near the village. Bard was waiting for him, apparently arriving here moments before Joe had.

"Morning, Joe," Bard called over cheerlessly. "That was ah right *nasty* beastie, huh? Ye... did ye change? Never seen ye without yer bathrobe."

Joe looked down at his armor, noting a distinct lack of a certain life-saving robe. "You've got to be kidding me. The bear *stole* my *robe*? I've had that robe since I joined the game! I thought that was just a weird animation! Ah! The message! I didn't even think about that; it said it was destroyed!"

Bard watched him with wide-eyes as Joe ranted and raved for a few minutes, yelling obscenities and kicking trees. It took a minute of melting the vegetation around him with acid, but Joe eventually calmed down. Bard coughed and tried to sound consoling, "Mayhap it were... for tae best. Time to move on ta better things?"

"Ugh. Maybe. Whatever. It isn't like I can do anything about it," Joe conceded grumpily.

Bard nodded, silently agreeing with him. "Shall we get back ta town? Ahm sure 'Lexis is waitin' on me, and you seem... upset."

"Give me a moment, I have a ton of notifications." Joe tapped the blinking icon that was waiting for him, and a golden halo of energy surrounded and exploded outward from his body. Euphoria filled him; he had reached level ten!

He looked over his quests, specifically 'Building a Specialization'. Now that he was level ten, he could go to the location Tatum had marked for him and find... whatever it was that would allow him to specialize. His face clouded as he once again saw the quest options for his newly gained Psychomancer class; that was going to be a very tough decision. Get training in a class that was *obviously* incredible, or *don't* piss off the Kingdom. He had a feeling that even if it wasn't specifically stated, getting the training would ensure that the trial wouldn't go well if he were discovered. Joe started feeling a bit ill.

"Let's go. Thanks for waiting, Bard. Plenty of things going on, as per usual." They started walking toward the transformed town, seeing the twisted stone walls as soon as they exited the tree line. From the look of the people out front, the dungeon was still active, and Joe's party wasn't the only one that had failed to survive after entering it. They met up with their party, Bard going directly into Alexis's embrace.

"I have to tell you, that was not an auspicious first trial run," Poppy told Joe with a hint of a smirk on his face. "I *do* hope this won't be indicative of our future time together."

"We have never had a full party wipe before, and I hope to never do so again." Joe rolled his eyes as Poppy pulled a face and pretended to be weighing his options.

Jaxon yawned lightly, scratched at his eyes, and looked around. "I thought that it was a very beneficial experience. Even after dying twice in there, I gained two levels when I re-entered the game. Something about doing the most direct damage to the Ghouls. I also gained a Title, it's called… 'Anything for the team' and has three dots on either side of it."

"Oh!" Joe exclaimed with wide eyes. "That's called a broken title, you can apparently combine them together to make more beneficial ones."

"Do you have any of these?" Jaxon asked in return. "How do you combine them?"

"Uh… hmm." Joe pulled up his menus, looking at his various titles. "You know what, I have a full ten titles; let me do something real quick." He tried to select one of the titles, and after a moment, it trembled and a small text editor appeared.

You are attempting to combine titles! You may align them as you like, but be sure that titles with ellipses are placed in the correct position. After arranging them, you have the option to make small changes, such as adding the words 'an, a, the, of' or something similar to create a sentence. The fewer changes that need to be made, the more potent the effect! Good luck!

Joe was a bit concerned that the notification was wishing him luck or that it seemed cheerful at all. It made him trust this entire process a bit less, so he took several minutes to finalize his decisions. Taking a deep breath, he added 'The Chosen of Tatum', '...I choose to be…', and 'Legend' together. In the text editor, he added small changes. The final title became: 'As the

Chosen of Tatum, I choose to be a Legend.' He pressed 'accept' and waited to see the outcome with hitched breath.

Title accepted! Calculating… Title condensed, Title effects boosted 10% due to consumed title 'I choose to be'. Calculating…

New title gained: Tatum's Chosen Legend. Effect: You are the Legendary Chosen of a deity and have earned his respect. +20% speed of learning any water or darkness related abilities. -10% learning speed of any fire or light based abilities. +20% favor gained with Occultatum (retroactive). +30% damage against opponents who have a higher level than you. -15% Damage against opponents who have a lower level than you. Reputation gained at 2.5x normal rate and lost at .25x the normal rate. Capturing places of power now proceeds 31% faster. Caution! You will be worth 50% more experience and favor gain to champions of other gods who manage to kill you.

Quest completed: Earn a God's Favor. You have reached the reputation rank of 'Ally' with deity Occultatum! While being an ally with a god will have many hidden benefits, there are also instant rewards! You have gained 5 free skill points, 'Query' is guaranteed to give results once per three days, and you gain one divine boon based on the deity in question.

Divine Boon: You may ask for one of three rewards. +5000 experience, one random Unique item useful to your class, or creating one ritual without the need for components (Mana cost remains). You do not need to choose now.

"That was worth doing." Joe was almost salivating at the titular and quest rewards he had just received. "Just, yeah, just think about combining them if you want. Really easy and intuitive system. I'd recommend putting powerful ones together; I did just now and it… yeah. Wow. Awesome effect and a new title. Even completed a quest. Those were *really* high-level titles. I didn't realize how potent that would be."

"If you are done messing around and drooling on yourself, I think we need to go back into the dungeon," Alexis announced firmly, to everyone's shock. "I know that sucked for all of us, but the boosted experience is too high *not* to go back in."

"It will be even harder this time," Jaxon pointed out unhelpfully. "You leveled up. The creatures in there will be even stronger than before. Those spiders will be ready to attack. I will still be fairly useless in combat."

"I think you would have been very helpful against the boss monster," Joe attempted to placate him. "It was a giant bear. Big, thick joints. Paw finger-bones the size of my arm."

"Good *lord*." Jaxon swallowed a mouthful of saliva, holding himself back from diving through the entrance alone. "Be that as it may… until that point, I'm a hindrance at best."

"Ye may nah have ta be." Bard rubbed at the beginnings of a beard on his cheeks. "Ah saw a weapon at ta shops yesterday that screamed 'Jaxon' to me. Ah didn't think much of it at the time, but ah think it'll be what ye be needin."

Bard had the entire group intrigued, so they followed him to where the merchants had set up shop. It was still early in the day, but business waits for no man; the shops were open. There was a small line in front of them, but Joe thought that it would be cleared up soon if the shouting was to be trusted. "No, I *don't* have any more arrows right now! You do know that there are other people that need arrows, right? For actual *combat*?"

"Right, but we're using them for a *better* reason, right, Dave?" One of the roguish-looking men said to the other.

"Absolutely, Paul!" Dave replied chipperly. "How are we supposed to keep Taj believing he's cursed if we don't fill him full of arrows? You can't be cursed with 'unending arrows of over-encumbrance' without having plenty of arrows! At this rate, he'll be able to move at a normal speed soon!"

"You are filling his bags with arrows?" The merchant wiped his face with a damp towel. "Is he at least an archer?"

"No sir, he's a Bard," Dave replied seriously, holding out a silver.

"Get out of here!" The merchant waved his arms at the two men, who took off with a laugh.

"Odd." Joe looked over at Alexis. "They are spending a ton of money to mess with a *friend*?"

"You don't get out much, do ya, Joe?" Poppy chuckled

almost nostalgically. "That's what buddies *do*, man. Gotta mess with your best friends or they don't think you care."

"Men are *strange*," Alexis whispered her comment with a hefty eye roll.

Bard pulled Jaxon over to the agitated weapon vendor who had a wide smile spreading across his face as soon as he saw Joe.

"Hello there, unknown merchant man." Jaxon cheerfully waved. "I am told you have a weapon here that screams my name?"

"Oh, come *on*, Jaxon! I meant tha' *figuratively*!" Bard pointed out a pair of gloves, almost more akin to gauntlets than anything else. With the merchant's permission, Jaxon pulled on the gloves and tested their weight. He frowned as he found that his movements were a bit slower, but the merchant had him test his attacks on a training dummy that had obviously been set up for this purpose. Jaxon punched, nodding as he felt the blow cleanly. He could tell with a single punch that these would not reduce his capabilities at all. "Keep going!" the merchant told him with a grin.

"Oh? There is more to these?" Jaxon hit once more, then again. As the third blow landed, blades shot forward a full inch, penetrating the wood easily. They retracted as fast as they had elongated, slipping back into place easily. "I like that *very* much."

"Every third hit, blades will pop out." The merchant wiggled a brow at Jaxon enticingly. "You ever hit with less than your full fist? Try that."

Jaxon nodded at the man, hit twice more, then drove stiffened fingers into the dummy. Two needles shot forward from his fingertips, making a far smaller hole than the blades on the knuckles had. "For pinpoint attacks, I presume? I wonder how I can use this with my chiropractic pursuits? Perhaps… adjustments and acupuncture all in one? I'm so excited that I may need to find a bathroom. I'd settle for a room with a lockable door."

"Gross, and maybe test that weapon out on *enemies* first?" Joe said in a slightly worried tone.

"Hitting with an open palm won't count toward the number of hits, but it *will* reset the hit count, just so you know." The merchant was openly smiling at the group, knowing he was making a sale today. "This is also only the basic version and has great armor penetration, but at level ten, you will be able to buy and use enchanted versions as well. They are artificed weapons; using them before meeting the requirements could kill you."

"Wonderful! I'll take these right away! How much?" Jaxon was reaching into his fanny pack because *of course* he used a fanny pack instead of a backpack. The merchant stated a number, and Jaxon frowned, his intimidation skill lacing his voice as he spoke again, "I am with the guild; *how much* did you just tell me these weapons cost?"

The merchant's eyes flickered to Joe before he paled a bit. "Ah, yes, guild rates! Here… let me just… adjust that price…"

They walked away from the merchant, several of them shaking their heads in disgust. Jaxon was happily punching at the air, skipping alongside with Joe, who also needed to skip just to keep up with the others. "I like this form of travel! Much less effort for a much better return."

"Looks weird as all get out though," Poppy said under his breath to Bard, who simply nodded as the two men skipped forward together. Jaxon kept pace exactly with Joe so that he could show off his striking forms.

"I'm gonna need an hour to prepare before we go back in," Joe told the others. "We need a way to take down that big baddie at the end."

Alexis called to Joe as he started to walk away, "Don't sink him under the ground like you did that rock monster! We need to loot him, Joe! I'm sure we will get something off him, and if not, I'm sure some of his body parts will be worth a lot to either us or various other jobs. Tanners, perhaps? That would be a lot of leather at the minimum."

"I wasn't going to *sink* him. That isn't *always* my go-to

option!" Joe replied indignantly. Not a single person in the group looked like they believed him, and Poppy had never even seen him activate a ritual. "Fine! I need *two* hours then."

"Called it," Alexis smirked as Jaxon flipped a silver coin to her.

CHAPTER TWENTY-FOUR

Joe grumbled a bit as he sat with his books and notes, trying to come up with a new ritual that had combat applications. "I could be learning how to make spell scrolls right now, but no~o~o, I decided that I need to lead a party and get combat experience."

Despite all of his complaints, Joe quickly got to work on building a combat-oriented ritual. Keeping the massive bear in mind, he tried to think of ways to incapacitate or outright destroy it without giving it the option of killing them or burying it a kilometer underground. "Huge strength, lots of stamina and health… how can I use that against him?"

Joe pulled several symbols out of his other rituals, mixing and matching them. "What if I use the stamina drain from my ritual of containment, use the single-target spell circle, and maybe…" he trailed off as he reworked a few of the general-purpose ritual diagrams he had worked so hard to create before now. They were modular and easily mutable; he simply pulled one command out and reworked it into the form he wanted before replacing it. Creating the effects he needed took the entirety of his first allotted hour, but he came up with a workable ritual diagram.

"I have all of the components needed, but there is no time to optimize this. It's gonna cost more than it should have to." Joe sighed at that thought, but he needed this to work more than he needed it to work perfectly. He could always fix it later. This was a Beginner-ranked ritual, so he decided that he should be able to complete it by himself fairly easily. With that thought in mind, he got to work on actually drawing out his intended spell work. Aten had gifted him with a dozen thin slates, and not only were they easily transportable, they worked as a canvas for his work better than anything he had used in the past.

Joe intended to work on the slates later, drawing out his general-purpose diagrams on them so that they could be altered at a moment's notice. For now, though, he had to content himself with doing all the work at once. Twenty minutes later, he was putting the finishing touches onto the glorified chalkboard. He quickly placed the needed components and started pouring his mana into the drawings. As expected, the strange patterns and runes in the diagram lit up easily, his personal power supply easily able to keep up with the demands of the ritual. What was *not* expected was the bolt of power that arced from the spell diagram and shattered the slate, releasing the accumulated mana in a single blast of raw force.

Woozily sitting up sometime between a second and a minute later, Joe saw that his health was in critical condition. After trying nine times to heal himself, he finally managed to make the healing stick. Not understanding what had happened, he opened his blinking notifications and read through them.

Blah blah. Blah blah blah, 10 yoo-hoos.

Well, that was new. It looked like all of his notifications had similar text in them, so he ignored them for now. Joe really had no choice but to stay where he was laying as others came running to find the source of the blast that had rocked the interior of the temporary base. His situation was noted by a few people, but when they came over to him all he could hear was, "Bork bork? Blah blah bork? Meow moo bahh?"

When all Joe did was look at them with obvious confusion, they started to mill around and talk to each other. After ten minutes, a few words of the conversation became understandable, and he took another look at his notifications.

*Blah concussion has turned into bork concussion! -40 int-*bork *until woof. 10 minutes. 80% chance for pew pew to fail.*

Alright. So, it looked like he had a pretty serious concussion, and it was impacting his intelligence. Right now he was sitting at a grand total of four intelligence if he was reading the notification correctly. Joe tried to heal himself again, but nothing happened. He kept casting the spell, and it eventually worked… but he had no physical injuries to fix. So maybe the rest of that message had been that he had a high chance for his spells to fail right now? Joe tried to think of a better way to do things, but thinking was *so* hard to do right now, as if he had a fever, a hangover, and the flu all rolled into one ball of nastiness, and it was sitting behind his eyes.

"Joe? Bork bawk boop?" Joe looked up to see a concerned pair of eyes locked with his. Poppy offered him a hand, pulling Joe to his feet.

Joe tried to tell him that he would be okay in a few minutes, but to his horror, when he opened his mouth, all that came out was, "Yolo, dab it, pokey-boi."

Poppy visibly startled, then tried and failed to hide a wide smile. As the remainder of the team walked over, Poppy called out to them, "Joe took a boop to the snoot! He's as dumb as a square of pebbles!"

Joe knew, intellectually, that Poppy was not saying the words that he was hearing. His mouth movements didn't match the words, for one. For another–hey! They were laughing at him! He wanted to say something in his defense but knew that opening his mouth right now was a bad idea. Waiting for the next ten-minute block of injury to wear off was difficult because no matter what the others *actually* said, all Joe heard were vague insults. If this was how warriors felt in the game all the time, it was no wonder that there was such a high population of berserkers among them.

Severe concussion has turned into moderate concussion! -30 intelligence. 10 minutes until moderate concussion turns to mild concussion. 60% chance for spells to fail.

His intelligence was now sitting at a very helpful and useful fourteen. "Alright, not going to lie, that sucked pretty bad. Give me a few minutes guys; my head is killing me."

"Can't you heal it? Or whatever Cleanse counts as? I thought that healed status effects," Jaxon blinked a bit too much as he spoke, but he got his point across easily.

Flushing a bit and blaming the concussion for forgetting about his spells, Joe used Cleanse on himself, thankfully completing the spell on the first attempt. Relief literally washed through him, and the pain in his head faded like a bad memory. He looked at all of the notifications waiting for him, surprised that not all of them were about his recent exploding ritual. Only *most* of them were.

Status ailment fixed: Concussion removed. Ability to cast spells set to normal values. Intelligence returned to normal values.

Ritual failed: Instability reached 60% (non-recoverable) due to incorrect placement of variables, components, and inconsistent sympathetic link width. Ritual destabilization resulted in catastrophic failure.

You have encountered a new component of rituals: Instability! New menu options are available. Remember, knowing something and understanding are very different things. While you do have a bonus 10% spell stability thanks to one of your skills, you have never felt the ill effects of instability!

Skill combination complete! You have encountered a branching skill, and your choice here will determine your growth in many areas! Please choose a new type of magical defense.

Option 1) Skill: Titan's Armor (Novice III). Effect: For every point of mana in this spell, negate one point of damage from primary sources of magic and one point from primary sources of physical damage. Increase conversion by .025n where 'n' equals skill level.

Option 2) Skill: Exquisite Shell (Novice III). Effect: For every point of mana in this spell, negate .75 damage from primary sources of magic, .75 damage from primary sources of physical damage, and .75 damage from elemental effects. Increase conversion by .02n where 'n' equals skill level.

Joe hadn't expected a choice like this. Either of them were better than his previous skills if taken as a whole. Titan's Armor seemed to be a mash-up of the two skills, giving the good portions of both and taking away the lower values for physical and magical damage. On the other hand, Exquisite Shell *added* some functionality while averaging the damage reduction for physical and magical damage. What all counted as elemental effects? Burning? Hitting the ground? Joe had to go with his gut on this one. Even if Titan's Armor gave more direct benefits, Exquisite Shell was the clear winner in his mind.

He made his selection and the skill seemed to flare before being sucked into his eyes. Joe suddenly sneezed, then again and again. "Ugh. I'm ready to go now, guys. Let's make like a librarian and book it. Wait, what am I saying? Hang on." Joe pulled out a fresh slate and began drawing on it while the others groaned. "Yes, well, I'd really like to beat the boss. Groan all you like, but if any of you have better plans…"

"I need to restock on reagents anyway. I almost forgot! Maybe if I use holy water as a base it would work better against the Ghouls?" Alexis wandered off to see if there were any merchants selling potion and poison supplies.

Joe took extra time setting up this ritual, looking for anything that could have been causing instability. When he didn't find anything, he got a bit worried. He hadn't seen any issues in the first one, either… he placed the needed components in their spaces, arranging them so they were more symmetrical, and stopped. Just to be on the safe side, he activated Exquisite Shell and poured a thousand mana into the spell. It took nearly five seconds to channel so much power into the low-level protection, but the shell would absorb eight hundred and ten points of damage. Well worth the wait.

After waiting a minute and a half for his mana to fully recover, Joe placed his scepter into the ritual and activated it. There were a few arcs of power–showing a non-inconsequential instability–but nothing that destroyed or delayed the ritual. It was really too bad that making a ritual on a chalkboard didn't let him use his occultist profession skill to see how accurate it was. He needed to work on his penmanship so he could use ink and paper. Joe shook his head, returning his thoughts to the ritual. Twenty seconds later, it was complete.

New ritual created! Would you like to name this ritual? Yes / No.

"Stamina poison," Joe said out loud, making the nearest people glance at him curiously before shuffling away from the man who had caused an explosion for no good reason.

That name is already in use. To avoid confusion, please try again.

Maybe this was why everything seemed to have grand names as they became rarer? Like 'Heavenly Breath Elixir' because the system didn't allow for common-sense name schemes? He had a few alchemists and crafters to apologize to. "Ritual of Poisoned Vitality?"

Name accepted!

Joe looked at the others who had decided to come within ten feet of him now that the ritual was complete and didn't appear that it was going to randomly detonate. That might be the real reason. Bard looked at Joe, nodding at the obvious signs of power he was displaying. "That's some pretty makeup ye got on. Ye look like the main character from that sappy vampire movie."

"What are you talking about?" Joe looked around at the smirking faces. "Anyone? Please explain."

Alexis took pity on him, pulling out a small mirror and handing it over. Joe looked at his reflection in shock. He looked like the victim of a glitter bomb, if glitter was the size of a quarter. "No! I'm sparkly! Stupid spell, why do you have to be so effective! I'd toss it away right now otherwise!"

"Oh? What does it do?" Poppy asked after smothering his chuckles.

"Stab me," Joe replied unenthusiastically, mind in shock from his *pretty* spell.

"What? Are you sure?" The Duelist seemed shocked at this command.

"Do it."

"Alright." Poppy pulled out his rapier and stabbed Joe in the arm. A splash of blood shot out; he had hit an artery with his attack.

Joe screeched and slapped himself with a healing spell, glaring at Poppy for a moment. His eyes widened, followed by rolling them *hard*. "Right. You have amazing armor penetration, don't you? For feces' sake, Poppy. Bard, can *you* please hit me?"

Bard shrugged and swung an axe at Joe, which hit his arm and skid off with a tinkling sound like a bunch of little bells ringing. "Look at tha'! Ye even *sound* pretty."

"…I hate that I love this spell." Joe held out his unblemished arm. "It's a magical defense that allows me to use mana to make armor for myself. Basically, a force field."

"A force field that does jack against *me*," Poppy smugly stated, twirling his rapier in a fancy flourish. Joe showed him a rude hand gesture in reply.

"It blocks physical, magical, and elemental damage. The armor is also *apparently* still weak against armor penetration, so that's fun. It did block some of the damage, but his rapier still got through. Obviously." Joe rubbed at his arm, where he was still feeling some phantom pain from the unexpected stab. Well. The stab itself wasn't unexpected, but the damage was.

"That's our Mr. Pokey for you!" Jaxon clapped Poppy on the back, causing him to stumble. His words caused the others to laugh softly, but Poppy vehemently opposed the nickname instantly. Of course, this simply made it stick. "Can we get going? I'd like a chance to defeat some Ghouls without becoming a martyr. The dungeon will vanish in an hour, so…"

"It'll stop letting people in at the end of the timer, but it'll stay active until everyone is out," Alexis informed the group.

"We *really* don't want to be the last group in, though; remember how the enemies got smarter when there were fewer instances?"

"Yup, yup. Let's make like an egg and scramble," Bard quipped, making everyone but Joe laugh.

"Oh come *on*! My 'book it' joke was better than that, and I didn't even get a pity chuckle!" Joe complained empathetically. Sadly, he was ignored in favor of the high-charisma Skald. Joe grumpily followed the others to the dungeon and, from the perspective of people outside the gate, seemed to vanish as he crossed the threshold.

CHAPTER TWENTY-FIVE

"Alright, same strategy as before?" Joe looked around to confirm with the others, but Jaxon raised a hand. "Not the fire and poison strategy, I meant the 'pick them off one by one' version." Jaxon lowered his hand, seemingly very relieved.

"The Ghouls went up a level." Alexis had moved around the corner, scouting ahead for the team. "I think it's a good idea to draw them elsewhere. Can you imagine what would have happened if we fought them under the trees like that? We would have been swarmed by spiders *and* Ghouls all in one go."

"What we really need is a building with two exits that can be blockaded. Then we can pull the majority of the Ghouls into it and let the poison do its work." The group looked surprised that it was Jaxon saying these things, but then… his intelligence had never been in question.

"Good call, Jax." Joe nodded his appreciation. "Has anyone seen anything like that?"

"Ye know, it might be ah bit ironic, but ah think tae smithy would work." Bard pointed toward the corner of town the smithy had been located in before being transformed.

"Let's do that then." Joe started carefully walking toward

the smithy, doing his best not to alert the horde of Ghouls patrolling nearby. It was a bit strange to him that the dungeon entrance was right next to the boss, as well as the highest concentration of monsters. They had walked for a little over a block when a roaming Ghoul turned the corner in front of them. Both the adventurers and the monster stopped, startled by this turn of events. The Ghoul recovered first, and a horrific smile coated in drool crossed its face, showing knife-sharp teeth. It charged them, obviously expecting an easy meal.

"Allow me, please," Jaxon strode forward calmly. When they reached the halfway point between each other, the Monk shot forward at high speed. Jaxon ducked under a wild swipe that—past experience informed him—would have torn his head off. He struck the wood-covered elbow of the Ghoul, once, twice, and on the third blow, a thick blade sunk into the joint. The Ghoul hissed in pain which turned into a shriek of rage as Jaxon activated his ability. The blade had severed a tendon, so when the joint twisted… its entire forearm popped off.

"That works *excellently*." Jaxon seemed to be treating this all very academically, even as roots wiggled into the severed arm and pulled it back together. "Hmm. I guess I need to work faster, else my *treatment* won't be very effective." Joe's group remained watchful, ready to help if needed, but it seemed that Jaxon had this duel well in hand. The Monk avoided devastating blows that shattered cobblestone, repeatedly punching the Ghoul in the neck. Every third blow the blade would jump out and penetrate through the wood protecting this weak point.

Jaxon suddenly jumped back and turned around, putting his back to the surprised Ghoul. "Fifteen blows to get to this point. Far too long. How can I improve my undead fighting capabilities?"

"Jaxon!" Bard barked. "Thing's not down!"

"Hmm? Oh, right." Jaxon activated his 'adjust' skill with a snap, and as the Ghoul reared back to attack… its head twisted and tore off. One of the best things about fighting undead enemies was that no blood sprayed out, but it was still shocking to see. Joe jumped forward and tackled Jaxon to the ground as the headless Ghoul continued to swing, missing and trying again. "What in the…? I tore its head off!"

"Right, but the armor is alive, too," Poppy stated as the armor made another wild swing.

"No, I mean I was only expecting the *neck* to snap. I didn't hit many tendons that time," Jaxon explained as he hopped to his feet.

"Must have been extra rotten. Stand back!" Alexis tossed a small orb that exploded into a cloud of poison around the armor, eating away at it and seemingly rotting it to pulp within thirty seconds.

"The relationship must be more symbiotic than expected." Jaxon looked at the remains of the Ghoul, curiosity filling his eyes. "Before now, we have always either destroyed the Ghoul or the armor entirely. I wonder how much they *actually* feed off each other."

"Let's postulate on the biosphere balance of cursed dungeons at a later date, shall we?" Poppy patted the Monk on his back like a dog as they continued onward. Only Alexis and Jaxon had gained experience from the fight, once again reminding Joe to treat every battle like he was the one fighting it. They continued on, having to stop and fight three more times, only coming close to death in one of them.

There were three Ghouls, and they seemed to work well together. They had jumped out in ambush as the group approached the smithy, and only Joe's high perception saved the team from losing at least one member just as combat started. The three Ghouls constantly attacked the same person, only deviating from their intended target if they needed to block a blow. Whoever was fighting them had to hold off all three while the others did their best to damage and distract them.

When all three of the Ghouls turned their attention to Bard, Alexis abruptly shouted, "Bard, get ready to hold your breath! Joe, get ready to heal Bard! Sorry, sweetie!" She threw one of her prepared orbs, and a nova of poison exploded from it with a ringing **pop**. All four combatants were slightly hidden in the haze of toxins, taking damage at a high rate. The wooden legs of the Ghouls gave out just as Bard began coughing violently.

Joe cast heal with one hand while casting acid spray with the other. The acid coated the Ghouls, finishing off the heavily damaged armor while the healing spell latched onto Bard and propped his health up through the damage the poison inflicted. Jaxon and Poppy closed quickly, stabbing the now-vulnerable Ghouls and quickly ending combat. Joe switched over to using Cleanse, directly removing the poison from Bard's system.

"I'm so sorry! It was the only way to finish them quickly!" Alexis was wringing her hands, waiting for Bard to stop hacking up a lung.

"Ah, now *that* is love." Jaxon leaned on Poppy and wrapped his arm–covered in specks of rotting meat–around the Duelist. "Understanding your partner so well that you can include them in your attacks, knowing that at the end of it, they will have persevered. Beautiful. Truly touching, that level of trust."

Poppy shrugged off the filthy arm that was staining his clothes but nodded along with his words. "You have a point, Jaxon. Hey, Joe, you wanna peek in the building and let us know it there is anything we should know about?"

"Can do." Joe went up to the door, peeking through the oversized keyhole. His eyes widened, and he became as silent as possible. Gulping, he activated intrusive scan and did his best to remember the information he saw.

Name: Betrayer. Class: Dungeon Boss. Title: Cursed Blacksmith.

Highest stat: Constitution.

Ongoing effects: Agony. Shattering Blows. Forced Servitude. Jailor.

Joe shuddered and reeled backward as the smith seemed to stiffen, slowly turning toward him. Joe instantly stopped using his scan and began running back to his group. "Hey, guys… this is… there is a boss monster in there. The smith is a boss, now."

"Oh," Alexis was the first to speak. "It kinda makes sense. The bear was a *raid* boss, right? Do you think we can beat the smith?"

Joe was confused by her easy acceptance of another boss existing in the dungeon. "I… it will be easier than the bear, for sure."

"Then let's do it." Alexis looked around at the others, but they only nodded at her.

Bard nudged Joe as he passed him. "Looks like tae party leader spot is still *undecided*, eh, Joe?"

"Not cool, man." Joe waited until Bard passed him, then kicked him lightly in the butt. He grinned at Bard as he turned around with an aggrieved look. "Better watch yourself, I can kick your butt any time I want."

"Boy, ye better *watch* yerself," Bard growled playfully in return. "Yer funny, but looks aren't everything."

"Guys! Focus, please!" Poppy's words brought them back to reality. Or, well, back to the game. Alexis went up to one of the holes in the wall that must have been a ventilation shaft, opening a small cask and stuffing it in. The gurgle of running liquid reached their ears, and after a few moments, a hacking cough came from the interior of the building. At first, they thought that the cough was powerful enough to shake the entire structure, but then they realized it was something else as a shockwave of pain washed over them.

"What in the…?" Bard shuddered as the strange pain passed.

"*You've got a pretty mouth*," Jaxon whispered almost lovingly into the Skald's ear.

Bard eyed the Monk. "Jax, that might be yer sucky charisma talking, but ah will straight up slap ye if ye say that again."

"I think that pain was the effect 'agony' that he has going," Joe told the others, unaware of the side conversation happening. The door to the smithy was blasted out into the street, entirely ripped off its hinges from a single attack. A tortured scream filled the air as the now-eight-foot-tall smith shambled out. He had clinking chains all over his body, connected at various points directly to his skin. It created a sick sort of armor, a chainmail bodysuit fused to his flesh. A hammer was dragging behind him, so heavy that it left a gouge in the earth as he stumbled forward. Various colored needle-legged spiders scuttled across his skin, but it didn't seem that they were there to attack intruders. No, they were doing… *something*… directly to the smith.

"His health pool is *massive*," Alexis announced after staring at the smith for a long second, obviously using a skill. "He took several *hundred* damage from the poison in there, and there is only the tiniest chunk missing from his health bar."

"Constitution is his highest stat; I don't know much else about the way he fights. He has a few active effects, but I think 'agony', 'shattering blows', and 'jailor' are the ones he can use on us," Joe quickly informed the others as the smith's madly rolling eyes finally landed and focused on them. "Don't know what they do, though."

"Ahm sure we will find out. Gonna boost our damage real quick; try hard not ta get hit. That'd be bad," Bard muttered as he held both axes out in front of himself. "*Victory or death!*"

Damage dealt and received increased by 25%!

"Oh, that's just *wrong*." Joe winced as the smith swung his hammer around at a speed he could barely see. It was like fighting the bear all over again. Poppy dropped to his knees to avoid the boulder of black metal, while Jaxon jumped over it and flattened himself in the air to increase hang-time. Bard was too far away to be hit, but he closed the distance quickly and joined in on attacking the oversized smith. Blood poured out of the boss, showing that unlike the other monsters in the area, he was a living being.

"Oh, *abyss* yes." Alexis opened fire with her crossbows, missing both shots. Joe looked at her with open-mouthed concern, even as he created a shadow spike that impaled the Betrayer. "Just, ah, need to get closer. My crossbow skill is only Novice…"

Joe realized that anytime she had been attacking something, it had basically been at point blank range. "Oh, you are sneaky. How did I not notice that?"

His inattention was costing them; Bard took a solid hit to the chest that audibly cracked several ribs, dropping him to just below half health. Luckily, that was the first damage their team had taken, so Joe was able to start healing him right away. He was a healer before anything else, dang it! Joe watched as Jaxon's attacks were blocked by the smith's giant hands, but it seemed that Jaxon didn't mind too much. After his blade had poked into the thick skin of the smith on his third consecutive strike, Jaxon winked, and the finger he had been exclusively hitting twisted and broke.

A deep bellow of pain exited the Betrayer, and a wave of agony washed over all of them. Poppy shuddered, stabilizing as a healing spell splashed against him. "Agony must take a portion of the damage we do to him in a given amount of time and return it to us! Looks like mostly magical damage with a bit of true damage mixed in! Watch out for that!"

Joe realized that the others must be having a much harder time with the agony skill than he was if their health bars were any indication. Joe's eyes flicked to his shield, noticing that it had already dropped ninety points during this fight. So it *was* protecting him, there was just an extra type of damage involved that the shield didn't counter. Joe started circling to the other side of the street as the battle between the physical types raged on. He wasn't trying to run; Joe simply had a very specific goal in mind. When he got to the spot where the battle had started, he dipped down and touched his taglock to a small pool of blood.

Final ingredient added! Activate 'Ritual of Poisoned Vitality'? Yes / No.

Joe tapped yes, and a beam of light shot from his scepter and onto the cursed smith. The boss paused for a moment, allowing Poppy to roll away from an attack that would have otherwise crushed him. A brightly glowing, illusionary ritual circle appeared under the smith's feet, and he seemed to become enraged as the light and ritual sank into him. He stomped at the circle, howling as his body took on a sickly green tinge. When his tantrum did nothing, he turned furious eyes on Joe and charged straight at him.

"Oh, fecal matter." Joe tried to get out of the way, but his physical stats were nowhere *near* the Betrayer's. The hammer came down on him, driving him a half-foot into the ground like a tent stake. Joe lay there, stunned, as the smith seemed to grunt in approval and charge at someone else. The Ritualist coughed up a bit of blood then quickly healed himself. Not *too* much of the damage had made it through, but his Exquisite Shell had been utterly *annihilated*. Sure, it had been weakened by the waves of agony, but the Betrayer had smashed through the rest of it with a *single* attack. Joe felt much less cocky about his Novice-ranked magical protection right now.

"What did you *do* to him?" Alexis chuckled and helped Joe get back on his feet while he was spitting out blood. "He was *pissed*."

"Used the ritual on him. For ten minutes he loses three percent of his total stamina every second and takes half that as magical damage." Joe moved over to Jaxon, using his lay on hands spell to fix an arm that had been crushed. "I think he regains enough stamina to stave off exhaustion, but the more he moves, the more likely it is that he will only be able to make one attack every few seconds!"

According to Alexis, the Betrayer's health bar was steadily declining now. Just as they were celebrating that fact, one of the spiders crawling on the smith stabbed into his arm. The spider died instantly after that, but the smith's arm began to writhe. His muscles bulked up as if he had been taking steroids for years, and his attacks with that arm became too fast to dodge without serious effort and forethought on their part. Howling with agony once again, the smith started swiping back and forth with his giant hammer.

Agony's area damage washed over Joe, causing his health to drop by three-quarters in an instant. For the others, seventy health was not exactly fun but was certainly manageable. For him, it was almost a death sentence. Spitting out yet another mouthful of blood, Joe healed himself and sent a shadow spike into the smith's legs. "He's starting to slow down!"

Of course, the shout coupled with the spike brought the Betrayer's attention firmly to Joe once again. Using his 'jailor' ability, he swung at Joe with his off hand. A chain unraveled and wrapped around Joe's torso, pulling and cinching tight. The Betrayer's hammer came down, driving a spike through the chain and into the ground. Right about then, the boss's stamina failed. Over the course of three seconds, the smith slowly walked toward Joe, ignoring other attacks even though he needed a rest break after each long, heavy step. Joe struggled to get the chain off of himself, and he had almost succeeded... when a shadow covered him from above. Joe looked up, just in time to see the final movements of a hammer being brought down on his unprotected head.

You have died! Calculating... you lose 2000 experience! You will respawn in 10 real-world hours. Seriously? You charged back into a dungeon where you cannot fight any *of the monsters on your own?*

"I could fight the *spiders*!" Joe uselessly shouted a clarification into the air of his respawn room. Unsurprisingly, there was no answer.

CHAPTER TWENTY-SIX

Ten hours with not much to do. Joe amused himself by prank calling a few people since there was no way to trace calls and harassment back to him. It was fun for all of five minutes, then he decided to do some searching into the game. He really wanted to understand how crafters like Alexis were allowed to level up so quickly. He felt that the game was putting them into a bad position, and it was a trap he would have fallen into without Tiona pushing him to join in combat.

What he found out was surprising, but it shouldn't have been. Crafters can level extremely fast and make incredible money but only for a short while. At a certain point, they began needing more… *specialized* goods. Then they had to go out into the world and get those resources themselves, buy them from people that already had them, or steal them if things got really bad.

This would either turn them into an adventurer who was behind everyone else with their terrible combat skills or would cost them a majority of the cash that they had made selling low-level items to other adventurers. Meanwhile, all the other crafters that had been following a similar playstyle would reach that point *at the same time*. Because of this, long-term gamers were rubbing their hands together, hoarding goods for the day that the market would begin correcting in their favor.

"Game economy is nuts." Joe shook his head at the implications that were rearing their ugly head. Pretty soon, around the time they specialize, crafters were going to start needing a ton of material to continue leveling. Rare or unique components were going to skyrocket in price just like mana potions had. Joe decided that it might be time to start dipping into his savings when he got back into the game. He was almost... *glad* that he hadn't survived the dungeon. If he had learned about this much later...

He thought about calling his mom, but from her perspective he had only called... what, five hours ago? Ugh. He felt like a failure. Joe sat through some more online classes, determined to get better at his skills one way or another. This time he focused on paper making, chuckling about the fact that just about anything could be found online. Most of the information the class contained was fairly useless to him, as he didn't have industrial equipment. Some was *quite* useful, though, such as ways to make primitive binding agents work as well–or better–than mass-produced paper. Only on a small scale, of course; it was far too expensive to use some of these methods on a large scale, but for Joe... this might be exactly what he needed to get an edge on his skills.

Taking as many notes as possible, Joe worked right up to the deadline of the portal allowing him access to the game again. He would need to sleep in-game, but that would be a more effective use of his time anyway. Getting a full eight-hour sleep in four hours or sleeping for only a couple out here? Easy choice. When the portal opened up for him, he stepped through, full of ideas and plans for the next few days. The shrine was empty, and the darkness proved that there were obviously a few hours before dawn. Joe was having trouble keeping his date and time straight; dying could really mess with your inner clock.

Before moving on, he noticed that he had plenty of blinking icons waiting for him. He braced himself for the deluge of information and opened the first one.

*Exp: 900. (2 * 225) * Sapling Ghouls x2).*

*Exp: 2000. (2 * 1000) * Triplet Livingwood Ghoul Miniboss x1).*

*Exp: 360. (2 * 30 * Phobic Spiders x6).*

*Exp: 5000. (2 * 2500 * Betrayer x1).*

As recompense for the failure of a quest giver to pay upon completion, you have been given partial ownership of the quest giver's most valuable holdings. You will receive 25% of the value of material sold from a nearby mine, which has been marked on your map.

You have gained enough experience to reach level ten! Now that you have reached level ten, you are able to specialize into a more powerful version of who you want to be! You can look at specialization options at any time!

How odd. You should have received this message at your previous level, which was... ten. Calculating... you have died twice in the last day. Potential for level loss. This matter deemed unnecessary to elevate to a higher level.

Joe breathed out slowly, mentally looking for the menus that would let him see specialization paths. Look at that, his team must have finished off the smith! He hoped they had been able to escape the dungeon after that.

Your sigh of relief has been noted.

Drat. That wasn't ominous at all. Joe rolled his eyes and marched toward the town, hoping that there would be no further looking into this matter. From what Tatum had told him, there could be serious repercussions for his meddling. For no good reason either, in his opinion. He had gained enough experience to put him at the correct level soon after... Joe decided to stop thinking about it. He had other things that he needed to do. For instance, being partial owner of a mine seemed pretty neat. With his Darkvision, he had no issues following the path, but when the town came into view he stopped and stared.

The walls were still high, twisted, and black. Hadn't the dungeon only been scheduled to last a single day? Then he noticed that there were people moving freely through the gates;

obviously, the instant dungeon had vanished. Joe walked over to the gate and made sure that it was a normal town again before walking in. It wouldn't be a great day if he walked into a dungeon by himself. He actually shuddered a little at that thought.

"If they are still out of their minds, bring them to the *weaver's* place. Plenty of blankets, and if that isn't enough to calm them down we have a lot of rope stored there." Joe recognized the commanding voice, so he walked over to see Tiona barking orders to large swaths of her guild members. He paused and simply took in the sight; it was good to see her again.

After waiting for a lull in the conversations, he walked over and said hello. She turned toward him with a frown on her face that transformed into a weary smile as she realized who was talking to her. "Joe! Good to see you. I'm sorry, though, I don't really have time to catch up. I'm only here right now because I have a twenty-four-hour leave from my training with the Kingdom, and this place is a mess."

"What's going on, and how can I help?" Joe instantly got into a working mindset.

She nodded appreciatively but declined his offer. "No, you look like you are about to drop. Go get some sleep. If you *must* know, the people that were transformed remember their time as monsters. They are... *most* of the people that had been living here are pretty messed up. The ones that were killed *most* often are the best off, contrary to what we would have expected. Dying kept their mind together."

The revelation left Joe a bit sick to his stomach. "What's going on here then? Are we helping them?"

"As much as we can. But if they don't get better..." Tiona shrugged a bit. "Makes me glad I'm not the one that has to make that call. We *are* taking over the town, though. These walls are better than anything except the city walls of Ardania. We don't know what they *are*, but we do know that they offer serious protection. We can't even scratch them."

"Alright. I get that. Um, in that case, we should really have a few people guarding the gates. I just walked in here without getting a second glance thrown my way." Joe flinched from the look of anger that crossed her face.

"They aren't *there*? I swear, if they abandoned their post to go tease that Bard again, I am going to *lose* it! See you around, Joe, and thanks." Tiona waved at him and walked away with a stilted gait, obviously working to control her temper.

"Bye," he uselessly called to her retreating form. Well, alrighty then, time to get to work! No. Bed. Bed first. He asked around and was directed to… what appeared to be a campsite. Okay. At least it was within the walls. He found a bedroll that was available for use and fell asleep almost as soon as his head hit the pillow.

He didn't sleep *well*, but as morning arrived and the sunlight stabbed his eyes mercilessly, he found that he had gotten enough sleep to *function*. Upon waking up, he went to the picnic tables that had been set up as an outdoor eating area, drank the guild-provided coffee with delight, and turned his focus to his puzzle cube. Joe had already lost two days of work on it and didn't want to get distracted and forget about it again today. He twisted and flipped, solving logic riddles and challenges, and was almost startled when he got the notification he had been working toward.

Characteristic point training completed! +1 to intelligence, wisdom, perception, and dexterity! These stats cannot be increased further by any means other than system rewards, study, or practice for twenty-four hours game time.

Name: Joe 'Tatum's Chosen Legend' Class: Mage (Actual: Ritualist)
Profession: Scholar (Actual: Occultist)
Level: 10 Exp: 55,599 Exp to next level: 10,401
Hit Points: 100/100 (50+(50))
Mana: 1276/1276 (12.5 per point of intelligence, +100% from deity, -11% from mana manipulation)
Mana regen: 13.35/sec (.25 per point of wisdom, + 9% from Coalescence)

Stamina: 95/95 (50+(25)+(20))

Characteristic: Raw score (Modifier)

Strength: 14 (1.14)
Dexterity: 18 (1.18)
Constitution: 15 (1.15)
Intelligence: 46 (1.46)
Wisdom: 49 (1.49)
Charisma: 18 (1.18)
Perception: 35 (1.35)
Luck: 18 (1.18)
Karmic Luck: +1

Joe read through his stat sheet and was excited to see that his wisdom was about to cross the next threshold. When had his Karmic Luck dropped? He scrolled through notifications, but there didn't seem to be anything that explained the odd loss. Joe thought about looking into his specialization menu, but something told him that he needed to finish his quest first. There were likely going to be great options, and he didn't know if he would be able to stop himself from picking something that might end up being suboptimal.

He left the dining area, deciding to find his team and see what they were up to. Joe really wanted to know what he had missed after he had been sent for respawn. After searching around for a while, he found that Jaxon had set up a stall to sell adjustments to people–which essentially amounted to charging for buffs–and Alexis was restocking her poisons and working on a few items. Bard was having serious drinks with a few other charisma-based classes, leaving him with only Poppy as a valid option for discussion.

Joe found the Duelist working on his technique at a small training area the guild had set up. Training dummies with various armor were thrashing around, moving chaotically like a mechanical bull at a cowboy bar. Poppy would pull back his rapier, thrusting forward every few seconds. He didn't rush his attacks, but he still missed openings in the armor fairly frequently. Still, when his attacks connected correctly, the training dummy would stop moving entirely. They had been designed to do that only when the attack 'killed' them. Joe felt a newfound respect for the methodical attacks of his newest teammate.

After the last dummy stopped moving, Joe stepped forward. "Hey, Poppy! Got a moment? I was hoping to hear about what happened in the dungeon."

"Joe? Welcome back!" Poppy grabbed a cloth and wiped off his face, then went over to a whetstone and began sharpening his weapon. "Heard anything from the others yet? No? M'kay. Well, after you got nailed into the ground, we had a much easier time taking out the boss. After it demonstrated its jailor technique, it was fairly simple for us to avoid it. We whittled it down to a quarter health when one of those spiders scuttled to his chest and–speculating here–it seemed to inject adrenaline right into his heart. His stamina went from nil to half-full over three seconds, but that also let your ritual do a bunch of damage to him."

Poppy took a drink out of a canteen. **Cough** "Woo, sorry, wrong pipe. Anyway, we basically turned it into a war of attrition. Alexis dropped right at the end because of agony and I *almost* went down, but we finished him before the skill could proc again. We found a bunch of gold in his shop, as well as a bunch of rare-ish metals and tools. At that point, we were offered the chance to warp out with the full knowledge that the dungeon would vanish. With only three of us left, we took the deal."

"Dang. That sounds like it was awesome. Sorry I got caught." Joe grinned sheepishly.

"No worries. By the way, we looked up one of his abilities, shattering blows? It makes attacks do triple damage against shields, armor, and structures. Don't get too worried about your magic armor; it will still be good in a normal situation." Poppy noted the look of relief on Joe's face and stood up. "What's the plan for today? I think the others decided that they wanted the day off, but I don't mind hanging out if there is something on your mind."

"Hey, thanks!" Joe opened his menu, looking at the *very* basic map included in it. The mark Tatum had added looked like it was a few hours walk away, but Joe decided that they could likely make the trip with just the two of them if they didn't start fights with any packs of animals. "I have a class quest a couple hours away, and I could really use a walking buddy if you are willing."

"I don't mind." Poppy started strolling away. "If it's just the two of us though, you're buying the meals! Drinks, too!"

Joe couldn't think of a particularly good argument against that; Poppy *was* going out of his way to help him. Or could he not think of a good argument because…? Ah-ha! Poppy's blasted *charisma*! Joe followed the Duelist with a knowing grin, glad that he had seen through the man. "Works fine for me."

CHAPTER TWENTY-SEVEN

After a bit of preparation and buying a few easily-transportable meals, they left the gate which was manned by a few slightly familiar but now-bruised faces. Joe waved, speaking to the man on the left. "Hey, Dave, we are going off on a quest. We should be back tonight, hopefully before dark. Just in case anyone comes around looking for us."

"Sounds good!" Dave smiled as best as he could with a busted and bleeding lip. "One thing, though, *who* are you?"

"Oh. I'm Joe; I'm a cleric. Actually, let me..." Joe healed both of them easily, and their faces showed obvious relief. "What happened to you?"

"Tiona found us-"

"Got it," Joe interrupted with a grin while walking away with Poppy. They had planned on a quiet walk together, but as they started down the road, they met up with a large group from the guild going on a quest together. Joining them as far as they could to mitigate risk, Joe and Poppy didn't get much of a chance to chat. After around an hour of speed-walking–speed-skipping in Joe's case–they separated from the large group and turned away from the road to follow a simple animal path.

From there onward, there were a few encounters with some wildlife, but if the creature was alone it was easily dispatched. Not too many natural animals could survive a hundred points of damage through the chest when he used shadow spike on them. Luckily, they were walking through the wilds in sparsely populated areas with no real historical value. Otherwise, Joe was certain they would be stalked by something far more powerful.

"It feels too… *easy*." Poppy confessed after another hour of walking. "We are mostly being left alone, but we're getting almost no experience for what we *do* kill. Even that bear dropped pretty quickly. Sure, it was held in place by a chest-high spike and was easy prey for me, but I feel like we should have taken *some* damage by now."

"We would have been in trouble eventually if we hadn't gotten the cub, too. Seriously, don't think too hard on it, or you'll jinx us. I know what is going on, and it is pretty common: your mind is still in battle-mode. It used to happen all the time when we got back from deployment." Joe quieted as his memories of his time in the Army washed over him.

"The military now *enforces* a couple months of 'normal' activity and relaxation after really stressful situations. It's for the best, and I should have given us more downtime to recover. My bad, I'm still not used to being a leader. Think about it a little differently; we were only in the dungeon for a few hours, but it was likely more intense than any combat you had ever been in before, right? Your mind is just stuck there for now. That's not a bad thing when we are in unknown territory like we are currently, and it is likely that… that you will get over it *quickly*." Joe nearly growled the last line, remembering that this game was able to influence their mental state directly.

After a moment of consideration, Poppy responded in a more positive tone, "Huh. Thanks, that actually really helps. It's always nice to know *why* I feel like I do. Makes it easier to manage. Why do I know nothing about you, and how close are we getting?"

"Well, Poppy, we just met. I'm not trying to hide myself; it just hasn't come up. Also, if we keep going at this pace and the terrain is this easy the whole way," Joe looked at the map again and judged the distance they had already traveled, "three hours or so."

"I should have asked for money," Poppy jokingly complained. "Worst escort quest *ever*." The conversation died down to a companionable silence after that, the two of them focusing on walking and staying alert for ambushes. Three long hours of relative boredom and several very minor encounters later, they were nearing the location marked on Joe's map.

"Two hundred and sixty-two experience for all of *that*." Poppy spat to the side. "Long walk, substandard results. Where is this place?"

They were now standing at the entrance to a flat, open grassland. As far as Joe could see, an ocean of green grass extended into the distance. "I have no idea. Maybe it's underground or hidden by the grass? This could be a misdirection, maybe that grass is *really* high."

It was a combination of his assumptions. Even with his supposition, he hadn't expected to be correct to this degree. As they got closer to the grassland, the ground sloped downward though the height of the turf stayed the same. By the time they were at the edge of the grass, they realized that the weeds were as tall and thick as trees. Poppy looked at the plants that made trees look small, and at an insect who made a brief appearance. "Did we shrink, or was that ladybug *really* the size of a hippo?" Joe stepped into the verdant grass forest, and both of them received a notification.

Achievement unlocked: Exploration! For being the first Travelers to enter the Gargantuan Grasslands, you are awarded 500 experience! Being the first to walk a path can have great rewards!

"I like *that* a lot," Poppy cheerfully commented. "To be fair, I wouldn't normally have entered what looks like an endless plain with nothing in it either. It's entirely possible that other explorers came here and just… turned around in total disappointment. An optical illusion like that could be a great defense if we did it right."

"You aren't kidding." Joe looked at his map, which had updated after they entered the grasslands. "We are close. I'd say… ten minutes?"

"Lead on, boss man."

They walked deeper into the area, flinching every time a truck-sized bug lumbered by. A few times they had been evaluated by the bugs but were deemed not to be food so the insects continued on their way. Poppy, on the other hand, was evaluating the bugs as potential gold mines. "How much experience do you think that one is worth? Do you think we could use their exoskeletons to make chitin armor?"

"I think that until we have a full party, I don't want to see what happens when one of those things gets mad," Joe replied bluntly. "We are on a *mission*, remember?"

"A *boring* mission." Poppy pouted at him, "Boo. Boring!"

Joe rolled his eyes and marched onward. A few minutes later, they stopped after circling a small area for a while. Joe was looking at his map, a bit confused. "It should be right here. We are *on* the dot." There were no structures, no holes in the ground. There was no difference in this area except perhaps a slightly thicker cluster of grass. "Should we dig…?"

Poppy was looking around, and he tapped Joe to get his attention. "Digging would be going the wrong way." He pointed upward, and Joe followed the direction with his eyes. A few stories above them was a structure that had grass growing through it in a way that made it appear that it had been abandoned long ago. The tilting building gave lie to the thought that it had been *intended* as a treehouse. Grasshouse. Whatever this would be called.

"Up it is." Joe exhaled softly, eyes alight with excitement. The issue at this point was that there was no real way for them to scale the stalk of grass. There was a branching blade of grass about seven feet above their heads, but… Joe chuckled and *jumped* straight up. His stamina dropped to a quarter, but he easily got his arms over the blade and pulled himself onto the vegetation. "Whew! That was fun."

"How the heck did you just do that, and do you have any rope?" Poppy questioned conversationally.

"Ah, no, I don't. Also, Master jumper, remember? I do have a *few* skill levels in 'jump'." Joe looked for another way to get Poppy up with him. "Maybe jump as high as you can, grab my hand, and climb up?" Poppy waited until Joe had recovered his stamina then hopped up and grasped Joe's hand. The blade of grass Joe was resting on started to bend, obviously unable to support both of their weight at the same time.

The Duelist let go without needing to be asked, sighing wistfully as he landed on the ground again. "Just go… make sure to tell me if it is amazing in there."

"Sorry, buddy! I will definitely let you know, though. It'll probably be incredible and amazing." Joe waited for the grass to stop bouncing then got into position to make another leap. He jumped at a rough spot on the grass, catching himself at the fold of the next blade. Using that as a foothold, he once again refilled his stamina and hopped to the next safe spot.

"Fee-fi-fo-fum!!" Poppy called up to him in a deep voice.

Joe had paused to catch his breath, so he glared down at the grinning man on the ground. "You are going to feel *so* bad if I get eaten by a giant."

"Not as bad as *you* would feel. That would hurt like crazy," Poppy easily shot back. Joe shook his head and kept moving, getting higher and closer to the small building the entire time. By the time he was close enough to look into the windows, he was exhausted. After taking a bit longer to rest, he built up some speed and jumped the remaining distance. Right as his foot left the ground, the wind picked up and the entire building swayed away from him.

What should have been an easy hop turned into a flying tackle that allowed him to just *barely* make it onto the stairway that led up to the main entrance. He landed heavily, his legs dangling over empty space for a long moment, but with great effort, he was able to roll to safety.

Skill increased: Aerial Acrobatics (Novice VII). Practicing without a safety net is the best way to increase skills quickly! Do it more often!

Yeah, no thank you to *that.* He would settle for slow and steady skill progression if this was the alternative. After catching his breath, he walked up to the door and paused. There was no handle; instead, a simple and faded ritual diagram was etched into the wood. Joe looked at it deeply, searching for hidden meaning, but after finding none, he shrugged and input mana into the activation site that led to the commands for 'open'. The ritual flared and vanished, and the door opened.

Joe silently cursed himself. Even if that ritual had been simple, it was one he didn't have access to. Now it had vanished, and it would take quite a bit of research to re-make it. He resolved to take screenshots of any ritual he came across as he continued. Easing forward, he tried to make sure there weren't any traps or hidden dangers that he was about to set off. As his eyes ran over the interior of the building, his jaw dropped in wonder.

All around the single-room building were active rituals. These rituals had diagrams that were moving, spinning, and seemed to be hovering above the ground. Joe felt like he had just walked into a watch, so fluid and regular were the movements. What eventually caught his attention was the pedestal set against the back wall; a long tube sat on it and seemed to be the focus of the various rituals in the area. The walkway to the tube was clear, so he walked over to inspect the item.

Perception check + knowledge check success! This is a protective scroll case. It most likely contains some form of document.

"How… useful." Joe ignored the text and tried to touch the scroll. His finger stopped a few inches from the case as if he were pressing against glass. There was no pain, luckily, so Joe scratched at his chin in thought. "Force field? I could use a few of these."

He walked over to the nearest ritual, reading over the

diagrams and trying to understand what was happening. After a few minutes of study, he decided that this was the ritual creating the force around the case. He tried to touch it to stop the flow of power, but another dome of power blocked him. "So a puzzle then? I bet I need to find the first ritual in the chain then stop each of them without blowing myself up."

With that thought in mind, Joe activated his Exquisite Shell, pumping a thousand mana into the protections. He walked to each of the rituals, taking a picture of them and seeing where they sat in the hierarchy. He did find the terminus fairly quickly, but he made sure to check *all* of the rituals first. It seemed that a few of them were set as traps, designed to trick the unwary into a force field that would last for weeks before running out of power. Those ones could be activated either by messing with them directly or failing to correctly dispel the others. This could be a fun anti-theft device.

Joe went to the first ritual that he needed to stop, looking it over one last time. It was simple, a Novice ranked ritual. He needed to input power into it right as the diagram twirled into a certain position. Right… *now*! The ritual flared and halted, and in his peripheries, Joe saw two others waver like they had been caught in a heat haze. He walked over to the first and found that the shielding around them was gone. Perfect.

It seemed that this room was set up as a test of sorts for potential specializing Ritualists. Each layer of rituals had an impact on more and more rituals, and each layer also became more difficult to correctly unravel. The outer edge was simple Novice diagrams, spinning at a pace that was easy to discern. This was followed by Beginner key-rituals which had two spell circles spinning in different directions. An Apprentice layer followed this, *three* circles spinning. Clockwise, counterclockwise, clockwise. Joe's head was beginning to pound, and it took a solid ten minutes to finish this layer.

Taking a breather, he went to the door and yelled down to Poppy that it might take a while. A lazy reply drifted up, "Whatever, just wake me up when you are done." Joe snorted and returned to the rituals, happy to be on the final layer: Student circles. This is where things became tricky. Joe hadn't really created many Student-ranked rituals, and the ones he *had* made were nowhere near this complexity. The circles were spinning, but their diagrams were no longer simply spaced flat and further away; now they were at slight angles, taking up less room than they would have otherwise but enmeshed in a three-dimensional orbit.

Joe was gaining quite a bit of insight into the creation of higher-tiered rituals, even without ranking up. He had a sinking sensation that the Journeyman tier would include rituals that swirled as if they were set into a gyroscope, which incidentally is what he planned on purchasing to create his rituals on if he got to that point. These free-floating rituals… Joe had no idea if they were created with solidified illusions or if they were the after-effects of making this tier of rituals, but he knew one thing for certain: he had no idea how to replicate them.

Skill increase: Ritual Lore (Beginner V). Sometimes it is not about what you know, it is about admitting weaknesses that you can work on. You have a lo~o~o~t of weaknesses. Admit them all and see if this skill skyrockets! Intelligence +2.

Joe wasn't bothered in the slightest by the return of the snarky messages. His lore skill was amazing, and it had given him more statistic points when leveling it than any other skills he currently had. He needed to spend some time in research, really crank up the numbers in that skill. His eyes returned to the floating ritual in front of him, and he felt that he understood it just a *tiny* bit better. As it turned out, it was enough.

The four spinning circles stopped one by one. There was an audible hum that filled the room for a moment before fading, and the ritual vanished into motes of light. All the other visible rituals in the room soon followed, leaving particles behind for a few moments that made the room appear to be filled with fireflies. He walked over to the container, picking it up and popping off the end. Slowly, carefully, he pulled out the large sheet of paper inside. As he unfurled it, a smaller paper fluttered *almost* to the ground, stopping and flattening a few inches before it would have touched the wood of the floor.

Joe was looking at the large document, confused by what he saw. The paper seemed to be… blueprints? And the detail was, simply put, astounding. The same three-dimensional effect that had allowed the rituals to exist *filled* these blueprints. The plans on it seemed to stretch and turn. Staring at the same position on the page allowed you to see new details for a full five seconds before they began repeating themselves. What in the world did this *do*? Joe reached down and picked up the paper, reading through it as his eyes widened and a smile grew on his lips. Just… wow.

CHAPTER TWENTY-EIGHT

If you are reading this, my hopes and dreams have been answered, and the murdered art of ritual magic has been rediscovered and refined once more. I don't need to tell <u>*you*</u>*, obviously, but anyone trying to brute-force the rituals guarding this container would have slowly starved to death for their transgressions.*

"*This* guy was probably the life of the party," Joe muttered condescendingly, shaking his head before continuing to read.

This is my final work of art, the blueprints to a building whose existence has been forcefully hidden by the various guilds, sects, and unions. This building is the reason *that ritual magic became taboo or disparaged in the world. Guilds, Kingdoms, associations, and sects have hunted down any of the existing buildings, doing anything they could to either capture or destroy them.*

As far as I know, there is only one still left in existence deep in the most protected sanctuaries of the Dwarven people. Even they, with all of their skill in creating stone and metalwork, cannot replicate this structure, and so they guard it jealously. Any knowledge of its creation will die with me… unless you are successful in activating and using this ritual.

If you manage to make the building, the knowledge of how to make it without this blueprint will be lodged in your mind. You will be able to re-

create this building anywhere you want. Provided you have the requisite skill and needed materials, of course. Even in my day, the resources were difficult, dangerous, and expensive to acquire.

Following this paragraph was a listing of all the raw materials that would be needed to make whatever the building was. If Joe had been drinking something, it would have been sprayed across the room as he read over the list. Just… *no*. Where was he even supposed to get six tons of black marble or a 'Sunburst Beast Core'? He skipped the list and continued reading.

It goes without saying that you will need to protect this building. Included in the design are the plans for a mid-sized temple. I would suggest finding the cleric of a god you trust and have them dedicate the temple to the deity. Depending on which deity is used, the building will *gain extra effects and protections. Now, onto the actual building itself.*

These are the plans for a building that you will know as a Grand Ritual Hall. Everyone else will know it as a 'Pathfinder's Hall'. This building allows you to create and perform rituals that would otherwise be outside of your capabilities. These Halls used to be less than rare in the world, as the creation of the building imparts an otherwise unobtainable specialization path upon the Ritualist who leads the ritual to form this building.

Others will see this hall as a place to gain power in ways they never could before because the building will offer several functions to them. One: it will allow them to see the exact *requirements that were needed to gain their current class. Too much in the way of hard-to-obtain classes and skills is simply guesswork without this building.*

Two: by paying a fee that the building owner can set, people will be able to see what specializations they have met the requirements to move into and what they need to unlock more classes. This includes the needed titles, statistics, and experience. There is a caveat here, as the building can only offer knowledge that it currently stores. A third-tier specialist can offer *details of his class to the building, which will open his path to others, but he will not be able to find a way to the fourth tier unless that knowledge has already been offered by another at that rank.*

It is a travesty that these centers were destroyed so that certain classes could hide their progression paths from others that may seek them. This was a time of great greed and darkness, and I hope that in your time, these issues have faded into tales for children. Best wishes, and good luck, Student. ~Sage Cognitionis.

Quest complete: Building a specialization. You have found the steps needed in order to progress to a powerful new class! Good luck making it happen! You'll need it.

"Cognitionis?" Joe whispered reverently as he carefully stored the document and blueprints away in his ring. "He was literally 'Sage Knowledge'? Or was he the 'Sage *of* Knowledge'? Either way… *wow*. This is…"

"*Joe*!" Poppy's scream drifted up to him, and he suddenly noticed that the building he was in was falling apart. Joe turned and ran, getting out of the door just as the entire building wobbled and began to fall from its place in the tree-tall grass. As it happened, poor architecture wasn't the reason that Poppy had screamed. The building landed on a massive wasp, crushing it to the ground and killing it while a last agitated **buzz** came from the massive insect.

"Ding, dong, the witch is dead." Joe slid down the stalk of grass, the angle of it allowing him to avoid the rubble and still-twitching wasp. Joe looked at Poppy's damaged clothes and wheezing form. "What happened?"

"Giant *wasp*! Whaddaya *think* happened?" Poppy folded in half, breathing deeply with his hands on his knees. "I fought it off as long as I could, but that thing was so *fast*." Joe used Cleanse on Poppy, but it seemed he hadn't been poisoned, so Joe simply got him to well-hydrated and waited for him to recover.

"Alright. Thanks. Before we go, I'm getting that stinger," Poppy firmly stated. "I'm almost *positive* it can be used as material to make a rapier for me, and I bet it'll do some kind of extra poison damage. I'll get Alexis to work on it." Joe did what he could to help Poppy shove aside rubble, and luckily, the rear of the wasp was the part least covered by stone and wood. Poppy laughed as he cut out its stinger and made sure to carefully extract the poison sack as well. It would make a good bribe for Alexis.

They started walking back to the town, and over the course of the jaunt, Joe told Poppy about what the small building had contained. After describing the structure that he could potentially create, the Duelist was strangely contemplative. "Joe, it sounds like making that building is going to bring a whole lot of trouble down on our heads. I understand that you want the unique class that you can get from it, but… you'll make sure to go through all of this with Aten, won't ya?"

"...Of course. Yeah, for sure." The rest of their trip was covered in silence, at least the majority of it when no animals came sniffing around. The late afternoon sunlight was making them sweat heavily by the time they finally returned to town, and only liberal use of Joe's cleansing ability kept them from dropping from heat exhaustion. Joe thanked Poppy for his help and went off to bother the guild leadership.

Joe found Aten discussing with a few others what they should do with the most heavily transformed building, the town hall. It was huge now and surrounded by open land and manicured gardens. Sir Bearington apparently wanted to burn it down to the ground and rebuild the original buildings that had occupied the space, while the guild was discussing if they should offer to buy the opened space in its entirety. Joe almost turned and walked away but hesitated long enough that he was noticed. Aten waved him over after seeing that he had something to say.

When Joe walked over, Aten pulled him to the side to admonish him a bit. "Evening, Joe. Look, I can tell that something is on your mind, but you really shouldn't come to me for *every* little thing. Do you even know who the next officer is in the chain of command for you? She's very nice, I promise."

A bit taken aback, Joe tried not to neither laugh nor get upset. "Makes sense. Sorry if I've been bothering you recently, but this is important. This is something that is a bit… 'your ears only' at this point though."

"Oh no." Aten looked at the horizon as if he would spot smoke or something coming to fight them. "I haven't gotten any zone or guild notifications... you didn't attack any *royalty*, did you?"

"Why does everyone always assume the worst of me?" Joe grumped playfully. "No, this is better, but also potentially much more... world-wide infuriating?" Aten's hands trembled a bit, but he listened to Joe and asked pertinent questions. He nodded along and finally, simply rolled his head around his shoulders a few times.

"That's... I mean, it's *interesting*." Aten shrugged a little. "Sounds like a conversation we will *eventually* need to have, but as far as I can tell, this will be pretty far off in the future, right?"

"Not... necessarily." Joe smiled a smile that Aten had come to regret seeing. "I got a reward from completing a quest recently, a divine boon. It lets me complete a ritual without the need for components. All we need to worry about is the associated mana cost. That's where I am going to need your help."

Aten was a bit slow to respond, and his voice was grave when he did. "I admit that it would be amazing to have a building of this power under our control. I need to know, though, would it be under *our* control or *your* control? What is it that you would need from the guild?"

"Aten, I am a Wanderer through and through. Together, this guild is going to do amazing things in this world." Joe stuck an arm out and put his hand on Aten's collarbone. "That said, it would be a little of both. This is going to act like a giant conduit for me, letting me complete really powerful rituals and spells. I *need* to have access to it all the time, and I'm not sure how it works. There may be times I need to kick everyone out, but I'll try to do that in a way that is *scheduled*. At the same time, there is no way for me to guard it, control access to it, or charge others for the services it'll offer."

Joe relaxed a bit, retracting his arm. "If that works for you, then heck yeah, do whatever else you wanna do. We're a team.

In terms of the mana requirement though… well… it's pretty high," he admitted reluctantly.

"How high are we talking?" Aten was relieved; he was really glad that he had added Joe to the guild when he first appeared. He couldn't imagine what would have happened if the other guilds had gotten their hands on this walking goldmine.

"Well, after reducing the cost by a flat fifty percent, eighteen point five percent from the ritual magic skill, then an additional nineteen percent on top of that… oops, almost forgot Coalescence, so another nine percent, forty-six point five percent off the new total…" Joe was obviously stalling, so Aten crossed his arms and glared. "Alright, sheesh. One hundred seventy-four thousand, three hundred seventy-five mana."

"Well, this was a fun talk. Hope you had a fun day today!" Aten turned around and started walking away, whistling off-tune.

"Aten!" Joe followed after the physically powerful man. "Wait, wait, wait! *Listen*, this is a *Master* level ritual created by a *Sage*! If I am reading the information correctly, the building can even be upgraded two more times into a Grandmaster building… and then a *Sage* tier building! That means it would be an *Artifact* from the start and a *Mythical* by the end."

"Explain yourself," Aten resigned himself to the conversation.

"Alright, did you know there is a chart for rarity on the internet now?" Joe nodded even as Aten shook his head. "Alright, listen, there is a rarity rating for items, and I think for spells and classes as well. From worst to best it goes: trash, damaged, common, uncommon, rare, special, unique, Artifact. Um, special is kind of a catch-all for things like mana potions, which fall under 'artificially rare', or set items. I think something else I found, Restricted, lands there as well. After Artifact, you get Legendary then *Mythical* rarity."

"I get that there are rarity levels. What I meant is: what use is a higher tiered *building*? I understand how an Artifact-ranked sword could be useful, but…" Aten trailed off, leaving Joe to fill in the blanks.

"Ah! Well, these buildings will give the entire *guild* buffs! I don't know what will happen when we build this, but I know the castle in Ardania is at least Legendary ranked. I hear that combat skills increase at quintuple the speed in and around the castle. The wall around the castle is apparently the boundary for the area of effect. That's why it is so far away from the castle itself! I'm pretty sure the Mage's College is one as well; it has spatial magic in it that makes the inside far larger than it should be."

Aten paused, chewing on that thought. "You think that you can figure out how to get us a *Legendary* or even *Mythic* building?"

"Eventually… yeah."

"This is going to suck, Joe. I *really* hope you're right, or I'm going to have some very unhappy investors." Aten took a deep breath and walked over to his original meeting, pressuring the others to put in a bid for the open land in the town. A few hours later, everyone in the guild got a notification.

Quest complete: Base-ic operations! Your guild has found a new home, make sure to defend it well!

CHAPTER TWENTY-NINE

When Joe awoke the next morning, he was stiff and sore. He creaked out of bed and wobbled to where the glorious ambrosia named *coffee* lived. This was his favorite time of the day, early enough that the air was crisp and clear but late enough that the sun was up and warming up the area. Nodding at the few people that he knew by sight, he pulled out his cube and started working on it. There was a problem that he hadn't finished yesterday, and he was hoping that his rested mind could figure it out quickly. It was the *last* one he needed to do on this side of the puzzle cube, and completing it would put him at fifty wisdom.

What is the largest palindrome made from the product of two 2-digit numbers?

The answer cube was obviously the last one that he needed to use, but unless he did the work, he wouldn't get the reward. Not that he hadn't tried. The words on the answer cube were blurry and no matter how he looked at it, he couldn't make it out. Joe snorted and started doing the work; he started at ninety-nine, and worked his way down with the other number, hoping it would be that easy. Surprisingly, it was.

99 x 91 = 9009.

That was a palindrome, right? Joe looked at the cubes again, and to his delight, the answer cube now held that number. After spending far too long a time spinning the face, the cube clicked into position. The blue section of the cube flared with a gentle light, and the message he had been waiting for appeared with extras!

Characteristic point training completed! You have completed the (Novice) cube face! Rewards have increased! +2 to intelligence and luck! +1 wisdom, perception, and dexterity! These stats cannot be increased further by any means other than system rewards, study, or practice for twenty-four hours game time.

You have reached fifty points in both wisdom and intelligence! We suggest laying down to avoid damage as your mind is upgraded. Since you have both Mana Manipulation and Coalescence, you will be granted the opportunity to increase these while unconscious! 3...2...1…

By the time Joe finished reading the text, it had unfortunately already counted down to 'one'. His eyes rolled back in his head and he flopped to the table, spilling his poor coffee before slowly sliding sideways off the bench.

From his perspective, Joe blinked and appeared in front of the raging storm that was his center. The orb of swirling mana hadn't changed much since the last time he had seen it, and he felt a bit guilty that he hadn't kept up with the skill. Now, though, it was crashing against the barrier he had imposed on it, fighting against his control as hard as it could. *That* wouldn't do at all. He walked forward, imposing his will on *his* power. The hurricane spun faster as if angry, and the vaporous energy began to shrink down into a more compact form.

Joe pressed and pressed, determined to make as much improvement as possible in the time he had. A **crack** seemed to be felt, heard, and seen as the vapor *shifted*. Reaching a point of no return, a droplet of liquid mana appeared in the center of the gale-force swirling mana mists. This drop was spinning as well, seemingly pulling in all the mana in the area. In moments, the droplet had expanded to the size of the fingernail on his pinky finger and taken in all of the gaseous mana that had been in his center.

He was concerned at first that he had just done something stupid, but that tiny drop of liquid mana gave off an odd feeling, a *pull* like the sensation he got on a swiftly-twisting roller coaster. Gravity? Was he feeling a gravitational pull from this mana? There was no way to test it, but that was certainly the feeling he got from the shining drop of power. As he contemplated this development, more gaseous mana flowed in and was quickly absorbed by the droplet. Was that his mana regen kicking in?

Thinking of what else he should be doing, he remembered that the message had mentioned his mana manipulation skill. He looked around the area, at the other passages he could go through, but they all had an *impassable* feel to them. Right… it had said *upgrading* his skill. How could he…? Joe looked at the trail of gaseous mana that flowed out of the cavernous room he was in and tried to pull more mana from the droplet. The entire thing moved at once, and Joe was wracked with gut-churning pain.

"'Kay. Not like that. Got it." He looked at the spinning power and imagined a small portion of it vaporizing and following him as a cloud. The mana responded easily, and a thick fog billowed out of the orb and drifted toward him. He directed it to surround the current stream, integrate with it, and perhaps increase it in size. This… didn't work. The original stream seemed to reject it, staying separate no matter how he tried to combine them. But… maybe *combining* them wasn't what he should be going for.

In the next attempt, he used the cloud to envelop and *compress* the original stream. In his mind, he was picturing a set of bare wires being covered and insulated, protecting and directing the power. Somehow, it worked *perfectly*. Not only did the stream condense, it began to flow faster and stronger like pressurized water through a hose. Joe finished the entirety of the path, connecting it to his center just as a message appeared.

Mental attributes upgraded successfully! Base modifier for both Intelligence and Wisdom have reached '2'! You have come a long way from your humble mental beginnings. Someday you might even be able to call yourself smart and wise!

Calculating…

Skill increased: Coalescence (Apprentice I). You have reached the beginning stage of liquid mana! Your mana has gained an attribute, and as you increase in rank, this attribute will grow based upon your areas of focus. No longer will your mana be swept aside by another, blown by the wind like a morning mist. You have unlocked a character trait: Suppression resistance.

Suppression resistance will grow as your power does and gives you a 50% resistance to stun, silence, and paralytic effects. This does not mean you will not be impacted by these; it means that if these debuffs take effect, the length of time they will remain active is halved. Your mind has always been striving toward freedom, and your mana has taken on a bit of your resolve.

Skill increased: Mana Manipulation (Apprentice III). You have increased not only the skill but the rarity of this skill! New effect unlocked: Steady flow.

Steady flow increases spell stability by 10% and reduces casting time of all mana-consuming skills and spells by 10%.

Joe's eyes popped open as soon as he had absorbed all of this information, and he sat up smoothly. Around him was a cluster of his early-morning coffee aficionados, but seeing that he was awake, they simply nodded and returned to their routines. Joe blinked a few times, feeling like he was seeing the world for the first time. Information seemed to flow easily through his mind, and snippets of conversations and things he had read in the past seemed to come together and make sense in ways it never had before.

He stood up and started walking, but after a few steps, he stumbled. Joe steadied himself and kept moving, but every few steps, he would stumble. He frowned, looking around and trying to see if someone was messing with him. Someone was indeed looking at him and smiling, shaking his head. Joe cleared his throat and growled, "Excuse me, are you tripping me? Please stop, it isn't funny."

"Ha, that's a good one!" The man snorted and came a few steps closer. He looked Joe over, noting a bit of dried blood that had dripped from his nose as his brain overheated. "You passed a mental threshold, didn't you? Intelligence?"

"Wisdom as well," Joe affirmed, unable to stop a small grin of pride from appearing. "How is it obvious, though?"

"Oh? Very nice. It's good to get those two together, can cause issues otherwise." The man nodded to himself, a wry smile still playing around on his lips. "What's your dexterity at?"

"It's not my main area of focus… nineteen?" Joe waited for the man to laugh at the number, but he only grimaced.

"Gonna take more work, but you'll get there. High intelligence will help you make more dexterous movements, but until you get used to it, you are going to stumble *frequently*. Your mind is just moving faster than your body can keep up. Your brain is saying 'step, step, step', but your body can only complete 'step, step' in that amount of time. Get it? There was a whole segment on this in the new wiki. Good luck." The man shuffled past him to the coffee area, leaving Joe a bit troubled.

"Stats need to be balanced like that?" Joe could only keep moving; there was nothing else he could do right now to familiarize himself with his new bodily functionality. Needing to discuss a few of the details of the upcoming building with Aten, Joe set off to the command area. As he got back to the town square, Joe was waved over by a guild officer he didn't recognize.

"Hi there! Joe, correct?" She smiled at him brightly, a bit *too* brightly. Almost a *Jaxon* level smile. Joe was instantly suspicious. He didn't trust morning people. Terra, for instance, got up and went *jogging*.

"Good morning… sorry to be blunt, but who are you and what do you want? No, I don't want to have said that. I'm sorry, the coffee hasn't kicked in yet. Let me rephrase that. What can I help you with?" Joe felt like he had committed a faux pas from the way her smile crumbled.

She tried to plaster her smile across her face once again but failed. She sighed unhappily and let her face settle into a look far less pleasing. "Alright, listen up. I'm the next guild officer in your chain of command. Aten asked me to meet up with you and introduce myself so that you'll stop bothering him. My name is Daisy. If you are a team leader, then I am basically a manager. I manage several parties, helping out when they have conflicts or questions. Beyond sending me to get you off his back, Aten also wanted me to let you know that he sent a messenger to Ardania last night, and another guild comprised entirely of Mages is coming to help you with something. They should be here tonight."

"Oh. Um. Thank you… Daisy. That is great news and *way* faster than I expected this to happen. Where is he? We need to discuss details about that project. Nice to meet you." Joe nodded at her and started to walk toward the temporary headquarters the guild had set up.

Daisy's previously neutral face now displayed a frown. She grabbed Joe's arm and *yanked* him back hard enough to cause damage, catching him entirely off guard. He almost fell, only able to catch himself thanks to his mind working furiously to tell him where to put his feet. "Did you not just *hear* me? I'm your *superior* in the guild, so if you need to talk to Aten, you go through *me* and *I* set up a meeting if *I* deem it necessary."

Well, that was enough of *that.* Joe poured a thousand mana into the activation of Exquisite Shell, remaining silent for a few seconds as it settled. When he was fully armored, he looked directly at her once again and tried to speak calmly, "*Daisy*, please let me tell you something. You share a name with my ex-wife, who annulled our marriage while I was in a medically-induced coma. This makes me predisposed to disliking you. Now, I try not to hold names against people too much, but if you put your hands on me like that again, there will be serious consequences that I do not think you will like at all."

"Look, I don't care how self-important or popular you *think* you are. Sparkly or not, you are going to follow the *rules*," Daisy chastised him severely.

"Who made these *rules*, Daisy? Was it Aten who told you that I couldn't talk to him? Did he *really* not want me to talk to him? Or just maybe did he want you to meet me so that you could help facilitate details and keep things running smoothly?" Joe demanded calmly. This had been a trying few days, and he was not going to deal with petty garbage like this so early in the morning. He was reaching his breaking point though, and she needed to back off.

"That doesn't matter, *lieutenant*." Daisy's voice was filled with venom. Joe didn't know his guild rank until now so that part was nice at least. "I, *Major* Daisy, am telling you that your behavior isn't going to work anymore, and I have full authority to cut off your wages and hit you with command debuffs until you get the *picture*. You won't be able to bother Aten, or anyone else, until *you* get with it."

"Well, *that's* fun." Joe took a deep breath and stepped to the side, moving away from her. "Why is it that when someone gets a tiny modicum of power, it goes right to their heads? Aten had told me that you were a nice person and to look forward to meeting you. I feel pretty bad that you act like this; it makes me trust his judgment less. Get out of my way. First warning."

At that very moment, Aten was frowning as he tried to figure out where the slew of reputation loss notifications was coming from. He and the highest-ranked guild officers gained and lost reputation within the guild all the time, and this helped them keep track of how the guild was doing as a whole. Typically, it was fairly stable, so this was concerning. When he saw that the notifications were from Joe, he wasn't overly concerned. At first. Then he saw that he was losing huge swaths of reputation with the erratic man. Aten's eyes widened as their ranking went from 'Ally' to 'Friendly' in the span of about half a minute, and it seemed to be spiraling lower. He bolted out of his meeting, ignoring the confused shouts of the board members.

"I *told* the other officers that you wouldn't listen. *They* said that you were 'eccentric' and 'fun' but you would *listen* when I told you to do something." She scoffed and a glow appeared on her hand. "I knew I was right. *Command: attention!*"

Joe halted in place, his back going rigid as he was forced to stand at attention. A timer cut in half appeared in the corner of his vision. 5… 4… "Second warning. This is *really* the way you want to do things, huh, Daisy? You asked for it." As soon as he was able to relax, he turned around and prepared a shadow spike.

Spell failed! By the guild charter, you cannot willingly and intentionally attack a guild member in good standing.

"*Obviously*, this is the way I want to do it. *Command: attention!*" Daisy was smiling sweetly at him, but all Joe saw was a smug brat who had never had power before. "Are you going to stop bothering Aten now?"

"Last. Chance," Joe growled as the command spell began to wear off again. Aten's notifications told him that his reputation had now dropped to *neutral* with Joe, and he was frantically looking through the coffee area he knew Joe was prone to hang out at during his free time.

"*Your* last chance. *Command: front leaning rest position, move!*" At her words, Joe dropped down into the push-up position. "Gimme twenty, and we'll try this again."

Joe had already decided on his next course of action. He finished the push-ups and stood up, taking a deep breath. "Alright. I tried to be nice, Daisy. I'm done with you. System! I claim my right to leave the guild under subsection *six*, paragraph *thirteen*, clause *four*!"

Calculating… checking recent conversation history… checking recent spell usage. Checking game log. Confirmed! Three warnings given… Confirmed! 'Abusive relationship' clause activated. Contract destroyed! You have left the guild 'The Wanderer's.

Guild alert: The Wanderer's guild has lost 2000 reputation with Ardania! They no longer meet the requirements to remain a Noble Guild and will have that status revoked unless they are able to gain 1573 reputation in the next 72 hours.

Achievement unlocked: Leaving the wrong guild the right way. The guild failed you, but you knew your stuff and were able to make a clean break! You have shown that you won't be pushed around; you are made of sterner stuff than that! You have gained six ranks in skill: reading. You have gained 150 exp. +3 Constitution.

You have revoked fast-travel rights to members of the guild 'The Wanderer's.

"I. Am. Out." Joe growled into Daisy's shocked face, shoving her out of the way as he walked toward the gates. He left the town, walking directly toward the shrine… and the fast-travel point that it contained.

CHAPTER THIRTY

Joe was still fuming as he walked into the Mage's College almost an hour later. He stalked down the hallway, making five right turns and walking into the contract preparation classroom. Just like the last time Joe had been here, a head poked up above the shelves in the back and Master Slender smiled and walked over. "You came back! I thought I had scared you off."

"Not at all, Master Slender." Joe showed the man a weary grin. "A few things came up, but I hope you won't mind picking up where we left off."

"Not at all. Come in, come in." Master Slender grabbed a few things from a nearby cabinet and got down to teaching. Joe was an apt student, and soon, they were pressing freshly made paper, bottling new ink, and sharpening raven-feather quills. By the end of the lesson, Joe was feeling better, had gained six ranks in the skills offered by this course, and one in his scribe skill; he was even a bit ashamed by how he had handled things with the guild.

"Something on your mind?" Master Slender gently inquired.

"Nothing that I can't talk to the other person about." Joe

smiled half-heartedly at the Mage. "Well, I'll see you another time?"

Master Slender nodded. "I'm sure we will, but you have learned almost everything there is for me to teach you at this level of class. You'll need to register for the advanced course to learn more. Though, there is *one* last thing. I see that you are level ten; have you learned how to combine skills?"

"I have." Joe opened the menu and waited for instructions. "I'm guessing that we combine these three together?"

"Excellent. You know what's going on. Sadly, there is more to it," Master Slender told him. "You also need to learn the skill 'Magical Material Creation' and combine *that* as well as your scribe skill. Obviously, this is the hardest step because, well… our students have been exclusively Nobles for decades and were able to toss the needed funds to initiate the combination right away. Frankly, there is no point in registering for the next level until this task has been completed."

Joe nodded sharply, frustrated with the wait but understanding the need to have the pertinent skills. "I can see how that is an issue for most people. How do I go about learning the 'Magical Material Creation' skill?"

"You've been a great student, and you have gotten through the class in record time so I'll teach you the skill for free if you want to learn it now. I'm not a *Master* of the skill, but I'm… passable." Master Slender didn't wait for an answer, simply pulling over a jar of the ink they had just finished creating. "We are going to use ink because, for some reason, people tend to be able to imbue liquids with mana much easier than other substances. It is just as easy to do it with anything, but…" he shook his head to show his disappointment at the general lack of comprehension that others exhibited.

"As I was saying, take the ink and try to suffuse it with mana. *Really* pack in the power until it starts binding to the ink." The professor handed over the jar with an expectant expression. Joe took the jar without hesitation and tried to create a sheath of power around the entire thing like he did when upgrading his mana manipulation skill. Once there was practically a shell of power humming around it, he started pumping power into a tiny hole that he had allowed to exist.

Fifty mana. One hundred. Two. Two fifty. At three hundred mana, the entire bottle was vibrating hard enough to hurt Joe's hands. Master Slender coughed lightly, forcing Joe to divide his attention. "Joe, perhaps I should step in here. There is plenty of mana in there now, *far* more than is needed. Just hold it in place and allow the mana to merge. I'm not a fan of magical ink flying around and splashing across my books."

Joe closed the hole he had been holding open, and after a few seconds, the material started to glow. First, the ink turned from black to a midnight blue, brightening and seeming to boil. Then the *glass* of the container shifted subtly, actually shrinking a bit but becoming much sturdier. Master Slender nodded in appreciation. "Excellent, excellent! Not many are able to imbue glass; it is notoriously stubborn and takes a huge amount of fine control as well as dense mana. Now, very carefully open a hole and let any remaining mana leak out. A very *small* hole, mind you, or this effort will be wasted."

Mana rushed out of the opening Joe provided, hissing like a pressure cooker with a leaky valve. When the flow dropped to a normal level, Joe opened the hole wider and eventually removed the shell of mana entirely. He picked up the bottle, and it slipped out of his hand like a greased egg, its tighter molecular bonds leaving the surface almost frictionless. Joe watched in horror as the glass fell to the stone floor… and bounced.

"Imbued glass is *very* hard to break." Slender chuckled as he saw the obvious relief on Joe's face. "It is also expensive and the base version of 'warded glass' which is one of the hardest man-made materials. That you can imbue glass at your level is impressive in its own right; you could make quite the living providing imbued glass for enchanters."

"As fun as making slippery glass is, I'd rather be able to make a final product on my own." Joe carefully picked up the bottle he had dropped, handing it over to the professor and acknowledging the notification he had waiting for him.

Skill gained: Magical Material Creation (Novice IX). Having a huge amount of raw mana and no real use for it tends to lead to dangerous experiments. That's how this skill was originally created! Sounds perfect for you! Increase density of mana matrix by 1n% per skill level.

"This is pretty cool. Is there an actual use for it though? Beyond the glass you mentioned?" Joe read over the details one last time before opening his menu and selecting to combine all of the skills. Three, four, five skills. Each time he added another, the cost doubled. Joe looked at the eight hundred gold this was going to cost him, his finger hovering over the button. "Anything else I should know before combining these?"

"Tons of uses for the glass, from weapons, to armor, to architecture." Slender did a double take and gave Joe a strange look. "You can afford to do this *right now*? That's… well, frankly, it's unexpected."

"Not trying to throw this in your face or anything, but… I was given a hundred platinum for—*ahem*—helping the previous Archmage… retire." Joe felt no need to mention the hundred thousand plus gold still in the bank.

"Ah yes… that would do it…" Slender thought a moment. "No, nothing else to note, and with these skills, it doesn't matter in what order you add them in. So go for it!"

"The order you add them can impact the results?" Joe shook off the statement and pressed 'combine'.

Time until skills have combined: 60 hours.

"Also, by the look on your face, you saw how long you need to wait for your new ability." There was a wry smirk on Slender's face. "Just one of those prices that we pay to progress. Yes, the order of combination greatly changes the outcome in many cases. This can lead to new skill formations, titles, and… classes. Yes, skill combination is the easiest and most accurate method of gaining rare classes. I'm sure you have unlocked the option to gain a new class when gaining skills, and this is no different."

"I see." Now more than ever, Joe wanted to complete the

amazing ritual he had found. His ring felt hot, like the blueprints were trying to call his attention to them. After regaining the skill 'Magical Material Creation'–he had to pay this time but was happy to find out that he could indeed relearn lost skills–Joe thanked Master Slender and promised to return soon for the next level of his class.

Joe wandered the halls of the Mage's College, trying to figure out why he had reacted so poorly to the manhandling that had led to him quitting the guild. He had been through worse–much worse–during his time in the military. Was it just that he had finally had an *incredible* taste of freedom for the first time in his adult life? Hierarchy and regimented life was all he had known before coming here. Maybe… maybe the military-esk way she had handled things had shaken him worse than it should have. There was no question that he had overreacted. It would have been *so* easy to wait a few minutes, then talk to Aten or…

You know… it was probably a bunch of things: the fact that Daisy reminded him of his ex-wife, that she was bullying him and he wasn't in any mood for it, and that he is *free* in the game and he felt she was threatening that. Beyond the issues with Daisy, he died twice in the last twenty-four hours, he has to deal with snarky messages from the game, he was told he kept bothering Aten and thought that they were friends when it *clearly* wasn't true, he didn't need the income the guild provides… heck, he didn't even know how much he was paid for his position! It was probably a bunch of little things that made Joe respond how he did.

Perhaps it had something to do with his breaking into the fifties of Intelligence and Wisdom and having his brain altered. Conversely, perhaps something related to his recently unlocked Mental Manipulation Resistance skill or Psychomancer class was causing some outbursts from resisting the system's mental interference. The only thing he knew for sure was that he didn't want to be known as an angsty person who was ruled by his emotions. Daisy had *certainly* overstepped her authority, and the system had agreed to the point that it recognized her actions as abusive enough to destroy his guild contract. Still, he was also in the wrong. Joe *hated* being in the wrong, even if he was only *partly* at fault. Alright. Back to the guild. He had some groveling to do.

Of course, just because he was feeling a bit bad didn't mean he couldn't drag his feet the whole way. As a matter of fact, he spent an additional day in the city just perusing the shops and wasting time. As much as he wanted to make this right, he also wanted to make them sweat a bit. Gaining reputation with the Kingdom was *hard* to do. When he finally started wandering to the town square, he could almost picture skid marks along the entire path he walked. The air was a bit blue from all the grumbling and cursing he did, and a few passersby blushed at his language… but he did eventually make it to the square and select the shrine as his destination. Eyelid twitching and fingers cramping, he pressed the 'accept' button and vanished from the city.

A man appeared in the spot he had vanished from, looking around and frowning behind the mask he wore. His multi-hued robes swished, and a small notepad appeared in his hand; quickly, he traced out a message that appeared on all items linked to it. *Contact lost once again. Target neither captured nor eliminated. Returning to base for punishment.*

CHAPTER THIRTY-ONE

"That was a heck of a thing to do to us, Joe." Aten's voice was obviously being tightly controlled. "I know that your contract wouldn't have destroyed itself if we weren't somehow in the wrong, but if you would have come and *talked* to me we could have worked out whatever the issue was."

"Getting to you *was* the issue," Joe explained what had happened, sharing the log of his interaction with Daisy when she denied his words. Aten had an odd look on his face. On one hand, Daisy was a trusted guild officer who had never had a single complaint against her, on the other was *proof* that not only had she done this but that she was lying about it.

"Daisy, what… the *heck*? Is this *why* I've never heard anything negative from your people? They are afraid to try talking to me? You've been pretending to be a drill sergeant?" Aten looked at the sweet lady he thought he had known for months.

"Of course not!" Daisy was full of righteous anger. "No one else has a *problem* following the rules!"

"Neither did the Mages in the College, at least not until they were given the chance to be *free*," Joe sniped at her. Daisy showed him a rude hand gesture, unintentionally lending credence to Joe's words.

"Enough already." Aten fiddled with his menus. "Daisy, your command powers have been suspended for now. We are going to let *all* of the people in your section know that you don't have them, and if they have been targeted by you we will know soon enough. If this was the first incident, we will just move Joe out from under you and be done with it. Otherwise, we will have a *longer* conversation."

Daisy was ushered out of the command tent, and Aten locked eyes with Joe, a bit of hopefulness showing. "I assume that you coming back to the guild means that you want back in it?"

"I do, but we are going to need to talk terms." Joe sighed and sat down; he hadn't wanted to be in a submissive position when Daisy was glaring at him. "I know that leaving the guild put you in a bad position, and I also know that at some point you won't *need* my reputation bonuses and travel system. For now, though, I think you do. I also think that fact has been overlooked pretty *heavily*. I bring a lot to the table, and I'm sorry to say that I think I'm going to *have* to leverage that now."

"Somehow, even though I've been nothing but helpful, I have a reputation in the guild that isn't good. Listen, I'm fine with just being a party leader, but from now on, I need autonomy. I'm also going to need to get our deal about this building in writing. We are going to have to get a *lot* in writing. I am also going to need a list of all the officers, the positions they hold, and where they stand in the hierarchy so I stop stepping on toes. Sorry to say, Aten, I lost a lot of trust after this little episode," Joe finished his lecture on a forlorn note.

"I know all of that." Aten looked sadly at his reputation meter for Joe. It had dropped all the way from 'ally' to barely maintaining 'neutral' in only a few minutes. That was the main reason he believed Joe so easily; you could lie, but the system wouldn't lie for you. "We can do that, and we can put you outside of the normal command structure. You won't have more than your party under your control, but you'll basically have free reign to do your thing."

"Alright. Let's get to it." They went to the scribe the guild had hired on, and within a few minutes, he was able to write out an amended contract. Joe was amazed at the skill the scribe displayed; it was like watching a slightly outdated printer print out a document. Joe's fingers itched to start ranking up his own skills. After quickly reading through the contract, Joe nodded and signed, followed by Aten signing.

There was a notification to the guild that they had regained all qualifications to be a Noble Guild, and Aten sighed with relief, a smile crossing his face for the first time that day. "Alright, well, we have an entire guild full of Mages on standby waiting to see why they are being fed and relaxing instead of working like I paid them to. I'm sure they don't *mind*, but they *do* get paid by the hour so if we could get moving I would appreciate it."

"I was wondering about that," Joe admitted as he was led to the area his ritual was going to be carried out in. "Are they under contract not to talk about the work they are going to be doing here?"

"Yeah. They also have a great reputation for working hard and getting their work done really fast. From what I've seen, though, they are usually contracted by guilds full of non-magical folk to go and hunt monsters with them. They also have a few alchemists, so when I told them that the job was essentially going to be them throwing spells continuously for an hour or more… well, they've been stockpiling potions for a while, and they brought them all along."

"That'll be helpful." Joe looked around with interest as the people around them suddenly became homogeneous. Gone were mismatched armors and leather clothing, swords and bows; in their place were robes. Sure, the robes had different designs on them, but all of them were the same color. Instead of various weaponry, there were only staves, wands, and orbs. Joe could practically *feel* the mana humming in the air, and he really started feeling the loss of his own robe to that overgrown bear.

Aten walked directly to the only person who had more than two colors on his robe. "Guild Leader Snake, it's always a pleasure to see you. Are you about ready to get going? We will start the initial setup now and should be ready for you in no time flat."

The Guild Leader turned toward them with a smile. "Ah, Guild Commander, ready when you..." his eyes locked onto Joe, widening comically as he clapped his hands. "Joe!"

"What? Wait... Snake... *T*snake?" When the man nodded, Joe stepped forward and gave him a hug. "Tim? What the heck, man; you were supposed to meet me as soon as you could! Where have you been? Why is your face twitching like that?"

"*Me*...? I could say the same to you! I searched all the newbie areas, all the training grounds, no one had seen you! No one! Twitching...? Oh! Yeah, I got an upgrade after my guild got real popular. I'm in a pod now. Where have you *been*?" Tim seemed confused and happy at the same time, and since guys aren't fans of feeling mixed emotions, Joe hurried to explain.

"I'm a cleric, a healer. Got picked up right away when a certain guild noticed that I could rub some dirt in their wounds and it would *actually* fix them up." Joe grinned as he stole Tim's old catchphrase. "Also, you couldn't find me? I'm in one of the most well-known guilds, and my name keeps popping up in server-wide announcements!"

"Not sure what you mean by the announcements, but I didn't think you were so unimaginative that you'd use your own boring name! Ugh, and yeah, the game decided that I was more suited to hurting than healing for some reason." Tim barely got that out before Joe turned it around on him.

"Oh, what a *shock*. The infamous infected blister-foot epidemic of-" Joe's laughter was cut off by Aten coughing heavily and extra loudly.

"So, I take it you two know each other, and I do *hate* to do this, but you guys *are* paid by the hour… so…" Aten trailed off as 'Snake' waved his hand back and forth.

"Twenty percent discount today only. Not on the use of potions but on labor. I've been looking for this guy since he started the game." Tim, uh, *Snake*, threw an arm around Joe's shoulders and chuckled. Aten was entirely uncertain what to say as Joe and Tim started catching up. When Joe explained that it had been him who killed the Archmage and proved it with his title, Snake's jaw dropped, and he made an announcement to his guild on the spot. Cheers broke out, and so many people clapped Joe on the back or shook his hand vigorously that he needed to subtly heal himself after a short while.

Eventually, they stopped reminiscing and got down to business. When Joe explained what they were about to build, Tim went pale and got shaky. "You are going to use us to build an *Artifact* building? This thing helps to plot out rank-ups and skill lines? Aten, we should work on your bargaining skills. I'll drop our price by fifty percent right now if you agree to let us use this place too. Give *us* a fifty percent discount on using it, and we will call all debt paid, potions included."

"That is a lot of money over time, and to be fair, Joe here is the building owner." Aten grinned, knowing that he was about to save his guild a couple thousand gold. "Why don't we say-"

"Look, man, fifty percent off right now, or we will just use this money to put a *few* people through and have them write down what they know instead of sending a *bunch* of people through it." Tim's grin widened at the pout on Aten's face. "Deal?"

"Yeah, yeah. Deal." Aten heaved a disgruntled sigh after he looked at Joe for confirmation and got a nod in reply. "You know where we want it? Good. Our Mages are on their way over to help as well. Let me know if you need anything. Otherwise… I look forward to seeing something amazing soon."

Snake waited until Aten was an appropriate distance away before asking the question he had been waiting to ask. "Still want to be in *this* guild? With what I know about you and your obvious skills, you would start in my guild as one of the top brass."

"Thanks, but… I'm doing well here, even if we have our rocky moments." Joe patted Tim on the arm and reminded him to focus. They got to work, first ordering the gathered Mages not by level but by total mana pool and mana manipulation skill. Those with lower amounts of mana were to be positioned further away, but in general, all of them had substantial amounts of raw power. Unsurprising for a guild of Mages where power equaled rank.

"Glad that's over. You have the highest amount of mana in your guild, correct?" Joe questioned Tim offhandedly. When he nodded, Joe took a deep breath and activated the setup function of his blueprints. Massive illusionary circles appeared on the ground, causing a few screams to ring out from quickly embarrassed people. "Good. We need the person with the next highest pool over here with us; then we need to start getting into position. Here is how this is going to work: we need to have prime numbers on each layer, but it skips a few each time. There will be us three, then the next layer on the *same* circle will have five, then seven. The *next* circle has to have eleven, thirteen, and then seventeen. In total, we need one hundred and ninety-five people to fill all the spots. Do we have that?"

"We have one hundred and thirteen. Including the… *Mages* from your guild. Remember, until recently, being a Mage was a very expensive process. Most of *my* people unlocked the class at the start of the game during character setup." Tim pretended to be disparaging, but Joe knew he was just trying to catch Terra's attention. He had been ever since she arrived.

"Alright… well, the smallest mana pool we have here is about four hundred. Average is around five hundred, though, right?" Joe waited for confirmation before continuing, "That'll only give us about a third of what we need in total. What can we do about potions, and we should…"

Continuing the discussion, they eventually unloaded all supplies and passed out the goods to where they were most needed. It was a huge undertaking just to get people to stand where they needed to, and Joe was once again pleased that he wasn't going to be in charge of other people for long. His head was throbbing as he worked to convince yet *another* party leader that all they needed to do was stand here, in this spot, and not move. No, he *didn't* care that none of them had mana; they were only here to fulfill a requirement. Yes, this *was* important. Yes, they had to stay *right here* and not move.

The furthest spell circle had a radius of fifty feet, so there was plenty of space for all of the people to stand. Joe got into position and yelled as loud as he could so that the others could hear him. "Okay, we are just about ready to go! If you haven't yet added your blood to a chalice, don't worry, it's coming around! Let's see… oh! If you are on the outer ring, please make sure that you stay conscious as *long* as possible! Things are about to get *weird*! You just need to accept that fact now; we should all survive this, so don't panic!"

After getting confirmation that everyone had added their blood to the silver chalice–Joe glanced at the sloshing silver bucket that they were using instead of a fancy cup–he nodded and spoke up again, "Here we go, everyone! Sections one through six, please remember your roles. Everyone, please remember that if you stay where you are supposed to be, you will be *fine*! If you run away or leave your spot, only *you* will explode like a kernel of popcorn! Everyone else will be fine. *Do not* leave your assigned spot! Get ready!"

Joe opened his menus and selected to use his 'Divine Boon'. Choosing to activate the next ritual without component cost, he felt a wash of golden power seemingly well up inside himself. He took a deep breath, and as he released it, he allowed his mana to flow into the Master-ranked blueprints in front of him. A deep chime rang through the area like a bell being struck, and golden power flowed from him and coated each portion of the ritual where a component of some sort was supposed to rest.

Ignoring the fact that they were supposed to be illusions, the circles they were all standing in began to move, carrying each person like they were on a conveyor belt. Most people were able to handle this without flinching, but then the flat lines started to change, orbiting Joe and the two others at the center of the ritual. Tim, Terra, and Joe reached out a hand each, their fingers almost touching as they made a triangle centered over the diagram. As one, they began to feed mana into the ritual. A disk of invisible power appeared under their position and began to lift them; soon, they were ten feet off the ground. Twenty. Fifty-five.

Remaining stable at that height, they couldn't help but watch as the people in the outer circles whizzed around them. Two breaths later, they read the first line of the ritual's activation sequence, *"Hoc est ad nocere!"*

The three of them grimaced as a seemingly uncontrolled burst of power flowed out of them and into the blueprints. The trio at the center were pushed a dozen feet apart as a series of reddish-gold circles of energy surrounded the document and a column of seemingly uncontrolled power began to rush down into the ground. Lines of mana seeped out of the paper, looking and acting like mist until they reached the disk under their feet. There the 'mist' resolved itself into thousands of tiny strings, going taut and connecting to the bodies of the three people and the diagram. More power raced from them, and the 'mist' billowed out once more; soon, lines of power connected everyone in the first circle.

"This isn't too bad. Kind of like a freaky roller-coaster…" Joe heard a female voice comment in the distance. He knew better but didn't want to scare anyone unnecessarily. The ritual was still *unfolding*. It was still getting ready, and any mana invested so far didn't count toward the total they needed. Telling the butterflies in his stomach to calm down, Joe took a deep, calming breath. He hoped he didn't get sick.

CHAPTER THIRTY-TWO

A trickle of vomit sprayed from the second circle, and a few people loudly complained as the spinning orbit brought them directly into the shower of bile. "I get motion sick! How was I supposed to know-" their words drifted away as all the circles continued to rotate and twirl.

"We are about to begin! Remember not to drink your potions until you see the group in front of you sink to their knees! You will be feeling drained, but we need to do this *right*!" Joe shouted this information as loud as he could, hoping that the practice runs they had done would be remembered. "Three... two... *one*!"

Contrary to the countdown, it would be almost a full minute before most people even noticed a change. For the three at the center... the party was already in full swing. They would all be drained at the same rate, approaching zero together. Unfortunately for Joe, he had about one third more mana than the others. To him, this meant that the ritual drew from him longer than the others. When two of them had equal mana, it drew from the next, followed by the third. Soon, they were all grimacing, working hard to keep the power flow regulated. Any fluctuations drew power from the others faster as well, so a smooth flow was required.

Unlike all the other rituals Joe had made, this one didn't seem to activate the ritual circles from the outermost edge, working inwards as the outer circles activated. No, it seemed that the tiny lines of power connecting them to the ritual did something to direct the power. The once-white lines were filling with blue mana. As power trickled outward, the color and shape of the entire circle gradually changed as well. Most concerning was that the ritual didn't wait for the three at the center to be fully drained before beginning to pull power from the next layer.

There was a collective '*Oof!*' as the mana draw began with an almost physical blow to the second layer. The five people there were almost as mana-rich as the first layer, though, and easily controlled themselves and their power. Lines of light left their layer, connecting with the golden divine power that was going to be acting as their components. It didn't *do* anything just yet, but they were *connected.* The entire time, Joe kept up a chant, and the other two at the center echoed him a moment later.

"*Ducatur fortior*!" Joe tried to modulate his voice, no need to shout and ruin the pronunciation.

"*Ducatur fortior*!" Both Terra and Tim stated together. Terra seemed a bit more focused on the issue at hand, whereas Tim just seemed happy that his whole job basically amounted to *touching* a pretty lady's hand and speaking in what sounded like Latin.

Joe continued to chant, reading directly from the words that constantly appeared on the blueprints. Even as his mana waned and exhaustion from that depletion set in, he continued to read aloud. There must have been some sort of system help with the pronunciation of these words because they left his mouth with confidence and exacting perfection. The three at the center slowly sank to their knees, the only signal they could use to show that the mana draw was going to fall on someone else now.

They *almost* gasped in relief as the burden fell from them, and their natural regeneration went toward refilling their mana pools instead of empowering the ritual. They kept chanting, even as power began to crackle along the lines connecting all of them. As the final layer of people on their circle began to be pulled from, much larger versions of the small lines connecting them to their circle began to grow. These cables twined away, connecting to dots of mana floating in the air. A gem-like mana structure formed around the entirety of the first circle, seemingly solid but still mainly translucent.

Gaseous mana began to roll off of this structure, flowing outward until reaching the boundaries of the second circle where it stopped and began to spread out. The circle seemed to act as a containment device, and it appeared that a portion of the mana being generated by the first layer of the second circle was being used to maintain that barrier. It should be noted that even though the layers were being activated quickly, this didn't mean there was less mana being pulled from them or that they were collectively weak. In fact, there were eleven people on that layer alone, meaning that a low estimate placed them at contributing over five thousand points of mana on this pass alone.

"*Progressing smoothly. Good,*" Joe thought to himself as he continued working. Now he needed to add in hand gestures and slow movements, and the others carefully mimicked him. The third and fourth circles had activated, and Joe once again wondered how a Master-ranked ritual had only four circles... the *layers*! If looked at another way, they were obviously different, more complex and grand than any other ritual circle he had ever seen before. Mwah-ha-ha! He was positive that if nothing else, this would boost his ritual lore skill.

There was a slight hiccup as the final layer activated, though it was expected. As soon as the draw of mana began, all of the people were forced to their knees screaming in pain, some of them fainting instantly. No access to mana meant no mana channels, no practice keeping their power under control. No open mana channels meant, well… intense pain until blackout, so he had expected this. Joe winced in sympathy pain for them. The three placed at the center quickly drank their first potion, jumping from about twenty percent recovered to seventy in an instant, then a boosted regeneration adding on more per second. Mana poured off of Joe, once again taking from him exclusively for a few long seconds before adding in the others. If he hadn't been used to huge surges of power like this… he would have fallen unconscious at the minimum.

The ritual had dipped down a tiny bit, and the entire thing was now rocking back and forth as though it were on a pendulum. The outermost circle seemed to create massive scoops and tore into the earth. That circle currently looked like a bladed Ferris wheel and was tossing tons of dirt and stone out of the ground. It was… digging a foundation perhaps? When the massive plot of land had been cleared, the blades of the wheel became colossal flat hammers and pounded the terrain to create a solid base. As the second round of Joe's mana expenditure came to an end, he watched as golden power dripped from the accumulated divine energy.

Two shining drops landed on the ground and spread across hundreds of feet like oil in a pan, covering the bare rock and rising to fill the entire space. A streak of black appeared in the gold, and the energy *changed*. At the speed of a bubble bursting, the foundation had been converted into black marble with beautiful streaks of white running through it in an obviously-planned design. There were ragged cheers coming from the outer layers that were not currently under a mana-burden, but those died down quickly. After the initial laying of stone, golden drops fell as regularly as a leaky faucet. Each time they did, a new portion of the building was formed.

At first, it appeared that this building would be a pyramid, and there was quite a bit of confusion when that entire structure collapsed into itself and became level with the ground. Pillars appeared. Would this become an open-air structure like the Temple of Artemis? A castle? Was that a computer…? A twenty-foot gyroscope? All of it vanished, sinking into the black marble. Only Joe knew that these structures still existed, simply waiting for a Ritualist to call upon them for use. Just before the third round of mana-draining began, the Master ritual started to rise.

The outer ring began to drip golden power as it spun, and a structure began to form. Narrow at the base and widening, it wasn't until the structure began to come together that it was recognized as a huge sphere, no, wait… it was a-

Just before the structure would have finished and closed the hole, the floating ritual *dropped* through the opening. A few shouts of shock rang out, but the ritual continued unabated. The third ring began to shine, and beams of light–consisting of mana and divine power–began to create strange objects and fanciful shapes like an industrial-sized three-dimensional printer. A floor appeared over these connected objects, and the expansive area began to form into a funnel. After the funnel had formed–a huge affair that looked like a stone tornado–the second circle began to cut shapes into it.

The patterns and spell diagrams on the fourth circle of the ritual were pulled away from it, leaving a simple and empty round platform for the participant to remain standing on. The second layer of the building had incorporated these designs and magical symbols into the funnel, adding an air of mystery to it. A similar thing happened to the patterns on the third circle, and then a translucent floor appeared over all of it. Looking through the floor allowed you to see deeply into what appeared to be a portal into a black hole. Sunbursts, specks of light, and raw mana were visible below, adding an allure and mysterious feel to the place.

Small rooms with spell circles in them began to be created, the circles raised or etched onto the floor. The entirety of the outer wall and ceiling became a single mirror, curved and reflecting all the light in the area. A single pillar began to form using the remaining ritual diagram of the second circle; the pillar twisted and lifted, heading toward the opening still remaining in the roof over a hundred feet above them. Power rolled off the ritual, the draw of mana coming in spurts from anyone who was able to produce it. Joe was sweating a disturbing amount; they were almost done, but more and more people in the outer circles were falling unconscious.

As they approached the ceiling, the fourth circle became horizontal and lifted up. It plastered itself to the roof and began rotating, leaving small platforms behind for the people that had been on it. Those people were slowly pulled to the ground, being gently deposited. Not one of them was awake to see it. The third ring followed suit, but it seemed to sink *into* the ceiling partly, somehow visible behind the mirrored surface. The second circle stopped just as they passed through the opening, leaving a rotating circle for the tower growing behind them to thread.

As that group of people was deposited back onto the ground, the barrier that had been keeping the mana generated from the first circle in check began to fail. Joe and the others that were in the first circle were straining to generate more power, and they drank their last potions. It wasn't as effective as the others before it; after three potions in too short of a time, the ones following simply don't have as much of an impact. In fact, it was only a quarter as potent as the first had been.

It was enough. The tower formed around them, surrounding the gem-like structure that had appeared. Mana that had nearly escaped was sucked in and repurposed. At this point, the first circle fell off and all but the main three were pulled to the ground by an invisible force. Joe, Terra, and Tim were gasping for air as the intense pressure of the mana in the air around them *squeezed*. The accumulated power began to collect into a spot directly above them, sucking in all of the thousands of points of mana that had been in there only moments previously.

Shining brilliantly, the chaotic ball of pure mana seemed to contain an ocean of power and generated a breeze that pushed the air away in a constant motion. Windows formed around them: single-piece, perfectly clear crystals. Only a drop of golden power remained, and it zipped upward and sank into the center of the ball of mana. For a bare instant, it seemed that the mana had grown a layer of diamond around itself. Then the world went white.

CHAPTER THIRTY-THREE

You have created a Grand Ritual Hall (Pathfinder's Hall)! This building provides a service needed by all; it allows for storage and access to the skills, titles, and experience needed to specialize into a class or gain a class. As a Ritualist, you are able to access a portion of the building that none other may: the ritual room. This room is fully configurable, allowing for nearly any shape, size, or complexity of ritual. Shifting this room consumes mana from the structure.

Many rituals are three-dimensional and require significant effort without access to an area such as this. This building is a shining beacon of knowledge in the darkness of ignorance and greed; all skill training in the area of effect of 'Shining Enlightenment' is twice as efficient. More effects will make themselves known as the building gains mana and class information! Structural integrity: 2,500,000/2,500,000. Mana supply: 100/1,000,000.

You have created an Artifact Structure! Congratulations! This is a feat that many will never complete. As the leader of the ritual that completed this structure, a new specialization has been unlocked for you. It will be denoted in your specialization menu with '' around it.*

Achievement unlocked: Create an Artifact-rarity Structure. +5000 experience for each participant. You, specifically, have gained a new title: Architect of Artifacts.

Architect of Artifacts: Any action you take that will result in the construction of a new structure will boost the buildings' overall statistics and potential boosts by 10%! +5 points to each characteristic stat permanently. (Excluding Karmic Luck.)

You are the owner of an Artifact Structure! You have the right to admit/deny any entry, set fees for usage, restrict any of the knowledge contained within the building, and deny any the benefits it provides. Caution! There are some who will not take being denied entry gracefully. Your building can be attacked and broken into, though it will defend itself depending on mana levels.

Skill increased: Ritual Lore (Apprentice I). You have delved deeper into the secrets of rituals than anyone in an age. This requires both intelligence and luck with just a dash of blood loss. +1 intelligence, luck, and constitution.

"I can't see!" Joe called out in the otherwise fairly quiet room. "It's so *bright* in here!"

"Ow! You stepped on my hand!" Terra called from somewhere below him.

"Am I blind? Why does it hurt to have my eyes open?" Tim called into the echoing area. "It's like I'm staring at an arc welder no matter where I look!"

"Ow! That is *it*; both of you get on the ground! If I get kicked or stepped on *one* more time, I'm gonna start throwing fire around!" Terra promised the two of them. "Joe, how do we get out of here?"

"There should be a..." Joe thought through the blueprints that had etched themselves into his mind, "trapdoor! It should be to the right of where we landed, check along the wall and see if you can find the handle; it opens by spinning it, not by lifting or lowering it!"

If they could have seen themselves crawling across the floor scrabbling for any change in the perfectly flat floor, they would have been laughing. As it was, they were getting a bit frustrated. Terra was the first to find a seam in the otherwise flawless floor, and soon after that, she had found the handle. The others had to crawl toward her voice, hoping that she didn't fall through and leave them lost again.

There was a smooth **whirr*, and they felt an area open up. "There is a ladder. Try and find that; otherwise, it's only about seven feet down." After saying this, he pulled himself into the opening and fell the distance. His jumping skill allowed him to land correctly, but he was still having a hard time seeing anything. He healed himself just to make sure he wasn't blind and waited for the others to come down the ladder. Not able to direct them for obvious reasons, he wasn't able to tell Terra that her foot was in the wrong spot.

"**Oof**!" Air exploded from Tim's mouth as Terra crashed down on him, taking him to the ground but saving her from an awkward fall. As they got up, Terra began to apologize, but Tim stopped her with an easy, "If you *really* want to make it up to me, let me take you out to dinner the next time you are in Ardania."

"Um. Alright, but you should know that I'm a vegetarian." Terra was grinning at Tim, even though she couldn't see the crestfallen look on his face.

"Of course she is." Joe chuckled quietly. The next part was said a bit louder, "And she goes *jogging* in the morning, Tim."

"I'm willing to look past that," Tim proclaimed grandly, snickering at Joe and the silent fury he could feel building from Terra. "If she will look past our terrible humor and pick which restaurant to go to. I have no idea which of them have good vegetarian meals."

Joe moved over to the base of the ladder and spun a small wheel. The light from above rapidly vanished, but Joe left the door open a smidgen. It was more than enough to see by, but it still took a minute for all the spots in their vision to vanish. "Did you know that as the owner and creator of this building, I can open or shut almost anything in the entire structure with a mental command? This is the *only* door, trapdoor, or hidden wall I can't. No idea why. There's no lock on it; the trapdoor just needs to be opened and shut by hand."

"Which way is out?" Terra inquired, looking at the circular room they were in.

"Down," Joe pointed at the spiral staircase hidden from her view as he spoke. "No elevator, and of course, we are at the very top." They started going down the stairs, showing that the pillar they were in actually consisted of two pillars, an outer one and an inner pillar which the stairs wrapped around. Ten minutes of descending later, they came to a door. "Here we go. You guys want to make a grand entrance?"

"Sure?" Tim answered with uncertainty. Joe grinned and closed his eyes. The inner pillar began to glow, and it appeared that the entire thing was glass or something very close. Light shown down from above into it, illuminating the entire thing. It kept getting brighter and brighter, so Joe motioned for them to open the door and get out. The door swung open into a silent room where almost two hundred people were focused on the suddenly brightly lit area of the building. The entire structure had been almost fully dark, and people had been worried about finding their way out.

Joe stepped forward and cleared his throat before proclaiming, "Everyone… we *did it*!" Cheers broke out among the crowd–some confused as they were still groggy from being unconscious–and a bunch of people rushed forward to chat with the various silhouetted figures. Joe commanded the door behind them to shut and lock, and it vanished seamlessly into the stone. He glanced at the pillar behind himself, pleased to note that the light from the inner glass was only blazing out of mystical symbols and lines, and near the ceiling were swirling ritual circles that now also allowed light through. Just cool. It looked so… *magical.*

Joe set the buff of the building to 'anyone' for now and laughed aloud as a wave of silence followed. After reading the notification, people ran off to train instead of partying. An odd but understandable shift. He looked over at his companions and nodded, then let them know that there were a few things he needed to check on. He walked off with a wave, heading to the area that currently only he could access, the Ritual Hall. He wanted no interruptions; it was time to specialize.

A small section of the floor lifted as he approached it, revealing a hidden ramp leading downward, and once again, he thought about how cool this building was proving to be. Joe walked down the tunnel which spiraled a few times before ending. He would have been confused as to his location, but the blueprints ingrained in his mind let him know *exactly* where he was at all times. Walking into a huge and empty room, he gave a mental command, and the entire thing *shifted.* Now he was on top of a pyramid, sitting on a throne. Grandiose? Yes. Needed? Not really. It was a big moment, though! Joe settled in and opened his specialization tab with an expression burning with excitement.

Congratulations! You have met the requirements to further advance your class or choose to walk another path that you feel suits you better. You do not need to specialize now, but know that each level you gain could have had the bonuses of your specialization applied.

After reading that, Joe realized why Tatum had set his level ahead by one. He cursed softly; he could have gained... *something,* some kind of bonus. He needed to see what he gave up. He read on.

Here are the higher classes you have attained the requirements for. Some simple details are provided; click on them for more explanation.

Abyssal Mage: Powerful elemental darkness magic. Dark creature summoning.

Archcleric++: An enhanced, more powerful version of the Archcleric Class. All bonuses and abilities increased by a large amount.

Coven Ritualist: Large-scale magics become more powerful.

Dark Ritualist: More effective anti-personnel rituals.

Eldritch Ritualist: Access to otherworldly, twisted rituals designed to warp the mind and use the lives of others to empower rituals.

Enchanting Ritualist: Greater effectiveness of enchantments and buffs placed on an individual or item.

Micro Ritualist: Small, singular effects are vastly improved.

Overhealer: Able to heal allies or damage enemies with healing power.

Psychomaster: Change the minds of others. By force.

Research Ritualist: Creation of rituals and ritual effects is easier.

''Rituarchitect'*': Create powerful structures for boosts and defense. Shift places of power.*

Scripture Ritualist: Single use simple rituals on paper are 90% faster to create and activate.

Waritualist: Large-scale attack rituals are easier to learn, create, and use.

Witch Hunter: Extra damage against Mages, bonus mana burn, magic resistance.

"Nice lineup here," Joe muttered appreciatively. "Betcha money that half of them only appeared because my titles are better than their own requirements. Fairly certain I know what I'm getting, but I want more information on… you, you, and… this one." Joe opened a few for more information, and while reading them, tried hard to gauge their rarity. It took a minute of staring greedily, but one by one, the information appeared.

Eldritch Ritualist (Unique). This class grants you access to twisted rituals designed to warp the mind and use the lives of others to empower rituals. Focusing on the sacrifice of creatures ranging from pigeons to dragons, the path of the Eldritch is a brutal shortcut to power. All are excited to see the Eldritch work for them, and all fear the inevitable corruption it leads to. Automatically grants the ritual 'Overturn Graveyard' and the knowledge of how to properly sacrifice any type of creature. Per two class levels: +4 Wisdom, +2 Intelligence.

''Rituarchitect'*' (Artificially Artifact): Mana is the source of all rituals in this realm, and you have found a way to use mana to create* permanent *effects. Not only are you able to create powerful structures for boosts and defense, by taking this class, you automatically learn a ritual to scan any structure and create a blueprint ritual to help you make your own version. The creation of these buildings can shift places of power, creating wellsprings of mana over time. Per two class levels: +3 Wisdom, +2 Perception, +3 Intelligence, +2 Dexterity (Artificially Artifact bonus).*

Waritualist (Artifact): Standing behind your army and working large-

scale magics is the trademark of the Waritualist. Whether you are enhancing all *of your allies or dropping meteorites on your foe, you instantly become the single greatest contributor to any war effort. Automatically grants the rituals 'Boost All' and 'Low-Orbit Drop'. Per two class levels: +4 Wisdom, +2 Perception, +4 Intelligence, +2 Constitution.*

These were amazing. In terms of pure stats, Waritualist was the clear choice. It was also the highest *actual* rarity, and the rituals that came with it were pretty freaking cool. Joe clicked on 'Boost All' to get the information, and it told him that this spell would increase all stats of allies in a kilometer by *fifteen* percent. 'Low-Orbit Drop' seemed to be the little brother of a meteor spell, dragging debris and such from orbit and dropping it on the targeted location. He *itched* to take this class.

He took a deep, calming breath. Eldritch was out for sure; he had no plans, currently, to kill off others just to save costs on his rituals. Also, the ritual it provided made a bunch of uncontrollable undead. He would get experience for everything *they* killed, but it was possible that he would be on the menu. Even with the risks, it was quite honestly a tempting class. Joe could see how easily it could corrupt, how easy it would be for him to gain levels. If that were his goal… but luckily for the unsuspecting citizens of Ardania, it wasn't his *only* goal.

Frankly, the ability to make a blueprint and ritual for *any* building was incredibly exciting. His guild could start building a city and stuff it full of *Mythical* buildings. Sure, he would need to *find* a few of those first and scan them, but this would make them a superpower over time. Finding the resources would be a chore, but it was doable! Besides, time was something Joe had in spades. He was a digital entity now. The thought of creating something permanent instead of only ever making war was what decided it for him though. Selecting Rituarchitect as his specialization, Joe braced for the painful changes he was sure would occur.

You have chosen a specialization! Since you are now the only living Rituarchitect, the rarity of the class is Artificially Artifact. Being the first comes with benefits! You gain an additional +2 Dexterity per two class levels due to the rarity increase (Already shown in class description), and you are granted the ritual 'Architect's Fury'. All benefits from base class remain. This class gains experience by scanning buildings as well as building them with the assistance of rituals. Other rituals created and used may also give experience. The skill 'Ritual Magic' can no longer be increased with skill points! The increased cross-class skill cost has been removed; I hope you've been grabbing as many skills as possible! Good luck on your adventure, young Rituarchitect!

Withheld skill experience gained!

Skill increased: Ritual Magic (Journeyman VI). You are now stepping into areas that none have trodden in long centuries. As a Journeyman in ritual magic, you are able to teach Novice Ritualists effectively. Each tier of rituals up to and not including Journeyman are now faster to create, starting with 60% faster Novice rituals and decreasing in speed by 10% per tier.

Did that last message mean that Student rituals were thirty percent faster to make correctly? Neat. Joe opened his eyes and glanced around. No blood, pain, or crippling regret. This was a happy change of pace! He thought about the ritual he had just gained and was pleasantly surprised to notice that it appeared in his mind crisp and clear, though he was a bit disappointed to see that it was only the scanning ritual. He had thought it was a bonus ritual. One of the best things for him was the fact that there was now no cross-class increase in skill cost. He had wondered why it was specifically stated in his class that he could learn any skill when it seemed that *everyone* had the ability to do that in one form or another. Turns out that it was just a hint about specializing.

He opened his character sheet to take a look at the changes. Joe made a couple of quick adjustments to his sheet; he figured that he didn't need all the details on the breakdown of mana and stamina anymore, and he was getting sick of seeing them.

Name: Joe 'Tatum's Chosen Legend' Class: Mage (Actual: Rituarchitect)
Profession: Scholar (Actual: Occultist)
Character Level: 10 Exp: 55,599 Exp to next level: 10,401
Rituarchitect Level: 1 Exp: 0 Exp to next level: 1,000

Hit Points: 190/190
Mana: 1578/1578
Mana regen: 17.55/sec
Stamina: 165

Characteristic Raw score (Modifier)

Strength: 19 (1.19)
Dexterity: 26 (1.26)
Constitution: 24 (1.24)
Intelligence: 59 (2.09)
Wisdom: 58 (2.08)
Charisma: 23 (1.23)
Perception: 39 (1.39)
Luck: 26 (1.26)
Karmic Luck: +1

"Looking good, if I do say so myself." Joe thought for a few seconds about his stats. "I bet there is someone out there that grinds stat points exclusively. I bet there are a *lot* of people doing that, actually." He decided not to share his stats with others anymore because he was sure it would start a long rant about how he didn't 'maximize his character'. Sure, but he'd get there *eventually*. There were things happening! There were quests to complete, legends to research! He shook his head at the imaginary argument with people that might not exist, deciding to go do things that mattered.

CHAPTER THIRTY-FOUR

There was one more thing that he needed to do before he could go off looking for quests or other people to harass. Following the blueprints in his mind, he went toward the temple area of this building. He needed to dedicate the place of worship to Tatum, and the building would gain protections or extra effects. It was a nice, simple way to-

Joe's jaw dropped as he entered the temple. There was a person on their knees in front of the main altar. "-and so, great lord of fire and wrath, I hereby dedicate this temple-"

"*Hey*!" Joe's furious shout shattered the cleric's concentration, and a startled squeak erupted from his mouth.

"What? What are you doing?" the unknown cleric stammered, climbing to his feet. "I was just about to bless this entire building!"

"It's taken care of." Joe sent a command to the building, and an invisible wave of force picked the cleric up and deposited him outside of the temple. There were a few shouts of confusion and fear, but he landed safely and simply couldn't walk any closer. He tried, and it was like he was walking against a hurricane-force wind. Eventually, he simply sat and waited for something, staring through the large open area at Joe.

"That was *far* too close," Joe huffed as he walked up to the altar area. He placed his hands on it and said, "I dedicate this temple to Occultatum." Simple, no fluff, hard to interrupt.

You have found an unguarded, unassigned, mid-sized temple! Would you like to convert the main shrine to a place of power for Occultatum, the god of hidden and forbidden knowledge? Yes / No.

Joe selected 'yes', and a non-existent bell tolled in the air above him. A breeze came from the altar as it began to deform and shift, changing from a simple yet huge stone block into a book with shifting and mysterious characters playing across the open pages. Joe imagined his robe fluttering in the breeze... wait, that was gone. His hair fluttering in the breeze... Joe clenched his teeth and seethed silently. Not only was he bald and robe-less, but he literally *sparkled* when he had his magical protections activated. This game... *whatever*. Refocus!

The entire temple shifted, the amazing building they were in facilitating the transformation easily. Joe felt a *slight* reduction in his personal mana, but it was easily regenerated and replaced. The walls gained shifting shadows that hinted at maps and information, and the floor sank around the altar and created a moat-like channel that collected dark water which began pouring from the 'book'. Overall, the area became dark, mysterious, and exciting. Joe was *very* impressed by Tatum's choices of interior decoration.

Mid-sized temple converted! Beyond the main dedication, this temple can have up to four lesser altars in it dedicated to different deities. They can offer different boosts to the temple and act as interceptors to anyone attempting to wrest control of the main altar. The smaller altars must *be converted before the first in the event of an attack; this forces the deity of that shrine to act on your behalf lest they lose overall power.*

The Grand Ritual Hall has gained protectors! Four Divine Juggernauts have spawned within the temple! New effects have been added to the Hall: Knowledge Nova, Assimilation.

Knowledge Nova: The Grand Ritual Hall has been filled by a deity that is not content with waiting *for knowledge to be found. At the cost of devoting the building's mana to this spell, an active scan will be initiated from the top of the building. A wave of mana will ripple out, scanning anyone in its area of effect. Each time this happens, it will ignore anything that has not changed from the last scan, allowing the scan to reach further. This spell can be activated manually but will automatically activate whenever the building's mana is at its maximum. Scan range determined by amount of mana devoted.*

Assimilation: No longer does someone need to offer *their class information to the structure. Now, anyone entering the area of effect of this spell will automatically add all information needed to gain any classes they may have unlocked. This is a passive effect, and only tier-four or higher classes have a chance to notice its usage. This spell will also be a part of the spell 'Knowledge Nova' when it is used.*

"Oh, boy." Joe wasn't sure whether to laugh or panic. "*That* could be trouble." He looked over at the Juggernauts that had appeared, completely enthralled by their appearance. Standing eight feet tall with matte black armor covered in shifting, glowing runes, these beings certainly *looked* the part of an unstoppable force.

"Awaiting assignment," the deep, nearly demonic voice echoed from the depths of a helmet, the glowing purple light shining through the eye-slit turning the pale Rituarchitect lavender.

Joe coughed, hiding the fact that he was just trying to snap his mouth closed. "Right! Um, two of you stay and guard the temple. Anyone may enter, but slay all attempting to convert this altar. One of you guard the entrance to the building and the other… um, I guess *also* go to the entrance to the building. Feel free to slay anyone who attacks you, but if possible, simply subdue them and keep them contained until I arrive."

The beings gave no acknowledgment, simply moving to their new posts. Tatum's voice came into Joe's ear, "Nice job with the building! It kinda looks like a giant egg. Did you design it that way, or was that the Sage's design?"

"That's how it came. *Way* too advanced for me to mess with," Joe admitted into the air.

"At least you know your limits." There was a pause before Tatum spoke again, "Oh! This design allows for an easy transition into a Grandmaster working or a Legendary structure, as you call it. Very nice. The original building used five times the amount of resources it actually needed, just so it could be upgraded for next to nothing... comparatively. Most likely the very best decision you could have possibly made with that boon, but *I* am exhausted. If you could have the building divert ten percent of the resources generated to me—not money, just mana, stamina, health and such—it would help rebuild my power."

"Sure, let me..." Joe opened the menu and set up that option, Tatum highlighting the sections needed for easy use. "Done. What about that cleric impatiently waiting over there? Should we let him use one of the lesser altars?"

"God of fire and wrath, huh?" Tatum chuckled aloud, the sound making the floor rattle. "That'd make you pretty popular with berserkers and the like. He doesn't get many clerics; most of his devotees are raging fighters or vindictive assassins. Probably smart for you to get on his good side; it'll protect you from some nasty characters. Sure, bring him in! He'd also help balance the temple, giving fire and heat to counter the dark and water. A good fit, if he wants it. Good luck, I'm off!"

The silence stretched for a second, but then Joe allowed the other cleric access again. The man walked forward with a resigned look, stopping a few feet from Joe.

A champion of an unaligned deity has entered the Grand Ritual Hall's temple! Prepare to defend what is yours!

"Heh. I got a notification asking if I wanted to try and take over the temple, but I would need a *raid* group to fight off *those* things. I'm Crim, nice to meet you. I was a *little* upset at first before I realized that you were the guy that hired my guild in the first place. Then I felt a little bad that I tried to steal the temple out from under you. I *really* thought I was doing you a favor, my bad." Crim blushed crimson, making Joe wonder if that was where his name came from.

"Hey, Crim, not an issue. Actually, thanks, I guess? It *would* have been nice if I didn't already have plans for it. How did you get into the Mage guild? I thought they only took, well, Mages," Joe awkwardly responded.

"I have both the Mage and Cleric class, *really* great for generating mana. Doubles my mana capacity." Crim smiled at Joe, who had a knowing look on his face. "Listen, there are more altars in here, right? Can I…?"

"Already approved by my deity," Joe confirmed for him, making a sweeping gesture at the unused stone blocks around the room in the four cardinal directions. Crim walked over to one, and a minute later, a wash of flame came over the area, turning the altar into a blazing brazier that released blue flames. Sconces appeared on the wall, and the chilly room heated up to a pleasant temperature.

Rudimentary pantheon created! You have created an alliance with another deity! 15% of all devotions to the subordinate deity in this zone will go toward growing Tatum's power! Guardian Juggernauts power increased by 10%! Building's mana generation increased by 5%! Make sure not to start fights with the devotees of this deity; you will lose favor very *quickly if you do. New reputation with Tommulus, deity of fire and wrath: Reluctantly friendly.*

"Solid increases!" Joe smiled at Crim and thanked him, deciding to leave the building and look at it from the outside. It took a few minutes of walking to get near the exit; this place was *huge*. When he got out and saw the building from the outside, he had to snort. It *did* look like a giant black egg with a lighthouse sitting on top. Looks didn't matter though… right?

"That is a giant eyesore," Jaxon cheerfully stated as he walked up to him. "Hi there, Joe! Glad you are back in the guild and reassigned as our leader! The others were a touch miffed that you left without contacting us, but I'm sure they'll get over it."

Unsure of what to say—and feeling horribly embarrassed—Joe followed Jaxon back to his party and apologized profusely, needing to explain the entire situation as well as where they now fell in the hierarchy. That is, how they were essentially outside of it. There was a bit of residual anger, but to Joe's great relief, the issue was mostly dropped. He was sure they had already said what they needed to, just not to him. He started off the day by paying them their salary which was listed in the guild tab. That helped, he was sure.

Poppy tried to break the tension by changing the subject, "Joe, did you know that everyone who participated in making that building also unlocked their magic stat? Mana and such?"

Joe latched onto this conversation like a drowning man grabbing a door. "That's great! I bet I'll have no shortage of volunteers next-"

Like a person already on the floating door and pushing away the drowning man, Bard let his hopes die. "They also told everyone exactly how much it hurt. Said t'were like acid cuttin' inta their bones for a half hour."

"*Acid* on bones? So wasteful!" Jaxon cried in outrage.

"People are so dramatic." Joe heaved a sigh and looked around at his group. "Guys, I'm really sorry about that; I didn't mean to leave you hanging like I did. I should have at least come to talk with you first before running off in a tantrum."

"Yeah," Alexis chimed in. "Don't... um... don't worry so much. It wasn't *that* long, and we... got you a present when we saw that you became our leader again, so we aren't *that* mad."

"Alexis! That's not how you build the tension!" Poppy chided her, making Bard glare at him. "You need to make him squirm a bit and get really *worried*! Don't *lead off* with the present!"

There was a moment of silence, so Jaxon jumped in, "So anyway, we got you this!" Poppy gave a small shriek of frustration and stamped his foot as Jaxon handed over a long staff with a purple orb at the top of it.

Mystic Theurge Staff (Ironwood) (Special: Dual Class). Mystic Theurges place no boundaries on their magical abilities and find no irreconcilable paradox in devotion to the arcane as well as the divine. This staff helps to unite their power. Effect: Adds 10-20 blunt damage on strike. -12% cast time when casting either Cleric or Mage spells. Halves penalty for using cross-class (Mage or Cleric) skills. Note: This is a two-handed item, and only one spell may be cast at a time using it.

"This is *so* amazing!" Joe exclaimed happily while turning the staff to look at every angle of it. "What is this rarity? Does that mean you can't use it unless you have the two classes it works for?"

"Yes, which is why it is so rare. No one usually bothers to make them because Mages typically don't also get the Cleric class." Alexis walked over and motioned for Joe to hand her his scepter. He did, and with a tweak of her fingers, she undid his taglock augment and clipped it onto the staff under the orb before handing both back. Her expertise allowed her to shift augments like that without reducing their durability or effectiveness. "Also, it can hold up to four augments. I'd recommend finding a few more if you plan to hold onto this."

"It's too much. Thank you all." Joe looked around, feeling even worse about leaving without an explanation. "What can I do to-"

Guild Alert! The Kingdom of Ardania has issued a call to battle! The Wolfmen have been spotted hurriedly gathering in the north and seem to be targeting a town newly returned to the Kingdom's control! Though you have a quest for this, the quest has now become compulsory: All Noble Guilds are hereby drafted into the service of the crown! Desertion will add a maximum-tier Warlock title which will take two Title slots. As you read this, all non-noble guilds are being notified of the impending battle and being offered a quest to form up and attack the enemy. Time until start of assault: 168:21.

Alert! A message from the King! Cease all other activities! Alert!

A calm voice spoke, and it seemed that every human in the game heard him as though the King were speaking directly to them, "People of Ardania, hear my words. The Wolfman hordes have begun to assemble, far sooner than we were expecting. There are multiple contributing factors, but the main issue causing them to prepare their attack is the fact that they have lost a large portion of their civilians to creatures transformed by some form of dark magic over the course of ten nights."

There was a pause to allow the information to sink in. "The Wolfmen know that they are on the verge of starvation. They lost most of their workers, their cattle, and a large portion of their stored food. Morale for the average Wolfman is at an all-time low, and all they have remaining are fighters. They will be desperate, vicious, and unrelenting. But! Now we have a chance that we have not had in decades."

"Their monarch has appeared and plans to join the battle. If he is defeated by one of you, we will grant a tract of land and a title of nobility to the person or guild who slays him as well as five thousand platinum coins to establish their Noble line. The Wolfmen's likely destination will be given to you... now. Good luck, and know that you will be joined by the finest warriors the Kingdom has to offer." The words of the King seemed to echo in the area, but as they faded, other conversations began. True to his word, the location appeared in their vision. Tiny crosshairs on his map covered the marker that showed the town where Joe was standing, making him feel like a sniper was staring at his entire guild.

Even after taking a moment to think about the ritual that he had redirected back onto the Wolfmen and wondering if it were the cause of so much death for them, Joe was the first to break the silence, "I guess we know what we are doing next."

CHAPTER THIRTY-FIVE

"Alright everyone, calm down!" Aten called to the assembled guild members. "It looks like we only have a little over a week before we get attacked, so we need to hit the ground running. This is *endgame* level stuff going on, so we need to throw everything we have at these animals! *Mess with the best…*!"

"Die like the rest!" the waiting people shouted the end of the guild's motto in reply then broke up to meet with their direct leaders. You could practically see Aten's command skill increasing as he smiled and watched his people move to their tasks. The guild Commander caught Joe's eye and motioned him over, much to his relief. Joe had been worried that his team would be asking questions of him that he didn't have answers for.

"Joe, thank goodness. Anything you can do to help? Some kind of line or circle magic you can use to obliterate the incoming Wolfmen?" Aten sounded desperate though he kept his mask of confidence on. This was a side of him Joe hadn't seen before, and unfortunately for him… Joe was completely unable to think of anything he could use on a large scale to help out even a little. Thoughts of digging wells or pits all over the place crossed his mind, but it was completely impractical.

"I'm *really* sorry to have to tell you this, big guy, but I've got nothing." Joe was really feeling sick to his stomach with the fact that he could have been a Waritualist right now with literally *stellar* anti-army weaponry… and had instead chosen to fabricate pretty buildings. Could he create a defensive building before the enemy arrived? Joe dismissed this thought after a moment; it was probably too resource intensive for him to complete anything worth building.

"*Really*?" Aten's expression shifted to doubtful. "*You* have nothing you can use to pull our keisters out of the fire? Some random… thing that you found in an ancient ruin somewhere?"

Joe gestured at the giant egg-building they were standing next to. "Most recent acquisition from an ancient ruin, Aten. I have pretty much nothing at all. I'm *all* out of tricks."

Aten tapped his fingertips together for a second as he thought. "Here is how I see it. You run my 'hail Mary' squad, the last resort that insane people listen to; you are my Party Zero. So, your job is *finding* that last resort weaponry; use that *one thing* that no one else would think of or *use* without being desperate. *We* are going to work on defenses and prepare to be overrun by other guilds encroaching on our land. Get going." Aten nodded at him sharply and strolled away, leaving Joe feeling a bit dazed.

Was that… *trust*? He *really* seemed to think Joe could figure something out, and Joe wanted to prove that he deserved that trust. He should rush off and… Aten's leadership skill was messing with him, wasn't it? Hmph. Still, just because he recognized the source didn't mean the message was wrong. Joe walked back to his party and started discussing ways that they could contribute, to mixed results.

"Oh, come *on*, Joe! The Geneva Convention laws don't apply here! I just need a *few* live Wolfmen to perfect the poison recipe, a dozen at the most-" Alexis was cut off as Jaxon jumped in.

"What if you dig really deep *pits* all over the battlefield-"

Bard jumped in, "Let 'em come! They can taste mah axes!"

"Your *singing* would be enough, I bet," Poppy stage whispered 'quietly'.

"Guys, we need something stupidly large scale," Joe interrupted the devolving conversation. "This is supposed to be pretty much the entirety of the Wolfman race on the warpath. Pits aren't going to cover it, and a little poison isn't going to slow them down."

Alexis started speaking with a gleam in her eye, "What about a *lot* of poi-"

"Yes, if you can make it happen. You've got three days to make as much as possible, figure out what you need and get an expense report to the guild." Joe rolled his eyes as she beamed, kissed Bard on the cheek, and ran off. "She's a lot less shy nowadays."

"It's tae influence o' high-charisma people around her constantly. Pulls her out of her shell." Bard watched her fondly until she turned a corner. "She's great."

"I'm glad you get along with your *girlfriend*." Poppy snorted at Bard's glare. "Sorry to say that my abilities don't really add up to much in a large scale. I'd like the next couple of days to work on my skills. If you all haven't noticed, there is a giant bonus of increased skill experience coming off of that building. Add that onto a well-rested bonus, and you're looking at some insane increases."

"Go for it, but try to help out around here if anyone needs you." Joe sent Poppy off with a wave. "Bard?"

"Same thing for me, gonna work on mah skills, try ta eke out some large-scale buffs or debuffs." Bard nodded at Joe, heading off in the same general direction that Alexis had gone. Jaxon cracked his knuckles and started toward a small group of people that were improperly carrying some equipment.

"Wait. No, come back…" Joe's voice trailed off as Jaxon vanished at a sprint. "Alrighty, that covers about everyone, except… me. I guess I'll go… study? Make paper? I don't know.

Or… should I go make this ritual?" He was referring to the ritual 'Architect's Fury', of course. "I do have that other pet project I was working on a while back; I'd love to have 'feather fall'…"

Thinking of the things he wanted to get done spurred on his motivation, and he looked at the various components that he needed in order to make the rituals he wanted to use. For such a high-level ritual, Architect's Fury was surprisingly cheap to use. He needed to make a Student-ranked ritual–four circles–but the only components required beyond a large influx of mana were a mid-to-high grade beast Core and a 'magical blueprint'. Joe was fairly certain that he could learn how to make magical blueprints on his own, but for now, he needed to figure out where he could buy them.

Out of other options and not having any vendors in the area that were selling anything remotely like what he needed, Joe decided to once again head to the city. He started walking toward the shrine but stopped himself and stared back at the egg-shaped Grand Ritual Hall. "I'll bet a dozen gold that there is going to be a fast-travel point in there." He turned and started walking but was knocked to the ground by an unexpected blow to the side that was absorbed by the Exquisite Shell that he kept on at all times now.

"Get up!" Joe looked up to see Sir Bearington standing over him, eyes bloodshot and fur sprouting across his face. "You and I have unfinished bears-ness!"

Joe easily jumped to his feet and glowered at the 'man' who was slowly but obviously regressing into a bear. "Did you come here to finish me off, Bearington? Finish what we started in the dungeon?"

"What? No!" Sir Bearington drew back a few feet, looking a bit flustered. "I also didn't mean to bear you to the ground with such a light tap; I was only attempting to get your attention. No, I… I need your help. My deity, the Lady Spriggan, is beginning to fade. With no shrines, no altars, no positions in a temple and only one champion, her power wanes too fast. I am here to *beg* for a position in your temple."

"Sure, Bearington. How about this: we'll make a quest out of it! All you need to do to get a position in the temple is go around and ask each guild member if they would like to have you there. I'm sure they will ask for reasonable favors in return for their vote of confidence." Joe had no sympathy for this man-bear.

Sir Bearington growled deeply, and more fur sprouted across his face. "I have no time for these games. The time I spent transformed in the instant dungeon re-awoke my bestial self, and if I have no succor granted by the Lady Spriggan, my mind will once more become unbearably simple. I *will* revert to a not-so-simple animal. The form you saw in the dungeon is my true one. Do you wish an enemy of me?"

"So, let me see if I have this correct. You are threatening to become a raid boss in the middle of a cluster of guilds, all of whom are looking for *any* kind of method to gain a *bit* more experience or difficult-to-find materials? You are saying this to a champion who would likely gain a huge amount of favor and experience for your death?" Joe shook his head, and at his words, Bearington's face fell into frightened contemplation. Joe could see that he had shaken Bearington's confidence and made him realize how untenable his situation was. "Instead of threats, tell me *why* I would want you, or your deity, around my people."

Sir Bearington's eyes glazed over, and a green light shone in them. His voice, when he next spoke, was far more feminine and powerful, "In return for aid… I can offer you information that you need, a way for you to turn the tide of the upcoming battle. As it stands, you *will* be overrun. The timer you see is only the *main* portion of the Wolfman armies. The fastest of them, those that will test your defenses, will be here in three days."

"I know your true status, *Rituarchitect*, and I am willing to part with knowledge that you *will* need. Beyond that, my power over nature, limited as it is for the time being, will help to balance the temple further. Water, darkness, fire… rage. Those are the current aspects of this location. All that is needed for this place to turn into a center devoted to evil is a few evil acts to be performed, and corruption will swallow this area. With war looming… evil acts are sure to follow. Your deity may even become an aspect of the *eldritch* instead of darkness. *My* influence will turn the aspects from the current path and combine to bless this area as a center of natural law, survival of the fittest empowering natural growth and defenses. Not to mention that you recently tried to kill me, and this would go a long way toward restoring my good will toward you."

Now it was Joe's turn to contemplate the information he had gained. "What is it that you are offering me directly? I admit the other portions sound good, but I am sure that all I would need to do to find a cleric of a more *powerful* nature deity is to take a short trip to the city."

Sir Bearington's body sighed. "I offer you the location of a manual. It contains a ritual that is simple in theory but was one of the greatest weapons of Ritualists long ago. This tome details the method to turn any *spell* into a *ritual* with the same effect. You want a warrior to throw fireballs? Hand him the completed ritual. You want to enchant weapons? Create a ritual zone that-**ack**" Sir Bearington dropped to the ground, coughing blood. "I have said too much without the needed fulfillment of obligations. Now is the time to choose, Rituarchitect."

"Do I really have a choice?" Joe shook his head in frustration. "Save your power for now, Spriggan. Let's go get you a shrine." Joe helped Sir Bearington to his feet, or at least, he tried. The man was several hundred pounds and slowly growing larger. Together, they walked into the Grand Ritual Hall, making their way directly to the temple. Though there were a few people that watched them curiously, everyone was mainly focused on their training or assigned tasks.

Sir Bearington sprawled on the unadorned altar, scrambling for purchase as his strength began to fail him. He heaved a few deep breaths then turned his gaze on Joe. A capillary in his left eye had burst, filling the sclera with bright red blood. "We are… almost too late. I have no power. Please, donate your mana to make this work."

Would you like to use your mana to fuel the transformation of this unused shrine into a shrine for deity: Spriggan? As no power will be coming from the champion or deity, four thousand mana is needed over the span of two minutes. Yes / No.

"Sneaky little…" Joe snarled in impotent rage and accepted the prompt. Mana began to flow out of him at a manageable rate, his regeneration easily able to keep pace with the power draw. First, the altar melted away. Then a tiny and detailed forest seemed to grow from the puddle of liquid stone. Joe wasn't impressed until he saw that there were moving animals and that the trees seemed to sway in a breeze. It was a tiny forest, replicated to the smallest detail.

A feeling of *awe* in the air seemed to diminish. No… not 'awe', something… *darker*. The patterns in the temple became more wholesome, a feeling like being out in untamed nature filling the open space. Not *safety* exactly, but no longer a strangely overwhelming pressure. It was easier to breathe, possibly due to the plants that were growing around the room seemingly without rhyme or reason. The dark water flowing from Tatum's book-altar now had a purpose, and small trees sprouted along the banks of the moat and small river that had formed.

Sir Bearington began to rapidly shrink, returning to a fully normal human form over the course of ten seconds. He looked around the room and nodded solemnly. "Thank you. We are in your debt."

Joe cocked his head to the side. "I think that's the first time you have ever spoken without slipping a bear pun into your speech."

"Those foul *puns* were a sign of the Lady Spriggan's power waning. It was unbea- no, it was *terrible*." Sir Bearington seemed to fully relax. "Many thanks, Joe. Thank you for allowing us into your burgeoning pantheon. In terms of additional defenses, all of the plants in here have poison in the thorns and the small trees are very young treants. They will grow *very* strong and durable over time but for now must be protected. *I* will also be here to protect the area and will retain my mind during transformations now."

"I am glad that this area is better protected, but while I hate to be abrupt I *do* need to get moving. Can you please get me the location of that tome I was promised?" Joe felt a bit awkward, but… there *was* an army approaching. Sir Bearington held out a beseeching hand toward the altar, and with a flash of green light, a small map appeared in his palm.

"That will direct you to the book. I must pass on a warning to you: it is well hidden and protected. Getting to this information will *not* be an easy task." Bearington's face was severe, his voice grave, "Truly, following this map may lead you to a fate worse than death."

"All the more reason to get moving," Joe spoke these words with confidence, not with arrogance. "I need to speak to my guild lea- um, Commander. My party members, as well. Thank you, and good luck. Protect our interests well."

"No one will steal a shrine from *me* again," Bearington stated with a pointed glance. Joe chuckled nervously. At least Bearington's apparent lack of mana explained why the shrine hadn't been re-converted or fixed up.

Now to get back to the original reason he had come to this place. Joe sat in the center of the room and closed his eyes, listening to his instincts as best as he could. He felt a small pull as his Hidden Sense kicked in, and he slowly stood and walked with his eyes closed. When the tickle in his mind was almost infuriating, he tripped over something and fell face first into the dark water in the room. His eyes popped open, and in the brief moment he was submerged, he saw a runic pattern he had become increasingly familiar with. After getting his head out of the water and taking a breath, he went back under and activated the fast travel point. It appeared on his list of travel locations, making him smile. His travel range was growing nicely.

Skill increased: Hidden Sense (Beginner III). Trust those mystical senses! They'll never get you in trouble, I'm sure of it! Seems that closing your eyes is extra effective; do that extra often in dangerous areas!

Sloshing his way out of the water, he quickly went to talk to everyone he needed to, explaining both where he was going and to be watchful of preemptive Wolfman Assaults. By the time he was back in the temple, he was mostly dry and ready to go. The location he needed to go was deep in Ardania, far deeper in the city than he had ever needed to go before. Joe took one last excited breath and vanished.

CHAPTER THIRTY-SIX

The trip to the location of the tome had *not* gone as he had wanted. Not. Even. Close. As he walked closer, the map he had been given proved itself to be magical. It zoomed in on his location, but just as he got close to finding the location the map was pointing to, he was forcibly stopped.

"Halt, citizen, or die where you stand! What are you doing here?" Thirteen pikes were leveled at him, most pointing at his heart, but the taller people had their weapon a little too close to his eyes for comfort. Joe, having just walked through what he assumed was a park in the city, was taken completely by surprise.

"Wha… where is *here*? Isn't this a park? Who are *you*?" Joe stammered and coughed from a sudden attack of nerves.

"Another Traveler. *Of* course. Citizen, you are approaching the local prison dungeon of the Kingdom of Ardania. Unless you have business here or are a prisoner awaiting trial by the Royal Family, you are to vacate the premises *immediately*." The man was obviously a Royal Guardsman, a cut above the city guard in terms of power, equipment, training, and authority.

"Sheesh, almost vacated my *bladder* when those fancy spears came out of nowhere!" Joe shuddered as he took a step back. "I'm leaving, sorry to bother you. I had no idea. Thank you for the warning."

No response came to his words, but now Joe was faced with a serious issue. There was something in there that he needed, and he was uncertain if he would ever be able to find it elsewhere. Something the guard had said, though... Joe's face fell as he realized exactly what he needed to do to get into the dungeon. He took a deep breath and started walking. Before following through on his plan, Joe needed to accomplish a few *other* tasks beforehand. Retracing his steps out of the center of the city, he went to one of his favorite places, the library.

Boris was inside, pouring over a large book as Joe opened the door. The intrusive light made Boris look up, and he cracked a smile. "Joe! Our most recent addition to the ranks of the Scholars, how can I help you? I hear that it is thanks to *your* efforts that our library has recently grown in power and breadth of knowledge! You had the Mage's College grant us research privileges as a reward when you could ask for *anything*? When we heard that..." He wiped at his eyes to clear away a forming tear.

Boris stood and walked toward Joe, actually giving him a very uncomfortable hug. "You have no idea what you have done for us, but I can tell you right now that you have earned a hefty reward. This has been approved by the entire council, so get ready for a few ranks in your profession!"

You have gained 8308 experience toward your profession! You are now a level nine scholar! Having attained this level, books up to rarity 'Special' are available to you! Reputation with Scholars increased by 2617! You have reached the reputation rank of 'Friend'. You have gained two items: Blank Bestiary and weapon mod 'Classify'.

Blank Bestiary: This is a magical book that stores information on any Classified creature. Not the 'protected information' type, but the phylum and such. This book can also absorb other non-magical bestiaries to gain their information.

Weapon mod 'Classify': Equipping this to a weapon will allow you to

Classify a creature. A simple melee attack with the weapon will scan the creature, giving a linked Bestiary basic information. Multiple attacks will increase the detail while killing the creature will do a full scan of their body.

"That's... wow." Joe gulped as he was handed a thin book and a small, dangling weapon talisman. "I actually had something for you, as well. I found some information that I think you will *really* appreciate having a chance to study."

"Oh? Do tell." Boris was smiling happily, sure that Joe had already given them all the surprises he was going to. Joe showed him a crooked grin as a long tube appeared from his ring.

"I have the blueprints here for a structure... with *Artifact* rarity." Joe pulled out the blueprint and handed it to Boris who took it with trembling hands and a completely dumbfounded look of astonishment.

"*Artifact*? You are *giving* this to the Scholars?" Boris staggered back to his seat, sitting heavily as he looked over the shifting building plans. "But why? You could sell this for a *fortune*! A Noble title! You could..." Boris shook his head, unable to find the words he wanted to say. "This certainly counts as lost knowledge. I... this is as much as I can approve right now. Take this item. For any more... I need to go see the full council again. Twice in two weeks!"

You have gained 1100 experience toward your profession! You are now a level ten scholar! Profession rank increase! You are now a 'Tenured Scholar'. All scholarly skills increase 20% faster. It will now take a vote of the council for you to lose any scholarly privileges. Permanent gains: +5 intelligence, +5 perception.

Your true profession has reached level ten! Profession rank increase! 'Occultist' has been upgraded to 'Arcanologist'! You can now see the truth of material in books up to the 'Master' ranks!

Item gained: Combination Gem (Consumable). Use this gem to instantly combine any skills, negating cost and time to complete. (Bound to Joe)

"A combination gem?" Joe stared at the small, shining gem in the palm of his hand. "What in the world...?"

"They are *fairly* rare," Boris told him in a distracted voice, "too expensive to use routinely; normally, it is far cheaper to simply combine the skills and wait out the time needed. Fairly regularly, though, I have heard of people attempting to combine a dozen or more skills at once, obviously hoping for something amazing. And who wants to spend over a hundred thousand gold on an *attempt*? On an *experiment*? At five thousand gold each, a combination gem is far more palatable. Also, you don't need to use up space in your bag on it; you can store it in the bank and use it at will."

Joe made a strangled noise as he looked at the gem in a new light. If he had gained this at the start of the game and it wasn't bound to him, he would have walked out and sold it to the highest bidder. Now, he recognized the real value it held for someone who could learn *any* skill. With a trembling hand, he stored it in his ring for a rainy day. "This was far more than I was ever hoping for, Boris. Thank you very much, but I shouldn't accept this. I gave that to you as a gift."

"My boy, you may have pushed us into prominence once more. This is far and away less than you deserve, but it is all I can grant." Boris's eyes focused on Joe again. "Oh, by the way, if it is of any interest to you, the Mage's College handed over a large amount of books of spells that no one has been able to cast in decades or centuries. You now have access to them, and I have a feeling that if anyone can learn their secrets… it is you."

"As tempting as that sounds, I will be very busy for quite a few… let's hope only *days*." Joe ruefully chuckled. "Things are about to get not very fun for me. I… I'll see you soon, Boris."

The head librarian watched Joe go with a flicker of worry. What could this practically *immortal* Traveler be worried about? Perhaps it was time for the Scholars to branch out of studying history and see what was happening in the present. Boris touched a communication crystal and was soon engrossed in a conversation with very *interesting* people.

Joe next went to the bank, paying for a safety deposit box and storing everything in it that he thought could get him in trouble. He walked out of the bank in simple clothes; no armor, weapons, or storage ring. Joe *did* have on his Exquisite Shell at the maximum amount of possible mana investment, so he still looked like he was walking in a glittering glass suit. From the bank, he went to the training grounds and began looking for the Captain.

The Captain was in his office, sitting and filling out paperwork with rather poor handwriting. Grumbling as he was interrupted, he looked up and shifted his expression from unpleasant to gleeful in the span of a moment. "Joe! I've been looking for you; I have some *very* fun and exciting news for you!"

"I'm glad, Captain, but I am sadly not here for a happy occasion. I have some things I need to talk to you about." Seeing Joe's serious face, the Captain actually looked a bit... abashed?

"Now, Joe, it's not that bad. Really, this is good for *all* of us. I think that if you just give me a chance, we can-" the Captain was cut off by Joe.

"Sir! I am here to tell you that I *unintentionally* gained a restricted class." Joe's words wiped all emotion from the Captain's face, leaving behind only a cool stare. "I am turning myself in and will *fully* cooperate with whatever needs to be done."

"I... don't think that you actually *understand* what needs to be done." The Captain slowly stood, staring directly into Joe's eyes. "Tell me, lad, *what* class did you get?"

"Psychomancer."

Horror appeared in the Captain's eyes, and his mouth moved wordlessly until he forced a few words out, "What skill did you obtain that *granted* you this class?"

"Mental Manipulation-" as the words crossed his lips, the Captain moved faster than Joe would have believed possible, his sword appearing in his hand and whipping toward Joes neck, "-Resistance," the word tumbled from his numb lips as the sword hit his Exquisite Shell, bouncing away but reducing its protection to dangerously low levels.

"*Resistance*?" The finished skill name seemed to cause the Captain to relax, though Joe remained standing still in wide-eyed horror. How bad was this class that he would be attacked *instantly* and without warning even with a reputation of *ally*? Sheathing his sword, the Captain seemed far less apologetic than Joe felt he should be. "That's… we can work with that. I'll help you, give you a reference and collect references for you. Joe, you need to be escorted to the city's dungeon to await trial. I will try to expedite the trial but… we are at war. You need to be tried by either the King or Queen for this. It might be a while. Possibly a *long* time."

Quest Complete: Please Don't Kill Me. By gaining a Kingdom-Restricted class, you have set yourself up to be an enemy of the Kingdom and, therefore, humanity as a whole. You have found a government official you trusted and turned yourself in. Good for you! I'm thinking lawful neutral is a good descriptor of your personality, boring and bland. Reward: A fair trial by the Monarchs.

Quest Failed: I Do What I Want! You turned yourself in instead of seeking an instructor. Too bad. You could have done great things. Terrible things, yes, but great things nonetheless.

"If you think it'll help, the reason Wolfmen are marching right now is that I *built* an Artifact-ranked building and they want to get control of it. Since I forgot to meet up with my guild leader, I am the only person with permissions for the building right now." Joe was actually kicking himself as he had forgotten to give Aten the ability to run the defenses. Hopefully 'automatic' would suffice.

"That… you *built*… that, yes, that may actually be a little helpful. More than a little, now that I think about it." The Captain reached under his desk and pulled out a bottle filled with amber liquid.

"Stamina potion?"

"Whisky," the Captain corrected him as he poured two glasses full. "I know a few Royal Guards, so I'll try to get you light duty in the dungeon. Healing others and such. It's… it's not a fun place to be, Joe. You did the right thing, but… I need to call in the guards to escort you. Finish your drink quickly. *Guards*!"

"Surprise!" The door burst open, and a lovely lady with copper hair with just a touch of gray in it stepped through the open doorway with a wide smile.

Joe, mid-chug, looked at her and sprayed twenty-year whiskey across the room. A small rainbow appeared as the spray went in front of the window, but due to the circumstances, it wasn't noticed by anyone. "*Mom*?"

CHAPTER THIRTY-SEVEN

The entrance to the dungeon was just ahead, but Joe was still reeling from the revelation that he had just been given. Not only had his *mother* joined the game in a long-term pod to be able to see him more frequently, but she was *dating* the Captain! The conversation replayed in his head once again.

"Joe? Blas? Sweetie, didn't you warn him? I thought that was the whole plan! As soon as you saw him coming, you made me wait in the bedroom!" Joe's mother was looking between the two of them with great concern, but then her eyes squinted and she crossed her arms. "Alright, what's going on here?"

Three guards appeared in the room through the main door, looking at the occupants curiously. The Captain–Blas, apparently–ran his hands through his hair. "Oh, man. This is a little intense so early in the relationship. Guards, I need you to..." He looked at the two people standing next to him and swallowed with great difficulty. His next words were very strained, "I need you to arrest this man and bring him to the dungeon to await trial before a monarch."

The guards all recognized Joe and so were very reluctant to arrest him. They slowly pulled out manacles and clipped them around his shimmering wrists. The metal adjusted to fit more precisely, but Joe could still have easily slipped his hands out of them if he wanted since his Shell stopped them from getting too close to the skin. Joe looked at his mom in wonder and tried to shake some sense into his head. "I'll talk to you soon, Mom! This isn't the Captain's doing; something came up, and I came here for this *exact* reason, okay? He will explain everything, and we'll get this all figured out. It's *so* good to see you."

At that point, Joe had been gently pushed out the door and led to the dungeon. Once again, as they got close, Royal Guards seemed to materialize in a half-circle before them, but this time, they took Joe into custody. One of them also took the instructions that Blas had sent along, nodding in confirmation at the request for light duty and explaining that he had come of his own free will. There was also a whispered conversation that Joe was only able to hear snatches of with his high perception.

"No, really... good guy... *no* beatings... -ing *serious* right now." The guard had an aggrieved look on his face, and his voice got a bit angry. "Just treat him like a healer that is here to help you out of his own free will because that is what he is! He has the health of a ten-year-old; he'll fall apart at the first real attack!" Real confidence booster. That guard should change jobs to being a Bard.

That was all Joe got to hear before the entrance to the dungeon yawned before him, the odd, horizontally elongated opening reminding him of a pair of smiling lips more than anything else. As he was led in, he felt like he was being swallowed whole by a filthy abomination. The obvious looks of readiness on the faces of the Royal Guard surrounding him wouldn't have bothered him... but their gazes were directed outward, not at him. So they were keeping him *safe* from something in the area? Whatever it was didn't appear, and their expressions turned to relaxation as they entered an obviously man-made area. Wooden gates thickly coated in metal closed behind them, and Joe got an unfortunate message.

You have entered a prison colony dungeon! As a prisoner, your respawn location has been automatically set to this fortification. Players are unable to delete their characters while incarcerated. You will be released in: (awaiting trial) hours. Experience gains are halved for prisoners. Reputation gains are halved in the dungeon, reputation losses are tripled.

"Yikes," Joe muttered, earning him a wry, knowing look from one of the guards. If you were unable to delete your character, committing high crimes just became much more *unpalatable*. He needed to warn some of the thief types in his guild when he got out of here. Escorted into one of the nicer buildings, Joe was left standing outside of an ornate office door. The guard that had been given instructions went in, coming out and nodding at him after a few minutes.

"Warden wants to see you. In ya go." The guard held open the door as Joe walked inside. The Warden was sitting behind a desk, fingers steepled as he looked Joe over critically.

The first words out of his mouth were abrupt and no-nonsense, "You are a healer, I'm told? While you are under our tender care, you will be in charge of healing any guards or prisoners that become injured. Are you a journeyman healer yet?"

"Ah, no, sir," Joe hesitantly responded, unsure of the correct way to address the powerful man.

"I see. So you do not have a way to regenerate limbs? That's too bad. Can you do focused healing? Mend bones, clear away poison, or reattach limbs?"

"All of those things to varying degrees," Joe told him plainly. "I don't have too much experience reattaching limbs, but I *can* do it."

"Hm," the Warden responded noncommittally. "You are a Beginner-ranked healer then? That's fine. We will have you start with the prisoners first, in that case. Show us what you can do. Stay out of restricted areas. Don't do stupid things. Try not to make enemies. Get out."

Joe left the room feeling very… *inadequate*. Businesslike, professional, and a powerful intellect, those were the words he would use to describe the Warden. Himself? Joe looked inward and found that he tended to lose sight of the big picture for a short-term gain. He was doing side quests all over the place, and when was the last time he had made a new ritual? What the... Joe's brow furrowed, and he pulled open his active effects tab. He had a debuff, 'cowed'. As soon as he saw it and realized what was happening, the debuff shattered.

High-ranked leadership skill resisted!

Skill increased: Mental Manipulation Resistance (Novice III). You know that sometimes there are good reasons to follow the orders of another, but you just don't care! To anarchy! Onward, buttercup! There's (censored) to spread! Increase this skill to stop yourself from being censored!

Uh-oh. Joe hoped that increasing this skill wouldn't impact his trial. He was taken directly to the infirmary which was *absolutely packed*. In fact, there was a line of groaning people laying on the ground outside of the building. Joe saw a guard being carried, and when they skipped the line and a complaint rang out, another guard peeled off the procession and beat the already injured man to the point that he *couldn't* complain. Guards can do what they want. Message. *Received*.

Joe followed his escort in, and he was introduced to a harried healer. The man in blood-stained white clothes looked annoyed even as he used the opportunity to down a mana potion. The guard explained the situation, and the healer nodded and looked at Joe. "What is it? Something on my face? Go heal people! If you find something outside of your capabilities, call me over. I'll be working with the heroes, not the villains, so don't bother calling me over to save a prisoner. Get moving."

With no other option, Joe went to the front of the lines to get to work. As expected, the shorter line was filled with guards and had triple the amount of healers working in it at any time. Joe got to work healing damaged prisoners, getting into a battle rhythm of healing any life-threatening injuries and ignoring any other type. Broken arm? End of the line. Hole in your chest? Head injury? Deadly poison? Get healed.

By the time the line had been reduced by half, Joe was

mentally exhausted. His eyes darted to the side to check his notifications and widened as he saw what was waiting for him.

Skill increased: Mend (Apprentice III). For breaking into the Apprentice rank, an extra effect has been added! Bones are now twice as easy to repair!

Skill increased: Lay on hands (Apprentice III). As a subskill of Mend, this skill shares the additional effect Mend was granted.

Skill increased: Cleanse (Beginner IX). You sure are clearing out a lot of poison! Did you let your pet poisoner go wild or something?

"You there!" The abrasive healer that had put Joe to work tapped his arm. "I was told you were a *healer*. You're a *cleric*? Get out of this line and come fix up the guard; they need true healing more than *these* animals." He ordered one of the slower healers to go work on prisoners and motioned Joe into his vacated position. Before Joe could comply, he was tackled to the ground and a shiv was mercilessly and repeatedly stabbed into the area over his kidney. Luckily for Joe, his Shell was still in position and the damage was almost entirely negated.

"*You bastard*!" Joe's ear was screamed into. "I have another *month* in here! Do you have *any* idea what-" Joe didn't get to hear any more of the rant because the man was beheaded with a single clean slash. A wash of blood flowed over his Shell and slid off, leaving him clean.

"That's handy." Joe looked at the head on the ground, recognizing it after a moment. "Headshot?"

"That's the last of *him* we'll see for the next twelve hours. Moron. He must be approaching level one by this point." The healer that had been directing things inspected the scalpel he had just used, putting it back into an easily-accessible pocket when he saw no flaws. "You'll get that sometimes, no worries. I'm just glad you have some basic protections. Get back to work."

With Joe's help and seemingly instantly refilling mana pool, the remaining Royal Guard were back to duty within twenty minutes, and the last in the line of prisoners had been sent away about two hours after that. Each 'Lay On Hands' cost two hundred and forty mana, so even though he could heal each person quickly the spell couldn't be used constantly. Joe had gained another rank in his two healing spells, but the increase to Cleanse that he was seeking eluded him.

Joe was looking around for more patients when the healer came back over and started talking, "That's all for today. For *now*, I should say. Go get food, then come back and find a cot to sleep on. We don't make people like you sleep in the common area like the others. I'm told you turned yourself in just because you knew it was the law? Admirable. If more were like you, this Kingdom would be a joyous place indeed. Go."

Joe nodded and started following the stream of exhausted healers to the dining area. When he felt that no one was looking, he pulled a folded paper out of his cheek and glanced at it with mixed feelings. He hadn't been searched when he got here, so he could likely have held onto a few of his more useful items. But, it *had* kept the map safe… ugh. He opened the map, and sure enough, it had updated. There was now a floorplan for the entire dungeon and it–good lord it was three dimensional. The map floated above the page, showing a small room off a main hallway three floors down.

"Ugh," Joe grunted, sounding like a fully constipated man who had just polished off a wheel of brie.

"Right? They overwork us to a *horrible* degree." One of the healers that was walking in the loose formation tapped his hand on Joe's… Shell. "You get used to it, though. Plus, the skill increases are *excellent*, aren't they? Working on people that have a good chance of dying if you mess up, constant work, and the threat of death from all sides all adds up to skill gains out the *wazoo*."

"Don't get much of a chance to chat with other people down here?" Joe inferred with an eye roll.

"Not even close! We get beat for talking, draws in the monsters." The other man showed him a manic smile as guards closed in and gave them both a hefty wallop. Joe didn't flinch, but the other man now had on a creepy smile as he was beaten. "Harder!"

"Don't speak above a whisper and you are okay," another healer leaned into Joe's side and whispered. "He's a bit... off ever since he got a high-powered drop from in here. It's a cursed item called 'The Beard of Charles'. Gives you a big constitution bonus and makes you resistant to the effects of alcohol but switches random things that you are trying to say, kinda like Tourette syndrome. Makes you speak in ways that force you to seek out pain. Now he takes a beating at least once a week when the effect kicks in. I bet he didn't *really* want to say 'harder'." The man chuckled softly.

"Sounds terrible," Joe murmured in reply. "Lot of cursed stuff in here?"

"Yup*pers*. Don't put anything on without getting it checked out first. You get drops in here for, like, no reason. Sneeze too hard? Bam. Specialty item just for you that prevents sneezing when worn but reduces how well you can breathe by a quarter. I'd say ninety percent of any items in here are cursed." The healer spoke a bit too loudly, and a guard showed him his club at high speed. Quiet reigned once more after the meaty thunk.

Joe felt contemplative. Almost no creatures or beings he had fought before now had actually dropped system-generated items. Usually, they had to scavenge what their opponents were wearing or the bodies of their foes directly. Now he was *really* looking forward to seeing what this place had to offer.

CHAPTER THIRTY-EIGHT

Like any other day when he had slept and gone to bed at a reasonable hour, Joe woke up the next morning. While this may seem a bit arbitrary to mention, this time it was an *exciting* awakening. **Thud**. **Thud**. Joe looked at the man standing by his cot with resignation. "Are you trying to beat me with a sock full of soap?"

"Rocks." The man dropped the sock and looked seriously put out. "Well, *that* was a waste of time. Headshot wanted me to beat you up, and I owed him one. I tried; I'm calling it close enough and saying that I paid off the favor. Sorry about that. Nothing personal. See ya."

"And they say people are unreasonable." Joe stood and looked around then called after the inmate. "Where's the coffee?"

"You think we get *coffee* in here? No drugs allowed. Caffeine is a drug."

For the first time, Joe's hands shook and he realized that he was *really* in prison. He gripped his bald head with wild eyes and whispered, "I need to get out of this place. This place is the *abyss*. Abyss?"

"There are a few things you can't say; you should know that by now. The game turns them into the local equivalent. So lack of coffee is what drove it home for you? Odd." The thug started to turn away again but was stopped by Joe's grip on his arm.

"Alright, I need a few answers." Joe stared at the man, fire in his eyes. "Tell me about this place. Why can't people speak loudly outside? What do they do here? How can I bribe guards or the Warden to get me down to the third level?"

"*Third* level? You're out of your *mind*. There are only *two* levels, and even if there *was* a third level, you could never get to it. The reason that we can't speak loudly is that it draws in Shades. Think a shadow that was once a ghost but got lost in the dark too long. They are the only thing in here that just ignore the walls around the camp. They get close and stab your shadow, giving you a shock of nasty corrosive poison somehow. You need spells or enchanted gear in order to kill them. Do you know why the *rest* of us are here? Because we are louder than Mages. They need someone to take the hit so *they* can kill the Shades." The man was spitting mad now.

"And there other things out there?" Joe prompted impatiently.

"Minor annoyances, mainly. They hit hard but are pretty slow. Usually, they only land a hit on ya if you are going around corners, and they manage to surprise you. Dirt elementals, I think they're called. A good blow will blast 'em apart." He shook a bit, reaching for a weapon he didn't have. "Lots of 'em have spikes on their bodies; that's where you see the cuts from."

"Thanks, I think I've got what I need." Joe waited for the man to walk away before refreshing his Shell and walking near the wall. There weren't any guards around him, so he started talking in a conversational tone, slowly speaking louder until he saw a patch of darkness that was shifting. It looked like a human shadow, and it strolled along the ground while remaining totally flat. It was horizontal from his perspective. Joe could hardly take his eyes off the thing; that was a *very* strange way to move.

A guard finally noticed him and came running, looking

furious that Joe was standing near the wall. When the Shade was in range, Joe lifted a hand and used Shadow Spike on it. There was a sound like a balloon popping, and the Shade was rolled up and formed into the spike. Joe released the spell and looked, but it seemed that the Shade was indeed dead. He checked his combat log just to be sure.

*Critical success! Savage blow! Corrupted Shade takes 300 transformation damage! Corrupted Shade has died. Exp: 25 (50 * .5 * Corrupted Shade x1)*

The guard that was jogging at him slowed down, seemingly confused. "How did you kill that thing? It takes a half-dozen fireballs to put one down!"

"Shadow magic. Extra effective, apparently." Joe looked at the guard with a critical glance. "I need to speak to the Warden."

"*Shadow* magic? That's completely counterintuitive." The guard seemed like he *wanted* to believe Joe, but he *was* a prisoner. "If you want to go to the Warden though… I hope you have a good reason. The man does *not* like to be interrupted for minutiae."

Joe spiked another Shade, smiling slightly as it also died with a single attack. "I think he will want to hear what I have to say." The guard shrugged and motioned for Joe to start walking. When they got to the Warden's office, the guard knocked twice and went to sit down. Joe looked at him oddly, but the man simply shook his head and gestured at a seat next to him.

They waited for a good ten minutes before they heard a faint reply, "Enter… if you *must*."

"That's your cue." Joe nodded in appreciation to the guard as he opened the door.

"Good morning, prisoner five-nine-three-zero-zero-one." The Warden glanced over Joe and motioned for him to take a seat. "You have been here for a little over fourteen hours; why are you already in my office?"

"I have a proposition for you."

"Conjugal visits are not allowed, nor would they be something that *I* was interested in. If that is all, please see yourself out to the punishment station," the Warden spoke in a very collected voice, almost making Joe not realize what he was saying to him.

"What? No!" Joe's face may have looked a touch *too* disgusted because the Warden arched a brow and steepled his fingers. Joe hurried to pull out his map and allowed the three-dimensional image to appear over his hand. "I have a map of this dungeon and can easily slay Shades."

"We have plenty of Shade slayers." The Warden's face didn't change, but he couldn't hide the fact that his eyes were looking over the map carefully. "You seem to be misinformed. That map has three levels, and the dungeon has only two."

"I was given this map by a deity. It is leading me to a tome that has the possibility to turn the tables on the Wolfman army that is marching on my Guild's town. It shows my location, here. While I would be more than willing to go after this book on my own, I would prefer to bring along a group so you can test the veracity of my words." Joe was a bit out of breath after his little speech, but the Warden didn't seem to mind.

"No, you can go alone. That's fine," the Warden replied instantly. "Anyone is free to go *deeper* into the dungeon. They all come back, one way or another."

"How unpleasant of you." Joe took a breath and looked at the Warden, full of confusion. "You have no desire to delve deeper into this place? Learn its secrets?"

"None."

"I see. I'm sorry to bother you… is that coffee?" Joe saw the Warden take a sip of something that was hurriedly placed under the desk.

"Get out." After Joe left the room, a side door opened and the Warden glanced over at the Traveler standing there. "Pose as a prisoner. Go with him and report everything that happens." There was no response to his orders, but then… he hadn't expected any.

Joe was in a *real* foul mood. He walked around looking for a group that was going dungeon diving, but there didn't seem to be many motivated people. He had learned that if you didn't go into the dungeon, you didn't get to eat unless you did some other kind of work in the camp such as healing. It seemed that a lot of the players simply didn't log in until their prison term was over, allowing their character to die of starvation a few times. Joe shuddered at that thought; to him, they were *real people* that died because they didn't take care of themselves. Gross. He went over to the stacks, which is what they called the piled up limp bodies of players, and cast Cleanse on each of them, a few times to hydrate the worst-looking ones.

Skill increase: Cleanse (Apprentice 0). Sometimes the only way to grow is to do the right thing for no expected reward. Someone, somewhere, is bound to notice and thank you for it. Look at you, making strides toward being a good person! +2 Karmic Luck.

That was the first time he had ever gotten a notification for a change in his Karmic Luck. Joe was still not sure what it did, but he was glad to see that a higher amount was gained for doing good things. So more was better, and… that's all he knew. His thoughts were interrupted by a voice.

"What are you *doing* over here?" A man in heavy armor clanked toward him, creaking and squeaking loudly. "They have nothing to steal; you may as well leave them alone."

"Not stealing or trying to steal. Some of them are really dehydrated, so I was doing my best to heal them. They can survive a lot longer without food than they can without water." Joe stood and faced the man, unsure of what else to say. "Is your armor unoiled so that you draw more attention in the dungeon?"

"Ugh. *Yes*. Finally, someone who gets it without needing information spoon-fed to them. The guards provide common weapons and armor if you ask for them, but they take 'em back each night." The man shook his head, wincing at his own noise.

"You have room on your team for a healer and a guy who can kill Shades in one hit?" Joe asked with a hopeful expression.

Looking a bit uncomfortable, the armored man responded,

"No, I can't take two more people. If you have more than five people in a group, you get swarmed by at least double the amount of monsters out there. I could take *one* of you, but I'd prefer the killer."

"I was, um, yeah I was only describing myself. Both of those people were me." Joe was the awkward one now.

Just to move the conversation along, the other man spoke, "Yeah, that's fine. I'm Bill, come on. I gotta warn you, my group is pretty *touchy*. We are devoted to clearing this dungeon, though, and we think there is a way out of this place or at least a way to get a *good* reward. A dungeon wouldn't exist without *good* loot, right? It can't *all* be cursed junk."

They strode toward Joe's temporary new party, and the others walked over and took turns hugging him and each other. Joe looked at Bill, who was rolling his eyes. "So when you said they were *touchy*, you meant they are all about human contact. I was expecting… short tempers."

"I know you were." Bill showed a fox's grin. "Let's get going." Joe was shown to the armory where he was given a shoddy casting orb. They didn't have any cleric weapons, so Joe simply accepted the fact and got moving. In Joe's admittedly biased opinion, the first floor was *insanely* easy. With a single spike, he popped the Shades and the team could move on. His Darkvision allowed him to easily distinguish between the Shades and natural darkness, so surprise attacks weren't an issue for this group.

The others–once they began to understand that the Shades weren't getting to them–started to have a good time. They went full force at any elemental they found, blasting the misshapen creatures away with pure force of arms. Joe followed his map, allowing them to avoid wrong turns and branching tunnels. They passed several groups along the way, and Joe always made sure to pause and clear away any poison or serious injury.

"I'm feeling so *altruistic* today," Joe mentioned to Bill, getting a chuckle from the man in return.

Bill laughed as Joe finished healing a man, only to get a one-finger salute as payment. "I'm sure they *want* to thank you but don't want to seem weak in front of their team. This *is* still a prison. Don't drop the non-existent soap and whatnot."

"Sure, sure." They kept moving through the darkness, only a single torch carried by one of the others allowed the majority of the group to see where they were walking. "We are almost at the stairs; you ready for floor two?"

"I'm not sure, Bill," one of the others spoke up. "We got some good loot today. Two 'Charles' type beards and one 'Chatbeard'."

"That's new. What does that one do?" Joe questioned without stopping. He had found that if he talked and walked, the others would simply follow without really noticing that they were doing so.

They were on the stairs before anyone else really thought about it, but beyond a few groans and hugs for support, no one complained. "It's a cream, also the only way to remove the 'Charles' type beard without a powerful anti-curse spell. It gives you a two-week debuff that makes people think you are younger than you are, but at least you stop cussing and insulting people when you probably shouldn't."

"How fun," Joe voiced without any conviction. "You guys know anything about this floor?"

"Same monsters, just stronger versions." Bill loosened his arms with a few wide swings. "Shades have more deadly poison; dirt elementals become mud or ant elementals. Before you ask, ant elementals are regular dirt elementals that are filled with biting ants. You *can* beat them down with melee, but if you get too close you have a serious problem."

"Understood." They moved on, and Joe couldn't realistically understand why there were so many injured every day. He got the fact that he was somehow a hard counter for the creatures in here, but this was *clearly* a dungeon for novices. Especially with the weakness of these Shades now shown, it was likely that this could easily be a training ground for rapid skill development. Joe *refused* to believe that *everyone* had trouble in here. It was more likely that the prisoners were given zero information or ways to deal with the monsters, while the Kingdom used them to distract the monsters away from whatever they *actually* did in here.

"Ugh, that one dropped goop. Alright, someone's gonna need to grab it." Bill called to the others as he pointed to where a Shade had recently popped.

"Goop?" Joe got closer, trying to inspect the drop. "That's ectoplasm, a… rare, I think, alchemy compound. Probably goes for a few silver." Just like that, Joe knew at least *one* thing that the Kingdom was likely after.

"Eh. We can't keep it, but we get extra rations for turning it in. We get searched every other day. Magically, so there's no reason to put it somewhere *unfortunate* because they will still find it," Bill warned him with a downward glance.

"Unfor…? Gross." Joe pulled a face and looked at his map again. "This is actually a small floor, at least if you go directly for the exit to the next floor. Otherwise, it is just a bunch of curved tunnels that circle back to each other over and over."

"Wait, you mean… this floor is supposed to be massive! People get lost in here for days at a time!" one of the touchy-feely guys complained. "*I* got stuck here overnight once!"

"Look." Joe showed him the map. "Eight main tunnels that circle back to the start point, each with eight tunnels that do the same but also branch to go into each other. Looks like a drawing of a flower that I did when I was twelve and taking art class. We take a left, a right, then go straight. Boom. There's the exit."

"I don't know how long you are going to be here, but *please* make me a copy of that map." Bill was looking over the details and shaking his head.

They followed the route plotted by the divine gift, killing off a few Shades and what appeared to be walking anthills, but when they got to the location the map had been directing them to, there was no room like it promised. They set about looking for ways to get into what they assumed was a hidden room, but there were no levers, buttons, or secret latches. Joe's instincts were screaming that the room was there, so he looked at the map again and saw that there were tiny numbered locations scattered around the entirety of the second floor.

"It's a *puzzle.*" Joe shook his head in negation of the facts. "Nope. I have no time for this garbage. Stand back." With the others out of the way, he dual cast Acid Spray and channeled both spells until he ran out of mana. In front of them was a smoking tunnel that they could *probably* all squeeze through, and the fresh hole opened up into a small room. Joe went through first, looking around the empty room for any indication of an exit. The floor seemed patterned and interesting, so he crouched down to inspect it.

There was a quickly muffled shout of surprise from the others as they watched Joe vanish with a small clap of thunder.

CHAPTER THIRTY-NINE

"What odd patterns. Is this an enchantment? What do you guys think?" Joe looked up and around but quickly realized that the others had vanished. Or… *he* was somewhere else. That was more likely, as the wall wasn't melted away but instead opened into a hallway. "Oh. Um. Hmm."

Joe tried to read over the mosaic on the ground, but it was all formulas and magical symbolism. While it was *similar* to ritual magic, it was different enough that he wasn't going to be understanding this any time soon. How had he activated it? Joe stomped on the patterns, poked them, and then jumped on them.

"He's back!" Joe heard, almost making him fall over in shock.

"Joe, thank goodness. Shades are starting to group up and get close. *Someone* decided to shout in surprise, and you vanishing makes a sound like thunder." Bill got close and grabbed Joe, shaking him a bit when Joe didn't respond right away.

"Uh… I'm not sure how I got this to work," Joe finally spit

out. "All I did was crouch to read this, and-" Bill instantly crouched, vanishing with a **bang** that made Joe yelp.

"See! It's not just *me*!" The other three ran over to the enchantment and crouched, vanishing from sight. After taking a screenshot of the enchantment, Joe took the hint and did the same, popping down to join the others. While they were all in the new room on the third floor he got a screenshot of *this* enchantment and pulled out his map to look at where they needed to go. The map had updated again, showing the third floor in much greater detail.

"Looks like we go through here, and then it is a long hallway with rooms on either side. Huh, kinda feels like a hallway in a hotel," Joe looked out into the long hallway, revising his statement right away, "or it is the solitary confinement area for a long-forgotten prison. At the end of the hall is a room marked with a skull and crossbones, so let's avoid *that* for now."

"Joe, don't you get it? We are on the third floor of a dungeon that no one has found in decades!" Bill was extra excited about this. "There might *actually* be great loot here. The longer a dungeon exists without being looted the better the rewards will be! As far as I know, this dungeon has *never* been finished."

They walked down the hallway, looking through the slots of each of the doors. Most of them were empty, *fully* empty, but were opened anyway just to check for anything hidden. The doors were secured with complex bolts on the exterior, impossible to open from the inside but fairly simple from the outside. Then one of the others looked through a slot and stiffened, body going rigid and falling to the ground. Joe ran over, glancing into the cell only to be caught by two eyes full of blazing green flames that seemed to dig into his mind.

Joe stiffened as well but only for a moment as he forced the invading tendrils of thought out of his head. The eyes shifted away from the hole, showing instead a wide smile made of the same burning flames. The mouth moved, and a terrible voice echoed into the hallway, "*Ahh. A fellow practitioner of Psycomancy. A Novice! Did you come all this way to study at the feet of greatness? I had thought I had been forgotten by the world, but you even brought me tribute in the form of snacks. Release me, and we shall commence your training after I consume their memories and sanity.*"

You have found a class trainer that is willing to teach you the skills of Psycomancy! Would you like to release him and learn the true depths of your mental capabilities? Accept / Reject.

"Not a chance." Joe slammed the viewing hole closed, and the being on the other side began to smash against the metal, howling in rage. Joe could only hope that the creature was a typical Mage-type, strong in power but weak physically. He shuddered as his fallen teammate blinked and stood.

"What happened just now?"

"Powerful mind-twisting creature. *Really* don't look in there guys." Joe gestured at the door and shook his head. He pulled a small chunk of chalk out of his pocket and took a moment to write a warning on the door. They kept moving, much more cautious when they opened the viewing holes. None of them noticed the man who had fallen prey to the Psychomancer was looking back the way they had come… with a spark of green fire growing in his eyes. By the time they had reached the end of the hall and explored all rooms on the map, they had realized that they had been foolish for thinking there may be valuables in these cells. Who would give inmates powerful items?

"Great. Three hundred and fifty-one experience; we've gone through three levels of the dungeon, and there's nothing to fight that we can beat. At least we should get some decent experience from whatever is waiting in there," one of the men complained bitterly.

So there they stood, eyeing the door that loomed in their path. It was not overly fancy, but it was obvious that behind this door was not more of the same. Most likely, it held the dungeon boss, which was sure to be a powerful enemy. They were about to reach for the rewards they had been seeking since they arrived. The only issue… this door was keeping them from their goals. As a group they agreed: this dungeon boss was going down.

They opened the doors and stepped through, and only the fact that the door slammed shut behind them and began to shimmer with a shield kept them from turning and sprinting away as fast as their legs could carry them. It was *unlikely* that this boss was going down.

The room was large and circular, and the center of it was filled with an inky pool of darkness that Joe couldn't see through, indicating that it was *made* of Shades. Standing in the center was what Joe could only assume was an elemental. It stood only a bit taller than him but was fully coated in black metal armor that constantly released a billowing darkness. It didn't move or make noise but simply stared at them. Joe stared at it in return, activating Intrusive Scan as he did so.

Name: Warden of Souls. Class: Elemental Specter. Title: Undying.

Highest stat: Luck.

Ongoing effects: Bored. Dark Renewal. Bored. Jailor. Enhanced Darkness. Bored.

The Specter shifted slightly, and an echoing voice came from it, "Ah, prisoners. I have been *so* distraught over having nothing new to do for the last few decades. It is like the crown forgot about me and simply stopped giving me new detainees to reform! Well, come on over, and we shall begin."

A fireball raced from one of Joe's companions, slamming into the chest of the Specter. It didn't flinch at all, merely looking a bit annoyed by the interruption. A tendril of shadow launched out of the darkness pooled at his feet and impacted the offending party member, driving him into the wall before turning into chains and spikes. Fully pinned to the wall, but apparently not hurt, the man could only struggle.

"You can make darkness take physical form?" Joe gasped in wonder. This was something that he would eventually need to test. His apparent lack of concern for his team's well-being made a few of them glare at him.

"Oh, a Shadow Mage? How *lucky*." The Specter looked

more closely at Joe. "I had wondered how even the paltry amount of Shades I let wander this place were defeated so easily. So my talents intrigue you, hmm? Is skill in shadow manipulation something you would be willing to bargain for?"

"Perhaps, but… you don't plan to kill us?" Joe spoke before the others could think that he was betraying them.

"Why would I let you leave this place so easily?" The Specter seemed genuinely confused. "You are here to be *reformed.* You will not be slain until you have repaid your debt to society. The others will all die within a few days or so, but with you… I find a loophole for companionship. You have no limit on your sentence, and you *can't* unless you appear for trial."

"You want me to get you out of here?" Joe timidly questioned him.

"Oh, quite the opposite. *You* will be staying with *me* for a very long time." The Specter showed a disturbing smile, the interior of his mouth seeming to show distant galaxies. "I was just hoping you would make it easy on yourself and consider it a once in a lifetime opportunity to learn from the Sage Nocturnal. Not too many with our capabilities out there."

CHAPTER FORTY

"You know, I keep getting told that Sages are supposed to be rare, but they seem to be dang-nab everywhere." Joe looked over the Specter, trying to create a Shadow Spike to impact him. It did, but the tip of the spike broke against the film of darkness that coated the being.

In retaliation, all of Joe's companions ended up netted to the wall. Manacles formed around Joe and dragged him down to the floor. The Specter spoke again, "I won't hold that against you; I'm sure you felt that you needed to try. You all *will* be held here until your time is up, why not make this a *happy* occasion? I am sure there are even a few things that I could learn from you. For instance, what year is it out there?"

"Look, uh, Warden?" Joe looked at the writhing darkness keeping his new acquaintances pinned to the wall. They had been there for upwards of thirty seconds without the bonds appearing to weaken at all, so Joe had no reason to believe they would vanish unless the Warden wanted them to. "Is it alright if I call you that? Warden? Great. Look, I'd be happy to learn from you. More than happy, really; this is an aspect of myself that I feel has been fully ignored for far too long."

"Excellent. It is always best to start these relationships off in a positive light, especially as we might spend an eon down here together as these fools wither into dust." The Warden chuckled dryly. "Ironic, isn't it, that I wanted a positive *light* when we are going to be spending all of our time in darkness? Shall we begin?"

To his credit, the Warden was an *excellent* teacher. Joe had no doubt that it was due to his self-proclaimed Sage status. Joe started with only the ability to see in the dark and create a few Shadow Spikes, but he was fully entranced with what he was learning. The Warden directed him through a multitude of forms and techniques, from creating chains and binding agents to dancing with his eyes closed and using darkness to guide his movements. Any time Joe would have collapsed from exhaustion, the Specter infused him with a dark energy that fully revitalized him.

"I must say… for only a few days' worth of training, you are becoming quite adept at using the basic abilities of a Specter. I think that with only a few more years of training, you will be able to take my place here. I'd love to roam the world once more, see what has changed over the last few hundred years," the Warden's voice penetrated the fog around Joe's mind, jostling him to action.

"That's your goal? Wait a moment… we have been here for *days*?" Joe's mouth clicked closed as the Warden glared at him.

"What? You thought I was teaching you for *your* benefit, inmate? Nice inmate number, by the way. Someone must not have liked you at all." A scoff passed through the liquid metal armor the Warden wore. "Another year or so of dark infusions and your body will be prepared for the racial change into a Specter. Then I can bind you to this location, freeing me from the constant need to keep these Shades and other prisoners in line."

At that moment, Joe knew that he couldn't wait any longer. He needed to do something drastic or he was going to miss the war entirely and become a glorified prison guard on duty for *eternity*. He opened his menu and looked over the thick list of skills that he had gained while trapped down here for apparently *days*.

Skill gained: Spellbinding (Beginner V). The creation of magical documents is arduous and difficult, oftentimes deadly. Mitigating the risks is the best you can hope for. Effect: Each rank of this skill increases magical quill durability by 3%, magical ink purity by 4%, infused paper durability by 3% when it is used or created by you and decreases time to create desired magical ink by 5%. +2% writing speed and accuracy. Increases possible written spell diagram complexity and stability by 2n% per skill level.

Oh wait, that looked like the document-making skills he had combined. The other ones were what he really needed. Not even bothering to read over the skill descriptions, Joe began tossing all of his new skills into the combination menu. He tried to group them by what they did as he put them in but otherwise didn't care. Darkvision, Dark Infusion, Shadow Dancing, Dark Perception, Shadow Manipulation, Cloak of Darkness, Dark Binding, Shadow Spike… the list went on. Twenty darkness or shadow related abilities went into the mix, and Joe didn't even blink as he read over the cost associated with the combination.

A bit over twenty-six million gold to combine, nine and a half days to complete. *Nope*. Joe tapped a small icon that had been grey each time he had done this before but was now showing a shining gem.

Combine skills using combination gem? This will negate the cost and time needed to combine all skills but will consume the gem. Yes / No.

"Oh, heck yes," Joe breathed, smashing the 'yes' button with all the mental force he could muster. He felt like he had been kicked in the gut as the plethora of skills was torn out of his psyche and a wall of information flooded his mind.

Skill gained: Solidified Shadows (Apprentice VI) (Mythical). The ability to shape shadows to a desired form has always been excellent yet fleeting. No more! This skill allows you to take your shapes and make them into a solid. Maximum damage possible dependent upon mana invested. One point of damage dealt per mana invested. Maximum mana allocation: 10n where 'n' is skill level.

Class gained: Flawed Shadowmancer (Unique). A shadowmancer is an Elemental Mage who uses shadows in lieu of other powers such as fire. A Flawed Shadowmancer is one who didn't understand the power they were trying to wield, rushing to forge themselves without the tutelage or mastery needed to bring their power to bear. This weakens their power over Shadows but removes a few of the restrictions the full class would impart.

Skill gained: Almost Effortless Shaping (Darkness) (Apprentice VI) (Flawed Unique). Effortless shaping allows the user to use their powers to shape their element, in this case Darkness, into any shape that they can imagine. This can be used to form weapons, shapes, abstract thoughts… and so on. Darkness withholds no secrets from you, allowing your senses to be even better *in the darkness. Attaining the Effortless Shaping skill is the goal of any elemental manipulator, even if they don't know it. You came…* somewhat *close. Instead of being able to shape shadows for free, mana cost is 80-n per second, where 'n' equals skill level.*

"What did you just do? Something changed; the *system* poked its overgrown nose in here." The Specter generated chains and pulled Joe close, looking him over with empty eye sockets. "*Tell* me!"

"I got a new skill!" Joe told him breathlessly, his throat being squeezed just hard enough to allow him to answer. "It's a new shadow skill; it somehow created excellent synergy and combined, giving me a class."

"A *class* you say? Already?" The Specter released him, seeming to become contemplative. "It's far too soon for that. What does this *skill* do?"

"It does something similar to dark infusion but over the course of a few minutes. I'd demonstrate it, but it requires *components* to activate," Joe complained bitterly. "Empowerment of Shadows."

"Components? No… only the most powerful shadow spells require components… does it require a Core?" The Warden was almost shaking, and Joe knew that he had him where he needed him.

"It does; the spell calls for a low-grade Core at the minimum," Joe told him.

"A shadow spell I don't *have*? So it is likely not… but still… I must see it." The Warden looked into Joe's eyes with its own empty placeholders and made a decision. "Go into the treasure room and gather what you need. Feel free to peruse the room, but know that if I feel that you are trying to run you will be pulled back in here and tortured for a few days before making the trip once again."

A chain wrapped around Joe, looping over his chest in an 'X' and melding into itself. As Joe walked, the dark chains clinked over the ground behind him and scraped against his skin. The treasure room was indeed a *treasure* room, though, from the sign on the door, it had originally been used for confiscated goods. There was a small shelf of books that drew Joe's attention instantly, but those would need to wait for now. He was amazed by the breadth of compounds, potions, and ingredients. Was this what happens when you didn't clear a dungeon for a couple centuries?

He found everything he needed and even found that there was a drawer with various grades of Cores. He wanted to scoop them all up but held off and, instead, only took exactly what he needed. Carrying an armful of ingredients, he approached the Specter and started laying them out. "Alright, now all I need to do is start the spell and feed it mana after giving it a drop of my blood, and my control over shadows will… I… I mean, I'll get a small boost."

The Specter stared at him for a full ten seconds without shifting its position. "...No. You *will* use this spell, but *I* will be the one to receive the benefits the first time. There should be no chance of you overpowering me even if you were boosted *far* beyond your capabilities, but… you are far too *eager* to perform this spell."

"But… do you even *have* blood?" Joe hedged in a complaining manner.

"What do you think this liquid is? Yes, it is Shades and shadow, but it is also the essence of my being, which is what *blood* currently is for you. It should *more* than suffice." The

Warden was becoming agitated, so Joe simply hung his head and sighed, not an uncommon gesture for him over the last few days.

"Alright. So long as I can go next," Joe pretended to ask hopefully.

"We shall *see*," the Warden purred, motioning Joe closer. Joe stepped into the dark miasma around the Specter and almost gagged as the gaseous fluid caressed him and tried to press into his body. He stopped himself from coughing and strode along the area with the same exaggerated steps needed for slogging through a deep mud until he stood next to the Warden.

Joe placed a silver chalice on the ground, and it was soon filled with viscous darkness. "Are you ready to begin?" Joe didn't wait for an answer, taking a deep breath and trying to concentrate. He pulled open his notes, finding a screenshot of the ritual he intended to use. He scratched his finger, allowing a single drop of blood into the chalice to recognize that the ritual was to take mana from him.

Reaching out with Almost Effortless Shaping, Joe began to twist and contort the darkness at the outer edge of the dark pool. To the Warden, it must have felt like mana was billowing out of Joe into a powerful spell, heightening his excitement. Staring at the screenshot of the precise but relatively simple ritual, Joe recreated the exact image over the course of five minutes by pressing it to the ground and solidifying it piece by piece. The ritual was ready to be activated at a record speed, and Joe almost started dancing with glee at the ease and speed of its creation, somehow managing to maintain his composure. Maybe it was the thought of what would happen to him if the Warden caught on. Yup. That was it.

"This will drain most of my mana and may take a moment. Then there may be pressure as the darkness floods your system and empowers you," Joe stated as he activated the ritual and sank to his knees. Mana flowed from him like a river, seeming to the Specter to collect in a ring around them. The Warden was overjoyed; he hadn't seen a substantial boost to his power in decades, yet this man might be able to offer him power he thought he would need years to seek out!

Five seconds passed. Ten. Thirty. Mana stopped flowing from Joe, and he collapsed to the ground heaving, trying to breathe air instead of drinking darkness. "There we go, now the darkness is charged with power and will begin returning to us."

"*Us*?" The Warden hissed, tossing Joe out of the pool with a simple motion. "I think *not*."

Joe landed heavily, actually needing to take a moment to heal himself from the awkward impact. He watched as the Warden stood in the ritual diagram happily, feeling the pressure building all around him for a full minute. "Yes, *yes*. I can feel the power building! This feeling… the pressure is lessening, or… my power must have increased to the point that I cannot feel it!" Joe looked at the notification that was waiting for him and slowly got to his feet.

Ritual of Containment completed successfully! As the target participated in the ritual's creation and didn't know what they were actually *doing–you dirty dog–the ritual's power is increased by 20% thanks to the added effect gained at the Student ranks of ritual magic.*

"There we go." Joe looked at the pool of darkness, which lapped up against the edges of the ritual but no longer flowed across. "That should take care of *you* for now."

"What? What do you *mean* take…?" Joe couldn't see it, but he was sure that there was an expression on the Specter's face that hadn't been there in a long, long time… fear.

CHAPTER FORTY-ONE

Joe flinched as the shadows inside the ritual circle lurched, but he hadn't needed to worry. Instead of transforming into chains or spikes or whatever it was trying to do, the darkness only… twitched. Like an involuntary muscle spasm. The Specter floated toward the edge of the ritual, crossing the boundary and charging Joe. *Now* Joe worried, turning and running to the outskirts of the room. The Warden kept moving far longer than Joe had hoped for, only drifting to the ground and shaking when he tried to follow Joe into the treasure room.

"What did you *do* to me?" The Specter snarled, making wheezing noises. He looked back at the pool of darkness, pausing his words and sounding confused when he spoke next, "It… it isn't dispersing? Where are the Shades? This place should be *teeming* with Shades now that I am out of the pool."

"That wasn't a spell," Joe told the greatly weakened Specter. "It was a ritual, specifically a ritual of containment. It was designed to keep you inside of it, and that darkness is the essence of you, is it not?"

"Yes… and no." The Warden didn't move but still stared at the darkness. "How long will this last?"

"This ritual isn't really given a set limit. So long as it has mana, it will just continue to contain you–and that darkness–inside of it. It is drawing power from the darkness and is *made* of the darkness, so it will be *very* difficult for anyone to dispel or damage." Joe didn't mind explaining this; there was really almost no way for the Specter to surprise-

"Kill me," the Warden spoke to Joe with a voice full of longing. "I can finally be free of this cursed assignment without the need to force another to hold the Shadewell at bay."

"Why would I do that?" Joe questioned the being incredulously. "I have no idea if that would unleash the storm of creatures you seem to fear as much as you love to torment."

The Warden shook its head. "If they are not out right now, it is because they *can't* get out. If I am gone, that ritual *will* remain in place. I am the mind… *that* is the body. It generates mana, stamina, health. If you will not take my place… slay me."

"Is this why you are here? The only reason?" Joe prodded the Specter. "Or is there something else that will happen to the area with your demise?"

"The reason I am *here* is because of all the truly evil prisoners *I* put behind bars!" the Warden spat furiously. "I devoted my career to ensuring that only the guilty were punished, and what thanks did I get? A dagger in the dark and a *permanent* posting."

"Why does this sound familiar?" Joe muttered, deep in thought. "You… how did you ensure that *only* the guilty were punished? What were you, before you were… this?"

"I was the best investigator in this entire *world*. I created a spell, Dark Compulsion, which *severely* punished lies. Spells like 'Compel Truth' can be worked around, their gentle methods easy for the experienced to ignore. Some Nobles got scared as I closed in on their illegal trade, and the next thing I knew, I was free of my body and darkness was pouring off of me. My status as the Sage of Darkness–Sage Nocturnal–forcibly changed my race upon death." The Warden spoke bitterly, his story obviously something that still caused him great pain.

"Do you have a copy of this spell?" Joe bluntly verbalized.

"It's yours, as soon as you agree to kill me," the Warden shot back with a hollow tone. All of the black mist he generated was constantly being pulled into the ritual circle, so Joe was able to see the damaged body that lay beneath. He shuddered to think that this could have been his future.

Quest updated: Seeker of truth! An influential investigator met an untimely end due to his relentless pursuit of criminals. You have found him, but in return for his knowledge, he demands that you end his torment.

"I will," Joe promised, staring into the withered orbs this creature had for eyes.

"Excellent." The Specter chuckled softly. "There is a spell book detailing the spell's creation in the treasure room on the bookshelf. That will teach you everything you want to know about it."

Joe moved his hand in a very slow slap across his own face. "Oh, you sneaky thing. A deal is a deal. Are you ready?"

"For decades," the Specter stated softly. "I pursued immortality, but now... I know it is not for me. Perhaps it will work out for *you*, though."

"I can only hope." Mana billowed from Joe, wrapping around the Specter and collecting the darkness into a pillar around it. He took a moment to form the interior of the pillar into a variety of damaging spells then solidified it with all the mana that he could possibly use over the course of thirty seconds.

*One thousand mana invested! Oh-oh-Overkill! Seriously, he had ten health after being out of that ritual for so long. You have slain a Sage! The world at large weeps for the loss of a great pillar of knowledge, but one person... somewhere... begins to laugh. The benefit for the highest skill level in Dark Magic has been transferred! Exp gained: 8,000 (16,000 * .5 * Spectral Sage of Darkness x1)*

You have reached character level 11! Please note that your class level has not changed.

"Gah! I should have come back when I wasn't a *prisoner*!" Joe dropped to his knees and pounded on the floor. "Half *freaking* experience gained! No titles, nothing else? Seriously? This cursed dungeon!" He stood and went to the wall where the other members of his party had been pinned, but the days of inattention had proved fatal to all of them. After taking a few calming breaths, Joe turned and looked at the Specter's corpse. Walking over, he reached out to move the body just as it fell to ashes, leaving behind a few items. After holding the items and doing his best to inspect them, Joe sat down and had to chuckle.

Item gained: Robe of Liquid Darkness (Rare). Wearing this robe makes you look a bit wet but increases the power of dark affinity magic by 10%. Could use a wash, as it hasn't had one in ERROR years.

Item gained: Spatial Codpiece (Legendary). This functional piece of armor also serves a greater purpose; it is able to store thirty cubic meters worth of items. Goods must come within two inches of the armor to be stored but can be retrieved directly onto the body or into the hand as long as the codpiece is touching your skin. Adds 5 points to overall armor class and prevents blows from damaging your genitals entirely. Let's just say your junk is safely stored.

Item gained: Condensed Ectoplasm (Rare) x10. This is a thicker, more potent version of ectoplasm.

Still laughing, Joe cast and channeled Cleanse on the black leather codpiece, surrounding it in a bubble of dark water as he scoured the surface with tiny particles of solidified darkness. After five minutes–and one final panic washing–he equipped the item. It was a… *strange* feeling, to say the least. He stored the robe, unsure if his method of washing it would damage the fabric.

Then Joe walked into the treasure room. It took a while, but he emptied the place out entirely. If anyone else would have been able to see him, they would have been very concerned; Joe walked around thrusting his hips at things like Elvis. Those things then vanished. Not a super pretty mental image to have stored away.

Quest updated: Seeker of truth! You have found a spell book detailing the methods used by the investigator of old. Return it to Boris to complete this quest!

Right next to the spell book was a small and obviously aged ritual manual. Joe opened it, reading through it and nodding as he did so. Simple. It was such a *simple* ritual. He couldn't believe that he didn't think of it himself, but he was *sure* that he would have eventually. Just like that, Joe had learned the secrets of making spells into rituals.

He felt validated in his choices and intelligent decisions; one of the most important components of this ritual was a spell scroll for the spell you wanted to convert to a ritual. It was like something had been guiding him along this path… his eyes narrowed as he thought back on his conversations with Tatum. Now a few things he had suggested were making sense. Tricky, tricky deity. Tatum had probably been trying to get around whatever rules he needed to follow but was unable to tell Joe to pursue scroll making directly.

With the treasure room emptied, Joe looked around for an exit. First, he triple checked that the boiling pool of darkness wasn't going anywhere. Then he stepped into the small room adjacent to what he assumed was the Warden's very old office. Not finding anything worth looting in here, Joe was about to leave when he noticed that there was a familiar pattern on the floor in the corner. Stepping on it, he jumped lightly, vanishing with a clap of displaced air.

CHAPTER FORTY-TWO

"I recognize this place," Joe muttered as he looked around a room that would be filled with impenetrable darkness for anyone else. "This is where they took me when we first entered the dungeon. So the exit should be right over there…"

Going the opposite direction, Joe soon found himself walking up to the gates of the fortification. He knocked on the wooden defense, and the door opened to show some very irritated Royal Guards. "Prisoner, why are you on the wrong side of the gates?"

"I cleared the dungeon, and it deposited me near the exit," Joe explained succinctly, causing a few of the guards to appear concerned and the prisoners to perk up. "Since I am here *willingly*, I figured I should come back in here."

"Likely for the best, yes," the guard admitted reluctantly. "We have never had anyone escape before, and it would have sullied our reputation instantly and irrevocably. *_Ahem_*. Thank you."

*Feat of honor complete! 1100 (2200 * .5) Reputation gained with Ardania Royal Guard! New reputation rank: Reluctantly Friendly.*

The guard gestured to a building. "We have been waiting for you, actually; the Warden has been asking for you."

"The *Warden* is al-" Joe cut his panicked reply off. "Oh, right… the Warden. *That* Warden. Ha. Yeah, let's go."

A few minutes of walking and waiting later, Joe stood once again in front of the Warden of the prison. "I see you have returned. Empty-handed as well, though you were gone for days and *claim* to have cleared the dungeon. Not that I would believe an inmate either way, but do *try* to make your lies believable."

The Warden stopped, obviously trying to bait Joe into discussing his recent exploits. Joe certainly wasn't going to fall for that and so maintained his silence. After an uncomfortable amount of time, the Warden finally broke the unhappy tranquility with a deep sigh. "Fine. Your hearing is scheduled for 'immediate', so prepare yourself for transport. Your lack of willing cooperation ensures that the ride will not be overly pleasant for you. Guards, take him to the High Court. Take him in the *iron* carriage."

The guard who had entered at his words nodded slightly and pulled Joe away by his arm. When they had left, the Warden–still looking at the door–spoke softly. "The Specter is defeated? The tide of Shades contained? There are no more true threats to us in the dungeon?"

"Yes, Warden. The dungeon is fully under your control."

"Excellent." The Warden got back to his paperwork, never glancing over at his subordinate. If he had, he may have seen a gleam of green fire shining through the eyes of his most trusted spy.

On his way to the exit of the dungeon, Joe sighed at the thuggish look of the guards that were joining them. "Should I go ahead and assume that you were just ordered to beat me as we went to the castle?"

"That would be a reasonable assumption," the Royal Guard said without looking directly at him. "The iron carriage doesn't have windows or seats or anything in it that would even be called *remotely* comfortable. However, it *does* have chains that dangle from the ceiling that will—with any bump or turn—push you into the spikes that are there to stop you from 'escaping'. It is typically reserved for the most uncooperative of prisoners."

"Gotta tell you, I'm a *big* fan of walking. We could go for a light jog, maybe? Have you seen me skipping before? It's funny. The castle isn't *that* far away…" Joe tried to chuckle, but his voice was a bit too dry. Sounded more like a heavy wheeze.

"Mmm," the guard responded noncommittally as they exited the dungeon and spotted a heavy carriage trundling toward them. "Here we are; hop on in." As soon as they exited the dungeon, Joe got a notification.

Rewards for clearing the dungeon have been assigned! Achievement unlocked: Soul Survivor. Not only were you the only member of your party to survive the clearing of the dungeon, you survived the attempts of a Mythical-class Specter to convert you to his own race and destroyed him. You do not leave this place unscathed! His changes have left a mark on you! You have been infused by the darkness of a Sage, a process that not many can claim to have survived. In fact, it is only you, currently. Experience gained: 1000. +3 to all stats except Karmic Luck.

Title gained: Dungeoneer. Being the only survivor of a dungeon is not something that happens by chance. This title will help you do it again in the future. Your tenacity has been rewarded. Rewards: Accurate information shown in dungeon clearing progress bars.

Joe followed the instructions he had been given, noticing that the interior of the carriage was exactly as the guard had described it… though he had missed a few of the details. Namely, the bloodstains and other various material that had never been cleaned up. With his heightened perception, he could easily smell that there wasn't an attached bathroom. When the two guards got in with him, he tensed up and began sending mana into a fresh coat of Exquisite Shell.

The guards waved him down, dropping a couple of cushions on the floor. "Nah. Outside of the dungeon, the Warden has no authority. Typically, we might beat you out of respect for the others you've hurt but not only did you come here willingly, you came back when you had a chance to escape. Not many people earn the respect of the Royal Guard. Take a seat; we'll be on our way momentarily."

The ride to the palace was a cheerful one, the guards bantering amongst themselves, though they did include Joe from time to time. He did his best to keep a smile on his face but was leery of actually engaging in the jokes or taunts they were tossing around. He was only one hundred reputation points above being put in the clinking chains dangling from the ceiling, after all. At the end of the ride, Joe was deposited directly in front of a bathhouse. He was scrubbed by servants who complimented his lack of bruises and bleeding, then was given a clean white robe to wear to his trial. No one tried to take his codpiece, thankfully and for obvious reasons, though he did give it an extra thorough scrub with soap.

Then it was time for his trial. Nerves filled Joe as he was led into a small waiting room. He stared at a large, ornate door that reminded him far too much of the typical Boss room of dungeons. When it opened and he was led in, Joe was startled to see that a large crowd had been gathered into the… oh, this was the throne room? Great. He walked forward, unimpeded by the chains normally seen on prisoners coming from the prison dungeon. This inspired murmurs and chatter that quieted as Joe stopped moving and the door behind the throne opened.

For the first time, Joe was able to see that the Queen did indeed move on her own and wasn't a statue like the rumors suggested. Also, she was *entirely* terrifying, which was likely why she moved so little. Each footstep touched the ground silently, but the simple movements of her body seemed to *scream* about their new position. Joe knew it was only in his head, but each move told him that a predator was approaching… and there was nothing he could do to stop her. Her grace was beyond that seen by master swordsmen, dancers, or contortionists. There was simply no comparison.

When she sat down and went still, nearly everyone in the room started coughing, having held their breath a dangerously long time without noticing. Apparently, this was a common occurrence because the Queen waited patiently before speaking. "The trial shall now commence. Traveler named 'Joe', you stand accused of holding restricted skills and a restricted class. How do you plead?"

Joe had to swallow a few times before he could speak. "Guilty, Your Majesty, but there were…"

"Guilty plea understood. The sentence is death followed by the binding of your classes." A gasp swirled around the crowd, and shocked looks were on nearly every face. "I jest. As I understand it, there are extenuating circumstances, as well as the fact that the skills you earned are untrained, defensive only, and you have not been seeking out training in their usage. Is this all correct?"

Joe had almost fainted when she said she was joking. Not at *all* what he was expecting out of the Queen. "That… that is correct, Your Majesty."

"I have heard the report of Guard Captain Blas, your past actions, and have been given a report on your actions during your time in the prison dungeon. So long as you share your status with me willingly, and I am able to verify that you are not lying, this case will be dismissed. All details shared with me *will* remain confidential. If you ever gain offensive skills for this class or teach the skills to another, you will gain a maximum ranked Warlock title and need another trial to clear it. You will be admitted directly to the trial, bypassing prison, so long as your actions were not seen as treasonous. Do you accept these terms?" The Queen waited patiently for an answer as Joe tried to process the rapid trial.

"I do," Joe stated with great relief. The Queen nodded, and Joe shared his screens with her. She looked at it for a moment and muttered, "Absolute Inspection". Light shone from her gaze, and Joe knew for sure that she saw *everything* in his status.

Name: Joe 'Tatum's Chosen Legend' Class: Mage (Actual: Rituarchitect)
Profession: Tenured Scholar (Actual: Arcanologist)
Character Level: 11 Exp: 70,762 Exp to next level: 7,238

Rituarchitect Level: 1 Exp: 0 Exp to next level: 1,000
Hit Points: 220/220
Mana: 1792/1792
Mana regen: 18.45/sec
Stamina: 195

Characteristic: Raw score (Modifier)

Strength: 22 (1.22)
Dexterity: 29 (1.29)
Constitution: 27 (1.27)
Intelligence: 67 (2.17)
Wisdom: 61 (2.11)
Charisma: 26 (1.26)
Perception: 47 (1.47)
Luck: 29 (1.29)
Karmic Luck: +3

"Interesting. You have been a busy man during your time here. Your titles intrigue me." The Queen tapped a finger on her throne, denting it and causing everyone to tense once more. "It is obvious that you are a good man and that you had not intended to gain power in order to harm our people. I judge this matter complete. Case dismissed. Go do other things, I hear there is a war on." The Queen stood and left the room. After another round of coughing, the people that had shown up as a friend to see the trial cheered for Joe. With a gulp, he noticed that his mother was included in that list.

CHAPTER FORTY-THREE

"Hi there, Mom! Welcome to Ardania!" Joe smiled brightly as he walked up to the glowering woman.

"What are you, a city guide?" She snorted, pulling him into a tearful hug. "What in the *world* is going on? Blas told me why you got sent to prison, but…"

"I tried to tell her that you were going to be totally fine, but Brenda wouldn't listen to a word I said," the Captain ruefully informed him, shaking his hand in congratulations.

"Don't worry, she only hears what she wants to." Joe ducked a playful swipe from his mother. "She'd be a great scout and will probably be a Sage of selective hearing within a month."

"Oh, *please*!" Brenda stamped her foot. "All I ever heard from you was how wonderful this place was! As soon as you went away, I knew I had made a terrible mistake not following. I put in an order for the pod right away, and it still took a couple weeks with me paying triple the going rate. Then I get here and *you* are being *tossed* into the darkest pit these people have access to! Of course I'm upset!"

"I'm sorry. You're right. I'm sorry." Joe hugged her, twirling her around as she smacked him on the back and yelled for him to 'put her down'!

Smoothing the creases in her clothes, she grumbled a bit and looked him over. "I'm so glad that you are okay, and… well, the last time we were interrupted and…"

"You and Blas are dating?" Joe rolled his eyes and crossed his arms. "I didn't need a magical spell to see *that.*"

"It's still *Captain* to you, mister." The Captain growled deeply.

"Maybe someday it'll be 'daddy'." Joe sighed longingly as Blas sputtered. "I can picture it now, you training some new recruits, me running over and yelling 'Daddy, I'm back from a mission'."

"*I'll cut you,*" Blas whispered and pointed at Joe as Brenda pulled the Captain in for a kiss to distract him.

"Now, all I'll need to do is *find* something to do." Brenda pushed Blas away gently and looked at Joe. "Just like you, I brought in quite a bit of money, but I'd be bored as all get out sitting around and wasting it. I'm not overly fond of the idea of going out and fighting all the time, though; the news said that a lot of people are trying to sue for how much pain the game makes them feel."

Joe and Blas both nodded seriously, glad to hear that she wasn't planning on risking herself. Joe pondered over this conundrum for a moment. How could his mother thrive without putting her at risk, have fun, and–being realistic–gossip all day. "Let me see… you are actually perfect for a position an acquaintance of mine was offering. Let's go to the merchant quarters; it isn't too far."

Blas looked Joe over, but when Joe told him they would be at the 'Odds and Ends' store, he simply nodded and told Joe that he'd pick her up at five for dinner. Joe thanked the man, and they parted ways.

Brenda kept giving Joe curious looks, but he simply ignored them. If she had something to say, she would do so. She always had. Eventually she did, blurting out the question that must have been on her mind for a while. "You don't think it's weird? He… he isn't *real*, and we are dating!"

Joe was thrown off a bit by the question; he had been expecting something entirely different, but… "Mom, he is as real as we are. That's what you were worried about? Nah, not strange at all. This is my reality." They talked for a little bit, walking up to their destination right as a young lady was levitated out of the door, spun around, and dropped on her face.

"Ha! As if I'd let you work here sweeping floors, let alone *run* this place!" The wizened old lady that owned the shop sniffed at the deposit she had made on the ground, looking around and seeing Joe. "You! Weren't you telling me that you'd find me the perfect new employee?"

Never had Joe told her anything like that. He wasn't about to say that out loud, though, not with the mood she was obviously in. "Ah, but doesn't true art take time? Allow me to present to you the perfect coworker: my mother, Brenda!" Joe grandly bowed toward his mom, hamming up his performance and getting a smack over the head for his trouble.

Seeing Joe get a good whack over the head, the shop owner chuckled and ushered Brenda forward. "Shall we go talk?"

"Certainly! I bought a new type of tea that I am excited to try; do you have a kettle I could put on? Go have fun, Joe, but don't forget to check in with me every once in a while." She gave him a quick peck on the cheek and walked into the store, gossip mode already in full swing. Joe was sure that she would do well here. The next thing he did was go to the bank and retrieve his gear from the safety deposit box, looking over a notification as he did so.

Quest updated: Apprentice to a Sage! You have found a person willing to become a merchant and sent them to 'Odds and Ends' for tutelage. Rewards will be granted dependent on the results of their chain quest.

"Next up, a coffee shop." He started to walk away, kicking himself for not canceling the rental of the warehouse while he was at the shop. There was a new coffee shop in the location of the inn that his guild used to stay in before it was burned to the ground, and Joe went into it more for nostalgia's sake than anything. It turned out to be a good idea because for the first time since coming to this world he found an espresso! Good lord. He sipped it like a thirty-year scotch and shivered. Enough pleasure, to work!

Two of the books that he had raided from the dungeon appeared on the table. Reading through the first again, he found a few small details that he had forgotten about regarding turning spells into rituals. Joe nodded at his foresight, glad that he was able to take notes this time. Next, he pulled out the tome detailing the spell 'Dark Compulsion' and read through it. Joe frowned. Though it was a powerful spell, it was *twisted*. Whenever someone lied while under the effects, dark thorns would dig into them, causing intense pain. Once the spell was activated, only the person using it could deactivate it safely.

No wonder the investigator had been assassinated. Even if the family he was investigating had done *nothing*, Joe was sure that they wouldn't want their children placed under such a nasty spell. If he had kids and someone came around with something like this, he might take a few regrettable actions himself. Originally, he had planned on turning this into a ritual and gifting it to the city guard. Now… nope. Their reputation would plummet if they used this torture device masquerading as a helpful spell. Joe decided to go to the library and turn in this book.

Skill increased: Reading (Beginner VI). Wait a minute, you can read? Wow! So impressive for someone in your… situation.

Well, that message just didn't even make sense this time. Joe cracked his neck and stood; his coffee had vanished, and it was time for him to do the same. Going over to the library, he dropped off the book with a few notes about properly storing it, gaining another hundred points of job experience. Asking about the spell books that Boris had mentioned last time, Joe was directed to floor three and a half. Following the instructions given, he walked into a room that was about the size of an airport bathroom. The door must have had 'ignore me' magic on it because otherwise, Joe had no idea how people didn't accidentally find their way in here.

Looking around at all the spell books, Joe was impressed by the power their titles proclaimed to bestow. 'Ultimate mana blade', 'Skyfall', 'Endless Army', to name a few. He was *less* impressed by their accuracy. Most of them shone a dull grey with only a few having the telltale golden signs that proclaimed truth. Joe took three books that had the most promise, knowing that he didn't have a lot of time before the war began in full force.

If these were spells that no one had been able to get working in decades or centuries, he quickly understood why as he read them. Whoever had written these books clearly only had a *general* idea of what was going on. Perhaps they were writing down the information, having it dictated to them from the bedside of a dying Mage. The spellforms were sloppy, a few words were spelled incorrectly which changed the meaning of entire sections, and component cost was not standardized. A 'pinch' of powdered quartz? How much was that supposed to be?

The books he had chosen were 'Mass Enchant', which promised to enchant any weapons within a given area, 'Shielded City', which at its most powerful could apparently create a dome of force over an entire city but would most likely only be able to cover a single building, and 'Mana Battery'. The last one was more something that he had picked up for himself to use in the future. Using the spell on a Core would transform the potential experience inside of it into mana at a one to ten rate. That meant that a *low*-grade Core could be used for five thousand mana, and then up to fifty percent more mana could be added to it.

If Joe could create some weaponized rituals and set them up with mana batteries, he could make some seriously powerful siege weaponry. Or perhaps traps. Joe had been liking traps in recent days. First, he needed to un-spaghetti the spells. In other words, he had to get all of the mistakes unraveled and make a clean spell diagram. Then he could transfer that to a spell scroll and then transfer *that* to a ritual. Bleh. No, no, it was fine. The first thing to work on… Mass Enchant. Joe nodded to himself and walked through town, getting to the town square and vanishing, reappearing in the temple area of the Grand Ritual Hall.

CHAPTER FORTY-FOUR

"What the heck is going on?" Joe looked around at the carpet of bodies groaning and moaning on the floor of the temple. "Are you *all* wounded? Why is the temple the hospital? Why am I asking rhetorical questions?" He got to work healing the people around him, not bothering to get too close but instead just chucking balls of water at them. There were simply too many to be able to go person-by-person. This method of healing had an unexpected benefit. Since people were packed so close to each other, the healing water tended to… *splash.*

Skill gained: Group Heal (Apprentice VI). As this skill was discovered by using the skill 'Mend', it retains all current bonuses. Effect: Select a target to heal restoring 5n/T HP where 'n' equals skill level and 'T' equals number of targets. Cost: 5n mana.

Handy but nothing overly special, unless… well, he could channel the spell, couldn't he? He selected ten people and used group heal, an orb of water flying out of his hand and turning into water streaming through the air and connecting the ten people to himself. Channeling the spell for the maximum time he could left him totally drained of mana, truly an impressive feat. Panting, he looked at what he had accomplished. Not much, but… it was at least *decent.*

Connecting to ten people meant that he healed twelve health a second for each of them, and at the end of fifteen seconds–when he ran out of mana–he had been able to heal them for over four hundred health. There were a few drawbacks to this, namely that broken bones were apparently not fixed when he used the healing spell this way. Another issue that was *more* concerning to him was that these guys were fighters, meaning that they had put a significant amount of time into boosting their health. If they had fifty points of constitution that meant they had at *least* four hundred and fifty health. It was likely that they had also boosted their health with items, skills, or other methods.

The real question here: was this enough? Joe supposed that if he were healing a smaller group of people it should be plenty. He spent about ten minutes helping the people in the temple out, not maximizing their health but stabilizing them to a point that they could function. He could select up to twenty targets and dump his mana into them before it became too much for him, bringing all of his targets up two hundred health. Joe found this far less tiring than going to *each* patient individually and fixing every little thing. Much easier on the emotional draining aspect, especially. Eventually, though–and far sooner than the people he healed would have liked–Joe *really* needed to get to work on his other projects. Leaving the temple, he went directly to the ritual hall area, finding the solace intensely satisfying and refreshing.

With the barest hint of a thought, the room began to shift, and he was soon seated in a comfortable chair with his notes and books in front of him. Joe started walking through the steps he needed to take; the first and most pressing was cleaning up the shoddy spell diagram of 'Mass Enchant'. He went through it meticulously, copying over what he knew to be correct first, then adding new lines and scraping them off with a shadow-made razorblade if they were shown to be incorrect. This process took several hours, and Joe was *certain* that it was night outside by the time he felt that he was ready. By intentionally leaving a small sequence that he knew to be correct out of the diagram, Joe was able to finish everything else without the whole thing spontaneously combusting. Doing it this way, he was able to check his work and make adjustments until every *other* part of the sequence was also correct.

Pulling out a scroll, ink, and quill that he had prepared at the College, Joe started drawing out the transcribed spell that he had redesigned. This was a bit simpler with the template that he had made, but he needed to be sure to go very carefully. Even so, Joe's fingers were burned and healed over and over as the paper he had been working on went up in flames from his failures. Getting to three-quarters finished, Joe yelped as he got overconfident and the paper erupted in purple flames *again*.

Thanks to the mana invested into it, the more ink on the page, the more dangerous the flames would become if his transcription failed. Thinking it over, Joe reluctantly decided that his Exquisite Shell was keeping him from writing the scroll properly. After weighing his options, he dispelled his armor and tried once again. He got to the end of his notes and added the final small chunk that had been missing, wincing as the ink seemed to vibrate three times on the page after completion. "Don't explode, don't explode…"

You have created a spell scroll! As your skill 'Words of Power (Written)' is at the Novice rank, the most powerful scroll you can make is the Novice version of any spell.

Spell scroll created: Mass Enchant (Novice). This scroll teaches the spell 'Mass Enchant' at the Novice level, which allows the caster to enchant a compatible known spell onto multiple items. Cost: Variable. Exp: 50.

Skill increase: Words of Power (Written) (Novice VII). Wow, you made a scroll on your first try! Oh, wait, the first one burned. You know what they say, second… third… eighth time's the charm!

"It worked!" Joe jumped around and whooped when the paper retained its integrity. He looked back over the notification and got serious. "I get experience for *this* too? I think it's time to invest some of my skill points into my skills." Since his class had disallowed the input of skill points into Ritual Magic when he specialized, and Ritual Lore could only be learned by study... this was a pretty solid spot to add some points. He had... whoops.

It looked like he had forgotten about his skill points for a good chunk of time. There were twenty-three points waiting for him, almost half of all the points he had gained. If he was going to participate heavily during this war, Joe decided that he needed to commit to it fully. Taking a deep breath, he dropped six points into Spellbinding and twelve points into Words of Power, leaving him with only five for a rainy day.

Skill increase: Words of Power (Written) (Apprentice 0). Congratulations! You have met the requirements to be considered an Apprentice in truly powerful written word! You can now create magical documents up to the Apprentice ranks! Based on your use of the skill so far, a new effect has been added: Autocorrect. By investing three hundred points of mana at the start of writing a scroll, three errors will be automatically corrected if you make them. When *you make them, be honest with yourself.*

Skill increase: Spellbinding (Apprentice I). As an Apprentice of Spellbinding, you get nothing extra. You thought that just because you normally do, you'd get an extra effect all the time? This skill is already potent. Go use it instead of whining.

"I hadn't *planned* on whining," Joe growled in a slightly whiny tone, getting right back to work. It took all *freaking* night for him to make a single Apprentice ranked scroll of Mass Enchant. As soon as he had the scroll in his hands, he brought it down and stored it in his... codpiece. *That* was going to take some getting used to. Joe stood there staring or blinking at the floor for a few long moments... minutes... hard to tell. His eyes were bloodshot, with bags visible under them. The only consolation he had for his exhaustion was that he had the scroll and both the skills had increased three times.

All he needed now for the ritual was a... scroll... of the spell he wanted to use to mass enchant things. Dang it. Joe had a day or two left, right? He could rest his eyes for a moment...

Joe blinked and woke up, looking around at the reconfigured room. Had he made the floor into a bed while he slept? Dangerous effect, that. What if he had a nightmare about the walls closing in and…? Joe shuddered with primal terror. No more sleeping in the easily-shifting room.

All he needed to do today was create a spell scroll. Simple to say… harder to do. Joe spent the next few hours turning his knowledge of the spell 'Shadow Spike' into a formula. Yes, he had used the spell to create his shaping skill, but a simple spike was a part of shadow manipulation that was easily translated. *Another* few hours went into turning *that* into a spell scroll, but it was far easier with his increased skill and some practice. He had even been able to recognize some signs of the contained mana losing its stability and dodged the resulting flames.

For lunch, he ate some dried meat that had been stored in his codpiece. He grimaced and shuddered; *that* hadn't been a fun thought. Joe decided right there that he would never tell anyone what part of his outfit was the spatial storage—just in case he ever needed to give them some food. Checking his notifications, he saw that he had gained one hundred experience for each Apprentice scroll he had made. Not bad. Just under seven thousand experience to the next level.

Now he needed to create the ritual itself. He had everything he needed except for the required mana. Joe was going to need a hand with the actual activation of the ritual because this was a Journeyman ranked ritual even though it was only going to be adding Apprentice ranked effects. Turning toward the door, Joe paused. Might as well get the ritual *created*, right? Staring at the ritual diagram, he willed the floor to rise up and shape itself in the same way the diagram required. This took about half an hour to get correct, but it was still far faster than drawing it out by hand. After inspecting it and fixing any errors he could find, Joe pulled out his chalk and moved forward.

Once again, Joe stopped himself. He had a better method now, didn't he? He directed the room to add a sheath around all the lines, magical symbols, and diagrams. Once they were all fully enclosed and the same thickness–Joe grinned maniacally as he started the next step–he solidified the darkness that was enclosed within the tubes. He returned the room to a simple empty circle and manipulated the shadows, convincing the silhouette of a ritual to float before it fell to the ground. Then he set it down gently and walked out of the room to find ten thousand mana worth of people to help him out. He *really* needed to get a dedicated cabal together. Scavenging for help every time he wanted to do something was annoying.

There were strange echoes in the ritual hall, but they were coming from the entrance so he didn't need to change course to investigate. People were moving in and out of the building at a run, and it seemed that *anyone* coming indoors was wounded. Oh right, there was a war on. Joe checked the countdown timer; there was another day before the main forces of the Wolfmen arrived. Were the advance forces really pushing their defenses this hard? That didn't exactly bode well for the main battle…

Booming noises rang out as large-scale spells were launched over the walls like artillery. As much as he wanted to go and take a look at what they were up against, finishing the ritual *should* be the priority. He wasn't going to be much help in battle, even if he could skewer a few Wolfmen if they got too close. War was not his specialty, though he kicked himself as he remembered that it *literally* could have been. Joe made a beeline for the magical artillery, meaning that he had to twist, turn, change direction and go the wrong way a few times in order to reach them. As it turns out, bees don't fly in straight lines.

"Trouser snake! You stuck around!" Joe called as he got close. "I need a favor, buddy."

"Why is it that you always show up at strange times after vanishing for days on end? Where have you been? Also, I can't spare any help right now. My entire guild is working in shifts, and we are *still* almost getting overrun out there." Snake spoke with severe distraction and fatigue in his voice, so Joe didn't take the refusal personally.

"Look, I found a way to help out melee fighters. It'll take

about ten minutes to get this going, and I think I can convince Terra to join in." Joe's words must have hit the mark because Tim... *Snake*, seemed to perk up like Joe did after downing a triple espresso. Joe tried to remember to call the man by his in-game name; it was possible that some people might come after him in real life if they knew too much about him.

"Find her, bring her back here. If I see that she is actually with you, I'll join you with a couple of my top guys." Snake waved Joe away, "Right now, though, I need to get back to making giant balls of liquid fire fly at seven-foot-tall werewolves. Ahhh, things I never thought I'd get to say as an adult." Five people stepped forward when he did, and their mana joined together to create a ball of what appeared to be plasma. After five seconds of each of them pumping mana into the group spell, Tim stepped forward and made a tossing motion. The ball of fiery death flew away to find a new home, and soon after, a **boom** echoed back to them.

CHAPTER FORTY-FIVE

Joe started asking around for Terra, but apparently, no one in the general population had seen her recently. When he eventually *did* learn her whereabouts, he was confused as to *why* she was there. He went over to the smithy and found her working on creating an enchanted blade, which not only was his goal but also satisfied his curiosity. Interrupting her—much to her displeasure—Joe was only able to convince her to join him by sharing half the screenshots of the magical elevator that had led to the third floor of the prison dungeon. He promised her that she'd get the other half, but only after helping him out.

From there it was back to Snake, followed by a five-minute hike to collect the ritual diagram and bring it to the rest area. By the time it was in place, the people he had collected were shifting uncomfortably, knowing that they were missing out on experience and the battle. If he didn't do something soon, they were definitely going to wander off to go do other things.

"Alright, let's get set up." Joe started directing people into place, positioning the first four in a square pattern and getting himself, Snake, and Terra into a triangle pattern closer to the center. "Seven of us, perfect. Prime numbers help keep the magic from going wild." He placed the components for this ritual into position, and Terra began to get excited.

"Is that a *spell scroll*? Holy happy cows, where did you find those? And *two* of them?" She was staring at the scrolls intently, and her already large eyes went comically wide. "*Apprentice* ranked scrolls? You are telling me that I could take that and have a spell that I could use at the *Apprentice* ranks right away?"

"Yeah, but this is better in the long run. Trust me." Joe declined to answer her first question; he hadn't known that scrolls were *that* rare. At least not so much that the other participants were whispering 'quietly' amongst themselves of taking the scroll when he wasn't looking. "Here we go people, a drop of blood each, please."

The small silver chalice he had purchased to replace the massive tarnished one he used to use was quickly passed around and added to its spot. Joe pushed his arms out to each side with his palms facing outward and lifted the ritual focus into the starting position it required. With a burst of mana directed into the diagram, it stayed in place in midair and even began to spin. The ritual had begun. Slowly and carefully, Joe began the associated chant. Mana began to flood into the ritual and out of their bodies, making the weakest among them groan softly.

Pitch-black circles spun at dangerous speeds above their heads, and the components were absorbed into the whirling gyroscope of shadow. Seeing the scrolls disintegrate and vanish, Terra seemed to get a bit choked up. They passed the threshold of required mana and the ritual became operational, but Joe kept that to himself and had the others continue to pour mana into it as long as possible. One by one, the others took a knee and gasped for air, leaving Joe to hold the burden alone as long as he could. Finally unable to bear it, Joe dropped his arms and the ritual slammed onto the ground around them, solid rings of shimmering darkness that seemed to have a heat-haze coming off of them.

Ritual created: Mass Enchant (Shadow Spike). Weapons left in this ritual will gain the on-hit effect 'Shadow Spike'. By hitting a target, a shadow spike will come out of the target's shadow and attempt to deal additional damage. Damage dealt will be increased by four points per minute that it remains in the ritual, up to 260 potential damage. Each additional ten minutes in the ritual will increase the number of spikes generated (one per hit). After thirty minutes out of the ritual, damage possible will begin decreasing by two per minute until the enchantment fails entirely. When activated, this ritual will last for eight hours. Additional mana can be invested: one hour of activation per two thousand mana. Activate now? Yes / No.

Joe chose 'no' and looked around with a wide smile. He explained the effects and that it was likely that they would all get contribution experience whenever the weapons were used. *That* turned a few frowns upside down! Joe thanked them all, sent the promised screenshots to Terra, and turned away to look for someone to help out with the weapons that would surely be piled into this spot pretty soon. He was stopped by Terra who had a strange look on her face.

"Joe... *you* made those scrolls, didn't you? These rituals, too... you know I specialized into being an enchanter, right? Yet I can only make *one* enchantment at a time. Sure, it *is* a permanent effect, but this is cool, too. Can you teach me how to do this stuff or make me a scroll of Mass Enchant?" Her face was troubled, an expression he had never seen on her happy-go-lucky visage before now.

Looking at her, Joe thought quickly. He *did* want to make more Ritualists, but maybe now–when tension was high–wasn't the time. With her work ethic and mana pool, she'd definitely be a good choice. "I can do both of those things but *after* the war, okay? If you just want the scroll, realize that I worked on it for *hours* and getting the skills needed to make it normally costs over a thousand gold. At the apprentice rank like that, I'd likely sell a single scroll for a couple hundred gold on the market, but... I bet we could work something out."

"In a non-creepy way, yeah? I want the scroll, but not *that* bad." Terra glanced over Joe, her words a direct assault on his self-confidence.

"Yeah, thanks for that." He rolled his eyes. "We'll catch up later!" Joe asked around and finally found the command tent, patiently waiting for the meeting to end before finding Aten. After explaining the use of the ritual, Aten rubbed his chin and looked away deep in thought.

When he looked back, there was glee on his face. "Does it have to be swords or weapons like that?"

"Any weapon should work; I don't think adding it to armor would be a good idea," Joe smirked and shook his head. "Enemy hits your shield, you get spiked. Bad plan."

"I was thinking *arrows*, actually." Aten's smile stretched as he saw Joe's jaw go slack. "Oh yeah, Joe, I think *tactical*. I'll talk to a guy. Expect enormous bundles of arrows to arrive over there soon."

After returning to the ritual circles and waiting for a bit, a group trundled over and set up a large tent around the darkness-stained ground. Then people that had obviously invested heavily in strength began carrying stacks of crates into the tent until it was full. Another man walked over to Joe and bumped him with his foot to wake him up. Joe had fallen asleep in the sunshine, and the explosions were actually oddly soothing without screaming accompanying them. "You the guy that's going to turn all these normal arrows into magical arrows?"

"Yeah, that's me." Joe covered his mouth and yawned, finishing with, "My name is Joe." He held out his hand and got a brusque handshake in return.

"Great, I'm the quartermaster for the guild. I'm in charge of all of this stuff, so my question is this: do you want me to assign someone to take care of these, or are you going to sign for everything?" The quartermaster had a *far* too hopeful expression.

"*No* chance of me taking those." Joe shook his head and denied him instantly. An important lesson he had learned in the army was *never* sign for anything if you didn't have to. That was a good way to get in debt *really* fast when things started to vanish. "I'm here to press the button, then you can hand them out as needed. It'll take an hour and five minutes for them to get to max damage, and damage will start to fall after half an hour outside the circles. Swords and stuff should stay in there for a long time; every ten minutes after reaching max damage lets the effect happen another time."

The quartermaster nodded at these instructions and asked Joe to get the magic started. Touching the ritual, Joe activated it and smiled as wispy darkness began to travel from the ritual into each arrow. He couldn't wait to see how useful these were in the upcoming battle. Stepping out of the tent, he was shocked to see more crates piled up and more on the way. How many arrows did they expect to use in the… war. Right. This was an entire nation of people they were fighting at this point. It was a hard concept to wrap his mind around. They would likely run *out* of arrows by the time the fighting was over. Freaky.

It took a bit of time, but Joe was able to find and wrangle his team back together. Each of them had used the time to train themselves or improve themselves in some way, and the results were obvious. Poppy now sported a rapier that had incorporated the stinger from the giant wasp, letting him deal critical hits and inject poison easily. Luckily for him, running out of the dangerous liquid wasn't going to be an issue–thanks to Alexis.

She had been found in a well-ventilated room stirring a cauldron and cackling like a witch from old Shakespearean plays. There were *barrels* of poison surrounding her, and she had obviously slept very little in the last few days. *Apparently*, the guild had given her anything she asked for so long as they got to use up to ninety percent of it for the war. She gave them ninety-five percent and rubbed her hands greedily at the thought of the experience points she was going to earn from the next few days.

Bard had been in a tavern chanting to his heart's content and had apparently found a few mass-effect chants that he was excited about, and Jaxon had been tossed into a prisoner of war area and had been going wild learning the weaknesses of all the Wolfmen he could get his hands on. This had also apparently been good training for the healer that had been assigned to follow him, going by the man's exhausted face. He had cried tears of joy when Joe stopped by to pick up Jaxon, and a fearful cheer had erupted from the Wolfmen that had been captured as well.

The fighting had died down over the last hour, but it seemed like the silence was starting to get on people's nerves. After a couple days of constant bombardments and explosions, people were expecting violence and noise. The quiet was ringing in their ears, and everyone was nervously watching the countdown timer that was ticking downward too swiftly for comfort. Aten recognized the issues that were going to appear if he did nothing, so he stood up on the wall and cleared his throat, preparing for a speech.

"Listen up, everyone! Tomorrow is the big day! Over the next few hours, reinforcements should be arriving, and we are going to have to waste time with guild politics. Just try to be polite, and don't brag *too* much about how amazing we are!" This got a few chuckles, helping Aten maintain a wide smile. "If you are off duty for now, get some rest or work on your skills. We didn't build this gigantic egg so that we would scramble away from it and not use the bonus skill experience, right?"

"Was that an attempt at an egg pun? Disgusting," Joe whispered and shook his head. "Stick to fighting and administration; your jokes are fowl! You could have hatched all *sorts* of better yokes than that!" Alexis slapped him, followed closely by Poppy.

"You *stop that* right now!" Poppy hissed at him, massaging throbbing ears.

"Seriously," Alexis chimed in, "that was terrible."

Jaxon raised a hand. "*I* thought Joe made a few good points."

"Good luck, everyone!" Aten was finishing up. "Stay safe tomorrow; make sure to watch your health, mana, and stamina! Don't die due to negligence, or I'll hear about it and we'll have some classes on situational awareness! Have fun!" Some confused cheering followed his statements, but the general consensus was that there was going to be a battle and they should do their best without dying. Fairly standard. Huge groups of people shrugged at the same time.

Aten was certainly correct about one thing: reinforcements were arriving. The town was soon flooded by people they didn't know, and then the Kingdom's Army began to arrive along with the offensive-capable members of the Mage's College. In Joe's mind, this was shaping up to be an amazing battle! Apparently, the King wouldn't arrive until later in the actual battle. He had the same issue as the Queen; when he moved, everyone would be forced to hold their breath in terror. Apparently, he had an impossible to get fifth-tier class that had insane requirements. Someone had been told he was a 'Battle Tyrant', and people just accepted that since it was the only rumor that seemed to fit the feeling the Monarchs exuded.

With the addition of the Army and Mages, there was no longer space inside of the town, and less effective defenses were quickly erected outside of the walls of the town. No one who was shuffled into this area was happy with their new assignment.

All too soon, it was time to sleep; then it was their shift for guard duty, sleep again… and the day of the battle had arrived. As the first sliver of sunlight crested the horizon, a single wolf howl shattered the still air. That howl was joined by another and another until there were so many Wolfmen howling that the buildings around town began to vibrate. Then, continuing to howl, the Wolfman army in the distance began to march together… and the ground started to shake as hard as the air.

CHAPTER FORTY-SIX

"Brace yourselves!"

"Prepare to launch artillery spells!"

"Archers forward!" This command was one that Joe had been waiting for because it was his guild's archers that were about to fire. He—along with a good chunk of the guild officers—was standing on the walls to watch the opening salvo. Joe watched as quivers were rushed forward and handed off to the waiting archers. The commanding voice rang out once again, "Use the *black* arrows first and as often as possible! They have temporary bonus effects! Three… two… one! Fire! Fire at will!"

The first volley flew away, arching into the air and falling as a black cloud. Not a *single* arrow missed. Not due to any great accuracy, simply due to how densely packed the Wolfman packs were clustered. The volley worked excellently because as the arrows came down, spikes shot up. At the speed the Wolfmen were charging, it had the same effect on their ranks as a cavalry charge. That is, the first rank stopped dead as the trailing Wolfmen hit them, driving them harder into the spikes that only lasted a second. *Those* Wolfmen took a bit of damage, but the *really* helpful portion was that the line was broken. After that, the Wolfmen were staggered and easier to counter as they got closer.

Joe received a notification icon to tell him about earned experience and grinned. He ignored it for now and watched with hungry eyes as more and more of his ensorcelled arrows were used. Spells were being launched as the Wolfmen came within fifty yards of the wall, and more empty pockets were appearing in the wave of onrushing animalistic beings with each blast. The Wolfmen were continuing to howl, full a deep keening that seemed to be making them more powerful as the sound continued.

"Why don't *we* get a racial buff?" He snorted as the first of the Wolfmen reached the wall. They were apparently expecting to be able to sink their claws into the stone of the wall and climb it because they barely slowed down as they jumped and scrabbled to find purchase. Instead of racing upward, they slammed into the black and twisted wall and fell with a yelp. Joe chuckled at the shocked looks on their elongated faces. Unfortunately, this only slowed them slightly, as there were plenty of cracks that the Wolfmen could work their hands and claws into. They were able to scale the wall, just not as swiftly as they wanted. Most importantly, not fast enough for the humans to be overrun at the start of the battle.

Seeing an opportunity, Joe used his manipulation to create a thin lattice of shadows that looked very similar to the regular cracks the Wolfmen used to climb. Unlike actual cracks where a handhold was expected, behind these was only a dense wall. Claws snapped and Wolfmen fell with surprised howls as they bounced off the unexpectedly smooth surface. Joe was hoping for the Beastmen to take some damage from falling, but the creatures below caught their falling brethren.

"Hey, bub, keep doin' wha'cher doin'." A burly man stepped forward with a barrel on his shoulder, tossing it down at the thickly clustered beasts. There was an oily rag on the barrel that was burning, and Joe was able to witness the use of the largest Molotov cocktail that a human had ever been able to throw. It hit the group and shattered, **whooshing** into a cracking inferno that stank of burnt hair and skin. "Awright, a few more like tha' and I'm good."

"Thanks!" Joe looked down the wall and saw that scenes like this were playing out all over the place: oil being spilled, poison being dumped, and channeled spells all creating huge swaths of Wolfman corpses. Joe decided to get off the wall at that point and get back to his team. This turned out to be a great idea, enough so that he was shocked that his luck stat didn't skyrocket, since right after he was back on the ground… the Wolfman Shaman counterattacked against the defenders. It became obvious why the Wolfmen didn't seem to mind their losses. An utterly *devastating* spell was unleashed that used the collective death energy of the Wolfmen that had fallen thus far, and a thin scythe of energy slashed over the battlements in a straight line. Anyone caught in it was sliced in half through whatever protections they may have had.

"What the…?" Joe froze in place as pandemonium erupted around him. Dozens and dozens of Wolfmen poured over the top of the wall.

"Get some defenders up there, *now*!" Aten roared over the din. He had come down a bit before Joe had, luckily for the guild. "If you lost your squad leader, the assistant leader takes over! Get moving!" Not giving anyone a chance to follow his orders, Aten sprang into action by himself. A sickly green ring of light shot out from him, coating everyone in his guild. A quarter second later, the light had returned to him, now bright orange. Everyone the light had touched was moving slowly or not at all in the cases of the heavily armored. Aten shot up the stairs at far above human speeds and began holding off the entire wave of beasts by himself. For fifty-five seconds, he pushed back the entirety of the invading group, killing dozens of Beastmen and shrugging off blows as though they hadn't landed. He jumped backward over the stone wall, landing solidly on his feet in the courtyard just as the orange light faded from him.

"What are you all standing around staring at? Go, go, go!" Aten shouted at the assembled humans.

"Hey, Alexis!" Joe had to almost shout at her to be heard over the sounds of combat restarting. "You're promoted! You are second in command. Sorry, I didn't know it was a thing!"

"Make it retroactive so I get back pay, and I accept!" she shouted back as they moved into position.

"Better watch out, Bard!" Joe got out as they ran to return to the battlements. "Give her an inch, and she takes a mile!"

"He's given me more than an *inch*, Joe!" Alexis called back thoughtlessly, face instantly going crimson as she realized what she had said. "Oh my gosh."

"Oh, *really*?" Poppy started to make a joke at their expense, but his levity failed as more of the Wolfmen hopped over the wall. They were almost to the top of the stairs, but the trickle of opponents had become a flood. Poppy's rapier was suddenly in his hand, the tip *slicing* through the air into a neck to claim the first kill for the party.

Joe stumbled as a huge paw slammed into him, his Shell working overtime to keep him alive. Jaxon stepped under the extended limb and released a flurry of blows into the Scout, moving back and snapping his fingers after a moment. Sickening **snaps** filled the air as the Wolfman was twisted. He crumpled, blood leaking from multiple wounds where bones had pierced the skin.

"Still bothers me a bit to be using my craft to hurt instead of heal." Jaxon sighed as he stomped on the Wolfman's head to finish him off. "Ah, such is life. Quoth the raven: **Caw!**"

"What the *abyss*, Jaxon?" Alexis was firing her crossbows as fast as she could, and the Wolfmen she hit tended to drop to the ground twitching, spasms locking up their muscles and making them easy targets for others. A volley of black arrows screamed over the group as the guild worked to regain control of their defenses. A series of pained howls drifted over the walls as those arrows found their marks, creating secondary damage as their shadows drove spikes into allies.

"Move!" was all Joe heard before he was shoved to the side. A massively armored man holding two shields got in front of his group, crouched into a starting position for runners and bellowed, "*Juggernauts' Sprint*!"

"Is that *Dylan*?" Joe watched as his old teammate began to lumber forward, picking up speed until he was moving far faster than someone carrying that much weight should be able to. He held his shields as a wedge and let the Wolfmen in his path bounce off of him. The ones he hit were either thrown off the wall the way they had come or tossed into the courtyard where they were torn apart by the defending humans. Dylan vanished around the bend, barely able to make the turn with his insane momentum.

Their section of the wall was not *clear*, but they had a far more likely chance of retaking it now. Bard's axes were whirling in time with the continuous howl, and a chant was spilling from his lips as he methodically chopped at the Wolfmen in his way. Joe felt energized, his stamina and mana returning faster than it should have. He used the boost–and the sudden loss of pressure from his enemies–to start shifting the shadows on the exterior of the wall.

Shadows of thorns grew from the wall, foot-long spikes covered in smaller spikes to prevent grasping them. Spikes were easy for him as they were the most common direct damage-dealing magic he had used while in the game. With the sacrifice of the majority of his mana, he solidified the shadows in the area, creating a downward facing wall of barbed spikes that the Wolfmen unknowingly threw themselves into. They had appeared so suddenly that dozens of the climbing Wolfmen had skewered themselves and fallen, some of them taking fatal damage from the fall this time around.

Joe dropped to the ground gasping as his body worked overtime to restore his drained mana. He shouted to the others about the spikey defenses he had added, and Alexis perked up. She pulled a large bottle out of her bag and popped the cork, drizzling the poison over the edge of the wall without looking until it had emptied. A few drops landed in the eyes of Wolfmen that were looking upward, but the spikes, for about seven feet, now had poison glistening along their barbs. The increased difficulty of climbing the wall deterred a few of the attackers, but others were not stopped and used blunt weapons to start smashing the spikes out of the way.

Looking around the battlements, it was easy to see that breaches had occurred all over the place. They weren't the first to clear off their spot, but they also weren't the last. Alexis was now firing blindly over the wall, mumbling about skill increases with her crossbow and chuckling at the 'loophole' she had found to do it instead of learning to be accurate. Joe was still recovering, but he got to his feet just as his instincts *screamed* at him about something hidden. His eyes snapped to the side, locking onto a Wolfman a good distance from the wall that had a ball of grey, misty light forming above him.

There were other Wolfmen surrounding him and, apparently, channeling mana into the spell, but *that* one was the key, Joe just *knew* it. "Listen up! We have a new target! That nasty scythe spell is building up again, and I've got the caster in my sights. I need ideas on how we can take him down at range, and I need 'em *now*!"

"Do we have anyone that could throw me at them?" Jaxon intently inquired. "If I could just get close enough-"

"Ah've got an idea!" Bard barked, interrupting the inane line of reasoning from the Monk. "We need ah *really* good archer. Lexi, you got that *special* arrow ready ta go?"

"You want to use that *now*? This early in the battle?" Alexis seemed shocked for a moment but nodded as he stared into her eyes. "Alright, but it can't be *me*. I'm still only in the Beginner ranks for crossbows, and we need someone with a bow."

Joe knew the perfect guy. If Dylan had been here, then *Chad* was sure to be nearby as well. Cupping his hands, he yelled over the wall at the defenders below, "*Chad*! *Chad*! Get over here, right now!"

His voice was entirely lost in the cacophony of noise that

was suffusing the air, so Bard tapped him on the arm and stood forward. He grunted, pointed at his neck, and bellowed, "*Chad*! Get yer butt over here!" His voice, enhanced by magic, echoed like thunder around the enclosed space of the town. A few fights stuttered, allowing the more experienced person in each battle to quickly gain the upper hand or paw, in many cases.

Joe saw a familiar face running up the stairs to them, though he was impressed by the archer's new look. Chad was wearing light armor, a thin winged helmet framing his face. His bow had blades at each end and was glowing slightly. Seeing Joe, a tired smile appeared on his face. "Hey, man. Good to see you. What's going on, and please tell me it was worth abandoning my post or I am going to get a lot of grief later."

"I've got a target for you; it's the Wolfy casting that nasty spell that almost got us overrun. Big gray scythe?" Joe saw the recognition on Chad's face and continued, "We apparently have a special arrow to take him out, but we need someone that can make the shot. Are you our guy for this?"

"Let's see the arrow." Chad continued speaking as Alexis pulled out the projectile, "I specialized as a Royal Sniper. Tiona felt bad about leaving the group, so she hooked us up with some great contacts. Apparently, I *only* 'show promise' as a Journeyman archer, but they still took me in." Joe chuckled at that; it was unsurprising that the best snipers of the Kingdom had high requirements.

Alexis handed over a *very* strange arrow. The tip was beveled, the shaft was slightly corkscrewed, and there were no feathers on it. Joe had the feeling that it had been designed as a bolt for a crossbow, but Chad didn't seem to mind it. "Great, what effects are we looking at on this thing?"

"It has a strange flight path. Every ten feet it will have drifted a half foot to the right, but the corkscrew shape keeps it floating high. That means it'll drop only a half foot per twenty feet, so don't aim as high as you would with a normal arrow. When it hits, it'll go through magical protections like they aren't there unless they have anti-arrow wards specifically." Alexis took a deep breath and continued, "I call this a Screaming Sorecerer because it'll be *loud* as it flies. The arrow should arrive before the noise does, and it has a silencing component as well as poison that applies a mana burn effect. If this hits a Mage that is currently casting a spell… I highly doubt they'll survive it."

"Wow. I bet the guild will want *these* if I am able to make this shot." Chad tested the weight, felt the wind, and got into position. "How many do you have?"

"One." Alexis shook her head at his incredulous look. "It cost me about fifteen gold to design and make it."

Chad looked at the arrow with a new respect. "Joe, can you touch my bow as I fire? Just near the blade. *Very* lightly, please; I want to see if your anti-mage title will help me. Who am I killin'?"

Joe stood closer and did as Chad had asked, pointing out the Shaman directing the spell. "That guy, and we need to do this *fast.* That spell is about ready to go." The gray orb had condensed and was now pearlescent and shimmering ominously.

"Shhh…" Chad drew the bow and pointed it off into the distance, causing Joe's eyes to widen in fright. Chad wasn't even aiming at the right Shaman! Before he could call out, the string snapped forward and the arrow was away. It *screamed* like a burning man as it flew, arcing around a large swath of the battlefield as it flew much further than any arrow Joe had seen to this point. There was a shimmer in the air around the group of Shaman–reminiscent of the ripples in a pond after a rock was thrown–as the arrow punched through a mana shield. It penetrated directly into the chest of the lead Shaman, and multiple things happened at once.

The beast's hands went to his new wound, his mouth silently screaming. He didn't get a chance to even try to stabilize the spell before it fell on him and exploded outward. The power invested in the spell moved away from the impact site like a shockwave, decimating anything in its path. Dozens then hundreds of Wolfmen were cut in half before the power faded, leaving a huge gaping hole where the enemy had previously been most clustered.

Jaxon looked over the annihilated area and nodded approvingly. "Nice shot."

CHAPTER FORTY-SEVEN

"Solid understatement there, Jaxon." Joe rolled his eyes as he looked over the area. Trees had been felled and hundreds of Wolfmen had been caught in the blast. The area was already refilling with targets, but the human defenders had gained a much-needed reprieve.

"Actually..." Chad shook his head in disbelief as he looked at his combat log. "That shot did exactly *one point two* damage to him. Only the mana burn and silence actually made *that* happen. Also, physical damage was only done due to 'Legend' and 'Anti-mage' titular effects. Good lord, his protections must have been *insane*. If he wasn't a high-ranked general at *least*... I'd eat his ridiculous hat." Chad pointed at Poppy. No one had anything to say about the arrow, but Joe pretended to brag by throwing a fist in the air and kissing his bicep. It was best not to panic during combat.

The loss of the Shaman started a shift among the Wolfmen, who were probably forced to change tactics without the previous Shaman's direction. Warriors became much more prevalent in their ranks, and their Scouts also began using their ranged weapons more heavily, attempting to block the humans from creating a counter to their next attack. Long and heavy ramps on wheels where being pushed forward; apparently, the Warriors didn't have the same confidence in their ability to climb the walls as did their lighter brethren. Either way, they were coming, and the howling was reaching a fever pitch.

Joe chanced a glance over the wall and got an arrow to the face for his trouble. He cursed in shock, then smiled when he saw that his Shell had gained a rank from the life-threatening projectile. "Guys, I have no idea what I should be doing right now. Any suggestions would be really helpful."

Chad spoke up before any of his team could. "I'd suggest either getting *off* the battlements–my personal preference–or providing support up here for the ranged guys that are stuck up here. Your team seems to be mainly close-quarters fighters, and *you* are a healer. Go heal people that have arrows sticking out of them. *You* guys go and beat up those Warriors when they crawl over the wall."

Not having better instructions, Joe agreed with this plan, and his team got to work while Chad returned to his post. Far from being berated for dereliction of duty, his excellent shot was praised, and he was clapped on the back as the story spread from the people who had witnessed it. On the battlements, Joe's team worked constantly to fend off the attacks, and Joe emptied his mana pool over and over to heal the people around him. Any time there was a lull, Joe would rehydrate people by using Cleanse. He made sure to stick close to his group, not wanting to be separated if anything went wrong.

Every once in a while, Joe would glance over at where the fighting was most vicious, the gate. There was a constant assault on that location that made the climbing hordes they were dealing with seem like a small scuffle. The air was thick with arrows flying in either direction, often colliding with each other and exploding into splinters. Spells were constantly humming through the air as well, and the land was becoming pockmarked and deformed. Somehow, the walls and gate were surviving the brutal battle, and that they still remained was a reminder that they were the only reason the humans had been able to entrench themselves here even this long.

Four hours into the battle, Joe's team was replaced on the wall by the next shift of defenders. His group stumbled down to the rest area and attacked the prepared food with the same viciousness they had been attacking Wolfmen only a few minutes ago. Jaxon looked around with deep bags under his eyes and coughed. "So, uh, how's everyone doing today? Getting plenty of experience? If you think you are going to level, please let me know so I can get close and use the light as a quick shower. It seems that I am covered in filth."

Joe opened his notifications, noting with pleasure that he had increased Cleanse and Group Heal to Apprentice six, Mend to Apprentice eight, and Hidden Sense to Beginner eight. Then the experience began to flow in, and he moved closer to Jaxon to help the man out. He *had* asked nicely, after all.

Exp: 7,381 (Various activities. See full listing?) You have reached character level twelve!

Rituarchitect experience gained: 2,190 (Macro Micro ritual). See explanation?

Specialization Rituarchitect has reached level two! Your stats have increased due to class bonuses: +3 Wisdom and Intelligence, +2 Perception and Dexterity.

Perception has reached 50 points! Calculating... most focused sense: sight. You now have two vision modes: standard and zoom 2x! Find those tiny details that have always eluded you! All senses have increased drastically; be careful out there! Pain hurts! Smells are smelly! Brush your teeth because you can taste all the nasty in your mouth. Oh look, the howls are louder too! Good luck ever sleeping again!

"And hot water *hot*!" Joe mocked the snarky message. He chose not to see the listing for the first notice, but he did want to see the reasoning for the specialization experience. As a golden supernova washed out from him, he read over the notice and was intrigued. Apparently, a 'Macro Micro' was a type of ritual that let him enchant a *lot* of items with a single, small enchantment. So this was the experience for the enchanted arrows?

Excellent. Next, he tried out the zoom mode of his vision, getting an unfortunate close up of Poppy's mustache. It was nice and fluffy from a distance, but this close… and right after eating? Extra nasty.

Joe coughed and glanced around the table. "We have eight hours until we are back on duty, unless, of course, we are getting close to being overrun. Any thoughts on that? Should we be doing anything, or do you want to just go to sleep?"

The vote came back quickly. Sleep won by a landslide. They were finishing up when a messenger ran up. "Joe? Of the Wanderer's guild?"

"Yes, that's me. What's up?" Joe was on alert right away; the man seemed deadly serious.

"Message for you from Aten, given to me via Daisy. 'Joe, change the settings of your stupid-butt building so that the fudging Wolfmen stop benefitting from the deity-cursed boosted skill experience, you fudging poop-stain'." The messenger coughed into his hand and looked around. "This part is from me, I censored a bit of the message, but… I *can* give it to you exactly if needed."

"No, I got it. I appreciate your candor; no one needs to be insulted in the form that message would have been." Joe tossed the man a silver coin to show exactly how *much* he appreciated the censoring, getting a nod in return as he hurried off. Opening his settings, Joe selected the building and changed the benefits to 'allies only'. "Totally forgot that was a thing. Hope I didn't screw us up too bad."

The others didn't seem to think there was going to be a large issue; at least, no one commented. That was when he noticed that Poppy and Alexis were asleep, their faces inches from the food they had been attacking only a minute ago. "Alright, let's go get some sleep."

Bard picked up Alexis in a princess carry and walked toward the sleeping areas. Jaxon, seeing this and also seeing the sleeping Poppy, followed suit and carried Poppy in the same manner. Joe made sure to get a screenshot for future taunting and blackmail. Settling in for a few hours of sleep, they drifted off to dreamland with their backs against each other for protection.

Joe came to in pain, a strange man standing over him. This was becoming *far* too common for his liking. Why couldn't he wake up feeling extra nice with a lady standing over him? His head was itching in an *infuriating* manner, and the leer on the man's face seemed to suggest he knew exactly what was happening. He smirked and in a low voice, whispered, "A present from an *admirer*." He vanished from sight, and even Joe's high perception could only detect a faint shimmer as the man ran away.

Yelling in pain as the itching transformed into needle-sharp digging at his scalp, Joe grabbed at his head and tried to figure out why exactly it hurt so bad. Feeling at the foreign object, it seemed that he once again had luscious hair! He tried to yank it off, but whatever this was, it was *not* going to budge. His mana and stamina began to plummet, and he saw that his new total was now fixed at a *maximum* of one hundred! No! Joe stood on wobbly legs and fell over from the pain just as a notification appeared.

Item: 'Narcissist's folly (cursed)' counts as a wig. Incinerating in three seconds (effect from cursed title: Baldy). Remove this rare and expensive item if you want to retain possession of it!

A new wave of pain hit Joe as the cursed item on his head burst into flames, badly scorching him before being completely consumed. He actually vomited from the pain before he finally generated enough mana to heal himself. Poppy was kneeling next to him as Joe regained focus, not getting *too* close thanks to the puddle of vomit covering his prone leader. "What in the world happened to *you*?"

Groaning, Joe slowly stood and rested his head against the wall. "**Hurk**, pretty sure an assassin just tried to curse me with a nasty item. Gotta start sleeping in **ugh** protected areas again."

"Sorry, man. You good to go, though? We just got called over to assist some of the guys from the Mage's College." Poppy was edging away from him as watery bile crept down the slight slope they were on.

"Yeah, I'm good." Joe wiped his mouth and stood, quickly using Cleanse to get the stomach acid out of his mouth. It also removed some tartar and plaque buildup; then a little healing fixed up his encroaching gingivitis. He could put dentists out of business if he wanted to… Joe shook off the intrusive thought and hurried to catch up with the rest of his party.

Getting back on the battlements revealed a wasteland around the town. Charred siege equipment, blood, bodies, and destroyed forest were the only things visible through the choking smoke that poured out of the remainder of the forest that was burning nearby. The only thing that had not changed from the start of the battle was the howling, and the cumulative bonuses on the Wolfmen were starting to become more apparent. The opponents that charged toward them were faster, stronger, and harder to tire than they had any right to be. Now, getting into melee range with them was something that only the hardiest Warriors could endure, and huge wolves were accompanying the Wolfmen. They had begun hunting humans in packs.

While refreshing Exquisite Shell, Joe realized that his team was now positioned above the gate, the place where the most serious fighting was happening and where the most injuries and deaths had occurred. A bit nervous, he steeled himself to fight all *night* if need be. Joe recognized a few of the Mages from his time at the College, especially the Silence Mage in a purple robe that had walked him into the trial.

"Listen up, if you are just getting on duty!" someone was yelling. Joe focused in on him, not wanting to miss any pertinent details. "We have a report that the enemy has a battering ram coming this way, and it is apparently designed to take down the gates of *Ardania*. These gates *will not* hold if the ram gets to have free reign at it! The Army is busy on the West side of town; a huge wave of Elites punched a hole in our defensive line. We are the last line of defense, and we have no reinforcements coming! We *need* to stay strong!"

Joe's responsibilities didn't change much with his new position; he was on healing duty. His shadow manipulation had a range of about ten feet right now, so taking out targets down on the ground wasn't really an option. He could spray acid over the wall and likely would when the battering ram appeared, but until then, there were more effective countermeasures. The battle raged on just as it had previously, if a little more intensely. Then something changed in the air, and tension whipped through the defenders. The battering ram had appeared, and it was like nothing Joe had ever seen before.

The front of it was a giant metal wedge, and the entire structure looked vaguely like an upside-down boat. He couldn't see for certain, but he was *almost* positive that the bottom was filled with marching Wolfmen… who were now starting to *run* at the gate. Where he was defending. Oh boy.

"*Countermeasures*!" The man giving orders demanded. Chunks of earth started to rise from the land in front of the gate, creating an additional barrier for the ram. Though a good idea, the gesture was futile because the entire battering ram was a ruse. As the front wedge hit the stone in front of the gate, the boat-portion sprung forward and upward like a catapult, revealing dozens of Elite Wolfman Warriors that used the sudden stairway to launch a sneak attack at the unprepared 'soft' targets. The Mages and ranged fighters were cut through like a knife through hot butter as the Elites started their grizzly work. Only the melee fighters supporting the ranged group stopped the area from being completely overrun.

Joe activated Group Heal and latched his healing waters onto the most hard-pressed fighters, constantly healing the wounds they were accruing. It took ten minutes of intense fighting, but the Elites were *almost* cleared from the battlements. Defying expectations, one of them broke through. Ignoring the wounds he took and focusing on the Mages and healers, he was a whirlwind of rage and destruction. Three, four men died in as many seconds as the Elite tore through them. His sights were on Joe now, and as the man prepared to defend himself by collecting shadows around the Wolfman, two brutal attacks were absorbed by his now-splintering Shell.

Just as Joe started to invest the mana into his shadows to knock the Elite off the wall, his control failed him. He slammed both his palms into the unimpressed Wolfman's chest, doing zero damage. There… there *should* have been giant shadow hands that threw the Elite backward and off the wall. Joe looked up and up and up… into the eyes of the enraged Wolfman as he swung his sword. In the periphery of his vision, Joe saw a purple-robed man smirking.

You have died! Calculating… you lose 2,400 experience! You have lost a character level! Time remaining until respawn… 18 in-game hours, or nine real-world hours. Time until respawn has been increased by 50% for being in an active war zone!

CHAPTER FORTY-EIGHT

Joe stood slack-jawed, staring at the walls of his respawn room. When he started to move again, he flew into a rage. "That *Silence* Mage! He *murdered* me! I'm going to *hunt* you *down*! I wanted that to go better! I wanted that to go *better*!" Joe shouted the last sentence, slamming his fists into the wall. There was no pain, no bloody knuckles, no damage to the wall. This made him even angrier for some reason, and he full-on threw a tantrum like a two-year-old.

When he was standing again, he had calmed down, so he went over to the couch and pulled up information about what was going on in the game. To his shock and relief, there was a live broadcast of the battle that was happening right now! A few minutes in, he realized that watching it didn't make him feel any better. The war was not going well for the humans, even though it looked really cool. Everyone in the game looked like they were sprinting around, but it was only the two-to-one time dilation. You had the option to watch at regular speed, but Joe wanted to stay current. Since he had just woken up in the game, he watched for five hours before deciding to take a three-hour nap.

For the final hour, before he was able to return, the battle was starting to rapidly worsen for the humans. The full might of the Wolfman nation was arrayed against them, and it seemed like nothing could help. Then… in a flash… the entire scope of the battle shifted. At first, the human side stiffened. Then the attacking Wolfmen within a certain range stuttered, swiftly going still as well. That was the only warning before the Wolfmen began to die. Joe had to rewind and watch the battle in slow motion to see what was happening, but when he saw it… he returned to the live feed and created a bowl of popcorn for himself. This was going to be good.

The human King had joined the battle without fanfare, and Joe now understood why he was called a Battle Tyrant. He exuded an aura of killing intent supplemented with mana that caused anything within the area he was fighting to simply… give up and die. He moved around the battlefield at such high speeds that it was impossible to watch him fight at *regular* speed, let alone the doubled speed that Joe was subject to. Joe could only follow the King's movements by the trail of erupting gore that he left behind.

There was only a single choice remaining for the Wolfmen. The howling–the sound that had been a constant in the battle for a full day–began to taper off. Voice by voice, the call of the wolf began to vanish until there was only one voice remaining. That one, single, mournful howl grew and grew, until the Wolfman creating it stepped into view. Actually… *was* it a Wolfman? It looked almost like a middle-aged guy that had eaten twenty too many cakes. "Henry! You sniveling *politician*! I, Aidan Silverfang, challenge you to single combat!"

The regal voice that the man had been using suddenly *shifted* into furious animalistic snarls. "How *dare* you show your face! How dare *you* oppose *me*! I have taken the entirety of this land for my people, and you have only ever hidden behind your *walls*! Crawl away *now*, and you will live another day."

The King–who was apparently named Henry–didn't seem bothered by this speech. He turned toward the Wolf and spoke in a sorrowful tone, "Aiden, why did it ever come to this? You were my favorite hunting companion, the creature I spent the most time with in this world besides my family. I have not launched an attack on you because there was simply no *need* to do so. My people were safe; our city sustains itself. Why should I hunt you down when there was a chance that we could be together again? *Friends* again?"

The thin veneer of sanity that Aiden had been shielding his true self with vanished and his body began to bubble, twist, and morph. In a bare moment, he had settled into his battle form, and the beast he had become was enormous. Standing at least ten feet tall and four feet wide, the Wolfman Warlord picked up two massive two-handed axes that were tossed to him by attendants and called a challenge to the King in a guttural voice that was obviously not used to the human tongue, "Come, meat! Let this farce end! My people are hungry for *manflesh*!"

"That's what she said," Joe whispered before shoveling more popcorn into his face.

"We don't need to end it this way, Aiden." The King was beginning to sound *bored*, of all things. "Let's have dinner, maybe go play in the forest-"

"Enough of this foul tongue!" the Warlord bellowed, prowling forward and preparing to attack. "I am no one's *pet*."

"*I* never claimed that you were. That was your own pride and failures, and it seems that this is how you see yourself. So be it then. Come, *dog*." Henry raised his sword and swung forward, the air pressure from the swing released a scouring line in the ground until just before it hit the Warlord who stepped aside and avoided the lighting-fast attack. Then the battle between them started in earnest, and they were quickly shrouded in dust and free-floating particles of charged mana.

Joe was disappointed for a bare moment; he wanted to see what was happening. Then he saw that the attack on the town had resumed *far* away from the Kingly battle, and he began watching that. Just as it was getting interesting, the return portal to Eternium reappeared. He had completely forgotten to set an alarm! Joe scrambled to his feet and *dove* through the opening, reappearing inside the temple area of the Grand Ritual Hall.

He got to his feet and started running to the entrance, not wanting to miss out on the epic battle between mythical beings. Just before he got out, a small notification that he had never seen before appeared in his vision. It was a golden aurora of sunlight surrounding a rainbow arching between two books. He opened the notification and read over the information, a smile appearing on his face as he did so.

Grand Ritual Hall mana supply: 900,852/1,000,000. Would you like to activate the structure's ability 'Knowledge Nova'? With current mana supplies and this being the first scan, the structure will record all class details of beings within a two-kilometer radius. Yes / No.

"Yes, yes, *yes*!" Joe mashed the button. How likely was it that the King was ever going to be within range of the nova again? "Set all class information of second tier and above as classified, please." His settings adjusted themselves, and Joe continued his run out of the building to see what was going to happen. He turned and saw that the beacon on the building was glowing even brighter than usual, washing out colors like an extraordinarily sunny day and causing rainbows to shimmer to life around the area. Beyond that, there was no indication of anything happening. Good. That was good, right? Was it working? He checked the mana levels of the building and saw that they were flatlining, so… it was working?

Knowledge Nova Scan Complete! Information on 721 classes added!

"Yes!"

Server Message!

Joe's heart jumped into his throat as he saw that message; the game was giving him away! Traitor!

The Wolfman Warlord Aiden has fallen! Racial boons removed from Wolfmen until a new leader has united their people! Wolfman morale lowered by 80% for 80 hours! Strike now, humankind! Strike down your enemy, and prepare yourselves!

"Holy guacamole, it's *already* over?" Joe ran to get onto the nearest rooftop, his improved stamina allowing him to scale the stairs inside and pull himself up to the dungeon-twisted roof before needing to breathe deep gulps of air. It was true, the battle had been won! The Wolfman army was scattering, their nation now leaderless. Cheers rose from the walls, then the town, then all around the town as citizens, travelers, and all able humans joined in.

The King remained in the field cutting down a huge swath of Wolfmen as they attempted to retreat into their territory once again. After a half hour of killing anything that came into the open, any Wolfman that was capable of moving had run, escaping into what remained of the woods. The King didn't pursue, choosing instead to start walking back toward town. Joe watched all this with amazement, not planning on taking his eyes off this magnificent sight any time soon.

A large company of Warriors and Mages peeled off of the army, leaving the fortifications and riding out to the King, who went very still so that they could approach without suffocating. The group did indeed surround him, but… not in a *protective* way. At least it didn't appear so from where he was standing. Joe slowly began to feel a deep unease. The people were in a triangle around the King, and one of the men in robes was bowing to the Monarch while pulling an item out of a bag. Presenting his fist to the King, the robed man suddenly clapped his hands together.

A blast like a literal nuclear weapon blocked all vision of what was transpiring. Joe, almost as a reflex, dumped all of his mana into creating a Shell around his body, working to protect his head and chest first. Knowing that he only had seconds to find shelter to survive what was coming, he *jumped* off the wall, landing on his feet and running as fast as he could toward the only thing that he expected to survive the incoming blast: the Ritual Hall.

The first shockwave *still* sent him flying forward when it caught up to him, but he angled himself in midair to shoot through the entrance to the Grand Ritual Hall. A wave of fiery death followed the initial shockwave, roasting him alive. With a scream of pain and mental power he didn't know he had, he ordered the door of the building to slam shut behind him.

Landing on the cool, suddenly dark floor, Joe gasped and wheezed. He was crispy, his skin blackened and charred. He was *so* glad that he hadn't gone to rejoin the front lines! As he worked to reverse the worst of the damage, a new notification appeared.

Server alert! Regicide!

CHAPTER FORTY-NINE

Weep in shock and outrage, oh Humans of Ardania! Your King has been slain by a cult of anarchists! Until a new King has been chosen, human men face a 50% reduction in earned experience!

"I don't like that. This is not acceptable," Joe croaked, his lungs having been seared by the intense heat. If he hadn't been able to resist elemental damage… he would have certainly been fried. As it was… Joe looked down and saw that his shell had failed, and one of his legs was missing completely.

Skill increased: Aerial Acrobatics (Beginner 0). Hey, you did a flip with style *this time!*

Debuff: Lost Limb (right leg). -100% walking speed, -50% jumping power. +10% hobbling speed. On the plus side, you can always change your name to 'Ilean, Ihop, or Stumpy'! Would you like to change your name now? Yes / No.

You have met the qualifications to become a pirate captain! Would you like to assign your secondary profession now? Yes / No.

"No!" What the heck was the system trying to do to him right now? Forming a pair of crutches from the shadows around him, Joe stood up and swung himself to the closed door. It had been a few minutes, but maybe it would still be best to open the door slowly. Thoughts of explosive depressurization during house fires filled his mind. He needn't have worried, though; the door slid smoothly upward revealing a landscape free of anything but flat dirt.

The trees, houses, and northern section of the wall were gone or buried. There were no signs of life that Joe could see, and as he moved along his chosen path, it was obvious that most of the people caught in the blast or shockwave had not survived the experience. There were a few exceptions, but those moaning and charred folk that had invested nearly exclusively in constitution were assuredly regretting it right now.

Joe kept moving, intent on his newest goal. With their enemies scattered and his people fallen… there was only one thing for him to do. It took him a solid thirty-five minutes to find ground zero; it was only thanks to the ground being even more damaged than the surroundings at that point that he was able to do so in the first place. "I wonder how toxic the air is right now? Cleanse is gonna get a workout…"

Then he saw what he had been looking for. At least… he was *pretty* sure it was. Joe picked up the item on the ground, staring at it intently until he gained the information he needed.

Left foot of King Henry. This is all that remains of a great, powerful, and loving King. Return it to the Queen for a reward so that she will not need to mourn over an empty casket.

"Well, *that's* pretty dark. I *really* hope that I am still within the time limit…" Joe set the half-melted foot back on the ground and centered himself. Pushing out his mana, he moved in the required forms. With his palms outward, he *pushed* the spell into the foot. "*Resurrection*!"

Golden power flowed out of him and into the remains. Unlike when he had used it on a Traveler and a portal appeared for them to walk through, now the power coalesced into a shining silhouette of a man and slowly faded away. It left behind a startled face that didn't appear to be much older than Joe, but that face was swiftly hidden behind a liquid metal that poured up over the man and trapped him in armor once more.

"Who are you, and... what just happened?" The King seemed a bit confused. "Where did the venerable Lord Rodgers go? He held out a box, and then..."

Server alert! Rejoice and make merry! The King is alive! Long Live The King! Reductions and debuffs toward humans for the loss of the King are revoked.

"I died?" The King seemed a bit out of it still. "You saved me then... you, an unknown level *eleven* man, saved *me*."

After a quiet laugh, the King reached into nowhere and pulled out a small token. He pressed it onto Joe's forehead, and the token melded to his skin, leaving a small shining insignia. "You are marked *by my hand*. Let none of my people say a word against you lest they speak against the King and Crown directly. When you are able, please come to the palace for a chat. We will get you a *proper* reward."

Reputation increased! Your reputation with the Royal Family, Royal Guard, Human Guards, and Loyal Citizens of Ardania has reached new heights! You are now to be treated as 'Extended Family' no matter your actual reputation score!

"Thank you, Your Majesty." Joe bowed as deeply as he could manage while using his crutches, excitement gathering in his chest.

"There is nothing more for me to say. Good luck, and I will see you soon... *Joe*." The King's form blurred, and Joe was held in place with an intense fear until the Battle Tyrant had vanished from the area.

"Aten is going to lose his dang *mind*." Joe chuckled evilly and started hobbling back to the decimated town. It was going to be a good couple of days. Maybe he would take a vacation. Maybe he would go hide for a few months. Either way sounded good.

It took a full day for everyone in the guild to come back, so after the *majority* of his guild respawned, they joined the crusade to hunt down and slay the remaining Wolfmen. Joe spent that time working to grow a new leg and had needed to put three skill points and four days into learning how to reconstruct his body properly, even though he had the requisite skill. It was a painful process, as nerves were regrown inch by inch, but… he needed his leg. Nothing to do but grit his teeth and bear with it.

The information he had gained as his healing skill crossed into the Student ranks would make any surgical resident jealous to the extreme. Not that they didn't have the same—or better—information, no, it was how *clear* the information was *all* of the time. There was no forgetting this for him. Need to know something? Boom, right there in the ol' noggin.

Two days after his leg had been fully regrown, the long-awaited notification arrived.

Quest complete: Shatter a People. The Human Nation has prevailed against the Wolfman tribes! Congratulations to you all but especially to the participants. The top three players who contributed to the overall success of this quest will gain a Noble title and a gift of land. In order of contribution, please congratulate: Joe Anti-Mage, Aten Commander, and BackAttack Beastbane. You have each earned the maximum reward possible! Reward: 50,000 Exp, 100,000 gold to your guild treasury, and 10,000 gold to your personal account.

Anyone with the title 'Racial Traitor' has been given a maximum Warlock Title, which can only be cleared away by the King, Queen, or 20 deaths. These people will now glow red, and no penalty will be issued for their death. Root out the traitors amongst your people, because this world is going to become much. More. Dangerous.

Joe yelped as an incredibly dense aurora appeared around him and suffused his body. He shot up to character level fifteen and now had *fifteen* points to spend on his characteristic points, but more exciting to him was that his leg was back to normal! He had regrown it, but something had been missing, something that made it feel like this wasn't his real leg. That feeling was gone! He got up and jumped for joy, joining in the shouts of glee from all around the camp.

Humans. Please focus carefully on this next message.

The ominous tone of the message forced calm upon everyone, and they waited with bated breath for what would come next.

Server alert! Congratulations to all Humans! You have destroyed your determined racial enemy and are now able to move on to the next stage of the 'game'. Thanks to your actions, humanity will survive… for now. Let me be the first to say it: Congratulations on passing the tutorial!

"That… everything up until *now* was the *tutorial*?" Joe wasn't the only person to say these words aloud, and he wouldn't be the last. What in the heck was going on?

Players now have one month before continent restrictions are relaxed, and your continent and humanity as a whole will connect with two more races! At that time, you will individually need to choose a race to join in the war against the other. Good luck, and make wise choices! Your future allies will help determine your fate. -Cal.

EPILOGUE

"Joe?" Hearing the masked man's voice brought Joe out of his coffee and puzzle break. It also interrupted his hour of training, meaning that he would need to start over in order to advance his characteristics that had not gone over fifty. Before Joe could decide how to react to the intrusion, the next words entered his ears, and he perked up excitedly. "We've got him."

"Are you sure?" Joe didn't even wait for an answer before packing up and downing all the remaining coffee in his cup. He was on his feet by the time the man responded.

"Affirmative. Matches the description perfectly, and he was identified for us by one of his old coworkers." The man gestured for Joe to follow him. "I assume you are able to pay the bounty in full? There is a hefty incentive for us to hold onto him, so…"

"No worries there. I'm *that* Joe." Joe wasn't trying to be braggadocios, but he needed the man to know who he was dealing with. "You know, the one that held the number one spot for contribution during the Wolfman War?"

"No kidding? Guess you have the cash then." Joe couldn't see it, but the smile under the man's mask was a happy one at this point. They stopped outside of a small butcher shop, and Joe was waved in. "He's in there, just like you asked. Two others are waiting in there with him."

"Excellent." Joe strode forward, opening the door and walking forward until he saw who he had been hunting for. Purple robe, check. Smug look even though he was in a bad situation? Check. "Hey there. You remember how you silenced me in the middle of a battle? *Right* before that Elite would have been destroyed by me? Three more people died before it could be taken down. I'm here to return the favor, traitor."

"You can't kill *me*, brat. Just because you killed the *true* leader of the College doesn't make you immune to their laws." The Mage sneered and spit at Joe. The spittle struck a glittering Shell that Joe wore all the time now and slowly slid off. "I don't care what the *King* said, the College would never forgive someone who killed a member in good standing. You want to go back to being hunted like an animal?"

"I'd rather have someone hunting me openly than someone who betrays his people, and *of course,* you dislike me having killed the old Archmage. You basically had all the power you could ever want. This is making so much sense now. Anyway." Shadows had been building around the Mage, and only Joe's gesture to solidify them brought them to his notice. Before he could even scream, bolts of darkness penetrated his body from multiple angles and stole his consciousness.

"Did you catch his name, by chance? I'd like to inform the College of his passing." Joe inquired of the bounty hunters while waiting for the Mage to expire.

The two men looked at each other, and after a drawn-out second, the one on the left spoke, "Sure did. Master Mage of Silence: Reggie."

You have committed Reggie-cide! As the person you just murdered was a Racial Traitor, you have been granted a preemptive pardon for any action taken against them, though no experience can be gained. Keep up the good work!

ABOUT DAKOTA KROUT

Associated Press best-selling author, Dakota has been a top 5 bestseller on Amazon, a top 6 bestseller on Audible, and his first book, Dungeon Born, was chosen as one of Audible's top 5 fantasy picks in 2017.

He draws on his experience in the military to create vast terrains and intricate systems, and his history in programming and information technology helps him bring a logical aspect to both his writing and his company while giving him a unique perspective for future challenges.

"Publishing my stories has been an incredible blessing thus far, and I hope to keep you entertained for years to come!" -Dakota

Connect with Dakota:
MountaindalePress.com
Patreon.com/DakotaKrout
Facebook.com/DakotaKrout
Twitter.com/DakotaKrout
Discord.gg/mdp

ABOUT MOUNTAINDALE PRESS

Dakota and Danielle Krout, a husband and wife team, strive to create as well as publish excellent fantasy and science fiction novels. Self-publishing *The Divine Dungeon: Dungeon Born* in 2016 transformed their careers from Dakota's military and programming background and Danielle's Ph.D. in pharmacology to President and CEO, respectively, of a small press. Their goal is to share their success with other authors and provide captivating fiction to readers with the purpose of solidifying Mountaindale Press as the place 'Where Fantasy Transforms Reality.'

Connect with Mountaindale Press:
MountaindalePress.com
Facebook.com/MountaindalePress
Twitter.com/_Mountaindale
Instagram.com/MountaindalePress

MOUNTAINDALE PRESS TITLES

GameLit and LitRPG

The Completionist Chronicles,
The Divine Dungeon,
Full Murderhobo, and
Year of the Sword by Dakota Krout

Arcana Unlocked by Gregory Blackburn

A Touch of Power by Jay Boyce

Red Mage and
Farming Livia by Xander Boyce

Space Seasons by Dawn Chapman

Ether Collapse and
Ether Flows by Ryan DeBruyn

Dr. Druid by Maxwell Farmer

Bloodgames by Christian J. Gilliland

Unbound by Nicoli Gonnella

Threads of Fate by Michael Head

Lion's Lineage by Rohan Hublikar and Dakota Krout

Wolfman Warlock by James Hunter and Dakota Krout

Axe Druid,
Mephisto's Magic Online, and
High Table Hijinks by Christopher Johns

Skeleton in Space by Andries Louws

Dragon Core Chronicles by Lars Machmüller

Chronicles of Ethan by John L. Monk

Pixel Dust and
Necrotic Apocalypse by David Petrie

Viceroy's Pride by Cale Plamann

Henchman by Carl Stubblefield

Artorian's Archives by Dennis Vanderkerken and Dakota Krout

Vaudevillain by Alex Wolf

Made in the USA
Las Vegas, NV
26 March 2024